GREEK

GREEK

palm south university book 7

kandi steiner

Greek is the final installment in the Palm South University series, the "series finale" if you will.

It picks up right where book 6, *Hazed*, left off. As this book is part of a series, you will need to read the other books in the series before beginning this one:

Rush, PSU #1 (http://amzn.to/2vQcj7G)
Anchor, PSU #2 (http://amzn.to/2vLkDXN)
Pledge, PSU #3 (http://amzn.to/2vQ1m5R)
Legacy, PSU #4 (https://amzn.to/2yQDsML)
Ritual, PSU #5 (https://amzn.to/3cEwBqE)
Hazed, PSU #6 (https://amzn.to/3w7YTlG)

Welcome back to PSU... ;)

Tweet or post while you read using #PalmSouth.

Join the Palm South University discussion group here (https://www.facebook.com/groups/712042985606913).

EPISODE 1

Jess

IF ANYONE WERE TO look down upon this scene from an aerial view, they would likely remark that it's a lovely and serene sight to behold.

A stunning penthouse suite at a gorgeous Mexican resort, the sheer white curtains floating in the breeze, the expanded balcony with a private hot tub and plunge pool all so alluring and beautiful. The magical backdrop of a pristine white beach and turquoise water, currently reflecting the full moonlight overhead, and the distant sound of the waves washing ashore.

From the outside, it appears to be an absolutely extraordinary slice of paradise on Earth.

But inside?

It's a goddamn disaster.

"I... I... I'm a monster," Cassie cries to herself, snot and tears dripping down her face as she rocks herself back and forth on one of the daybeds. She sniffs, not even bothering to wipe away the mascara staining her cheeks. "How could I do that to Adam? How can I ever live with myself again?" She balked. "How do I tell him? Oh, God."

She covers her face and sobs even harder, and Skyler winces, rubbing her back and doing her best to comfort her Little as she falls apart.

Erin is pacing back and forth, arms folded hard over her chest as she shakes her head over and over, tossing between murmuring to herself and screaming curse words loud enough for the entire resort to hear. Something happened to her around the same time Cassie had her meltdown, about an hour ago amidst the thumping music of the beach club, but she has yet to tell us what, exactly.

All we know is she looked at her phone, screamed bloody murder, cried, and has been pacing ever since we all dragged Cassie back here to console her.

Ashlei disappeared into the bathroom as soon as we got back, and for how long she's been in there, I can only imagine she's ralphing up the fruity shots we've been knocking back all night.

And then there's me, swiping back and forth between two pictures on my phone, each depicting a different man I love.

Swipe.

Me on Kade's back, my arms wrapped around his shoulders, lips pressed to his cheek as my hair falls over us like a curtain. His warm brown eyes are bright with love and adoration, his smile megawatt in size as he snaps the selfie.

Swipe.

Me and Jarrett in bed, his beast of a body encompassing all of mine as I curl my back into his chest like a cat. The morning sunlight reflects on our soft, sated smiles, and his dark eyes smolder at the camera, promising he's nowhere near finished with the girl in his arms.

Swipe.

Kade.

Swipe.

Jarrett.

Swipe. Swipe. Swipe. Swipe.

Back and forth, over and over, I stare at those men — the men who own my heart — and feel it break at the realization that I will hurt one of them.

That I've *already* hurt them both.

I don't deserve the patience they've given me — the space, the time. And I definitely don't deserve their love.

But I have it, and though I love them both in return, I know there's no putting off the decision I have to make.

The decision I made long before I was ready to admit it to myself, if I was being honest.

In my daze, I don't realize Erin is screaming and Cassie is having a full-on panic attack until I snap out of the trance my phone has me in. I close the screen and drop it to the cushion beside me, popping up and running over to Erin first.

"It's not fucking fair! This whole system... this whole *world* is fucked!" she screams.

"Will you bitches shut up?!" Ashlei yells from inside the bathroom. "It's impossible for a girl to poop with all this racket going on!"

Skyler gives me a look that says she's got Cassie, so I grab Erin's hand and lead her to the edge of the balcony, letting the fresh sea breeze calm us both. I don't say anything, just hold her there and smooth my hand over her arm, letting her take a moment for whatever it is that's going on.

She opens her mouth to say something when my ringtone sounds from the chair I was sitting on, and Erin and I both look at the screen, stilling at the sight of Jarrett's name in bold above the new message.

My chest caves in on itself, and I close my eyes for a long moment before I open them to find Erin staring back at me.

"What are you going to do?" she asks, her voice just a whisper.

Before I can answer, Ashlei clears her throat from where she's now standing in the middle of the balcony between us all. Her hair is a mess tied loosely on top of her head, her arm still in a sling from the accident, and her face is ghostly pale.

She doesn't say a word.

But when I spot what she's holding in her hand, she doesn't have to.

Her eyes lock on mine, and I exhale, stomach roiling for a whole new reason. Skyler is the first to say what I know we're all thinking.

"Oh, shit."

Bear

Three Months Earlier

OF ALL THE BULLSHIT classes they made me take during my time at Palm South, they never forced one on me called *Life After College*. And only three months removed from being a student, I'm seriously wondering why that isn't the number one required credit for every single one of us.

I had no idea how easy I had it, even when it was hard. I didn't realize how having classes and finals was a piece of cake compared to maneuvering the oversaturated job hunt, how partying on a school night is a hell of a lot easier than partying on a work night, or how that degree doesn't mean shit once you actually get a job — for your salary or for your day-to-day tasks.

If anything, there should have been a class during every kid's last semester called *Welcome to the Real World, Where You Have Student Loan Debt and a Shitty Salary and a Job You're Not Actually Prepared for and a Boss Who Expects You To Work Double the Hours Required.*

Good Luck!

These are the thoughts that trickle through my mind like a leaky faucet as I eat lunch out of a plastic container in the break room, staring at the calendar on my phone with the list of shit I still have to do when I go back to my cubicle.

It had taken me all damn summer to get a job. It turned out that while I had a degree, my lack of on-the-job experience made me less appealing than those who had internships out the ass. Luckily for me, Erin helped me spruce up my resume, and Ashlei hooked me up with an unpaid internship for a couple months at her firm, working on graphics for her clients.

With a professional portfolio finally under my belt, I landed my first paid gig — Junior Graphic Designer at *Sparrow Creative*, a young but hungry advertising agency downtown.

As much as the journey to get here sucked, and as much as I'm not thrilled with the salary — even though I was able to negotiate a little higher than they originally offered — I'm thankful to be working, to finally be applying what I learned in school.

But something is... missing.

I thought it was sports. After all, I played all through high school and college, and now I'm a quote, unquote, *adult* and not a professional athlete. So, I joined a CrossFit gym, thinking that would fill the gap.

And it has, for the most part.

In fact, I've become so competitive and so knowledgeable about the culture and the training that the owner at my gym has been whispering in my ear about possibly coming on as a personal trainer or class instructor.

For now, though, I'm content just to train and compete on my own.

And still...

Something's missing.

I could argue that it's sex, being that Erin and I have been taking it excruciatingly slow. But that's been *my* decision — mostly because I know what she's been through, what she's *going* through, and when I do take her, it's going to be with nothing but reverence and a cherished understanding of how lucky I am to be the one she trusts to give herself to.

Besides, we've been doing plenty of other things that satiate my sexual needs, including me coaching her through sucking my cock, which might be the most erotic thing I've ever done in my life — and I've had a finger up the asshole, so that's saying something.

If I'm being honest, that woman is so goddamn hot, all she has to do is kiss me and rub that tight little body against mine and I'm ready to come.

So it's not the sex, and it's not the job, and it's not the lack of physical output.

But still...

Something.

The slam of the microwave snaps me from my thoughts, and I look up just in time to see a longing smile spread on my co-worker's face.

"*God,*" she says, shaking her head with her eyes on my food. "That looks so much better than the Lean Cuisine I have. Tell me what it tastes like." Her eyes flick to mine. "Slowly, so I can savor it."

I laugh, taking the bite of salmon and asparagus I have stacked on my fork before I set it down. "I won't submit you to such torture, Giselle."

She sighs. "I should probably thank you, but maybe I like a little torture from time to time."

She winks as I shake my head and stack up another bite. "It's just salmon. You could easily be eating this, too."

"Define *easily,*" she says, grabbing her frozen meal from the microwave once it dings and sitting across from me. "Because someone had to cook that salmon and those veggies, and I can tell you that after a long day here?" She shakes her head, peeling the plastic wrapper back from her container. "It ain't me."

I cringe at the sight of the rubbery-looking pasta she's unveiled. "I think I'd stay up until two in the morning meal prepping if it meant I didn't have to eat *that*."

She sighs again, stabbing the noodles with her plastic fork and twirling until she has a bite prepped. "It's awful," she admits. "But it's worth every savory minute I had on my couch last night."

I chuckle, and we hold our forks up in a sort of *cheers* before both taking a bite.

Giselle is a few years older than me, and though she's joking about being lazy, I know for a fact that she's not. For one, she's too toned and slim to not be active and watching what she eats, and for two, I've seen her bust her ass day in and day out in this office since my first day three weeks ago.

She's the youngest account manager in the agency.

And it doesn't take more than three days of working with her to understand why.

As if her boldly colored skirt-suits and matching high — *high* — heels don't command enough of a presence when she walks into a room, her light brown skin, cat-lined eyes and painted lips certainly do the trick. I've never seen her onyx hair down, it's always pulled back in a slick, tight bun, and the way she holds her shoulders square and back straight told me long before I ever talked to her that she took no shit from anyone.

The first time I was in a meeting with her, she single-handedly saved us from losing a client the agency had been working with for three years. Not only that, but she ran through a list of reasons it was *their* fault that their content was under-performing, and by the end of the meeting, convinced the client to invest double what they were before in the advertising efforts.

All without breaking a sweat.

So, while I could understand why she might not have the energy to meal prep every night, I wasn't foolish enough to believe she didn't work just as hard outside of this office as she did inside it.

"How are you feeling now that you're a little more settled in?" she asks when she's done chewing.

"Great," I say with a smile I hope is more convincing than it feels. "I'm excited to be here. I just hope my work is up to standard for the agency."

"You know it is," she says instantly. "Don't fish for a compliment when you already know."

I gape. "I... I wasn't—"

"Confidence, Mr. Pennington. *That's* what turns me on. You walked in here with it on the day of your interview and every day since. I understand you wanting to taper that down a bit, be modest around someone in a higher position than you, but I'll tell you right now that you'll get farther here — and everywhere in this field — by owning your talent and reminding every single person every single chance you get that they can't find that same talent anywhere else. If you're not demanding a raise in six months' time, you might as well quit and find a new job. Because unless you demand the respect and the pay you deserve in this career, you'll never get it."

I swallow, not sure if I should be flattered or scared.

But Giselle just lifts one eyebrow, nods, and continues eating. "Did I see you walking into BlackSheep last night?"

I pause with my next bite mid-air at the mention of my CrossFit gym. "Yes..."

She chuckles. "I'm not stalking you. I go to the yoga studio two doors down." She pauses. "I've always been curious about CrossFit though. Think I would like it?"

I take a breath, thankful for the subject change and the way my balls relax a little now that she's not grilling me. "Depends. I think if you're athletic and like a challenge, absolutely. But it's a little harder on the body than yoga." I pause. "No offense. I just mean you'll bulk up a little more, and get callouses."

Giselle takes a sip of her water with a slick smile on those painted lips of hers. "Oh, I don't mind getting my hands dirty."

My phone pings on the table, the vibration of it loud enough that both our eyes slip to the screen where Erin's bright, beautiful smile reflects back — along with a text that asks how my day is going.

I smile, feeling more like a little boy with a crush than a grown man with a serious girlfriend. Even though I know Erin better than probably anyone, and she knows *me* better than anyone, everything between us feels fresh and new now. Every night I spend with her is a new discovery, every conversation one I want to commit to memory, every kiss one that leaves its own permanent brand.

I'm still wearing that goofy smile as I type back a response.

"Girlfriend?" Giselle asks.

"The best one on the planet."

When I finish the text and look at her, she's wearing a smile laced with a million things she won't say. "Glad you found her before you found this place," she decides on, popping another bite in her mouth. "Because you damn sure wouldn't have found the time or energy to date if you'd come here first."

I'm not sure if I should laugh or ask her if she needs someone to talk to, but I don't get the chance before there's a knock on the door panel of the break room, and my boss peeks his head in.

"Sorry to bother during lunch, but can I get your eyes on this website?"

I nod, gathering my things. "I'm finished, anyway."

"Great. See you in my office."

He ducks out, and once I've cleared the table, I nod to Giselle. "Nice talking to you. Enjoy the rest of your lunch."

She holds her fork up to me with a wink, and there's something in her eyes still, like she's assessing every move I make, every word I say.

I can still feel her watching me even when I'm down the hall and out of sight.

Cassie

I SCREAM THE WORDS to our door chant loud and proud with my sisters, and then to a roar of applause from the potential new members waiting outside the door, we all scurry to our spots in the hallway, lining up in perfect order to receive the girls.

I've done this three times before now — once on the outside and twice on the inside — and every time, my stomach fills with butterflies. But this time, those butterflies seem to be flying with wet wings, slow and sad.

Because it's my last rush week.

Ever.

A thick knot forms in my throat at the thought, the same kind that blocked my breath when I clung to Adam in the Boston airport two weeks ago. Saying goodbye to him after spending half the summer with our families, and the other half getting him set up in his new apartment, and with his new job which felt impossible.

Just like saying goodbye to Kappa Kappa Beta does now.

Change...

I'm no stranger to it, and yet I've never been hit with so much at once. It felt like a dream, getting my acceptance email from Johns Hopkins, and now here I am just four months from graduating and leaving this sorority and this university behind me.

Tears well in my eyes, and I look up at the ceiling and fan myself to keep them from falling. I'm about to match up with a girl I'm supposed to convince to rush KKB, not run away thinking we're all a bunch of emotional weirdos.

Hands grab my arms as I'm still staring at the ceiling, and when I drop my gaze, I find Skyler smiling at me with tears of her own.

"I want to hug you so fucking bad right now," she says. "But if I do, we'll both lose it and ruin our makeup and chase the poor new girls away."

I bark out a laugh, swiping the lone tear that escapes from my cheek before it can mar my makeup. "This is it," I whisper.

Skyler nods, her bottom lip trembling, but then she quickly shakes her head and blows out a breath as the Recruitment Chair hollers back that the doors are opening.

"We can cry later. For now, plaster on that smile I love so much and find us some new sisters."

I smile and nod, and with a kiss to my cheek, she releases me and makes her way to the front of the hall to greet the girls.

As the president.

My stomach roils a bit at the tradition I'm breaking, the one that has been around longer than I can even wrap my head around. Every girl in our line has been president for years and years, but that ends with Skyler.

Or maybe, it just skips a generation.

Maybe *I* won't be president, but with my sights set on finding a Little, I find myself smiling at the thought that maybe, one day, *she* could be.

When the doors finally open, it's pure madness. Music blasts from our speakers, all my sisters clapping in sync to the beat as we file toward the door. When we get there, we're matched up with a girl rushing, the line-up planned by our Exec Board. They review the girls each night before and select who they think would be the best match to talk to the potential new member. It's all a dance, a beautiful, coordinated dance of courting.

If only dating were so lovely.

When I'm a few girls away from picking up my own match, I spot a potential new member on the other side.

Chewing her fingernails down to the nubs.

Her slicked-black hair is styled in two adorable space buns, a pair of oversized glasses slipping down her nose before she pushes them up and goes right back to chewing her thumb nail. She's wearing the cutest romper I've ever seen, navy blue with a white and yellow floral design and a small gap showing the pale skin between her breasts and her belly button. It takes confidence to put on an outfit like that, and yet she looks like she's ready to bolt at any second.

She doesn't look up at me when it's our turn, not until I step halfway out of the house and extend my hand for hers.

"Hi!" I say cheerily. "I'm Cassie. Welcome to KKB. I know it's a little loud right now, let's go inside and find somewhere we can talk."

Her eyes are a cloudy river, blue and green swirling together inside an iris lined with a thick, navy blue rim. They stun me so much I have a hard time not gasping and commenting on them right away. Instead, I hold out my arm for her to link with mine, and she does so hesitantly before following me back down the hallway.

I'm *supposed* to lead her to a corner in the main dining room, where we'll scream over the rest of the conversations happening in the house and strain to hear one another. But I'm already hoarse from the day before, and I can tell just by looking at her that this girl would appreciate some quiet. So, I lead her upstairs and back to my room.

"Whew," I say when we're inside, leaving the door open so we can still hear everything going on downstairs. "It's a little crazy out there, huh?"

She nods emphatically, her eyes growing a bit wider as she folds her hands in front of her waist.

"Sorry, it's kind of a mess up here," I say, looking around at the rogue hair extensions and makeup and clothing tossed this way and that. "During Rush, we open up our rooms to everyone — even if they don't live in the house. And with seventy-six of us getting ready every morning, there's not much time to clean up after."

She smiles. "This is your room?"

I nod. "It is. I have a roommate, Lindsey, who rushed last semester. She's really sweet. And my Big is the president, the one who greeted you before you came in. Her room is right down the hall."

The girl's eyes go wide. "Wow. That's so cool."

I smile. "What's your name?"

"Tera," she says. "Tera Rosebaum."

"Nice to meet you, Tera. I'm Cassie, in case you couldn't hear me downstairs. How's Rush going so far?" I grab my desk chair and pull it over to Lindsey's, sliding that one out for Tera to have a seat.

She hesitates at first, but when she finally sits down, I don't miss the relief she feels to no longer be standing in her wedges. "It's... going."

I laugh. "Kind of overwhelming, isn't it?"

"That's an understatement," she says, wincing a little as she rolls her ankles. "To be honest... I kind of feel out of my element here. All the hair and makeup, the dresses, the heels, the screaming, the music... it's a lot."

I nod, remembering all too well how it felt to be on that side of it. "I had those same thoughts when I rushed. I remember thinking to myself that I was among a bunch of walking, talking Barbies."

"Oh, my God. That's exactly what it is!"

"Like how did all these girls learn how to do makeup like this?"

"I can barely keep up with mascara and lip gloss."

"You should see me try to contour. Hideous. Like a clown."

Tera giggles, relaxing a little more in her seat. "How did you get over that initial discomfort?"

I sigh, looking to the side as I try to recall who I'd been at that time in my life. It feels so long ago now that it takes a lot of effort.

"Well, for me, it took meeting the right girls. Some of the houses I went to, I could just tell I wouldn't fit in. It was nothing against them, I just didn't feel that connection, that spark, you know? But when I came to KKB, I met a girl named Erin." I smile at the memory. "I didn't know it then, but one day, she'd be my GrandBig."

"Your what?"

I chuckle. "It's kind of like your family within the family of the sisterhood as a whole. After you Rush, a girl in our sorority will pick you for her Little, and you have to pick her for your Big, in return. Then you're part of a line. So, Erin was *my* Big's Big."

"Makes my head spin."

Another laugh from me. "We can get into it later. But yeah, for me, meeting her, and then a few other girls in this sorority... I just felt like I was home. I was torn, actually, on the night before bid day, and I talked to a girl down by the reflection pond who helped me pick. Come to find out, she was a KKB sister, too." I paused. "And she became my Big."

Tera smiles, but then the light goes out in her eyes, gaze falling to her shoes. "What if you don't fit in anywhere?"

I tilt my head. "Is that how you feel?"

She nods. "Don't get me wrong, I'm not like the girl who has no friends. I have a lot, actually." She pauses. "Had. Back home. But I don't know, I'm... different. I like anime, and romance books, and video games and cosplay." She clears her throat, smoothing her hands over the shorts of her romper. "And *look* at me. I look like I ate three of your sisters before I came in here."

My heart lurches into my throat, and I instantly want to reach for her, to pet her arm and say she's gorgeous, and that her size was the *last* thing I noticed about her. But I can tell just from this small interaction that Tera doesn't trust easily, doesn't open easily, and I want her to feel safe with me — not like I pity her, especially since from what I can see, there's nothing to pity.

She's a badass. I can sense it.

"Cosplay, huh?" I decide on. "What exactly does that mean?"

She laughs uncomfortably, grabbing the back of her neck. "It's really nerdy."

"Stop that. I bet it's cool if you love it so much."

She shrugs. "I mean, *I* think it's cool."

"And you have a whole slew of friends who do, too, right?"

She nods. "We dress up like our favorite characters from movies, or books, or video games or shows."

"Wow! Like, costumes?"

"Yes, but *way* more intense. I mean, especially for conventions and stuff, we go all out. I'm talking chopping our hair off, or growing it out for years to get a specific look, spending thousands of dollars on fabric and supplies to make our costumes."

"So you're not just buying them online or something?"

"*God*, no," she says, brows furrowing with the offense.

I chuckle. "Sounds like I have a lot to learn. Do you have any pictures of you dressed up?"

Tera bites her lip, like she's deciding if she can trust me, but in the end, she pulls out her phone and taps until there's an image so striking it makes me gasp.

I grab the phone out of her hand, pulling it closer and zooming in to inspect the intricate design of the fire-engine red costume. It's skin-tight, leather-like and hugging every curve she has. Paired with the badass thigh-high boots and her bright red hair — which I can't tell if it's is a wig or her actual hair dyed that color — she looks like a completely different person.

"Bitch!" I say without thinking, but she laughs, so I take it as permission. "Get out of here with that *I can't do makeup* shit. Look at you! This is incredible!"

"I was Asuka Langley Soryu. She's an anime character."

"She's iconic," I correct, handing her phone back to her. "And so are you."

The smile she's wearing now is her most genuine once since she walked in the room, but with a shout from below and a music cue, I know it's time to start walking her out.

I sigh, standing. "There's never enough time during these things."

"It's time to go already?"

"Afraid so," I answer as she stands to join me. "But I really hope I'll see you back here tomorrow. I'd love to get to know you better."

She smiles, her mesmerizing eyes flicking back and forth between mine. "I'd like that, too."

We link arms and walk downstairs, chatting a little until the music is too loud to do much other than smile and wave goodbye.

And when the doors shut, my sisters excitedly filling into the kitchen for lunch, I run around the house until I find Skyler, nearly toppling into her once I finally do.

"Whoa, whoa!" she says, catching my arms as we both find our balance. She laughs. "Slow down there, killer."

"I think I just met my Little."

Her mouth pops open at that, and her eyes search mine for a moment before her lips meet again and spread into a knowing smile.

"Tell me everything."

Skyler

I'M USED TO THE way lonely feels.

Growing up, I was an outcast, a nerd, the girl who hung out with her poor family and didn't have more than a handful of friends — if you could even call them that. When I wasn't playing poker with my parents, I was studying or coloring or listening to music in my room. Sometimes I would ride my bike around town by myself, just listening to the wind breezing through my hair.

When I came to Palm South, all that changed.

With a snap of my fingers, I altered that past and became a new me — the me I'd always felt like I was inside. I embraced my sass, my courage, my fearlessness and channeled it into being the girl I'd always known was simmering there under the surface.

With my sisters in Kappa Kappa Beta always around, and practically every boy on Greek Row begging for my time, I never had another lonely day.

Until this summer.

How I could have lived in such a blissful heaven for a full year only to tumble down from the clouds and slam into the dirt is beyond me.

Kip felt like the safest, most sure thing in the world.

Now, I don't know him at all.

The Kip I love wouldn't have forgotten our one-year anniversary, or the date *he'd* planned. The Kip I love wouldn't have had his hands on another girl's hips while she was naked in a shower, whether it was for work or not. The Kip I love would have listened to me, would have understood my anger and hurt.

And more than anything, the Kip I know would have found a way to make it right.

It wasn't that he didn't try, I suppose. He called. He texted. He came by the house. When I finally did decide I was ready to see him and hear him out, he apologized.

But not for what he did.

For how he'd made me feel.

It was a monstrous slap to the face. *"I'm sorry I made you feel that way,"* as if I was being irrational, as if he still stood firm in his delusion that he was right and I was wrong. I knew I wasn't a saint. I knew I could have handled that situation better than I did.

But he couldn't even see it, couldn't see Natalia for the games she played, couldn't see how him putting her and the show before our anniversary killed me.

The show about *our love*.

How ironic.

He went right back to filming, editing, producing — like everything was fine. It wasn't until he showed up one evening and tried to kiss me and I pulled away that I think he realized a simple apology wasn't going to be enough.

"I need some time," I'd told him. *"And some space."*

I could close my eyes now and still see the hurt in his eyes, the deflation of his shoulders, could still feel the way his lips pressed against my temple at the same time one lone tear slipped down my cheek.

That was the last time I saw him, almost two months ago.

I threw myself into recruitment, into my last semester as president, into making damn sure I leave this sorority in even better shape than I found it. Spending time with the girls helped, too, and now that we're in the thick of Rush week, I'm distracted.

Distracted, but lonely.

Even in a house full of my sisters.

Even at night when Cassie and I curl up in my bed and talk and laugh and reminisce.

Every minute I'm awake, every second I'm alive — I'm lonely.

Because my other half, that person who completed me and made me feel whole for the first time in my life is gone.

And I don't know if I'll ever have that piece of me again.

"Sky," a voice says, shaking me from my haze as I filter through the profile binders of the potential new members coming through the house tonight. It's the last night before we make our bids and hope they pick us for their top choice, in return.

I turn in my chair, finding Ava, our recruitment chair, with an apologetic grimace on her beautiful face.

"Sorry to bother," she says instantly. "But, um... you have a visitor."

I frown. "Is it one of the other presidents?"

"It's Kip."

All the blood drains from my face, my stomach roiling violently.

I clear my throat. "Be right down."

She nods, her eyes sympathetic as she closes the door and leaves me alone.

I take a moment to check my reflection in the mirror, smoothing my hands over my elegant, short black dress. It's a halter top with thin straps and a body that hugs all my slim curves. My favorite accent is the slit that accents my toned thigh, and the strappy high heels I paired with it. My hair is pulled back in a delicate braid, my makeup applied to perfection, natural and light, but with enough precision to stun.

Pref night is perhaps the most important of all of Rush week. It's our final chance to convince the girls we want that this should be their home for the next four years.

It's also the most emotional night for the seniors, as they realize *their* time here is coming to an end, and a new chapter is beginning.

Without them.

I blow out a soft breath, succumbing to numbness as my feet carry me blindly down the hall, the stairs, and out to the front porch where Kip is leaning against one of the tall columns, his hands in his pockets, eyes on the cement ground.

When he lifts those cerulean blue pools and locks his gaze on mine, my bones lock up, stopping me mid-stride a good four feet away from him.

My skin heats as he drags his gaze down the length of me, and he shakes his head slightly as he pushes off the banister to stand tall. "Sky... *Jesus*," he breathes, running a hand over his scruff. "You are so goddamn beautiful."

Everything in me wants to melt.

I want to swoon, to run to him, to fold myself into his arms and press my lips to his.

But my heart refuses, making me cross my arms and clear my throat, instead. "Thank you," I say flatly. "Do you need something? I'm kind of busy."

Kip doesn't wince, but I see the pain my words inflict regardless. He never was able to hide his emotions from me.

"We finished the show."

He waits for me to react, and when I don't, he presses his tongue into his cheek, steeling a breath before he continues.

"I mean, we finished filming. We still have some post-production to do, but it'll be done back at the school before we turn in the final product." He swallows. "I think the mini-series will be live on the web by the end of November."

"Congratulations."

I can't help how flat the word is when I release it, can't help that I'm already turning to leave, but Kip's hand shoots out to hook my elbow, stopping me in my tracks.

"Skyler, I'm leaving," he breathes against my neck, his body inching closer and closer. "I'm going back to California. Please," he pleads, his voice breaking. "Don't make me leave like this."

I close my eyes against the pain splitting my chest, against the urge to weep.

"What do you want from me, Kip?" I ask on a breath.

"Forgiveness."

I turn then, pulling from his grip on my arm. "Forgiveness for what, exactly?"

I need to hear him say it. I need to hear him say he was wrong, that he understands why I was upset — why I *still* am.

Kip rolls his lips together, pushing his glasses up the bridge of his nose before he hangs his hands on his hips and looks off in the distance down Greek Row.

I shake my head. "Kip, what happened that night... what happened all last semester... it killed me."

His nose flared, eyes watering, but he wouldn't look at me.

"Whether you realize it and want to admit it or not, you chose the show over me." I swallow. "You chose *her* over me."

"Natalia is a professional."

"Natalia is a bitch," I correct, not even a little sorry when he finally looks at me with a frown etched in his brows. "She's conniving and smarter than you give her credit for, and she knew what she was doing."

"Why are you attacking her? *You're* the one who picked her for the part!"

"And that was my mistake. Now, can you admit to yours?"

Kip pinches the bridge of his nose on a long breath. "Skyler, nothing happened. I was directing them through the shower scene so we could get it right. Natalia was there because I asked her to be, she wasn't trying to—"

"You forgot," I interrupted, and my bottom lip trembled as I waited for his eyes to meet mine once more. "You forgot to pick me up. For our date. For our *anniversary*. And then I walked in on you touching another woman, naked, in the shower. Let me ask you this, Kip. If it were me who forgot, who you had to track down, who you found holding another man in the shower — would you be okay with it?"

"Skyler, it's work. It's nothing—"

"Don't do that to me," I say curtly. "Don't make it seem like I don't support you, like I haven't *always* supported you. I understood when you needed to move across the country to go to the right school to get you where you want to be. I understood even when you came back here and you explained that I wouldn't see you much. I understood when your time was wrapped up in filming. I even understood why you didn't see it at first, the way Natalia looked at you, the things she was doing to make sure I felt threatened." I swallow. "But I have a right to be upset over what happened, and I deserve a proper apology."

"I'm sorry," Kip says quickly, reaching for my hands. He holds them up and presses his lips to the knuckles. "I'm sorry for hurting you."

I nod, biting my lip.

It still isn't enough.

"I have to go," I whisper, pulling my hands from his. "It's Pref Night and I have a lot to do."

"Skyler, please," Kip begs when I turn. "I don't want to leave like this. I... I don't even know what we are anymore."

I pause with my hand on the front doorknob, my breath hitched in my throat, tears swelling in my eyes until the wood panel blurs.

"That makes two of us."

I open the door, close it behind me, and press my back to the wood, smoothing my breaths as much as I can as I listen to Kip shuffle off the front porch.

Then, I lose it.

"WE NEED TO CALL the florist," my boss, Brittany, says in a slight panic through the phone. I just left the office not even an hour ago, and I hadn't even had the chance to put my leggings on before my phone was ringing.

But this is how it is working with Brittany Nova.

That bitch doesn't know how to *not* work.

"I called them this morning. The arrangements are all set, centerpieces complete, bouquets ready, they're just finishing up prepping for the arch, which they'll build on site," I say, grabbing a wine glass from the cabinet and a half-full bottle of Malbec from the fridge.

"Oh, good. Okay, next, we need to finalize the wedding cocktail."

"Already done. Bride and I decided on tequila, and the bartenders whipped up a few options for her this afternoon. She loved the one with grapefruit. We're calling it, *Rose in Love* and I already have the team making a sign for the bar."

"Rose in Love," she repeats. "I don't hate it as much as I thought I would. Okay, the seven-tier cheesecake — *God help us* — we need to—"

"Made to perfection. I stopped by the bakery on my way home. They made a smaller tier for me to taste and inspect. All the filling options are exactly as we asked, the colors are remarkable... although, I'll be honest, the poor team of bakers looked like they were ready to collapse from decorating it. They'll deliver it at four-thirty tomorrow evening, and I already made sure the venue has an entire fridge saved for it. They'll store each tier separately and assemble in the kitchen during dinner, rolling it out just in time to be cut."

"Brilliant," Brittany breathed, and I could hear the pen sliding across paper as she ticked that off the list. "The surfboard guest book."

"Set up with gold, silver, and black Sharpies right next to the Polaroid table."

"The lights—"

"Are all prepped and ready, along with speakers and mics, and the team will be bringing them over at ten tomorrow morning so we have plenty of time to get it all set up the way we need. The only thing I'm waiting to hear back on are whether the tree lanterns are too heavy for the limbs to support, but don't worry — we have gold bird feeder holders on stand-by if needed."

"Fireworks?"

"I'm pouring a glass of wine and am about to start tying the ribbons on the sparklers now. Buckets are already decorated. The team and I have a plan of attack for lighting all three-hundred-and-forty-five guests. And the pyrotechnics have forty-thousand dollars' worth of fireworks that will put Disney to shame and a boat to set them off of from the middle of the lake. We tested last night, and the lawn will be perfect for viewing."

There's a brief pause before Brittany lets out a dramatic exhale, and I can almost see her slumping back in her chair. "How did I get so lucky to find someone like you?"

"You say that now..."

She chuckles. "Okay, so I guess all that's left for me to do is—"

"Is to go to the rehearsal dinner and *have fun.*"

"That's never been a part of this job."

I snort. "Well, okay, maybe fun is the wrong term. But *relax*. Jenna and Howard will be there and they are well prepped to take care of everything. You just focus on making sure the bride is calm, and keep her mother away from the schnapps."

"That might be the hardest job of the evening."

"That's why we saved that one for you."

She lets out a puff of a laugh. "Thank you, Jess. For everything. Try to get some rest tonight, too."

"I plan on it, right after I put the final touches on the seating chart board."

"See you in the morning."

"Bright and early, boss."

When we hang up, I chuckle to myself and leave my phone on the counter, bringing my wine glass and the rest of the bottle over to the dining room table — which has been more of my craft table lately than anything. Since Ashlei moved out of our place and in with Brandon, and Erin spends most of her time at Bear's, there's never really any reason to clean it.

A ping of loneliness filters through me, but it's gone just as quickly as it appears.

If I'm being honest with myself, I've enjoyed the last couple of months on my own. I've been able to throw all my energy into the job I worked so hard to get, into making a name for myself with my boss and the rest of our team. Even though summer is the slowest season for weddings in Florida, we still had several weddings each month — all with affluent brides who expected the best from us.

I've been thankful to not have any distractions.

But just because Kade and Jarrett both respected my wishes and left me alone for the summer, doesn't mean I haven't been thinking of them every single day.

I don't know what I thought I was doing when I asked for the summer, as if them giving me some time and space would somehow give me clarity. Like I would have some sort of epiphany. Instead, I feel like I've sunk even deeper into thick, nasty mud that keeps seeping up, up, up. At this point, it's got to be at least chest-high and threatening to take me all the way under if I don't do something soon.

The issue is that I have *no* idea *what* to do.

I meant what I told the girls back in May — I love Kade and Jarrett both.

But just like the girls had so gently reminded me then, I also know I can't *have* them both.

And maybe that's the truth that's kept me latching onto this notion that somehow, space and time would help. Maybe, if I was being brutally honest with myself, I just didn't want to make the decision and was putting it off for as long as I could.

What a selfish, awful thing to do.

I'm halfway through my first glass of wine and first dozen sparklers when my phone buzzes loud on the counter, moving along the granite to the beat of my ringtone.

"Hey, Herb," I say when I see the front desk's number on the screen. "Another package?"

"Not this time, Miss Vonnegut. You have a visitor. A Mister Kade Brewer. Shall I send him up?"

Ice freezes my veins, and I pause for so long, Herb clears his throat to remind me to answer.

"Um, yes," I say weakly. "Yes."

I stare at the phone for too long after the call ends, unable to breathe, let alone fix my appearance or think about what the hell I'm going to say once Kade makes it up to our floor.

I'm still frozen in place when there's a soft knock on the front door, and I snap out of my daze, slamming back the last of my wine before I answer it.

The sight of Kade turns my knees to jelly.

His style has changed so much since I first met him. I've watched him grow from a boy into a man, from a silly flirt into someone who knows what they want and isn't afraid to go for it. Still, to see him standing here in fitted navy dress pants and a sleek white button down, a sports jacket folded over his left arm and mocha oxfords on his feet, it's enough to shock me silent.

His short hair is styled, his face clean-shaven, skin dark and smooth from the summer sun. I know as president of his fraternity, he's likely spent most of his days at the beach or the campus pool, and he has the tan to show for it.

And then there are his eyes, endless pools of honey gold and warm maple syrup brown swirling together.

And he's watching me like he's a sick dog and I'm the motherfucker with a gun about to put him out of his misery.

After a long pause and not a peep from either of us, he finally swallows, standing a little straighter as he says, "I know the last day of summer isn't technically until September, but school is starting back up next week, which signals fall to me." He shakes his head. "And honestly, I couldn't stand to be away from you. Not for one second more." His shoulders slump. "Please, Jess."

I close my eyes on a breath, and when I open them again, Kade's brows are bent together, his eyes searching mine for a response.

For permission.

So I simply take a step forward, and in the next breath, I'm swept into his arms.

Everything about him encompasses me — his big, muscular arms, his broad, warm chest, his hands splaying on my rib cage, his scent, earthy and strong. I feel like a little girl again in those arms, like I'm free.

Like I'm safe.

Kade exhales at the embrace, burying his face in my neck. "Fucking hell, I've missed you so much."

I squeeze him back. "I've missed you, too."

He doesn't release his hold on me for a long time, and when he finally does, he keeps his hands on my hips and just barely pulls back, watching me, waiting.

"Come inside," I say, grabbing his hand and tugging him out of the hallway. I close the door behind us and head for the couch, sitting down first and patting the cushion next to me so Kade does the same.

For a long pause, we just sit there, staring at each other, the silence somehow comfortable and awkward all at once.

"You look... weird," he finally comments, arching a brow as he takes in my attire.

I look down, realizing I'd only half-changed out of my work clothes, so I'm wearing an over-sized Kappa Kappa Beta t-shirt and a bright orange pencil skirt.

"Shit," I say on a laugh, running a hand back through my hair that's no doubt just as much of a mess. "It's been a busy day. Busy *week*. We have a wedding at the Hennigton Estate tomorrow."

Kade whistles. "Must be a fancy one if it's there."

"The budget was four-hundred-thousand dollars, if that tells you anything."

He balks. "That's a joke, right?"

"Not even a little bit." I slide a finger along the buttons on his shirt. "What are *you* so dressed up for?"

I didn't miss the way his Adam's apple bobbed in his throat at the touch, but his smile was quick and easy. "Had a meeting with the Director of Development and Chapter Operations for Alpha Sigma."

My eyebrows shoot up. "He came all the way from national headquarters? That doesn't sound good."

"It was very good, actually," he says, grabbing the back of his neck. "They're so impressed with how we've turned the fraternity around, they're giving us a sixty-thousand-dollar budget for house-expansion."

I gasp. "Kade! Oh, my God! That's amazing!"

"He said to put in a pool," he adds with a laugh. "The brothers are going to flip out."

"*I'm* flipping out. This is amazing!"

He nods. "Well, we mostly have Adam to thank."

"And Jeremy. And *you*," I say, pointing a finger into his chest. "You were a big part of it, too. Still are."

"Yeah."

I frown. "Why aren't you doing backflips from excitement right now?"

He blows out a laugh, shaking his head and looking out of the floor-to-ceiling windows behind me. "Jess, I haven't been capable of being happy for months."

My stomach sours. "Kade..."

"No, no, don't say you're sorry, okay?" He chews his lip. "I don't want to talk about the summer, or about *him*." His nose flares a bit with that word, and then his eyes are on me. "I just want to hear how you are, and talk to you, and fucking *hold* you in my arms. I just want to know I still have a fighting chance to make you mine. I have to know."

I was already nodding before he finished, and I climb into his lap, straddling his thighs and wrapping my arms around his neck as I press my mouth to his.

The moment our lips touch, we both shiver, gasping at the sensation of being connected again.

Kade folds his arms around me and pulls me even closer, swallowing my next breath and kissing me like it's the last time he'll ever get the chance to.

"I love you," I whisper, pulling back to look him in the eyes when I say the words.

He nods, brushing my hair from my face. "I love *you*."

"Consider the summer over," I add. "I don't want to stay away from you any longer."

"Oh, thank fuck."

I smile.

"I was actually hoping you would come to the A Sig karaoke event in a couple weeks. You know how big of a deal it is... I really want you there. I *need* you there."

"Then I'm there."

"Really?"

I nod, and when he pulls me in for another kiss, I wonder how I've stayed away from him this long.

Or how I could have ever walked away from him in the first place.

Cassie

"WAIT, SO THE PLEDGE *actually* streaked through class?" I ask Adam.

"Not only did he strip down naked in the middle of class — a class with almost a hundred students, I might add — but he ran up and down the stairs, his junk just bouncing everywhere."

"Oh, my God."

"The poor professor, she's seventy-four years old. She fainted."

"She fainted?!"

"His waving willy sent her right to the floor."

I snort, but cover the sound with my hands in shame. "That's awful," I say, but I can't stop laughing.

"She's alright, thankfully. But yeah... *that's* what I'm dealing with."

I shake my head. "Well, at least you're in a cool place. You'll have a fall! Unlike us here," I add with a sigh.

Adam chuckles. "I do love it here. But it reminds me of spring break last year." He pauses. "Makes me miss you even more."

"Thanksgiving," I remind him, pressing my fingertips to my laptop screen, right over where his lips are. "And I fully expect you to show me around. We were in the Rockies, but I've never been to Boulder. Or Denver, really, other than to fly in and out."

"I can't wait," he says, and his brows fold together with the sentiment.

It's only been a few weeks since we both left Boston — him to go to his first Alpha Sigma chapter assignment as a

Field Executive, and me to come back to Florida for my last semester of college. But after having the whole summer together, it's like torture, being in different states, living different lives.

I finger the AΣ letters hanging from the white gold chain on my neck, remembering the day he lavaliered me like it was yesterday instead of six months ago. Any time I feel lonely or distraught over us being so far from each other, over not knowing the next time we'll be in the same place, I reach for that charm and let it ground me, let it remind me that what we have is far too strong for distance to destroy.

"What about you? How's it going over there?"

I sigh. "Well, I survived Rush Week, so that's always something to celebrate. Classes are already kicking my ass, but with it being my last semester, that's to be expected, I guess." I frown. "It's weird. Since I already got into Johns Hopkins, I feel... less motivated."

"Hey, maybe for the first time in your life, you just skate by for a semester. Take it easy."

I laugh. "Yeah, right. Do you know me?"

"I do," he says with a smile. "You'll be busting your ass for straight A's like always."

Adam kicks back in his bed — an unfamiliar bed so different from the one we set up for him in Boston. He gave me a tour of his little room in the Alpha Sigma house in Boulder when we first got on the call, and it made my stomach hurt that he was having new experiences at a new university without me.

It also makes me long to be there in bed with him, to be held by him, touched... kissed...

I shift against the little tingle that thought sends between my legs.

"Are you happy with the pledges you picked up?" Adam asks.

"Yeah," I say genuinely, smiling at the memory of that crazy week. "It's always a blur, but I tried to really take it all in this time. My *last* time. And... there's this girl I really like, I really feel a connection to." I bite my lip. "I think I might try to take her as my Little."

"Really? Who is she?"

"Her name is Tera. She's..." I laugh to myself. "Unique. Different in the best ways. She's got this amazing style, and all these fun hobbies and interests that are completely new to me. She does cosplay."

"Whoa," Adam remarks, brows shooting up. "What kind?"

"I don't really understand it all, but she said like anime characters. She showed me a picture and holy hell, it was hot."

"Who was she dressed as?"

I arch a brow at his earnest interest. "I can't remember... Asuka or something?"

"Asuka Langley Soryu?"

My jaw drops. "Yes. How the hell do you know that?"

Adam grimaces, grabbing the back of his neck. "I *may* or may not watch anime sometimes..."

"You never told me that!"

He laughs. "It's not exactly something to brag about, especially in a fraternity."

I shake my head, sitting back on the bed and folding my arms over my stomach. "Adam Brooks. I learn something new about you every day."

But Adam doesn't respond. In fact, he doesn't move at all. His eyes are glued on the screen, and after a moment, he lets out a long groan.

"Your tits look amazing right now."

I bark out a laugh, looking down at the simple tank top I'm wearing and the way my cleavage is on display with my arms crossed under the wire of my bra.

"You're such a perv."

"Can you blame me? It's been so long."

"Too long," I agree. "Seeing you in bed makes me wish I was there with you more than usual."

"Seeing your legs in those little sleep shorts makes *me* hard as a rock."

I flush, tucking my hair behind one ear as my eyes fall to my lap. "Adam..."

"When does Lindsey come back?"

I look at the door of our room, as if I expect him saying her name to have conjured my roommate. "I don't know. She's at the Omega Chi Beta house."

"Maybe we should take advantage of the alone time..."

I blush even harder, but just hearing him say the words has me clenching my thighs together. "I... I don't really know what to do."

Adam grins, a devilish smirk that tells me he knows *exactly* what to do.

"Lie back into your pillows," he says. "Let me see you."

I swallow, heat rushing from my neck to my toes as I do as he says. I use my hands to scoot back more toward the headboard, and then I lean back, posing like I'm on display for him and him only.

Adam bites his lip. "You're so beautiful," he murmurs, and then he repositions his own camera, and I can see his hard-on straining against his boxer briefs.

"Adam..." I breathe at the sight.

"I told you you make me hard," he says, and he runs

his hands over the thick outline, moaning as he flexes into the touch. "Does this make you wet?"

My mouth parts. "Yes."

"Show me."

I roll my lips together, not sure if my face is hot from embarrassment, or from how insanely turned on I am.

"Come on, baby," Adam purrs. "Open your legs for me."

My heart pounds harder at the request, and I tuck my knees up to my chest before slowly letting them fall open, my feet spreading to opposite sides of the bed.

"Now pull your shorts to the side."

Adam strips off his shirt, and then lays back in bed, waiting for me to do what I was told.

Hesitantly, I run my fingers down the inside of my thigh, and then slip them under the thin, plaid fabric of my shorts, pulling them to the side just a half inch.

"More," Adam pants.

I can see my reflection on the screen, though it's small in the top corner and Adam takes up most of the space. But when I pull the fabric a little farther, there's no mistaking the pink glossy image I reveal.

"*Fuck*," Adam hisses, and he reaches into his boxer briefs, tugging them down just below his ass and freeing his length. It springs up, hard and ready, and he thumbs the bit of precum on the tip before rolling his fist over the tip, the shaft, all the way down to the base.

I don't realize I'm moaning at the sight until the sound is vibrating through me, and I snap my mouth shut as soon as it happens.

"Don't be quiet," Adam says.

"I have to. House full of sorority girls, remember?"

Adam bites his lip, and then he sinks down farther into his sheets, his back against the headboard, abs folding in on themselves. He kicks his briefs the rest of the way off, and now I have a perfect view of his hand around his shaft, his tight balls, and his face full of lust and wanting in the background.

"This is a really hot view," I comment.

"You're telling me. I want to tear those shorts off you and kiss my way down between your legs. I want to run my tongue along those wet lips and suck your perfect little clit between my teeth."

I gasp at the vision of it, as if I can feel it actually happening, and without him having to tell me to, I strip out of my shorts and my tank top, unlatching my bra and tossing it aside until I'm completely naked on the screen.

"Jesus, Cassie," he moans, stroking himself slowly as his eyes devour me. "What do you want to do to me?"

"I want to lie back on that bed and hang my head off the edge of it, and I want you to fuck my mouth the way you did in the tent that night at Boca Chita Key. I want to feel every inch of you sliding into my mouth, my throat, until I gag for you."

Adam stifles his groan, but he's already pumping faster, flexing into his hand time and time again. "I fucking love when you have me in your mouth."

"And then I want to ride you. I want you deep inside me."

"How deep?"

I don't even realize that I'm palming my breast, tweaking the nipple, that my back is arched and my fingertips are circling my clit softly. It's like watching him on screen transports me in time and space, like I'm there with him.

Like it's *him* touching me.

I slip my fingers inside myself, watching on the screen as they disappear. "So deep I see stars," I breathe, closing my eyes as I let the sensation of being filled take me under.

"Rub your clit for me, baby. I want you to come."

I do as he says, dragging my fingertips down from my breast until they're circling my tender clit. I'm still pulsing my other fingers in and out, but then I keep them as deep as I can reach, wiggling the tips back and forth to hit the right spot.

"You're so fucking sexy, Cassie," Adam says, picking up his pace. "I want to come on those perfect tits of yours."

"I want you to come in my mouth."

He groans his approval, pumping faster as I match his pace.

"I'm so tight, Adam," I find myself whispering, and I'm not even a little ashamed. In fact, I'm spreading my legs wider, arching my back, chasing my release.

"You're always so tight. Tight and wet and *mine*."

"Oh God… I think…"

But I don't finish the sentence before the spark I've been chasing catches fire, and a powerful orgasm rolls through me, pulsing and numbing and all-consuming. I have to hold my breath to keep from crying out, and as my climax starts to recede, Adam catches his, his face contorting as he tries not to be too loud. Watching him spill on his stomach makes me ready for round two, makes me want to be there to lick it up and beg for more.

Jesus, who am I?

Adam's entire body shivers when he's spent, and he lets out a long breath, shaking his head. "Fuck *me*, that was hot."

I giggle, my face heating as I grab my shorts and pull them back on, slipping the tank top over my bare breasts.

"Nooo," Adam whines. "Don't cover them up."

I laugh, but before I can even pop back with a reply, the door to my room flies open and Lindsey bounds through it.

"Oh, my God. The party is so fun, Cass! You have to come!" she says, ignoring the way I jump at her entrance.

Adam covers his mouth to keep from laughing, meanwhile looking around him for something to clean up.

"I just came back to change real quick. Some stupid freshman spilled her rum punch all over me." Lindsey rolls her eyes, strips off her shirt and quickly replaces it with another. Her eyes find me then. "You coming?"

I swallow, hoping like hell I don't have *I just had phone sex with my boyfriend* written all over my red face. "I'll catch up, just finishing up some studying."

Lindsey rolls her eyes. "You already got into your dream school, remember?" She checks the time on her phone. "If you're not there in twenty minutes, I'm coming back and dragging your ass out of that bed."

She doesn't wait for a response before she flies out the door, and Adam howls with laughter as soon as she's gone.

"That's not funny, Adam! What if she would have been even sixty seconds earlier!"

"She would have had *quite* the view, and would have understood why I'm so obsessed with you."

I narrow my eyes and flick him off, but then I'm laughing, too, relaxing back against the headboard again. My eyes soften, and Adam's smile turns sad, too.

"I miss you," I whisper.

"Miss you more."

Bear

ANYONE WHO KNOWS ANYTHING about me knows that I don't get nervous.

That word, that state of being? It doesn't exist for me. Put me in the game with thirty seconds left and an impossible play to make. I'm your guy. Put me in front of a room full of angry fraternity brothers with the mission to get us all on the same page again. I'm your guy. Put me in front of the most drop-dead gorgeous and unobtainable woman in the world and watch me woo the panties right off her.

I'm. Your. Guy.

Nothing phases me — there's no amount of pressure you could put on me that would make me feel anything but completely confident that I can do whatever the fuck I want to do or need to do to get the job done.

But they say when you graduate college, things change.

And boy, are they a changin'.

My palms are so slick I can barely hold onto the handle of the pan as I sauté the mushrooms for the recipe I picked out, and I can't count the times I've double-checked that every candle is lit, that the flowers are in the perfect place, that my tie is on correctly, that the music is just the right volume. I also may or may not have restarted the album three times now, because the song I want playing when Erin gets here keeps coming on before she's arrived.

There's no denying it, no faking like I'm calm, cool, and collected.

Because Erin wants to have sex tonight.

And I have absolutely zero fucking chill about it.

It's not like it will be our first time. No, our *first* time together consisted of entirely too much alcohol and a sorority formal that neither of us remembers. That night has a black ink smudge over it, and if you asked either of us what positions we were in or who came first, we'd have no answer.

All we know is we woke up naked in bed together, and not too long after, Erin found out she was pregnant.

So, clearly, we didn't use protection.

My hand pauses mid-stir over the mushrooms, heart thrumming in my ears as I remember the choice Erin had to make. I can't imagine what I would have done if I'd been in her shoes, and as much as it angered and upset me for a long time, now, all I have in my heart is respect for her.

And love.

God, I love that woman so much it burns me.

So no, it's not our first time, but it's the first time since mountains and mountains of shit piled up between us — pain and longing and miscommunication.

Plus, I'll be the first man inside her since the ones who violated her, who took something from her she'll never get back.

The memory of walking in on that scene, on seeing Erin with mascara marring her cheeks and her dress hiked up over her hips, those monsters prowling out of the room like they were kings instead of scum...

I nearly break the spatula in my hand, but shake off the thought before it can sweep me under, tapping the spatula on the edge of the pan. I set it to the side and mix in the heavy whipping cream and melty mozzarella cheese.

And then there's a knock at the door.

Wiping my hands on the kitchen towel hanging from

the stove, I fidget with my hair and my tie one last time, and then I swing my front door open, losing my breath at the sight of Erin on the other side of it.

She's always beautiful. She's always poised and classy, always naturally glowing — even in her worst moments. But tonight, there's a sparkle behind that glow, a magnetic light in her eyes, a sensual smile on her soft pink lips that makes my rib cage squeeze tight around my lungs. Her hair is down and curled, the dark blonde tendrils flowing over her shoulders, and a pastel yellow sundress hugs her breasts, her waist, her hips, cutting off mid-thigh to reveal her tan legs and the nude heels strapped to her feet.

"I think this is the part where you invite me inside," she comments with an amused brow.

"Shit, sorry," I say instantly, opening the door wider and ushering her inside. "Ah, sorry for cursing, too."

She chuckles at that, hanging her purse on one of the hooks I adhered to the wall just beside the door. And then she's in my arms, pressing up on her toes, her lips on mine.

"Since *when* are you sorry for cursing?"

I breathe a laugh against her lips, my shoulders releasing a little now that I'm holding her. "I don't know. I just…" I pause, shaking my head. "You're radiant, Erin. As always."

"Thank you," she says with a little blush playing on her cheeks. "And *you*," she comments next, holding my arms as she pulls back and lets her eyes trail down the length of me. "Are wearing a suit." She looks at me again. "In your own house."

I didn't think it was funny until she said it, and now, I feel about as idiotic as any guy can.

I laugh, kissing her cheek before I release her. "Can't a guy dress up for his girlfriend for date night?"

"You can dress up for me any time you want," she says, looping her arm through mine. "But just so you know, you could have worn sweatpants and I'd have loved it just as much."

"Oh, I *know* why you love my sweatpants," I tease.

She giggles, hiding her blush as she presses her face into my chest. But then, she pulls back, sniffing at something in the air and frowning. "Um... is something burning?"

I balk, eyes nearly bulging out of my head as I rip from her grasp and jog across the entryway back to the kitchen.

"Ah, Christ," I curse when I make it back to the stove and see the burning, ruined sauce in the pan. I cut the burner and pull the pan over to a burner that's not on, sighing as I debate whether the sauce is salvageable.

It's not.

Erin chuckles when she comes up behind me, her arms wrapping around my waist, chin resting between the lower part of my shoulder blades. "Whoops."

I shake my head. "I'm so stupid."

"No, you're not."

"I am."

"You were distracted."

"Still, I knew I had it on, I should have turned the heat down or come back over or—"

Erin tugs on me until I turn and face her. "It's okay, Clinton."

The sound of my name on her lips has me closing my eyes and letting out a soft breath.

"We can order in," she continues. "I have to pee, but when I get out, I'll look on my phone and see what's around here. Okay? It's all good. We'll find something to eat, I promise."

I nod, but still don't open my eyes, not until she kisses my cheek and hurries off to the bathroom connected to my bedroom.

The house I found to rent after graduation is small, old, built sometime in the 1940s. It's a two-bedroom, one-and-a-half bath with a small fenced-in yard and a porch. The floors creak and the plumbing needs updating, but it has charm, and the landlord gave me a price that even Erin said was too good to be true for this close to downtown.

Scrubbing a hand over my face, I finally move from the spot where Erin left me, grabbing the pan like it's a poor bastard I'm about to pulverize in a street fight. I hastily scrub the charred contents into the trash can and then toss the pan in the sink, turning the water hot as I fill it and squeezing a healthy amount of soap in to soak.

Erin comes back into the kitchen silently, and when I turn and find her watching me with a soft smile and a red rose petal in her hand, all the blood drains from my face.

I completely forgot I had the room all set up — candles, rose petals, music. I thought if she used the restroom, she'd use the half bath in the living area.

"Shit..." I murmur mostly to myself, shoulders deflating as I pinch the bridge of my nose.

I just stay like that, unsure what to say, unsure whether I should try to explain myself or just pretend like I don't see her standing there. But with a chuckle, Erin crosses the room and sneaks her way into my arms, forcing me to release the hold on my nose so I can wrap her up, instead.

"Hey," she whispers, waiting until I meet her eyes. "Talk to me. What's going on?" She frowns then, grabbing ahold of my biceps. "You're shaking."

"Because I'm nervous as hell."

She barks out a laugh at that. "You? Nervous? I didn't think you were even capable of that emotion."

"That makes two of us."

Her brows fold together over her soft brown eyes as they search mine. "Talk to me."

I sigh, folding my hands behind the small of her back, but my eyes are across the room. "I just wanted everything to be perfect tonight."

I swallow, unsure what else to say. The right words don't exist for this moment, and I've already fucked it all to hell, so I don't even feel confident enough to try.

Erin slides her hands up my chest, over my shoulders, up still until she's cradling my face and angling it toward her. My nose flares as I drop my gaze to meet hers.

"I don't need a fancy dinner or rose petals or candles or you in a suit," she says, glancing at my tie as she does. "Although, you *do* look sexy as hell in it."

I smirk.

Her eyes find mine again, endlessly warm and inviting. She slides her fingertips back to hold my neck, her nails brushing the tender skin and setting off a wave of chills.

"I just need you," she whispers.

I nod, dropping my forehead down until it meets hers on a long inhale from both of us.

"Clinton?"

"Mm?"

"Take me to bed."

Fuck, the things those words do to me, the animalistic way my body responds — gripping her tighter, heart racing, cock already thickening in my slacks. It's like she owns me, like those four words were a snap of her fingers, and now I'm at her beck and call, ready to do whatever she wants.

Whatever she needs.

With something between a growl and an exhale, I bend down and swoop her into my arms, my lips on hers just in time to catch her giggle of surprise as I carry her down the short hall to my room.

This girl is my drug.

I realize it distantly as I carry her back, chasing her tongue with mine, savoring each little gasp and moan along with the little buzz they give me. I could never put into words what it is with her, what it's *always* been with her. All I know is that in the very depths of my existence, there's one thought that overcomes me any time I'm with her.

Mine.

Even when she wasn't.

Even when I wasn't sure she ever would be.

Neither of us had a choice in the matter.

She belongs to me and always has — just as I belong to her.

My bedroom is dimly lit from the candles and smells like teakwood and bourbon. I lie Erin gently down on top of my dark comforter, right on top of the rose petals, making a handful of them float up and back down like feathers on her skin and in her hair. She backs up until she's resting on her elbows against the pillows, her legs crossed, eyes big and soft as she watches me and waits for what I'll do next.

The night is completely in my hands.

I'm not fool enough to not realize how fucking lucky I am, and how much I must mean to her for her to trust me this way.

The soft, sexy sounds of the Tank album I put on filter around the space between us, and I turn the volume up a little more before I tug at my tie, releasing it first and then working every button on my suit jacket until I can shrug it over my shoulders.

Erin watches me with her bottom lip pinned between her teeth, her knees pulling up toward her chest.

I don't take my eyes off her as I strip off my dress shirt next, and then make quick work of my belt, shoes, and socks. When I unfasten the top button of my pants, Erin snaps up, sitting on the edge of the bed and placing her hands on top of mine to stop me.

"Let me," she pleads.

I let out a pained breath through my nose, because the way she looks up at me when she says those words, the flush on her cheeks, the way her fingers tremble as she struggles with the button and then the zipper and then helps me pull the slacks over my hips, my ass, down my thighs... it's the most erotic sight I've ever seen in my life.

I'm so fucking hard that I've pitched a tent in my briefs, and Erin gulps as she runs her palm along the length of me, the cotton fabric still between us.

I hiss, letting my head fall back, flexing my hips into the warm touch.

"Clinton," she whispers, and when I look back down at her, she doesn't have to say more. I can see it in her eyes.

She's the nervous one, now.

I nod in understanding, leaning down until my fists hit the bed on either side of her and my mouth captures hers. Then I'm backing her up into the pillows again, one arm swooping around her waist to hoist her up and set her back down.

"Look at me," I whisper when she's settled, when her trembling fingertips are digging into my shoulders. "You are safe. Okay? You're safe, and you're in control. You don't even have to say anything, I'm listening to your body."

Her eyes gloss with tears, but she nods, grabbing my neck and pulling me in for a long, hard kiss. I kiss her back just as earnestly, sealing my promise.

And then I trail those kisses down, down, down.

Over her chin, her neck, across every inch of her collarbone, I kiss. My lips leave little invisible marks across the petite swells of her breast over the fabric of her dress, and then on the lace covering her ribs, until I'm settled between her legs on my elbows.

I grab her ass firmly and lift her up just enough to free her dress, and then I push it up over her hips, hands gripping her thighs as I press a kiss sweetly over the thin, silky fabric of her beige thong.

She gasps, fisting the sheets and arching her back.

We've taken it slow over the summer, but if there's one thing I know about my girl, it's that she tastes just as sweet as she looks, and enough time with my tongue on her will have her open and panting and pleading for more.

Or coming, if I'm not careful.

I take my time stripping her panties off, kissing each part of her leg the fabric slides down before I discard them to the side. Then, I press my lips to the arch of her foot, her ankle, dragging my tongue along her calf and inner thigh until I'm settled in and ready to eat again.

Just the first lash of my tongue against her makes her writhe.

I smirk, teasing her mound before I run my tongue flat along the length of her, soaking up her taste and how much she wants me already.

"Oh, *Clinton*," she breathes, her hips grinding, seeking more friction when I do the same thing again.

I answer by pointing my tongue and circling the tip around her clit — once, twice, three times, quick and slick, before I lap her up long and slow.

I love that she calls out my name — my *real* name — not Bear, not God, not the myriad of things I've heard before. When she says my name, I'm like a dog snapping to attention for its master, the syllables of it from her lips a reminder of who I belong to.

Sliding my hands under her ass, I grip where her thighs meet her hips and tug her closer, feasting on her perfect, swollen, pink pussy as she squirms. She's twisting her hands in the covers and breathing so hard I almost wonder if she wants me to stop, if she's trying to get away, but any time I let up on the pressure, she mewls like a kitten, whimpering for more.

When her legs start really quaking around me, she snaps up suddenly, pressing her hand into my chest to break my contact. And when I bring my eyes to hers, sliding the back of my wrist across my damp lips, she flushes before calling me up to her with one *come here* wave of her finger.

I fist the front of her dress and yank, pulling her to sit so I can strip it up overhead in one fell swoop. I unclasp her bra next, sucking each perfect, pebbled mound between my teeth as soon as they're exposed. Erin clings to me, holding me to her, moaning and soaking up every touch.

When my lips are on hers again, I blindly reach into the drawer of my bedside table, fumbling a bit until I withdraw the golden foil packet. I bring it to my teeth and rip it open, making quick work of my briefs, and when I sit back on my knees, Erin's hand covers mine once more.

"Can I?" she asks, her eyes on the condom, and then on my length.

My answer is simply to give her the condom, and then we both watch as her shaking fingers bring it to my tip, stretching it over with a slow, rolling motion. She inches it down, and then wraps her hands around my shaft and the condom completely, rolling it the rest of the way until it covers me as close to the base as it can get.

I nearly come just at the sight of it, the feel of her hands squeezing and working me with her perfect little breasts heaving with each breath.

When the condom's in place, she swallows, sitting back a little and bringing her shy gaze to mine.

Leaning over until I can press my lips to hers once more, I sweep my arms around her and gently lift, sitting in her place as I hoist her up and over until she's straddling my lap. When she's there, I keep her up on her knees, holding her hips with my hands and kissing her long and soft.

"You're safe," I remind her when I break the kiss, trailing my lips over her jaw. "And you're in control."

She nods on an exhale, but before I can do anything else, she grabs my face in her hands, holding my gaze to hers.

"I love you."

The words slam into me, but not from surprise and not from fear — from relief. Because I've always known it, haven't I? I've always known Erin loved me, just as I've always known I love her.

I press my forehead to hers. "There is no measurement for how much I love you."

Even with our foreheads connected, I see the way her lips curve into a smile, the way a lone tear leaks from her eyes. When she pulls back, I thumb it away easily.

Then my hands are back on her hips, waiting, holding her steady and letting her decide what to do next.

Erin presses her hands against my chest, the tips of her fingers folding over each shoulder. I reach down between us just long enough to position me where she needs me, for the tip of me to glide into the shallow entrance of her.

We both stiffen and steel a breath at the feeling, the most sensitive part of me stretching her open just a centimeter, but enough that we both tremble and quake.

And then she sinks, just a half an inch, and we both moan in sync.

My hands wrap around her hips even more, encompassing her entire waist, and I hold onto her for dear life as she stretches a little more, letting me a little more inside her.

Stars. In my room and my head and swimming in every vein of my body is a galaxy of stars.

My cock pulses inside her, and she slips down a little more before she's grimacing and squeezing my shoulders tight.

"Are you okay?"

She nods, letting out a slow breath. "It hurts a little," she confesses. And then her sass makes an appearance, her brow popping into her hairline as she adds, "I've never had anyone this big before."

I can't help the cocky smirk that blooms on my face at that.

"You *technically* already had it once before," I remind her. "Remember? Oh, wait..."

She pinches my rib, and then we're both laughing, and kissing, and all the tension floats away on a nonexistent breeze.

Erin pushes up on her knees just a bit before she drops back down, sinking a little farther, another grimace warping her face.

"Go slow," I tell her, and I hold her hips to help, guiding her down so slowly I'm afraid by the time she sits all the way, I'm going to come twice over.

She's so fucking tight, so wet and slick and *mine*.

Slowly, Erin starts to take over again, picking up her pace. Up and down, sliding off my length just to sit back down and take more of me inside her.

Up, down, up, down.

A pant, a moan, a kiss, a sigh.

And then she sinks all the way, opening wide and gobbling me up so that I'm balls deep inside her.

We both still again at the sensation, holding onto each other with slick chests and shaking limbs.

It's like coming home after thinking we were dead, like finding the part of ourselves we never knew existed and yet always sensed was right under the surface.

Now it's my turn to take control.

I grip her hips tight, lifting her all the way up before gliding her back down, and we both moan again, louder, more urgent, Erin's fingernails digging into my skin. Again, all the way up, and all the way down, our climaxes building like a wildfire.

"Oh, my *God*, Clinton," Erin cries, her legs quaking violently. "This... I... it feels so *good*."

I groan my agreement, and then I capture her next moan with my mouth, eagerly sucking it down and kissing her hard. My tongue swirls with hers as I help her ride me, faster and faster, but I refrain from slamming into her the way I desperately want to. And *God*, do I want to. Every feral part of me is begging me to lose control, to obliterate that pussy and make sure she doesn't walk a day in her life without remembering what I feel like inside her.

But tonight, I let her drive, let her call the shots for how deep and how fast and how hard. She wants me tame? I can do tame.

The beast inside me will live.

Something happens, and the walls of her tighten even more, squeezing every inch of my cock so hard I grunt and hold her tighter. One look at her face tells me what it was — she's on the brink of coming.

I kiss her harder, urging her on, and then I wrap my arms full around her and pull her closer, so that her hips open more, her back arched, body tilted.

And every new flex has her rubbing her clit against my pelvis.

Her moans are wild now, completely uninhibited, and she rocks faster and faster, keeping me inside her for the most part until that pussy clenches around me again and I know she's finding her release.

I give myself permission to follow, moving her hips the way I need them to move, but continuing that pressure on her clit so she can ride out her wave. And just like I saw when we first connected, stars blast me from every angle again, my climax a shocking, power-drunk punch to the gut that leaves me still and holding onto Erin for dear life as it shreds me apart.

For a long moment, I'm in outerspace — floating, numb and intoxicated by an all-consuming pleasure.

Slowly, the room comes back to me, starting with the soft sound of Erin's haggard breaths, the feeling of me growing soft inside her, of her slick chest against mine and her hands twisted in my short hair.

She drops her forehead to my shoulder, and then her shoulders begin to shake — softly at first, and then uncontrollably, sobs racking her body there in my arms.

I don't say a word.

I just hold her tighter, let her cry, and press my lips gently to her shoulder, her neck, her cheek. I don't rush her to talk or to look at me. I just wrap her up and pray that she knows she can feel whatever she needs to feel with me — good, bad, or in-between.

You're safe.

You're in control.

I seal those silent promises with every kiss.

EPISODE 2

Ashlei

MY MOM USED TO call me her little bird when I was a kid.

I had a knack for getting into trouble, for getting into precarious situations, and for getting hurt — mostly because I had such an appetite for challenge and a competitiveness like no other. Boy or girl, older or younger, it didn't matter. If someone challenged me to do something or said I *couldn't* do something, I'd prove them wrong.

I had more stitches than Barbie dolls by the time I was ten, but Mom always said I was her little bird, always flying from the nest without fear of falling.

I knew I would fly.

And right now, I feel like I've never soared higher in my life.

The last four years have taken me through some major ups and downs. From the drug escapade and getting caught up with the wrong people, to trying to turn my life around only to sleep with my boss, then fall in love with him, then lose him along with my job because I was stupid, then win him back and move in with him... you could say it's been a whirlwind.

But as it often does, the sea has been settling in my life, the storm gone, waters calming and breeze gently blowing through my hair. For the first time in a very long time, I feel completely at peace.

The summer only brought on more clients and more responsibility for me at *Ball & Pen*, and my boss, Celeste, became more and more comfortable handing me the more challenging events. She also gave me a bigger budget to hire more staff, including a *second* assistant for me in addition to Jeannie, who has become my right-hand woman.

Brandon had tried desperately to get me to come back to work at *Okay, Cool* when we'd made up, but as much as I love him *and* his company — *Ball & Pen* felt like the right place for me to be. It was a chance to build my name outside of Brandon, to not be seen as his previous intern-turned-employee-turned-girlfriend. Although we'd embraced our relationship head on and no one seemed to have a problem with it, I wasn't naïve enough to think the rumor mill didn't run behind both our backs.

Besides, Celeste sees my potential, and she trusts me with the responsibility I've always dreamed of having — ever since I decided event planning was a career I could see myself loving.

And *boy*, do I love it.

I work tirelessly every day and night, sometimes into the weekends — much to Brandon's dismay — and even on the most stressful days, I feel so alive, so *in love*, that I don't mind.

The only things that fuel me just as much as working are loving Brandon and pole dancing.

It amazes me still how easily the transition was with Brandon, from fighting and breaking up, to not talking for months, to fucking and dating like nothing had changed at all. The little games we played in the spring were maddening, but I'd go through them all again if that's what it took to have him. The truth is that Brandon's just as full of pride as I am, and it took playing those games to break him down and get him to realize he still loved me — even if he *was* mad at me.

And he had a right to be.

It isn't always easy. Even now, the pain I caused him surfaces and I have to smooth his worries about me possibly betraying his trust again. I never would, not in a million years, and I have no problem continually proving that to him.

But for the most part, the summer was pure magic for us — and I've never been happier or more in love.

And as much as I love work, and love *him*, there's a special kind of love I hold for this place — my pole studio — where I can get out of my head and fully into my body, where I can challenge *myself* and continually be humbled and find a way to rise again.

"That combo is fucking sick," Leona says when both my feet are on the hardwood floor again. She's a younger student, a perky, curvy little thing with pixie short hair and more tattoos on her pale skin than anyone I've ever known in my life.

I bend over and grab my knees, panting, chest heaving as I try to catch my breath. "Thanks," I say with a smile.

"Seriously, how the hell do you bend like that? And the Iron X... I'll never be able to do that." She shakes her head, wrapping both hands around her own pole and staring up at it like it's both the only thing she's ever loved, and her biggest enemy.

It kind of fits, to be honest.

"You will," I assure her. "Trust me. I've been doing this for four years now, off and on, and everything I can do now felt impossible to me at one point or another. Just keep working," I say. "I promise, you're stronger than you realize."

Leona smiles and nods at me in thanks, and then she's climbing up the pole again, working a layback combo I remember being a bitch to conquer myself when I was in my intermediate stage.

Leona is just one of the students I've come to love at the studio. From taking classes and attending almost every open pole practice, the girls here have become like family. Now that I've started to compete again, I've even roomed with some of them at competitions and conventions, and I've been both challenged and inspired by every single woman here.

"Has Karen convinced you to come on as a teacher yet?" one of the other girls chimes in from the back. "Because I'm dying to take a class with you."

I smirk, grabbing my water bottle from the cubbies on the far wall and taking a big swig. "Not yet, but she's getting close."

That earns a few gasps and excited claps from the room.

"Oh, my God, *please*, Lei!"

"I NEED to learn from you."

"Can you do a dance class? Your flow is insane!"

I laugh and hold up my hands to calm them all. "I'm still thinking on it. My big girl job is pretty demanding, and this is where I come to release. I don't want to lose that."

Silence falls over them before Leona says, "That's fair. But if you ever *do* decide to teach, I'll be the first one to sign up."

There's a chorus of agreement that makes me flush, and then the girls are all back to climbing and practicing their tricks.

I grab the bottle of Dry Hands out of my bag and squeeze a small amount in one palm, rubbing my hands together with my eyes on the pole as I debate what I want to work next. I'm nice and warm, and after nailing that last combo, all I can think about is that I'm ready to work my nemesis.

Bird of Paradise.

The twisty move is an absolute freak of nature, and one that my body hasn't particularly loved since I started training it over the summer.

It's an outside leg hang variation where you wrap your inside arm around the front of your inside leg, that's extended toward your face, by the way, and wrap your outside arm around the pole to grab that inside hand. Then, when you've got *that* bitch of a back breaking twist achieved, you release the outside leg and extend it back in a split, balancing everything while you hold on in this anatomy-defying pose.

All while upside down.

And spinning.

No big deal...

I first saw the move at a competition back when I competed for Leslie's studio, and I remember how loud the crowd cheered when the girl did it, how much my jaw dropped, how furious my little voice was in my head.

I have *to do that move!*

I didn't realize how much went into it, how flexibility and strength training had to combine for it to be achieved.

But I've been working tirelessly at it for almost a year now, and particularly hard over the summer.

Maybe today's the day...

I clap my hands together one last time, making sure the Dry Hands is sticky and ready to go, and then I launch myself at the pole.

Gripping tight, I power climb up, using only my hands and bicep muscles, legs swinging out behind me. When I'm up three climbs, I hold a pencil pose, body in line with the pole, and then tuck the chrome into my armpit and lift my legs up and over my head.

Chopper.

Leg hang.

For a while, I lie back and enjoy the brief rest. I remember a time when a leg hang was so painful, I thought my inner thigh was on fire. But now, it's a breather, a chance to let my body relax before I go for the next move.

Inhale.

Exhale.

Slowly, I grab for the pole and maneuver my shoulder into position — one that's extremely bendy and difficult, even with being warm. I take my time, and when I feel confident, I swing my inside leg around and grab hold with my inside hand.

This part is always sketchy, inching my shoulder under the pole more and more, centimeter by centimeter, my hands reaching for each other to lock behind my shin and hold me in place. I breathe through it, eyes closed so I won't get too dizzy.

And finally, my fingers touch.

A few more breaths and I've got my hands locked together, though my shoulders are screaming.

"You've got this, Lei!" someone shouts, and a few other girls cheer me on as I go for the last part to clench the move.

Squeeze everything tight.

Breathe.

Relax.

And when I feel ready, I unhook my outside leg and send it back behind me, straight and extended, toes pointed.

Bird of Paradise: unlocked.

The girls roar their approval, and for a moment, I'm smiling and internally freaking out that I actually fucking did it.

But the next, I slip, just an inch, just enough for all the joy to drain from my face, for my heart to race into my throat, and for me to realize I'm not secure.

Shit.

It's not easy to come out of this move, and I don't have enough time to think about how to do it properly, to save myself from slipping all the way down. I try to bring my outside leg back in to hook, but it's too late.

I can't squeeze hard enough.

I can't re-grip the pole.

And in the next second, I'm free falling — desperate hands grasping for chrome that I never quite find.

Cheers turn to gasps, and I hit the floor with a nasty *snap, rip, crack.* There's a brief shot of the most agonizing pain I've ever felt in my life.

And then everything goes dark.

Adam

THE SUN IS HIGH and blinding as I walk University Hill, taking in the crisp Colorado air with each breath. September at Palm South always meant pool parties and sweating every walk to class, but here? The days are pleasantly warm, the evenings cool, fall constantly whispering in your ear that it's well on its way.

I've got my hands tucked into the pockets of my light jacket, one branded with the Alpha Sigma letters and given to me when I joined the national staff as a Field Executive. The summer in Boston was a crash-course of learning — not necessarily the fraternity rituals or standards, which I already knew well — but rather how I would take my knowledge and experience from the last four years and apply them in my new role.

A role they did everything they could to prepare me for, but I'm not stupid enough to think it'll be so easy.

In their eyes, Field Executives are welcome with open arms, but if I know anything about fraternities, it's that having someone from nationals visit is hardly ever a good thing — and I wouldn't be anyone's favorite guest of honor.

Every chapter I visit, every group of guys I seek to mentor will need me for some reason, whether they want to admit it or not.

And the group here in Boulder *definitely* falls under the *not* category.

There are a few brothers sprawled on the grass when I reach the A Sig house, a monstrous Neo-classical beast that puts every house at Palm South to shame. Aspen University is older than Palm South, more prestigious, and has four times the amount of students. They also have more money, and their "Greek Row" is spread out all over The Hill, giant mansions with letters proudly fixed to the front like Easter eggs you can't help but hunt as you walk.

The brothers I pass by give me nods of hello, most of them friendly, most of them glad I'm there. The past two years of recruitment haven't gone so well, and though I was able to help them get a better turnout this year, my work had only just begun.

Through Rush Week, I'd become close with a lot of the brothers — the president and recruitment chair, the philanthropic chair, who I was most excited to work with, and a number of brothers of various ages. The new pledges knew me as if I was the House Director, and I intended to earn everyone's trust by the time I left — and to leave them in better shape than I found them.

Oddly enough, the current brothers aren't the issue.

It's the alumni presiding over the chapter that take the cake.

It's standard to have older brothers governing each Alpha Sigma chapter. After all, leaving a national organization in the hands of a bunch of rowdy college kids wouldn't work out in anyone's favor. Still, the goal of the alumni members is simply to ensure order. They may be present at chapter meetings to make sure everything is done correctly, may sign off on philanthropic or social events, and may step in to take care of punishment should one of the brothers, or all of them, need it.

But it's the current brothers who run exec, who make decisions, who hold their brothers accountable and make a name for the chapter on campus.

Or at least, it's *supposed* to be.

I pull my shoulders back as I walk through the front door of the house, preparing myself for the meeting ahead.

I can't help but smile at the various pods of brothers as I pass through the house — some playing video games, some studying, some in the backyard playing beer pong. On the surface, everything looks right, looks in place, looks successful.

But this chapter has slowly gained the reputation for being dull and old school, for not performing in athletics, scholarship, *or* social activities, and for just being lackluster, in general.

And it didn't take me long to figure out that the alumni were the reason for most of it.

That's why I called this meeting, and though I know it won't be easy, I pray the guys will hear me out and make changes to better our presence on the Aspen University campus.

I take my time setting up the meeting room, setting the donuts I picked up from the popular spot on The Hill right in the center of the boardroom table. There are four alumni chapter advisors who preside over this particular chapter, and one by one, they all file in.

There aren't technically supposed to be titles among them, but when I met them the first time, they introduced themselves as Shawn, Secretary, Derek, Treasurer, Jared, Vice President, and Corey, President.

Corey was, so far, the biggest pain in my ass.

As they sit down and mutter among themselves, I find myself wishing Cassie were here. I would give anything to have had her in my arms before this meeting, to be kissing her senseless before running out the door, to know I had her just down the block when the meeting's over.

As it is, I'll have to settle for texts, phone calls, and the occasional video chat.

Memories of our *last* video chat bring a whole new slew of thoughts to mind, but I clear my throat and tamper them down, saving that energy for later.

"Gentlemen, thank you for joining me," I start, and that quiets the room.

Corey, the president, and Jared, the VP, both watch me with bored, suspicious glares, but the other two offer smiles and their full attention. I could tell after the first twenty minutes with them that they're divided, but with the two snarly ones being the oldest and regarded as the highest roles, they seem to make all the rules.

My plan is to change that.

"I'll try to make this as brief as possible, as I know you all have jobs and lives to get back to."

I make sure I say that last part firmly, because I want to remind them that they are *not*, in fact, frat brothers anymore.

"As you know, recruitment went well, all things considered, but having a great pledge class won't erase the hard work ahead of us. I have put together a plan that attacks three main categories of focus this semester: athletics, scholarship, and social activity," I explain, watching the room as the guys read over the binders I've put together in front of them. "I think we should focus on athletics and social activity first and foremost, with scholarship and philanthropy being introduced but more heavily focused on in the next semester."

"That doesn't make sense," Corey says instantly. "Why wouldn't it be scholarship and philanthropy first? What, are we trying to be the party boys now?"

"No," I assure him. "However, these are kids. Think back to when you were eighteen, nineteen, even twenty. Did you care about your grades or giving to the community as much as you did about partying with your brothers, making out with girls, and winning championships?"

Shawn snorts. "God, no."

Corey glares at him, then says, "Maybe this is how things were run in Florida, Adam, but we have more prestigious goals here."

"That may be," I say, not giving him the satisfaction of thinking I give a rat's ass about what he thinks of me or my chapter. "But these brothers need a win. They need to throw a great party, as weird as that sounds. A *safe* party, but a rager, nonetheless. And they need to feel like they're gaining popularity, like they stand a chance at being known on The Hill."

"I agree," Derek says. "But honestly, I don't see how these goals are achievable." He reads from the list. "Win the IM football championship, create a new annual Alpha Sigma event with high Greek Life attendance, host a social at a new and exciting venue?" He shakes his head. "We need actual athletes. And money."

"You've got more talent here than you give yourself credit for. I've been watching the guys, and I think if we talk to the Athletics Chair, we can get them to gather the new pledges as well as the older brothers together and get a good team going. We have two weeks until the sign-up date, three weeks until the first game."

"And what about this fancy new event?" Corey asks. "Who's going to come up with that?"

"The brothers, of course," I say without blinking. "This is their chapter. They're young and creative, give them a shot to come up with some ideas that we can sign off on. That's our role, after all," I remind them.

There's a pregnant pause before Jared sighs and drops his binder to the table. "I think this is a terrible idea."

"Listen, guys, I know it's hard to step out of the comfort zone, to throw all our eggs into baskets we can't even see yet. But I've been trained," I say, trying to earn their trust. "Give me a chance to prove I know what I'm doing. And if you still feel like I'm a nutcase by the end of the semester, I'll write to nationals myself and ask them to place me elsewhere."

"I don't know why they sent you in the first place," Corey mutters, which earns him an eye roll from Shawn that I smirk at.

"Let me talk with the Athletics Chair," I say calmly. "We became fast friends over Rush Week. And at our next chapter, I'll introduce the event, get the brothers excited and thinking."

"I guess we don't really have a choice," Jared says.

I smile and nod, letting them know the meeting is over.

Because no — they *don't* have a choice.

I saw Ricky, the Athletics Chair, playing beer pong in the backyard on my way up to the meeting, so I stop to talk to him on my way out the door. As I expected, he's pumped about the challenge, and a few brothers in the yard are already chomping at the bit to help him put the team together.

I clap him on the back and leave them to it, then check my watch, deciding I should head to the Student Union to fill out paperwork and get a date reserved for our on campus event.

On the way, I text Cassie, and I'm so locked into our conversation that I don't notice the poor girl crossing my path until I run her over, literally knocking her over and leaving her sprawled out on the lawn below me.

"Shit, I'm so sorry," I say, hurriedly putting my phone away before I reach down a hand to help her up.

The girl has long, thick, messy black hair and tattoos lining both her arms. When she looks up at me, I'm knocked silent by shocking blue-green eyes outlined by dark charcoal and lashes. Her dusty-pink lips curve into a smile at the sight of me, and she lets me take her hand and pull her up.

She's wearing a tight, crop t-shirt with some band name I don't recognize, and I swear on my life her tits are bigger than any I've ever seen in person. Pair that with her slim waist, thick hips, and ripped-up black jeans, and she's in a whole league of her own. My eyes flick to her combat boots that I'm hoping she doesn't want to stomp me with, but she just dusts herself off with a chuckle once she's fully upright, arching a brow at me.

"It's all good. Maybe keep an eye on the road there, though, eh?"

I try to smile against the grimace coming to me naturally. "Sorry," I say again. Stupidly.

The girl just nods, and then with a curious smile, she leaves me and continues on her way.

Stitched into the pocket of her backpack are the letters $\Delta B\Gamma$, and I can't help but shake my head, because I would have bet money she was at least a grad student, if not older.

I think of when I met Cassie, how sweet and innocent she was, how she was naturally beautiful without a stitch of makeup on, how she looked so young and full of life. This girl was built like a woman, with eyes that told me she had stories and scars alike.

But times are changing, and young girls don't look as young to me as they should, I guess.

I shake my head, pulling out my phone again as I continue on my way to the Union.

But this time, I decide to call instead of text.

Erin

THIS ROOM IS TOO stuffy.

Brown and dark, wood and leather, shelves of boring books and even more boring documents proving their worth hanging on every wall. The windows are too small, not allowing enough light through for my tastes. This has been my most dreaded thought when it comes to the career I chose — finding a firm that doesn't make me want to crawl out of my skin with its architectural and interior design.

"Erin," my lawyer says — softly, tenderly. "I know this is hard."

I blink, tearing my blank stare from the law books on her shelf and meeting her eyes, instead. Candice is striking — tall and curvy, dark skin and even darker hair, long and filled with small braids that grow red in tint toward the ends. Her makeup is always flawless, red lips powerful, and every suit she has — pants or skirt — is tailored to fit her perfectly. Sometimes she's in kitten heels, sometimes flats, but no matter what's on her feet, her energy is tall and loud enough that she commands attention from everyone the second she enters the room.

Everyone but me, it seems, because I can't help but zone out during this meeting — mostly because I don't want to hear what she's telling me.

"And I also know hearing me say that doesn't make it any better," she adds, her brows bending together. "But look, this will all be worth it. Justice waits for these boys, and we might have to crawl through some muck to get it, but get it we will." She leans over the glossy mahogany table and folds her hand over mine. "I promise."

I swallow, nodding, which gives her permission to continue talking about the next steps.

Candice and I first met back in May, as soon as I told the girls what happened to me and decided I was ready to finally report the incident. Going to the police was the hardest part — detectives and bright rooms with questions being fired at me. I knew quickly that I needed a lawyer, and Candice stepped in ready for battle.

She showed me a long list of cases she'd fought — most of which she'd won — and promised me she would give me her all.

Of course, that was just the beginning of a hellish summer, and now, hearing what we have to do next, I realize the worst is yet to come.

"The detective they've assigned to your case is a hard ass," Candice says, filing through some paperwork before handing me a small profile on Gene Riley. His headshot smiles back at me as I fight down the bile rising in my throat. "But he's fair. I've seen him make the right call countless times. He's got a strong moral compass, which means if the evidence is there? He's got no problem pushing the case forward to court." She pauses. "But... it also means that if the evidence *isn't* there, he's not willing to send what could be an innocent man — or in this case, multiple innocent men — through the system."

"They're not innocent," I say, almost growl, my eyes hardening as I meet her gaze.

"I know," Candice insists. "And that's why we're going to cooperate with Mr. Riley on whatever he wants, so we can make sure he sees that, too."

I sigh, looking at the bio again, at the file of paperwork in front of me that I refuse to open because I know there are four other faces in there that I would like to never see again in my life.

"This step is crucial, Erin, and I need you to understand that before we move forward. He's going to question you, Clinton, your family, your friends — they need to know this is coming." She pauses. "He's also going to be questioning the defendants, and *their* family and friends."

"Who will lie," I say without hesitation. "They're never going to admit to it."

"Of course not, who would?"

I grit my teeth, biting down my urge to scream.

"That's why it's important that we tell Mr. Riley *everything*. Be as detailed as possible. We need to give any and every possible shred of evidence we have."

I close my eyes. Just thinking of reliving that nightmarish night makes me want to jump out of the window of this thirty-seven-story building.

"You can do this," Candice says earnestly, knocking her knuckles on the wood. "We *will* make those boys pay for what they did to you."

My next swallow is thick, tongue like sandpaper in my mouth, but I nod, trying my best to actually believe her and not just fake like I do.

A cheerful little melody from my phone breaks the tension, and I frown when I see Ashlei's name on the screen. She should be at work right now, and we almost never call each other — it's either text or in person.

"Mind if I take this?" I ask Candice.

She waves me on, picking up her own phone and tapping away on the screen as I slide a thumb across mine and answer the call.

"Hey, babe. Everything okay?"

There's a long pause of silence before she sniffs. And then, a whispered, "No."

My heart stops in my chest before kicking back to life, and I swivel in my leather seat, turning away from Candice altogether. "What's going on? Where are you? Are you hurt?"

That breaks Ashlei into full-on sobs, and I curse, grabbing my things off the table.

I cover the phone with my hand to mute it. "I'm sorry, I have to go. I'll call you," I tell Candice.

She nods, questions and concern in her eyes, but I don't have time to assure her things are fine — mostly because I don't know that they are.

"Where are you?" I repeat when I'm out of the room and dashing through the firm for the elevator.

"Palm Medical."

I stop short. "The hospital?"

"I was at the pole studio yesterday and..." She sniffs, another long pause breaking between us. "There was an accident."

I close my eyes, saying a silent prayer before I punch the down button to signal the elevator. "Hey, it's going to be okay. Alright? You hear me? I'm going to pick up the girls and we'll be right there."

"Hurry," is all Ashlei says, and then the line goes dead.

The girls are still in a tizzy when we blow through the doors of Palm Medical. It doesn't matter that I spent the entire drive here reminding them that we needed to be calm for Ashlei, that we don't even know what's happened yet. There *is* no calm when it comes to one of us being in trouble or hurt, hence the literal tornado of us entering the hospital, papers flying in our wake.

The poor nurse at the front desk doesn't know who to listen to as Cassie, Skyler, and mostly Jess talk over each other to try to get information. Finally, I hold up a hand to stop them all mid-sentence, and calmly explain to the woman who we're looking for.

As soon as we get the floor and room number, along with the clearance for visitation rights — which wasn't easy, considering there are four of us and our lame attempt at convincing her we were Ashlei's real sisters went over about as well as a lead balloon — we were in the elevator and on our way to the surgery wing.

"I'm going to remind you all one more time — *calm*," I say on our ride up, and though I know it's hard, the girls all nod in agreement. And true to their word, we stroll at a softer pace in the surgery wing, speaking to the nurse at the desk there before being led back to Ashlei's room.

When we see her, we all stop dead.

She's laid up in the hospital bed in a gown that she somehow still makes look pretty, her hair greasy and piled on top of her head, dark circles under her eyes, and her arm in a massive sling that covers her entire shoulder and most of her chest. Brandon is in a chair beside her bed, his eyes glazed as he pretends to watch the TV.

"Well," Ashlei says when she sees us, attempting a smile. "Am I a beauty queen, or what?"

Cassie covers her mouth at the same time Jess curses, and Skyler and I just deflate, shoulders slumping.

"Oh, Lei," I say softly, and then wish I hadn't, because those words immediately bring tears to her eyes, her bottom lip quivering like a child.

We rush her in an instant, enveloping her in a group hug and holding on for dear life as she sobs. Cassie cries softly, too, but Sky, Jess, and I exchange understanding looks that say we need to hold our shit together.

"I'm going to get some coffee," Brandon says when we pull back, and he leans down to kiss Ashlei's forehead before leaving us alone.

"What happened?" Jess asks as soon as he's gone, taking his seat and pulling it close to the bed.

Ashlei wipes her nose on the back of her wrist. "I was doing a complicated leg hang move, and I just... I lost grip. I fell, landed awkwardly on my arm, banged my head pretty hard." She pauses, rolling her lips together. "Shredded my rotator cuff, broke my collarbone, gave myself a nasty concussion."

"Fuck," Jess says, shaking her head and instantly reaching for Ashlei's hand.

"When did this happen?" Skyler asks next.

"Day before yesterday."

"And you're just now telling us?" Cassie squeaks. It earns her a glare from me and Jess alike, but she just shrugs like *what, she should have told us sooner!*

"I was in and out of consciousness for a while," Ashlei admits. "And then after some X-rays and tests, monitoring me overnight, and measuring my pain... they decided I needed surgery. So I couldn't really call yesterday, either."

"How do you feel now?" I ask.

"Terrible," she admits, her eyes glossing again. "Everything hurts, and I'm stiff as hell. I keep getting dizzy, and I feel super nauseous. The best time is when I'm sleeping." She blinks. "Except for the nightmares."

A long pause falls over us, and Skyler sits on the edge of the bed, wrapping her hand around Ashlei's ankle. "So, talk to us. What does this mean?"

Ashlei sighs. "Well, short term, it means I miss some work and get to wear this lovely accessory for at least a couple months," she says, gesturing to the monstrosity of a sling fixed to her shoulder and holding her arm. "Long term?" She shrugs. "Physical therapy, I guess."

There's a relieved sigh from all of us, and Cassie leans against the bars of the bed, brushing Ashlei's hair from her face. "Well, that's all good. I'm so happy it's not worse."

Ashlei nods and tries to smile, but her lips quiver again, and then tears slip free and slide down her cheeks even though she hastily wipes them away.

"Lei?" I ask, frowning as I sit on the other edge of the bed opposite Skyler.

She shakes her head, more tears falling as she furiously wipes them away. "No, you're right. I'm lucky I'm alive. I'm lucky it wasn't worse. It's just..." Her face warps, and she looks at her lap instead of at any of us when she says, "I might not ever pole again."

A violent silence suffocates us all, and our eyes jump around the room, because we know there's nothing we could ever do or say to comfort her when that's a real possibility.

Finally, I lean forward and fold my hand over hers, waiting until her eyes meet mine. "We're here," I say.

Because if nothing else, I know that one thing for sure.

Jess

"DOES IT FEEL WEIRD, being back on campus?" Skyler asks me as she delivers our drinks. She taps her clear plastic up against mine and then we both take a sip, grimacing in equal measure at the awful taste.

"Very," I admit. "And the drinks suck."

I make a gesture with my tongue and Skyler snort-laughs.

"We just make 'em stronger here. Plus, it's an Alpha Sig event. What do you expect?"

"I've become so spoiled by good martinis downtown."

"Poor baby," Skyler mocks with her bottom lip protruding.

I shove her on a laugh from both of us, and then we're watching the stage as the next sorority takes over, ready to karaoke and go for the gold.

It's been a hard couple of weeks. With work being bananas and finding out that my best friend is in the hospital, it's been hard to find anything worth smiling over. I debated bailing on Kade a million times before tonight, but he'd given me my space since showing up at the condo that evening, and this was all he'd asked of me — that I come to his first big event as president.

He needs me, and I don't want to let him down.

As if I've conjured him, Kade jogs up on stage, taking over the mic and introducing the sorority about to perform. He's looking fine as hell tonight, his tattooed muscles popping out under his tight Alpha Sig shirt — a royal blue one made especially for the event tonight. He's paired it with a light gray, flat-billed hat and matching Chubbies, and they're just short enough to show his thigh definition.

He looks like Frat Boy Royalty, and I hate that it makes me so hot for him I have to fan my neck to keep from sweating.

I'm smiling like a loon as he does his bit as the emcee, and when he jogs off the stage again and the girls start singing, Skyler leans into me with her shoulder, shaking her head.

"What?" I ask.

"You're so fucking smitten."

I blush, but don't deny it.

Skyler takes a sip of her drink before casually asking, "What about Jarrett?"

My smile slips like a sandal on a freshly mopped floor, and the joy I felt reverberating through me a moment before is doused instantly.

I sigh. "That *is* the question, isn't it?"

"I can't believe they both left you alone for the summer," Skyler remarks. "Does he know you're seeing Kade again?"

"No."

"Are you going to tell him?"

"I don't know."

"Are you going to *see* him?"

I sigh, turning to face her. "Sky, I don't know. Anything. Like, at all. I'm flying by the seat of my pants here and just trying to hold on. As soon as I know something... you'll know. Okay?"

She grimaces. "Sorry. I was just trying to be a good friend and ask the right questions."

"Don't be sorry," I tell her. "They *are* good questions," I confess, turning back to the stage and taking a long pull from my cup. "I'm just not ready to answer them yet. Just like I'm sure you're not ready to answer questions about Kip."

Skyler offers me a sympathetic smile and a *touché* before we're rocking along with the performance, and at least for the moment, the conversation is dropped.

The longer the night goes on, the better the show seems to get. Not only are the fraternities and sororities battling it out for the karaoke title, but Kade has planned game-show-like events in-between each act that keeps everyone engaged. Prizes are flying like crazy, drinks are flowing, and there's a massive foam pit dance floor keeping the party going.

It really is an incredible event — and pride for Kade swells in my chest.

When I'm teetering on the line between tipsy and drunk, I suddenly hear my name blast over the speakers, and I snap my gaze from the foam pit up to the stage to find Kade grinning wickedly and waving me up.

I instantly shake my head.

"Oh, come on now, J-Love. We all know you're not shy."

That earns some laughs and cheers from the crowd, along with a few whistles that make me laugh, too, before I flip them all off.

"Someone's playing shy. Come on, guys. Help me out. *J-Love, J-Love, J-Love,*" Kade starts chanting, and Skyler is the first one to join in before the rest of the crowd follows.

I pinch her ribs, but she just giggles and scurries away from me before snatching my drink and giving me a playful shove toward the stage.

I sigh, knowing the argument is pointless. So I throw my hands up and yell, "Alright, alright!"

The crowd cheers and parts for me to make my way through, and then a couple younger Alpha Sigma brothers I don't recognize help hoist me up onto the stage.

"There she is," Kade says with a wide, lazy smile. He pulls me into him for a kiss far too inappropriate to have thousands of people witness, which earns us a slew of cat calls, whistles, and *get a room!*'s before he pulls back with a grin. "Ready for our duet?"

I blanch. "I'm a terrible singer."

"Prove it."

Before I can save myself, the music starts, and someone is shoving a microphone into my hand as Kade takes his off the mic stand and starts snapping along.

To "Don't Go Breaking My Heart" by Elton John and Kiki Dee.

I burst out in a laugh as Kade jumps up, crosses his feet before he lands, and then does a full spin as the crowd goes wild. Then, he belts out the first line, and I don't have any choice but to follow with my part.

Back and forth, we sing the lyrics, my eyes drifting to the teleprompter more than his. After the first few, he grabs my hand and spins me into him like he's a professional dancer, somehow holding me steady when he twirls me back out. I'm laughing through my next line, and then he drops to his knees in front of me to belt out the pre-chorus bridge, which everyone else sings along with us.

The more the music goes on, the more I loosen up, letting my hips sway and playing into Kade's antics. Before I realize it, it's just me and him up there, the stars shining bright above us, the crowd and the music gone altogether. All I hear is my heartbeat in my ears. All I see are his warm eyes and playful smile. All I feel is his steady grip on my body, his muscles under my hands, the familiar, comfortable buzz of energy flowing between us.

And by the end of the song, I'm mesmerized by this man, wondering how the hell the douchebag, cocky sonofabitch I first met became this coolly confident sex pot that I'm so fucking obsessed with I can't stand it.

When the music finally cuts off, the crowd erupts, and Kade picks me up and throws me onto his shoulders. I toss my hands in the air, one still holding the microphone, as he takes us for a lap around the stage.

He starts running so fast I have to hold on for dear life, and then with a wave and a breathless, "We'll be right back with the announcement of tonight's champions. Until then, enjoy this special performance by Red Leather Chains!"

The crowd goes even more crazy at the announcement of an up-and-coming band that's been all over the music charts. I gasp, too, and try to scream over the noise to ask Kade how the hell he got them for this event, but I don't get the chance before he runs us backstage. Darkness hits like a train, along with a strange kind of quiet. We can still hear the music, the crowd, but it's slightly muted, like it's far, far away.

My ears ring as Kade carefully helps me off his shoulders and drops me to my toes on the ground in front of him, my body sliding down every inch of his along the way.

We're both panting, the music blasting from the stage, crowd cheering — but in the little pocket we've found ourselves in backstage, it feels like we're the only ones in the whole universe.

Kade's eyes flick between mine, and then he splays his palm across my heaving chest, running up the slick skin to wrap his hand around my throat. I gasp at the touch, letting my head fall back, and watching him through hooded eyes — eyes that dare him to keep going.

He squeezes a little harder, leaning in to hover over me as his gaze falls to my lips. "I know I promised you space," he husks. "But I lied."

His mouth crashes onto mine before I can tell him I don't give a fuck what I said and that space is the last thing I want right now, so I pull him into me, meeting his kiss with equal need. He grips my throat even tighter, cutting my oxygen short, but I fucking love it, so I drag my nails down his back and beg for more.

I yelp as Kade bites my lip hard enough to draw blood, and then I'm in his arms being carried backward in the blinding darkness until my back slams against something hard — a ledge or a shelf or a speaker case, I don't fucking care. All I know is my ass is half-propped on it, half hanging off, and I've got my legs wrapped around Kade like an anaconda.

"Do you know how mad you've driven me this summer?" he asks, snapping his hands over my wrists and clamping them to my sides, my fingers curling on the edge of whatever I'm sitting on. "How badly I've wanted to call you, see you, kiss you." He forces my mouth open with a demanding sweep of his tongue. "Taste you." His hard-on grinds against my core, sparking a trail of chills down the length of me. "*Fuck* you?"

"Show me how badly," I dare him, and then with a monstrous growl, he rips me off the ledge and whips me around, slamming my chest into the metal this time.

I have no idea if we're hidden from view, if we're safe back here, or if a pledge is going to walk through at any second and see us. But I couldn't care less — not when

Kade grabs my skirt and rips it down my thighs like a beast, not when he bends down and grabs my ass, spreading my cheeks and making me arch more so he can eat me out from behind, and *definitely* not when he stands again and spanks me so hard I see stars.

"I'm not going to be easy with you tonight," he promises.

And I just spread my legs a little wider and look over my shoulder with a grin that says *promises, promises.*

Kade smirks, shaking his head as he makes quick work of his belt, his shorts, his briefs, pulling them all down far enough to whip out his thick, glorious cock. There's no time for a condom or foreplay or so much as a warning. He just roughly rubs his fingers between my lips, slicking his hand with my desire, and then coats himself with it before lining his tip up with my entrance and ramming it home.

Kade covers my yelp with another bruising kiss, and then he grabs my elbows in his hands, holding them behind me like handlebars as he rails me. When his mouth releases mine, my cheek pressed against the metal of whatever object we're fucking against is the only thing I have holding me upright — the rest is all him.

His hands grip my arms so hard I know they'll bruise, and every thrust is a punishment — a lashing I'm desperate to receive. I want it hard. I want it brutal.

I want him to fuck me *all* the way up.

I'm so turned on from the fact that we're in a public space, that one brush of my clit would send me over the edge, and as if he senses it, Kade slows his pace just enough to reach around with one hand and rub my sensitive bud.

My legs instantly tremble and shake, and the hand he freed flies up to slap against the metal and hold me upright as I chase my orgasm.

It comes on like a tsunami, the wave building savagely quick before it topples over and takes me under. Kade bites down on my shoulder to remind me not to be too loud, and holding in my screams only makes the orgasm that much more powerful. My face is fiery hot, body full of numbing stars.

And then, all at once, I fall limp, panting, a tremor shaking me from head to toe.

"We're not done yet, baby," Kade promises, and then he withdraws so quickly, I nearly fall from the sensation of losing his warmth. He spins me, grabs my cheeks between his thumb and fingers and kisses me forcefully.

Then, he guides me down to my knees.

"I can't make a mess back here," he explains with a wicked grin, swiping my hair out of my face. "So open that pretty mouth wide."

It shouldn't turn me on so much, the demanding arrogance in his voice, the degrading act of bending to my knees on a dirty floor for him.

But it does.

God, it does.

And as I take his cock in my mouth, I can feel my desire building again, and I'm literally dripping between my legs.

Kade groans as I swirl my tongue over every inch of him, teasing him a bit before I take him all the way inside. I don't waste time, coating him with saliva before I use both my hands, each of them rotating around his slick shaft while my tongue tortures his tip.

I know exactly what he likes, exactly what to do to get him to release.

His hand fists in my hair, and then he holds my head still, pumping his hips and fucking my mouth. I close my eyes and try to remember to breathe, to open my throat and relax.

And I don't gag until his cum shoots out and hits the back of my throat.

The groan that leaves him is guttural, hungry and wild as he holds me there, his cock deep in my throat, my tongue flat and splayed out so far I can nearly lick his balls. I open my eyes and watch him from below, which makes him curse under his breath, and then with a shudder, he finishes, slowly releasing me, slowly withdrawing.

After I swallow, I want to grin, wipe my lips, and spout something sassy at him, but I don't get the chance before he reaches down and grabs my arms, hauling me up to stand. He grips my cheeks in one hand again, and crashes his mouth to mine, kissing me senseless before he releases me.

"You're fucking *mine*," he says, his dark eyes hooded, jaw set.

Then, he pulls up his shorts and like nothing happened at all, strolls right back out on the stage just in time for someone to hand him an envelope with what I assume is the winner information for the contest.

And I can't help it.

My jaw drops, and then I belt out the loudest laugh of my life.

That fucking asshole...

Goddamnit, I love him so much.

When I finally come to my senses and realize there's a breeze in a place where there shouldn't be, I grab my panties and skirt off the floor and hastily pull them on, smoothing my clothes and then doing my best to fix my hair with no mirror. I know it's going to be damn near impossible to make it look like I wasn't just thoroughly fucked, but part of me doesn't care at all.

Let them all wonder.

Let them all know *I'm* the bitch who gets to have him.

I make my way back through the crowd to Skyler in a daze, a stupid smile fixed to my face.

When she sees me, her mouth pops open and she folds her arms over her chest, shaking her head as she eyes me up and down. "You dirty skank, did you just pull a quickie backstage?"

"I'll never tell," I say, but my words are slurred, a little from the booze and a *lot* from being completely drained after that romp with Kade.

Skyler snickers, and then hands me my clutch and asks if I want another drink. With an affirmative, she leaves me at our spot to head to the bar, and I fish through my clutch for my phone.

When I pull it out, my heart stops in my chest at the text waiting for me on the screen.

From Jarrett.

I open it with a knot in my throat blocking my airway, and when I see a screenshot of a picture of me and Kade on stage from Skyler's social media post, I nearly pass out.

I guess summer is over.

When's my turn?

Ashlei

I PUNCH THE PILLOW that's supposed to be propping me up, huffing again when I lean back and still feel uncomfortable. I lean up again, shifting for another *punch, punch* as the ice I have balanced on my shoulder slides off me, the bed, and then onto the floor with a *thwack*.

"Ugh!" I growl, letting my hands flop down on the bed and rolling my eyes.

I nearly cry at the thought of having to get up, bend over to get the ice, and then get situated again. Thankfully, Brandon comes into the bedroom with a soft, knowing smile and picks the ice up for me, helping me get it in the right place on my shoulder as he sits on the edge of the bed.

"I hear a lot of grunting coming from in here," he comments.

"How the hell am I supposed to try to sleep like this?" I whine. "Have you ever tried to sleep propped up? It's awful. My mouth keeps falling open, and then I'm snoring and my throat is dry and I'm drooling on myself."

"You're sexy when you drool."

I glare at him, but he just chuckles, rubbing my thigh sweetly and leaning in to press a kiss to my lips — which I return with a half-hearted pucker of my own.

"Who needs wine?" Skyler purrs, coming in through the door right behind Brandon.

A little whimper is all the answer I give, but it's enough, and Skyler hands me a damn sippy cup full of Sauvignon blanc.

I begrudgingly take the first sip, but feel marginally better afterward.

"I figured the nap wasn't happening," she remarks, climbing into bed next to me. She snuggles in under the covers and leans her back against the headboard. "Are you sore?"

"Yes. And irritable."

"No, really?"

I give her a flat look.

Skyler smiles, patting my arm and sharing a glance with Brandon before she says, "You're sad, babe. And it's okay to be sad."

That permission nearly breaks me, and I sniff, looking down at my bright orange sippy cup. "I just can't stop thinking about my life without pole."

"You're going to pole again," Brandon says quickly. "You heard Doctor Long after your surgery. He said once you get through these two months of recovery, you can start up at PT, and there's no reason you can't eventually get back to pole."

"Except he also said my shoulder will never be the same again," I remind him. "And that I may never get the full strength I had back. And that I might injure myself further."

"Only if you don't take recovery and PT seriously," Brandon argues.

"Wait," Skyler chimes in, brows popping up. "You really had a Doctor *Long*?" She smirks, waggling her eyebrows.

I snicker, too, which earns us an eye roll from Brandon.

"I'm just saying, we will get you the best physical therapy money can buy," Brandon promises me, and he waits until I look at him, until I'm watching as he brings my knuckles to his lips and presses a soft kiss to them. "We will get you back to pole, okay? I promise."

I close my eyes on a long exhale when he leans up to kiss my forehead, and I wish I could rewind to even two weeks ago, to when we were coming off the most perfect summer of my life. I wish I could go back to coming home and being ravaged by him before I could even drop my purse, wish I could go back to events at work being my biggest concern, go back to knowing at the end of every day, the pole studio was waiting for me to decompress.

"I love you," Brandon whispers, and I don't miss how Skyler smiles shyly down at her lap at the words of affirmation.

"I love you, too," I say, but it comes out more of a whine that makes Brandon smile.

His phone buzzes from his pocket, and when he pulls it out, he frowns at the screen, standing. "Excuse me," he says simply, and then he's out the door and answering the call.

I turn to Skyler immediately with a dramatic sigh. "Tell me about your life so I can forget about mine," I beg, taking another sip from my cup.

"Hey, go easy on that," she says. "You can't have more than one glass with the pain meds you're on now."

I flick her off.

"My life is boring," she says with a shrug and a smile at my gesture, but the smile slips quickly. "Rounding out my final classes, recruitment is over. I've been focusing on new member events so we can get the pledges lined up with their new Bigs. Cassie has her eyes on this one girl, so I've been trying to get them in the same places as much as I can."

"Little matchmaker, huh?"

"Something like that," she muses. "I've been talking to my guidance counselor about what to do next, whether I should go for my MBA or start applying for jobs, or maybe formulate a business plan and try to get investors to get started."

"Don't you have enough money to do it on your own from winning second place in that tournament?"

Her face goes ashen, but she doesn't miss a beat. "Sure, but I think I'd like to have at least one other partner in on the project with me."

She doesn't have to say so for me to know she was originally planning on that partner being Kip.

"Have you talked to him?" I ask softly.

Again, no name needed. She shakes her head, eyes on her wine glass.

"Do you want to?"

"Of course, I do," she says, finally lifting her eyes to mine. "I miss him every second of every minute of every hour of every day."

Her eyes gloss with the words, and I frown, reaching over to grab her wrist. "So *call him.*"

Skyler shakes her head, sniffing away the tears that hadn't quite formed yet. "No. I know it may not make sense to anyone else, and maybe it looks like stubborn pride." She pauses. "Hell, maybe it *is* stubborn pride. But he still doesn't see it. He still doesn't understand what he did wrong, how badly he hurt me. He apologized, sure, but he doesn't even know what to apologize for. He's blind to Natalia's true motives, blind to how he walked right into her trap, blind to how he put me behind everything else in his life and expected me to be fine with it." She shrugs. "He's sorry he lost me, but if he doesn't even understand why he did, then what would I be walking into if I just brushed this under the rug and said *okay*?"

My frown intensifies because she's got a point I can't really argue with.

I open my mouth to at least attempt to ramble through some sort of positivity speech when there's a soft rap of knuckles on the doorframe.

"Sorry to interrupt," Brandon says, and the look on his face makes me sit up a little straighter. "Um... you have a visitor."

If it was one of the girls, they would have just plowed right in by now. And if it was someone from the office, Brandon likely would have told them I'd see them next week when I came back. So I just answer with a confused frown, not sure what to say.

And when he moves to the side and Bo Hán walks under the arch, I drop my sippy cup, thankful for the child-proof lid as it hits my leg and bounces off to the floor.

"Holy shit," Skyler says, popping up first with a wide grin. "Bo?! Oh, my God!"

Skyler runs to Bo, who's smiling uncomfortably, her eyes flicking to me and then back to Skyler just in time to catch her crushing hug. I don't miss the relief that washes over her the longer Skyler squeezes her, and the way her shoulders relax, her smile widening.

"I haven't seen you in forever! How are you?" Skyler asks, pulling back to frame her arms. "You look amazing."

And she does. Her sleek, sable hair is short and edged at her chin, her warm brown eyes highlighted with gold, lashes long and sleek. She's as petite as I remember from college, only now she seems to stand taller, more confident, like she's not hiding a damn thing about herself anymore. The long-sleeve, white, lace top she's wearing buttons all the way from her chin to the hem of the little black flare skirt she's paired with it, and though the heels she's wearing are slight, they're strappy and bright red and just enough pop of color to tell you you're in the presence of a bad bitch.

"I'm good," Bo says, tucking her hair behind her ear. Her eyes dart to mine then, and she holds my gaze, a soft smile spreading on her smooth, peony pink lips.

Skyler looks between us, then at Brandon — who looks majorly confused and marginally concerned — before saying, "Brandon, can you come help me with something in the kitchen?"

She doesn't wait for his response before looping her arm through his and steering him down the hall. He gives me a questioning glance, but I smile and blow him a kiss, hoping it soothes whatever concerns he might have.

And then I'm alone with Bo Hán.

In the bedroom I share with my boyfriend.

Bo swallows, stepping inside a little bit as her eyes take in the length of me. "Do I want to know what happened to put you in that hardcore of an arm sling?"

"I fell off the pole," I say, a little breathlessly, a little too quickly. I just keep blinking over and over like she'll disappear with the next opening of my eyes.

Bo's face falls slack at that. "You're... you're doing that again?"

I shake my head. "Not like you think. I got out of that situation, and I never looked back. But, once I got my career on track, and found Brandon..." I shrug. "I found my heart missing that piece. So, I found a new studio. I've been dancing and competing... they even asked me to teach," I add with a small smile. Then, I nod down to my arm. "Until this, anyway."

"I'm sure they'll still want you," Bo offers quickly. "Especially if you're even half as amazing as you used to be."

I nod, trying to smile, but the frown etched in my brows overpowers it.

"I never thought I'd see you again," I finally whisper.

Bo's eyes well with tears, and she moves closer, letting out a long exhale as she leans down to retrieve the sippy cup of wine I dropped. She places it on the bedside table before sitting on the edge of the mattress, hands folding in her lap.

"I thought the same," she admitted, her eyes searching mine.

A long silence passes between us, no words necessary as we took each other in. I wonder if the memories are flashing in her mind the way they are in mine, but the way her eyes stay watery, the way her smile quivers a bit — I know I don't have to ask.

"I graduated in the spring," she explains. "My parents sent me to a tiny university in Montana, of all places. Can you believe it?" When my only answer is a deadpan look, she chuckles. "Yes, I suppose you can. But... strangely, I grew to love it. The mountains, the pastures, the quiet. I had space to think, and to grow, and to come into myself."

I nodded. "You seem happy."

"I am," she says earnestly. "I really am. And I... I finally got my parents to understand. I mean, I know it's still hard for them, but I brought someone home — someone I met in Montana who I love very, very much," she adds.

There's a strange cracking of my heart, a splintering of a piece of it I'd forgotten even existed. That piece will always belong to her, I realize — no matter what.

"I know it's not easy for them, but they love me, and I think they're beginning to realize that that matters more than anything else." She pauses, brows folding over her warm eyes. "I'm just so sorry you had to bear the brunt of their shock and confusion at the beginning of it all."

"Don't be," I tell her quickly, and without thinking, I reach out to cover her hand with mine.

We both still at the touch, eyes falling to the contact before we meet each other's gaze once more. But it's not a touch born of desire or lust, it's one of true, unyielding love and understanding.

Of sisterhood.

She squeezes my hand, and I close my eyes, a single tear breaking free and rolling down my cheek.

"I'm not here long," Bo says. "Just passing through, really. The company I'm with right now just secured a client in the Brickell Arch building, so we're here to court them a little and go over how our technology will integrate into their systems."

I arch a brow.

"Oh," she says with a chuckle. "Yeah, I changed my major. I'm a coding engineer."

"Not even a little bit surprised, you little baddie."

She laughs. "Anyway, I just... When I found out I was coming here, I knew I had to see you. I wanted to explain where I went, wanted you to know I didn't have a choice, and that I thought of you every day for quite some time." She pauses. "I *still* think of you. And I'm just so happy *you're* happy. You know — all things considered," she adds with a smirk at my sling.

I smile, too, and nod vigorously. "I'm happy you're happy, too. And thank you, for coming to see me, for... for caring enough to give me this closure I didn't realize I still needed."

"I needed it, too," she says. "And... hey, maybe instead of closure, it's a new chapter. I'd love to have a friend here in Miami. If you'll have me."

I pull her in for a long hug as my answer, closing my eyes at the way it feels to have her back in my life — even in this small way. "Always."

When we pull back, I shoo her off the bed so I can wiggle my way out and stand, too. Then, I loop my good arm through hers.

"Come on, I need you to get better acquainted with the man who swayed me to the more phallic side of my sexual desires."

She barks out a laugh at that. "I don't want to impose..."

"Nonsense. Stay for dinner. Stay the night, if you want to." I squeeze her. "We have a lot of catching up to do."

And with a smile from each of us, we venture down the hall to join Brandon and Skyler, and I find a bright gold lining on the dark cloud that had been hovering over me ever since the accident.

Adam

"I THINK WE SHOULD do it."

I stifle a laugh at how serious Cassie's face is as she says it, how wide her bright green irises grow at the thought.

"Come on, aren't you even a little curious?" she asks.

"I've done it before."

"Oh…" She waves me off. "Well, you've never done it with *me*. And you know… I heard the sex when you're high is…" She makes a chef's kiss gesture with her fingers and lips, waggling her brows at me as I laugh again.

"Hey, no need to convince me. I'm in. Do you think you want to smoke it?"

She shakes her head. "Maybe a chocolate or gummy or something? And I want to just hang out in your dorm when we do it." She blinks. "Or maybe my hotel room. I'm sure they don't allow it on campus."

"They don't, but that's not a rule that's exactly strictly followed," I add with a smile. "But okay, it's a plan. When you come for Thanksgiving break, we'll get you high."

"And you. Oh! And we should load up on yummy Thanksgiving food and munchies for the occasion."

"I'll order from a restaurant, that way we don't have to cook. And get some Twizzlers."

Her eyes grow even wider. "My favorite."

"I know."

She sighs, leaning her chin on her hands as her eyes wash over me. "I miss you so much."

"I miss you, too," I say, and my chest aches with the truth of it. "Are you going out tonight?"

"Nah, I think Skyler and I are going to court that girl I was telling you about who I want as my Little. Skyler invited her to come hang out in the president's suite, and we're going to make her introduce us to anime."

My brows shoot up. "That should be... interesting."

"I'm actually really excited! The characters seem so cool."

"You're the biggest nerd."

"And *you're* obsessed with me."

I sigh. "Also true."

"What are you doing tonight? And where are you?" She looks at the scene behind me. "It looks gorgeous."

I tap the part of my screen that makes the camera switch from facing me to facing my view and show her around. "I'm just hanging out in this little park on The Hill. The sun is starting to set over the mountains," I say, showing her the orange glow in the distance. "See it?"

"It's beautiful."

"We'll get up for a sunrise hike when you're here," I tell her, putting the camera back on me. "It's even more breathtaking."

"You'll have to peel me out of bed."

"Oh, I can be *very* persuasive when I want to be."

She bites her lip against a smile. "I'm well aware of those particular talents of yours."

I chuckle, leaning back on the blanket I'm on and propping my phone up against my water bottle so I can relax. "How is Skyler, by the way? I haven't talked to her since..."

I don't finish the sentence, but Cassie frowns, a heavy sigh leaving her that tells me all I need to know.

"She's... I don't know. Numb, I think. She barely talks about it, about *him*. She's just been focusing on the pledges and her last semester as president, talking to the girls who want to run for office, finishing up classes and making her plan for after graduation." She pauses. "Have you talked to Kip at all?"

"I tried calling him, but no dice. He texted me a few days later apologizing, and just said things were crazy busy in California right now but that he'd get back to me when he could."

"Ugh! So he's just living it up," Cassie says, throwing her hands up. "Just being *busy* when he's left Sky back here with a broken heart."

"Babe," I say with a smile. "I know you love her, but if I have my facts correct, Kip *tried* to make things right with her, and Skyler essentially said too little too late."

"Well, he clearly didn't try hard enough, then."

I laugh, but before I can argue the other side of it again, I'm nearly run over by a frantic tornado of hair and arms and legs.

"I need your help."

I squint up at the silhouette of the girl I ran into on my way to the Student Union last week, frowning in confusion.

"Now. Please. I don't know what to do. She's... she's fucking wasted, and I think..." She swallows, running her hands back through her long hair, her chest heaving. "Please."

"Who is that?" Cassie asks.

"I'll call you back," I tell her, and I end the call, jumping to my feet to grab the girl's arms. "Okay, it's alright. Just take a breath here and tell me what's going on."

The girl looks so different than she did the first time I ran into her. Her tattoos are covered by a long-sleeve pink cardigan, a matching band in her hair, and she's wearing long, slim, cream dress pants with small brown kitten heels. Her makeup is subdued and natural, and the combination of it all is what made it so hard for me to recognize her at first.

"I'm an Educational Leadership Consultant for Delta Beta Gamma, and I've been here with the girls all summer and they've been working so hard. They wanted to have a party at the house today and I... I covered for them and let them and... there's a girl, a young girl — freshman — she's... she's really drunk." She swallows, her blue eyes wild and animated. "I have her propped up in the bed, but I'm worried she might need to go to the hospital."

"Let's go," I say instantly, and then in a flash, we're flying up The Hill to the Delta Beta Gamma house.

The party is still raging when we run through, but we bypass all the games and shot taking and dancing, running up the stairs where it's a little quieter. The girl guides me down a long hall, and then into a bedroom where the girl in question is propped up against the headboard.

Her head is lolled to the side, mouth hanging open, and there's vomit on her shirt.

I cringe, rushing over to her side and taking her hand in mine before sweeping the hair from her face.

"What's her name?" I ask.

"Martina."

I nod, then start saying her name softly, shaking her gently until her eyes peel open like it takes all her strength to do so.

I know that feeling.

"Hey, Martina," I say as soothingly as I can. "How are we feeling?"

"Mm...okay," she slurs.

I nod. The fact that she's responding is a good sign. "Just feeling a little drunk?"

She nods, making a horse sound with her lips before her head lolls back again.

"Stay with me for a moment, Martina," I tell her. "I know you're tired, but can you just talk to me for a bit?"

She sighs, but holds her head up, her eyes bouncing between mine.

"Good girl. Can you tell me how old you are?"

"Nineteen."

The ELC curses from where she's standing behind me, but I hold out my hand to calm her so I can focus on my task.

"What's your major?"

She makes a sticking sound with her tongue and the roof of her mouth. "Accounting. But, youknowha?" she adds, holding up a finger. "I really wanna study litratrer."

I smile. "Literature, huh?"

"Mm-hmm," she says with an over-exaggerated nod. "I wanna edit booksh."

"Who's your favorite author?"

"I read romance," she says, shaking her head. "You wouldn't understand."

"I like romance."

Her eyes pop open. "Really?" Then she sighs, dropping her head back against the headboard. "I wish Josh liked romance."

She pouts, and I relax a little more. The fact that she can remember names, that she's talking to me, that her skin isn't cold or clammy and she's breathing normally are all very good signs that she's going to be okay.

"Do you like Josh?"

"Sadly," she admits. "But he's oblivion."

"Oblivious?"

"That," she says, pointing at my chest.

I chuckle again. "Well, any guy who has your attention is a lucky one."

She nods, but then I see her start to doze again, and I sit up from the edge of the bed, turning to the ELC who looks like she's just killed a puppy.

"She's going to be fine," I tell her.

"Oh, thank God," she says on a long breath. "What do we do? Should I get some Advil or water or?"

"No," I say, shaking my head. "We just need to get her lying on her side. Nothing but time can make her sober up — not food or water or a cold shower or any of that." I glance back down at Martina and her stained shirt. "If I step out of the room, do you think you could change her top? Just get her in something clean and maybe wipe her mouth a little?"

The girl nods, and then I step out for a few minutes until she calls me back in.

"Okay, let's get her on her side, just in case she gets sick again. We need to prop pillows and maybe bags or whatever we have around her so she can't really move without difficulty. And if you can, stay here with her and make sure she stays on her side. Check on her every now and then. As long as she's breathing normally, not too slow, and she's waking up and answering your questions... she's alright."

When we get Martina situated, the girl slumps down in one of the desk chairs in the room, and I grab the other, sitting on it backward with my forearms perched on the top. I extend a hand for hers. "I'm Adam, by the way. Adam Brooks. I'm a Field Executive for Alpha Sigma."

She takes my hand and shakes it gently before running a hand back through her hair again. It takes the pink band off when she does, and she looks at it begrudgingly before throwing it to the side and raking her nails over her scalp. "I'm Chandler. Chandler Simmons."

"Nice to meet you."

"I wish it was under better circumstances," she remarks.

"You mean like when I ran you over last week?"

That makes her smile. "Even that was better than this."

"Hey, I'm just glad I could help."

"I am, too. They didn't teach us this during training."

"Really? I'm shocked. We went over it several times in mine."

"Well, you're a guy," she shoots at me with pursed lips. "It's acceptable for fraternity guys to get hammered. But as a sorority girl, you're supposed to be a lady, to uphold a certain standard. They won't even talk about what to do if a girl gets too drunk because it's never supposed to happen."

"That's just naïve."

"Welcome to the patriarchy."

I frown. "I'm sorry. But consider me here to help however I can."

Chandler relaxes a bit, and then she smiles, her eyes running the length of me. When she finds my gaze again, there's nothing but true gratitude. "Thank you."

I nod, and then a slightly uncomfortable silence falls between us — mostly because I'm remembering the tattoos hiding under her sleeves, and the well-endowed breasts hiding under her cardigan.

"Well, I should get going," I say, standing. "Need to call my girlfriend back and explain what happened."

I think I see a flicker of disappointment in Chandler's eyes, but it's gone as quick as it came, and then she stands, too. "Apologize on my behalf for stealing you away. If she ever comes to visit, I'll take you both out to make up for it."

"It's all good." I clear my throat, heading for the door, but I pause at the exit and say, "See you around?"

Chandler nods on a smile, gives me a little wave of her hand, and then I'm out the door and pulling out my phone to call Cassie back.

Erin

"I DON'T WANNA," I whine, sticking out my bottom lip as far as I can and batting my lashes for good measure.

Clinton chuckles, kissing my knuckles before he stands and tugs on my wrists to try to get me to stand. "I know you don't wanna, but that's exactly why we should."

"It's been such a long week. With the detective and school and tests and poor Lei being laid up and I just..." I sink farther into the couch, despite him holding my hands. "I really don't wanna."

He gives me a gentle tug until I finally groan and reluctantly stand, and then he sweeps me into his massive arms, encompassing me in his classic Bear Hug that instantly fills me with warmth. I sigh, leaning into the embrace, my head resting on his chest as I clasp my hands behind the small of his back.

"Tell you what. Give me one hour. If in one hour you still want to come back and get in these sweatpants, I'll cuddle you all night and deliver wine on demand."

"I want to cry just thinking about that."

He smiles, pulling back to search my gaze. "What if I told you wine is still involved?"

"I'm listening..."

"And food."

I tilt my head to the side, sighing. "Fine. But I'm not putting on makeup or doing my hair."

"Good because you look perfect without doing a damn thing," he says, kissing my nose, and then he releases me and practically skips into his kitchen, telling me to get dressed.

It still takes me a while to drag myself back to his room where my weekender bag is, and I dig through it, pulling out a pair of linen shorts and a loose, comfortable blouse to go with them. I tug on my Sperrys and put my hair in a ponytail, grimacing when I see my reflection in the mirror.

Perfect, my ass.

The long week of studying and tests and meeting with my lawyer is evident on every inch of my face — namely in the dark circles under my eyes. I debate putting on makeup despite what I said, but I don't have the chance before Clinton calls my name from down the hall and tells me to hurry up.

With one last sight, I flick the light off in the bathroom and let him lead me out into the sticky, humid night.

We're quiet on the drive to wherever he's taking me, but he's wearing a wide smile and singing along to the songs on the stereo, one hand on the steering wheel, and the other tucked possessively around my thigh.

I stare at that massive dark hand, the way the fingers curl easily around me, the way I know exactly what they feel like on every inch of my body and like clockwork, my neck heats, mouth watering a bit at the thought of what he might do to me tonight.

We took it *excruciatingly* slow over the summer — which was half my idea and half my own personal torture. But after Gavin, I wanted to be sure Bear and I were serious before I opened that part of me to him — especially since I hadn't been with anyone since the night I was raped.

A little shutter goes through me at the thought of the word, but I'm getting better at saying it, at accepting it, at remembering that it's something that happened to me — not something that defines me.

So the summer was slow, but we still played and touched and kissed and laughed. I still explored him under the covers just as he did with me. And then, a few weeks ago, we finally broke the barrier and went all the way.

And *God*, it was all I wanted to do nowadays.

It's hard for me to keep my hands off him, to not kiss him longer and deeper every time, knowing that if I kiss him just the right way, he'll grow hard without being able to control himself.

I love that I have that effect on him.

I love that he wants me so badly he can barely stand it.

After a slow, calm cruise through town with the windows down, we pull up to a small park by the beach. Clinton climbs out before I can even unbuckle, opening my door for me and helping me out before he grabs a big cooler and duffle bag out of the bed of his truck.

"Did you pack us a picnic?" I ask, eyeing the bag as he slings it over his shoulder and carries the cooler in that same hand so he can hold mine with his other.

"I did, indeed."

"Wow," I comment as he steers us toward the water's edge. "You've become such a romantic."

"I blame you."

I smile, but can't help but lean into him a little more as we walk, into this man who I always knew I loved, but never thought I'd actually ever be with. Thinking about all we've been through, the obstacles we've had to overcome… it's enough to make me want to cry and rejoice all at once.

Clinton picks a spot under a tree, spreading out a large blanket and unpacking the contents of the cooler and bag while I settle in. He pours me a plastic tumbler full of wine, and then one for him, and after we cheers and take a sip, he leans in to kiss me, long and sweet.

The sun is already setting, just ten minutes or so left before it will dip behind us and dusk will move in. We sip our wine and munch on the different cheeses and meats and fruits Bear packed for us as we watch the colors change in the sky over the beach and the water.

"Have you ever seen a sunset on the west coast?" I ask him.

"Of Florida? Or like California?"

"Both. Either."

He frowns, thinking. "You know... actually? I don't believe I have. I mean, we went to Tampa a couple times for Gasparilla, but that was mostly drinking — never really cared to watch the sunset."

"We should go."

He smiles. "We should. Where else?"

"Hmm..." I nibble on a piece of sharp cheddar, thinking. "I've always wanted to see the Red Woods."

"Sounds like we'll be seeing the sunset in California, too, then."

"Oh! What about Greece?"

He chuckles. "That's a big leap from California, but yes. Add Greece to the bucket list."

I instantly pull out my phone and start a new note, titling it *Erin and Bear's Epic List of Adventures*.

"Okay," I say after writing down what we've discussed so far. "Your turn. What do you want to add?"

He sighs, eyeing the cotton candy clouds that are now turning a deep shade of purple. "Well, first... I want to take you home."

I roll my eyes. "Okay, perv. Focus."

"No, I mean *home* home," he says, and when I look at him, his eyes are sincere. "To Pittsburgh."

Butterflies zip through my stomach so fiercely, I place a hand over my navel to soothe them. "You do?"

He nods. "I want to take you to all the spots I went to as a kid, show you where I grew up. You've already met my family and hung out with them, so I know you can survive the crazy."

I laugh at that. "I love their crazy."

"So, that's a yes?"

I smile, typing on my phone. "It's at the top of the list. And you know what? I want to take *you* home, too."

Bear frowns. "To Kansas?"

I laugh. "That's where my *grandparents* live," I correct him. "My parents live here in Florida. Jupiter Beach."

"Oh," he says, relieved. "Alright, then. Add it to the list."

We spend the evening drinking wine, snacking, and laughing while we add places to our list. We daydream about what we'll do, the things we'll see, the people we'll meet. And before I know it, it's been two hours, and I haven't thought about wanting to go back home once.

Except now, with the night heavy around us, and Clinton holding my back to his chest as he leans up against the tree, I can feel a certain part of him at the small of my back, and the urge to go back to his place is strong again.

I nuzzle into him, wrapping his arms even more around me. "So, I'm thinking it might be sweatpants time again," I say.

"Oh? Done with being out?"

I bite my lip, reaching behind me and down between us to rub him over his basketball shorts. He stiffens at the touch, and then stifles a groan as I rub the length of him, which grows hard instantly as if I've commanded him to do so.

"Very much so," I whisper.

I turn in his arms, finding his heated gaze just as yearning as mine. He pulls me into him, framing my face for a deep kiss before he stands, yanks me up, and smacks my ass. "Help me pack this shit."

I laugh at his haste, even more so when I see him adjust himself in his shorts with a shake of his head at me. With lightning speed, he tosses everything back in the cooler and the duffle bag, not the least bit concerned with whether things were packaged correctly or standing upright.

And then, we're back in the truck and speeding across town.

I can't help but watch him as he drives, his grip tight on the steering wheel, jaw clenched, and that bulge ever present under his shorts. When we hit a stoplight downtown, I tug on my seatbelt enough to loosen it so I can lean over the console, and I hesitantly smooth my hand over his abdomen, the band of his shorts, until my hand folds over his hard-on and squeezes.

"*Fuck*, Erin," he hisses, grinding his hips into me.

I lick my lips, eyes on his growing length as the light turns green and I squeeze him a little harder, rolling my palm over the slick fabric of his shorts. When we hit the next light, I tug on the string tying his shorts at the top, freeing the knot.

"Can you take these down a bit?"

Bear's head snaps in my direction, and he gapes for just a millisecond before he presses his foot into the brake and lifts his hips enough to slide his shorts and briefs down to mid-thigh, freeing his cock.

I moan at the sight, biting my lip again before I lean even farther over the console. Clinton adjusts, holding the steering wheel high with one hand so I have enough room to peek my head in, and his other hand is holding his pants out of the way.

Careful not to hit his arm, I run my fist over him — one pump, two — and then I cover his large tip with my lips, spreading them wide until at last my tongue tastes him, swirling and sucking and teasing.

He groans loud, but keeps his eyes on the road, his focus steady as I take him a little farther inside each time. I feel wild and free, sexual in a way I haven't in a long time — if ever. He makes me feel this way... comfortable, confident, desired.

Safe.

It's hard for me to take Bear all the way in my mouth even with the best positioning, so being at this awkward angle with his pants in the way, it's impossible. But I slick my tongue along the walls of his shaft, curling it over his tip and moving in time with my hands as best I can. I know I won't get him off this way, but I also know I've got him so hard, his balls so tight that he's ready to burst.

When we pull into the small driveway of his house, he slams the truck into park and instantly reaches over to unbuckle my seatbelt. In the next breath, he's pulling me on top of him, flipping the center console up and out of the way so my knees have more room to steady myself. I straddle him as he crashes his mouth to mine, hand at the back of my head and crushing me to him like that kiss is his lifeline.

"You are everything I've ever wanted," he breathes against my lips before bruising them with another kiss. "Everything I need."

I kiss back in earnest as my answer, frustrated that he's exposed but my shorts are between us. "Take me inside."

Blindly, he reaches for the handle and shoves the door open, holding me to him as he stumbles out of the truck. He doesn't even bother to pull his pants up, doesn't give a shit if anyone in the neighborhood is watching. He just holds tight, my legs wrapped around his waist, and shuffles up the few stairs to his porch, fumbling with his key in the door, and then we tumble inside.

My back slams against the wood the second the door closes, and Bear pins me there, kissing my neck, my collarbone before frantically tearing my shirt off and sucking the swells of my breasts where they heave above the shell of my white bra.

A growl seeps from his throat, and then he drops me to my feet long enough to yank my shorts down to my ankles. He reaches for my panties next, but they're just a thin scrap of a thong, and without meaning to, he shreds the threading, quite *literally* ripping them off me.

"Shit," he says, looking at the lace in his hands, his chest rising and falling in erratic huffs.

"Whatever, I have more," I say quickly, and I grab the lace from his hands and throw it across the room before leaping back into his arms.

Our lips fuse together, and we're on the move again, though I can't see where. Suddenly, my ass is placed on top of the cool countertop, and Bear tugs me forward until I'm hanging off the edge and leaning back on my hands to steady myself.

He doesn't even take the time to remove my bra, just tugs the cups down until my breasts pop out, and he devours both, sucking the nipples and swirling his expert tongue hard and fast. I let my head drop back, legs already quivering at the need to have him inside me.

Suddenly, he stills.

His forehead drops to my chest, and he shakes his head, meeting my gaze with an apologetic look in his eyes. "I'm sorry," he says, swallowing a gulp of air. "I... I want you so bad I..." He shakes his head. "I'll slow down, I'm sorry."

"No," I whine, and I press up until I'm kissing him just as hard and desperate as before. "Don't slow down, Clinton. Don't stop."

He curses, sucking my lip between his teeth before releasing it with a pop. "I want to fuck you right now, Erin. Hard. Brutally. Do you understand?"

My pussy clenches at the words.

"I want to slam into you. I want to feel you stretch open for me, and then I want to fuck you hard and fast. This is how animalistic you make me. So if I don't slow down now, I won't be able to."

"Don't," I whisper again, scooching closer, my ass hanging off the edge of the counter now. I reach down to stroke his long length, coating him with the pre-cum on his tip. "Condom."

In a flash, he's gone, reaching into his shorts that he'd abandoned by the door without me even realizing. He fishes out a condom from his wallet, slides it on, and rips his shirt overhead, stalking toward me like a hungry beast.

Yes, my body hums.

I don't want tender. I don't want gentle and careful. I don't want to be something everyone thinks will shatter in a moment's notice, some fragile, doll-like thing.

I want to be the powerful woman who drives him wild.

I want to be the source of his every desire.

I want to feel every ounce of his lust-driven madness.

He must see it in my eyes, too, because the second he reaches me, he runs his large hands back through my hair, tugging until my neck is arched, chin turned skyward, his mouth crushing down on top of mine. He steals a soul-shattering kiss, and then he holds my hair there in one fist so I'm watching his face as he reaches down and positions himself at my entrance.

Then, without warning, without care for gentleness — he impales me.

The burning sensation of stretching open makes me cry out, but it's gone in a flash, replaced by an all-consuming desire as Bear picks me up off the countertop and holds me in his arms as he rams into me again.

How the hell this man can hold me, balance me, *and* fuck me to the hilt is beyond me, but I know one thing — he's in control this time.

So I just hold on tight and let him take me for the ride.

"*Fuck*, you feel so good," he purrs, kissing me hard as he wraps himself all around me. One arm holds the small of my back, crushing me to him, and the other firmly grips my ass, helping me ride him as he bends into a bit of a squat. His hips thrust, in and out, slow at first but quickly picking up speed. "So fucking good."

I can't say anything in return.

It's all I can do to hold on, to moan, to cry out and keep breathing as he pummels me. He gives me exactly what I asked for — all of him, no holds barred.

Without me realizing it, he's walked us to the couch, and he lays me down into the cushions, dropping to his knees and pulling my ass to hang off the edge. He reaches up to palm my tits, and then he's pounding me again, harder, faster, relentless and menacing.

I come without warning.

There's no slow building, no little spark that catches and softly tingles through my limbs. No, one second I'm holding on for dear life, the next I'm screaming so loud I feel like a porn star as the unexpected waves topple over me.

My cries only fuel Clinton more, and he keeps his pace, growling something like *yes, baby* but I can't be sure because I've completely blacked out. Stars are in my veins, gravity doesn't exist, I'm floating and free-falling all at once.

With a grunt, he slams into me even deeper somehow, holding me there with him buried inside me. I feel his cock pulse between my walls, the emptying of himself inside the condom as a lion-like roar rips from his throat.

And then, as if we've been running for miles, we both collapse.

He falls into me, I sink farther into the couch, wrapping my legs around him and holding onto his slick shoulders with my still-trembling hands. We stay like that a long while, just breathing, existing.

Slowly, Bear starts planting soft kisses on my shoulder, my neck, until he tilts my chin with his knuckles and captures a long, slow, sensual kiss.

Safe.

I am so safe with him.

"Fucking *Christ*, Erin," he pants, smiling before he kisses me again. "That was... you are..." But he can't finish the sentence, just shakes his head and folds me in his arms, maneuvering us until we're lying on the couch — him on his back, me on my side with my head on his chest.

"I loved that," I admit, trailing my fingertips along his chest.

"I didn't hurt you?"

"God, no," I snort. "Can you not tell?"

A devilish smirk breaks on his lips. "You *were* screaming my name pretty loud."

"I think I screamed loud enough for the whole city to hear."

"Good. Let them hear," he says, twisting until he's facing me. "Let the whole damn world know you're mine."

My heart flutters.

"And you're mine?"

He shakes his head, one corner of his mouth lifting as if it's the most obvious answer in the world.

"Haven't I always been?"

And then he kisses me, his hand roaming down to trail the sensitive skin on my hip, and we slip easily into round two.

EPISODE 3

Cassie

"WHAT ABOUT THIS?" I ask the girls, holding up a shiny, silver vest. "I could wear it over a lime green tube top!"

"Ooooh, yes!" Jess says with glee, grabbing the vest from me and holding it up over my chest. "If you button this top one, it'll push your titties up all nice and pretty."

I snort as Skyler adds, "We *have* to put LED lights on your cowboy hat."

"Duh," I say with a flip of my hair. "And star earrings. Every space cowboy has star earrings."

I grab the vest from Jess and toss it in our cart, and then we move along.

"I love thrift shopping," Erin says, dragging her fingertips along the rack of clothes as we walk. "Especially when it comes to planning for Halloween."

"What are you going to be again?" I ask.

"We're going to be a doctor and a nurse," she says with her cheeks shading red.

"*We*," Jess repeats with a cock of her eyebrow. "As in, you and Bear?"

Erin nods.

"God, I'm obsessed with you two," Jess says with a shake of her head. "I think I ship you more than any celebrity relationship I've ever followed."

"I think Bear just wants to see me in a little nurse uniform," Erin says.

"Obviously," I chime in. "But hey, that's half the fun of Halloween — get all dressed up just to have someone else strip it all off."

The girls laugh at that, but mine is cut short when I remember I *won't* have that part of the night this year.

This will be the first Halloween I haven't spent with Adam since... well, since coming to college.

Of course, half of those Halloweens, I was with another guy. The first time, Adam was with Skyler and I was with Clay. Then, there was Grayson. Truthfully, we've only really had one together.

And this year, we'll be on opposite sides of the country.

"What about you over there, mopey pants?" Jess asks Ashlei — who has been quiet all day long. She's just dragged along behind us, eyes dull, hands not even bothering to reach for a single article of clothing.

"A mummy," she deadpans, making a dramatic gesture to her slung-up arm.

Skyler chuckles, looping her arm through Ashlei's healthy one. "You know, we could probably make that hot. Just wrap a thin layer of gauze around your titties, a tiny skirt around your waist... show of that lean tummy of yours."

"It won't be lean for long with all this sitting around I'm doing."

The joke falls flat when Ashlei delivers it, because it doesn't have bite or any semblance of sarcasm. It's just... sad. Pitiful. The way she has been ever since the accident.

"I'm sorry, Lei," I say softly, reaching out to squeeze her wrist. "I hate this for you. Do you have any update when you start PT?"

"Not until I'm cleared from wearing this thing," she says, again gesturing to the sling. "And that won't be for another six weeks or so."

"It could be less," Skyler tries.

"I don't want to get my hopes up," Ashlei responds. "I can't afford to."

The girls and I share glances, knowing our friend is in a rough patch and there's not much we can do but just be there for her.

Sometimes, things are so dark and bleary, the last thing you need is someone telling you it'll be alright or to look on the bright side. Sometimes, you just need someone to lie down in the darkness with you and remind you you're not alone.

Jess wraps her up in a careful hug. "We'll make you the hottest mummy yet. And if you want to call off Halloween altogether and watch scary movies on the couch with some junk food and wine? I got you."

"Me, too," Skyler says. "Honestly, I don't have any plans other than make sure our new pledges don't get into too much trouble."

"I told Tera I'd take her to Ralph's, but I can totally cancel," I say.

"No, you can't," Skyler throws at me. "Big-Little Reveal is soon, and you're not the only one with eyes on Tera."

"Besides, every KKB sister *has* to experience Halloween at Ralph's," Jess chimes in.

I sigh. "I know, and I'm excited to take her and show her the ropes. Really, I am. It's just…"

"It's just that Adam won't be there," Ashlei finishes for me, and when our eyes meet, a soft nod is all I can give as a response.

"How has it been going with him gone?" Jess asks.

"Fine, I guess," I say, stopping at a rack with neon colors. I hold up a pair of hot pink fishnets, and before I can even ask, Skyler grabs them from my hands and throws them in our cart.

"*Fine* never actually means fine," Ashlei assesses.

"Well, it *was* fine. At first. I mean, we had the summer together, and then when he got sent to Boulder, we would text and call and video chat all the time. But lately... I don't know. He's been busier, and I keep seeing him tagged in pictures with all these girls. I know it's part of the job — he's helping the brothers throw events, working with other executive members in the fraternities and sororities, but..."

"But he has a whole life without you," Jess finishes, her eyes understanding. "That was the hardest part for me with Jarrett."

"Yes," I agree, rubbing a velvet jacket between my fingertips as my gaze loses focus. "He just feels... distant. He always has to go. He always has something to do. And there's this girl he keeps mentioning, Chandler. They met when he helped her with a girl in her sorority who was entirely too drunk, and now they're kind of like... I don't know, mentors for each other? He's been helping her out and she's returning the favor. It sounds friendly, but..."

"It's natural to feel jealous and intimidated and scared," Jess tells me, squeezing my arm. "But listen to me — Adam is all yours. I mean, you're wearing his letters. That might as well be an engagement ring around your neck."

I finger the necklace as she says the words, heart thrumming at the memory of the day he gave it to me.

"Don't make the mistake I did and make a bigger deal out of something than it is. Trust him. He loves you. Okay?"

I nod. "Thank you."

"Speaking of that... what's going on with the boys?" Ashlei asks Jess.

She sighs, throwing her hands up. "God if I know. Taking the summer away from both of them didn't help anything — I think I was just trying to avoid it. But Kade came over and we've been talking so much, and I had such an amazing time with him at the A Sig karaoke event."

"Oh, we know," Skyler says with a smirk.

Jess flicks her arm. "But now Jarett wants his turn."

"Are you going to give it to him?" I ask.

Jess stops at a rack and leans into it, the clothes and hangers groaning with the weight of her. "I know it sounds fucked up but... I *have* to. I have to see him. I have to talk to him and ask questions that have been eating me up. I have to see if what we had is still there." She pauses. "He was my first real love. He was my first real heartbreak, too. And I... I don't think I can let him go."

"Ever?" I ask.

She shrugs. "I don't know. All I know right now is that I have plans with him on Halloween, so we'll see what happens."

"Well, now I'm *definitely* not asking for a girls' night," Ashlei says.

"I'd bail on him for you," Jess promises.

Ashlei smiles, kissing her cheek. "I know. But this drama is too good for me to pass up on. It'd be like missing a week of my favorite TV show."

Jess flicks her off, and with a soft laugh, we all start perusing the clothes racks again.

Skyler avoids the Kip question when it comes up, and Ashlei falls back into her silent, glazed state of being.

The KKB girls aren't in the best shape right now.

But at least we have each other.

Bear

"**I FUCKING HATE YOU**," Giselle says from the floor where I'm standing over her. Sweat covers her neck, her chest, drips off her hairline and into her eyes.

"Kick your legs up like you mean it," I challenge.

She grits her teeth, and then with a grunt, she sends her legs up, straight and together, her core firing up before I grab her sneakers and throw her legs back down toward the ground. It takes a focused breath from her not to let them hit the ground, and then she pushes them back up to me.

Again, and again, and again.

I finally call it, and she flops out like a fish, chest panting as I grab a towel and hand it to her. "Get some water," I say, doing the same. "I think we're done for today."

"You think?" she pants, groaning a bit as she sits up to grab her water bottle. She takes a long swig, shaking her head. "When I asked you to be my personal trainer, I imagined jumping jacks and high knees and some pushups. I *didn't* picture a full hour of unimaginable torture."

I chuckle. "You're already stronger than last week, and remember — you asked for this."

"Yeah, yeah," she says, extending a hand up for mine. "I only do it so I can stare at you without a shirt on."

I grab her hand and help her stand, laughing off the comment. When she's up, I don't miss the guys on the benches behind her letting their eyes wander every inch.

She's wearing tiny black workout shorts, similar to those a volleyball player might wear, and a matching black sports bra. It's strappy in the back, but otherwise plain. But it's not the outfit that draws everyone's attention — it's the body wearing it.

I knew Giselle was fit. I could tell even under her suits she wore in the office. But seeing her rippled midriff, her toned arms, her muscular legs with nothing covering them? There's no doubt in my mind that while I may be pushing her or challenging her with different exercises than she's used to, she's no stranger to hard work in the gym.

After toweling off her face, she lets the white cloth hang around her neck, squirting a healthy amount of water in her mouth. "You're really good at this, Clinton."

"Thank you."

"No, I mean it. *Really* good. I've worked with other trainers, and they're not like this. They don't check in, they don't offer nutrition guidance — at least, not past what I can easily research myself online. I feel so much stronger ever since you calculated my macros, since you taught me how to give my body the proper nutrition it needs."

"You were starving yourself before. It doesn't surprise me that you were tired all the time."

She shrugs. "I thought caloric and fat deficiency was the key. Thanks for teaching me otherwise." She pauses, assessing me. "How many other clients do you have?"

"Just a few. I can't take on too many — not right now, anyway. I need to stay focused on my real job."

"What if this *was* your real job?"

I blanch at her question, toweling off my neck before I take a seat on one of the benches. When I don't answer, Giselle crooks a smile and plops down next to me.

"Think about it. You understand fitness. You understand nutrition. You know how they work together. You get joy out of helping others, right?"

I nod a little more with each statement.

"And you have a degree in graphic design, with experience in client management and a little HTML knowledge, too. I mean, you could literally run your own business." She pauses. "If you wanted to."

I lift my brows, turning to face her. "I never thought of that."

"Well, now you have," she says with a smile. Her eyes are warm, almost playful as she watches me. She opens her mouth to say something else, but before she can, my phone rings, the sound making both of us jolt a little.

"Hey, babe," I answer. "Finishing up training with Giselle. Can I call you right back?"

"Of course. I've got about forty-five minutes before my next class."

"Give me ten."

When I hang up, I know there's a goofy grin on my face, and Giselle pokes her finger right where I know my cheek indents a bit when I smile like that.

"Whew, you are *smitten*, aren't you?" she teases.

I blow out a breath. "You have no idea."

"She must be something."

"She is," I say, showing Giselle the picture on my background. "And let's just say the road here wasn't an easy one."

Giselle whistles, taking my phone and studying Erin. "She's gorgeous. I'd say you're a lucky guy, but since I know you, I think the luck is mutual between you both."

"Thanks," I say with a shrug, taking my phone and tucking it away again. "But trust me — I'm *very* much the lucky one."

Giselle doesn't say anything but smiles and looks at her watch. "Alright, I guess I should get going. Dinner meeting with a client," she adds with an eye roll. "But let's touch base about the next month — because I'm officially hiring you as my trainer *and* nutritionist."

"You already paid me."

"Well, I'm going to pay you more."

I grab my neck. "Well, thank you, I guess. I'll make a plan for the next four weeks. Just so you know, I'm doing a little traveling at the beginning of November."

"Oh? Where to?"

"Just going home for the weekend. Pittsburgh," I clarify when I see her frown of confusion. "Erin's never been, and I want to show her around where I grew up."

"Erin is the girlfriend, I presume?"

I nod. "It's just for the weekend, though, so it shouldn't affect our training."

Giselle frowns, standing when I do. "You're flying all that way just for a weekend?"

"No paid time off yet," I say with a shrug.

Giselle's mouth tugs to the side, then she waves her hand in the air like she's batting away a fly. "Take a longer weekend, maybe a Wednesday to Sunday."

I frown. "But I—"

"Don't worry about it, I'll work it out with Henry."

Henry my *boss*, she means.

"You've been working your ass off and you deserve it."

My head is spinning a little — first from the idea she put in my head about my own company, and now from this. "Um... I guess if you're sure."

"I am. And remember what I said about the confidence thing?" She smacks my ass with her towel. It's playful, along with the grin on her face, but I admit it makes me a little uncomfortable. "Stop acting like you're surprised when I tell you how great you are. It's kind of annoying."

I smirk, but don't have anything to say in response.

"See you at the office," she says, and then she grabs her water bottle and struts away toward the locker rooms.

Every guy she walks by has to fight not to watch.

Ninety percent of them lose.

My thoughts are still whirring when I pack up my own gym bag and head out of the gym. I pull my phone out to call Erin back, and that's when I see the text from Skyler.

I know you have plans on Halloween, but are you free the night after?

I could really use a Bear Hug.

My chest aches. Skyler and I haven't had the chance to hang out much, what with her in her last semester as president and finishing up school, and me working and focusing on my new relationship with Erin.

I've got a big one with your name on it, I type back.

Her only response is a heart emoji, and I make a mental note to pick up burritos from her favorite spot off campus on my way to see her.

Once the text is sent, I call Erin back, and count down the hours until she's in my arms again.

Jess

THIS MIGHT BE MY most boring Halloween costume to date.

Blame it on the fact that it's my *first* Halloween out of college, or that I'm exhausted from work and didn't have time or creative energy to think of something better, or perhaps that I have no idea what I'm walking into tonight — or what I want to walk into — but this year, I'm a classic witch.

My long, blonde hair is curled and flowing over my shoulders, the highlights fresh and bright under the black pointy hat on my head. My makeup is dark and fierce — smokey eyeshadow, long, fake lashes, black glittery lips. The dress I picked for my witchy vibe is an old black sequin one that I wore on New Year's Eve one year. I shredded the bottom of it, ripping it in triangle strips of different shapes, sizes, and lengths, and I ripped holes in the midriff and chest area for good measure. Wide fishnet leggings and pointy-toed high-heeled boots finish the look — along with a broomstick I paid some kid two condo doors down to spray paint and glitterfy.

And while I didn't aim for sexy, as I usually do, I think I landed there, anyway.

It's classic and simple, but the darkness of it matches my mood completely.

I'm fixing my lipstick when my phone lights up with a text from Kade.

Have fun tonight.

My stomach tightens at the words because I know he's not saying them genuinely. I know there's a bit of jealousy underlining them, a bit of worry, a bit of unmanageable rage at the fact that he has to share.

I wonder how he doesn't already hate me — how they *both* don't. Ever since Jarrett confessed he still had feelings for me, the two of them haven't so much as talked, let alone been in the same room.

I've driven brothers apart, and what's worse are the head games I know I'm submitting them to.

I should just let them both go. I should tell them that they're better off without me, that they'll both move on and find someone better. Because I don't see a single way this can end where someone won't get hurt.

And yet, I can't let them go.

I groan, typing back a response before I slump down in the barstool at the kitchen island. "I'm the fucking worst," I mutter to myself.

My phone rings again, and this time, it's Herb downstairs.

Jarrett's here.

I tell Herb not to send him up, that I'll be right down, and then I stand as tall as I can in front of the full-length mirror by the front door.

"Okay, bitch. This is the night. You figure out what the hell you're doing and either choose Jarrett or cut him loose. No hanky-panky, okay?" I say to myself, making a peace sign and drawing a line between my eyes and the girl's in the mirror. "It hasn't even been a month since you fucked Kade. Don't be a whore."

I swear, I see the girl in the mirror wink before I turn for the door.

My palms are slick on the elevator ride down to the lobby, and when the doors slide open and I see Jarrett standing in the middle of the marble floor, my mouth goes dry.

His back is to me, lean and muscular, his hands sitting easily in his pockets. His head is smooth and freshly shaved, and he must sense me, because he turns — ever so slowly — until his dark eyes lock on mine.

He's wearing an all-black outfit, just like me.

And he looks like every sin I'm trying not to commit.

A black tunic is tapered at his waist with a belt, the chest of it ripped open to show the muscles and tattoos underneath. He's shoved the sleeves up to just below his elbows, showing off his tanned, toned forearms and the ink that covers them, too. His beard is neat and trimmed, salt and pepper gray touching the dark brown of it, and the leather pants he's wearing are something out of a *GQ* photoshoot — fitted, but that slouchy kind of casual that makes your mouth water on sight.

He smirks when my eyes make it back to his, no doubt loving the fact that I just ogled him and almost had the elevator doors shut on me in the process. I step fully out, standing tall as I stride over to him in my heels, and that's when I see the tastefully painted blood dripping from one side of his mouth.

"Vampire," I muse, arching a brow when I notice he's wearing blood-red contacts. "I'll be honest, I thought you'd show up as a beach bar bartender."

"Didn't want to turn you on too early in the night. Although, I *can* drive my truck instead of us catching a cab, if you'd like. Just in case."

He doesn't wink, doesn't make any facial expression with the tease other than to smirk just a fraction more. But the memory of that first time fucking in his truck makes my neck heat, my core tighten.

I flick him off and shove past him before he's on my heels, chuckling as he catches up.

"Where are we going?" I ask.

"Dancing."

And then as if it's the easiest thing in the world, as if I belong to him, as if he never left me or hurt me or pulverized my heart — he takes my hand in his and leads me to the waiting cab.

The Lemon Club is one known for its bustling nightlife, often hosting well-known DJs and never closing before four in the morning. It's already bumping when we finally get through the line outside, and in the doors, orange and purple lights thumping with the music and fog filling the floor. Above us, aerial artists hang from hoops and silks, and all around us, girls and boys alike dance in go-go cages, their bodies moving in time with the heavy bass.

The club is packed, people squeezed in at the bar and dancing on every inch of the dance floor. Jarrett pulls me into a dark little corner before looking around with a mixture of amusement and annoyance.

Then, he slips his hand around my waist, tugging me closer.

Again, as if it's the most natural thing in the world.

My breath hitches at the contact, at the way it feels to be held by him after all these years, to have his hands on me, that familiar energy buzzing through my veins just with that simple contact. My traitorous body hums to life, pussy throbbing, nipples pebbling and aching for more.

I really am the fucking worst.

"Sorry it's so loud in here," he yells over the music,

leaning in close enough to my ear that his warm breath brushes my lobe.

I swallow. "It's okay!"

We stand there for a long moment, Jarrett dragging his gaze down the length of me, his jaw tight.

"You look incredible," he says, and though I know he had to scream it for me to be able to hear, it feels like a weighted whisper in my ear.

"So do you," I say, and it's almost a pout — enough so that Jarrett chuckles and lifts a brow.

"You say that like it's a bad thing."

I offer a slight smile in lieu of answering that *yes, it is a very bad thing*. Because taking the summer away from him numbed my brain to the power he exudes over me. I'd forgotten his rugged, earthy scent, his thick, muscular arms, his devilish smirk, his dark, hypnotizing eyes. I'd forgotten what it felt like to be pinned by his gaze, to know without him saying a word that he wants me — desperately.

But with him standing right in front of me, his hand possessively holding my half-bare waist, I'm all too aware of everything I'd tried so hard to forget.

Jarrett's expression is a little more solemn when he says, "It's been excruciating staying away from you."

I close my eyes, letting out a slow breath like it'll somehow save me.

"Did it help?" he asks, leaning in even closer, his breath on my neck. "Did you find the space you needed to think?"

A wave of chills runs over me at the feeling of him being so close, and *thinking* is about the last thing I can do.

"Let's dance," I say instead of answering, and I grab his hand, pulling him deep into the middle of the dance floor.

I know immediately that it was a mistake.

I didn't want to talk, didn't want to answer his questions, didn't want to look him in the eyes and admit that I'm more confused than ever. I didn't want to confess that I still love him, that just like he told me — I never stopped. Because I also love his brother, and it just doesn't seem fair or right or sane for both of those things to be true.

But now that we're on the dance floor, his hands snaking around my waist and pulling my back flush to his chest, I realize that talking or crying or literally *anything else* would be safer than this.

The music seems louder out here — thicker, heavier, like a physical presence pulling both of us in. Jarrett grabs my hip hard with one hand, the other splaying over my midriff, and then he's moving us, hips swaying slowly at first before finding the beat.

We haven't even had a drink yet. I can't blame it on the alcohol that the moment his body lines up flush with mine, I moan, biting my lip and letting my head fall back against his chest. I reach one hand up to hook behind his neck, the other covering his hand where it spreads across my stomach. Lights pulse overhead, blinding me from time to time as we dip and sway and move together.

It's intoxicating, that buzz of desire that shoots through me with every new touch. His hand moves from my hip to my thigh, and I gasp. His other hand slides up just an inch, his thumb pressing into the hollow space between my breasts, and I arch my back, grinding my ass against him.

He's hard as a fucking diamond, and the way he rolls that impressive length against me, I know he couldn't care less about me or anyone else in this club knowing it.

"Your costume is very fitting," he rumbles in my ear, sucking the lobe of it between his teeth. "My little witch, spinning her web, keeping me under her spell."

His words stroke me like expert fingertips, and I grind against him more, grabbing his hand and moving it up until it fully palms my breast. His moan is guttural, a menacing growl as he bites down on my neck like it's the only thing he can do to keep his composure now that he's touching me.

In front of everyone.

But who cares? Who's looking? And even if they are, maybe I want them to. Maybe I need to feel this connection again, to remember what we had, to let myself have everything I once took for granted like I never lost it at all.

It's selfish and fucked up, but I can't find it in me to care.

Before I can talk myself out of it, before the angel on my shoulder can get a peep out, I whip around in Jarrett's arms, crushing my mouth to his.

He catches the kiss with intention, one hand coming to the back of my head to hold me there. My witch hat flies off in the process, which only gives him permission to run his fingertips more through my hair, to grab the back of my skull and kiss me like it's his chance to mark me, to claim me for good.

His arm wraps around me like a boa, squeezing tight, holding me to him so I can feel every breath, every muscle, every inch of his rock-hard length. And the moment our lips meet, I feel every memory rush back in a furious wave.

I remember that first time in his truck, and that last time in the hotel — the time I didn't *realize* would be our last. I remember him caring for me when I was sick, remember him taking all my friends out for dinner, remember how every time his fingertips ran along my skin, my entire body came to life. I remember how fiercely I loved him.

And how utterly destroyed I was when he left me.

I wince against the pain that memory brings, and Jarrett seems to sense it, because he kisses me harder, slicking his tongue along my lips until I open up and let him inside. We both moan, and I press up on my toes to get more, Jarrett's hand sliding along my ass, my thigh until he hooks his hand behind my knee and hikes my leg up.

The kiss is deep and bruising, tied up with emotions of love and lust and pure fucking hatred. Slowly, we start to move again, grinding to the beat with his thigh between my legs and my dress hiked up over where he holds me in place. All of my weight is in his arms. I have no choice but to move the way he dictates, to sway the way his hands tell me to, to rub where he wants me to rub.

Holding me steadfast with one arm around the small of my back, he snakes the other one between us, sliding up my hiked leg along the tender skin of my inner thigh.

I shiver, barely breathing the words, "What are you doing?"

His only answer is a wicked grin, and then his fingertips slide up and up, higher and higher, dangerously close to where I know I'm slick for him.

Suddenly, the music is too loud. We're too close. The kiss is too hard. My heart pounds in my chest in a warning, reminding me how much this man hurt me, reminding me how dangerous it is to play with a fire that burns so fucking cruelly.

I snap back away from his mouth, shoving my hands into his chest and pushing with all my might until he has no choice but to let me go. I stumble backward once he no longer carries my weight, but I don't take more than a second to watch the stunned look on his face before I'm squeezing through the crowd, running over anyone who doesn't move at the first muttered *excuse me.*

I have to get out of here. I can't do this to Kade. I can't do this to *myself.*

I want him.

I want him so fucking bad it hurts.

And I love him.

I still fucking love him.

Tears sting my eyes, not just at the admission, but at the realization that the love I have for him burns just as hot as the love I have for Kade.

Someone will end up broken.

The someone who deserves it most is me.

I push and shove and tear through the thick crowd until I finally push outside, stumbling over my heels in the process. But I catch my footing, straighten my dress, fix my hair and strut on once I'm on the sidewalk. Sniffing, I keep my eyes focused forward.

I have no idea where I'm going, but I know I can't stay still.

I hear him calling my name after a moment — softly at first before he's jogging up and hooking my elbow to rip me around. I expect to find anger, to find a man who was cock-teased and is now pissed off about it.

What I find breaks me even more.

Jarrett must have removed the stupid red contacts he was wearing, because his natural dark brown ones are flicking between mine, brows furrowed over top of them as he searches me for where I'm hurt. There's nothing but care and concern and pure fucking love, and it instantly makes those tears I've been holding back build and rush over before I have the chance to stop them.

"What's wrong? Are you okay? Did I hurt you?"

I laugh at that last question, which makes him frown more. Slowly, tentatively, he pulls me into him, wrapping me in a soft, sincere hug. He holds me like that for a long while, and I just let the tears come, let them soak his tunic and the street we stand on.

"Yes," I finally breathe. "You did hurt me."

With my head on his chest, I see the way his throat hollows out, the way a thick swallow strains his neck. I pull back, breaking all contact and swiping at my face before I fold my arms over my middle and stand a few feet away from him. It's far from fall in Florida, no matter what the date on the calendar, but the nights are cooler than they were before, and the breeze chills me to the bone as I look around at the people laughing and talking as they walk by us — oblivious to the turmoil raging inside me.

"You hurt me worse than anyone ever has in my entire life," I continue. "I loved you, Jarrett. I trusted you. I gave you everything I had to give. I put up with the long distance and the lack of communication because I knew, at the end of the day, that I wanted you — no matter the cost."

I sniff, more tears building in my eyes that I refuse to let fall.

"And then you tossed me to the side."

Jarrett shakes his head, pain etched in his features as he reaches for me, but I pull away.

"You did. You let them get in your head, let other people convince you I was crazy. You left me like some silly part of your past."

"It was a mistake," he says quickly. "The worst fucking mistake I've ever made. I was stupid. I was *wrong*."

"All I wanted was for you to come back," I admit on a strained whisper, rolling my lips together and shaking my head. "And now that you have, I hate that I wished for it."

Jarrett tries reaching for me again, but I flinch away.

"I wish you'd have stayed gone. I wish you'd have never shown back up and turned my life upside down as soon as I figured out how to right it again."

"No, you don't."

I cry at his words, covering my face and forcing a breath to stop the tears as much as I can before crossing my arms and lifting my chin to face him again. I don't want to break, but goddamnit if he doesn't undo me.

"I never left you."

I laugh under my breath, but Jarrett moves in closer. I back away, but he doesn't relent. He just keeps closing the space until my back is against a brick wall and his chest is touching mine.

"You've always had me and you know it — just like I've always had you."

I swallow, staring at him through bleary eyes, but already I can feel it — my pulse quickening, thighs tightening, head pounding as every molecule of my body swirls at the way it feels to be watched by him.

"This?" he says, gesturing between us. "What we have? It's elemental. It's... *transcendental*. It doesn't matter what happens, what mistakes we make, how much time we have apart or who might come between us."

He shakes his head, stepping into me more, his entire body pressing against mine as his hands snake up my arms, over my neck, up my jaw to cradle my face between them.

"It's always going to be us, Jess." He licks his lips. "For me, it's *always* going to be you."

His mouth is on me in the next second, stealing any response I had.

And I let him take it.

Let him take *all* of me.

We're in a cab back to my place less than sixty seconds later.

Hands.

Hands *everywhere*.

Grabbing my hips, my thighs, my ass, my back, my neck. Gripping my hair. Shredding my clothes.

And lips.

Lips everywhere.

On my mouth, my breasts, my neck, the sensitive skin along my inner thighs.

I might as well be drunk, or high, or in a fucking meditative state for how time passes, how I lose track of everything as that man sweeps me away to a universe all his own.

It's all a sensory-overdrive blur until the moment he rips his briefs down.

He's already on the prowl for me, crawling his way up the bed where I wait for him propped against the pillows. Before he can reach me, I press my toes into his chest, pushing back until he's on his knees so I can get a good, long look.

A good, long, *hard* look.

A good, long, hard, perfectly shaped, perfectly thick, perfectly *mine* look.

Jarrett crooks a smile, tilting his head a bit. "Someone likes what they see."

"Someone hasn't seen it in far too long."

In a feat of movement my brain can't comprehend, Jarrett flips me onto my back, stands at the edge of the bed, and grabs me under the arms to drag me until my head hangs off the mattress.

"Maybe someone should taste it," he husks, carefully moving my hair from my face and gently, tenderly tilting my head until my throat is long and exposed, head hanging completely off the bed.

Jesus fucking Christ.

He doesn't wait for my smartass answer that I'm sure he knows I have on the tip of my tongue. Instead, he grabs his cock and presses it to my lips, arching a brow and slicking his tip along them until I grant him entrance.

The gentleness is gone.

He presses inside before I'm ready, slicking himself with my saliva as I force a breath and open my throat wide so as not to gag. He curses when he's fully inside me, and then he's palming my breasts, pulling out again only to slide back in nice and slow.

I kind of wish I had his view, kind of wish I could see his dick bulging in my throat, my tits under his hands, my thighs spread, body writhing with need.

This is what he does to me.

This is that elemental, carnal connection he was referring to.

It's the most powerful high.

"Goddamnit, Jess. Do you know how many nights I've laid awake thinking about this, about you?" he asks, withdrawing just to push inside my throat once more. "Do you know how badly you've ruined me for any other woman, how dull and lifeless their touch is compared to yours?"

I threaten with a little bit of teeth when he mentions other women, and it makes him yelp a little before he chuckles, pulling all the way out and yet again flipping me on the bed. He picks me up—

Picks. Me. *Up.*

And throws me into the pillows, dropping down on top of me before the mattress has even adjusted to the weight. He kisses me hard and long, our teeth clashing, and then he's trailing little bites and sucks of skin all the way down.

Before I can prepare for it, he drags the flat of his tongue along my slick pussy, groaning as he laps up my desire. "Fuck, I never forgot how much I loved breakfast in bed with you."

"It's nighttime," I remind him.

"It's after midnight, technically. And besides," he adds with a quirk of his brow. "Haven't you ever had breakfast for dinner?"

He steals my breath to answer with another lash of his tongue, and then his fingers are spreading me wide, creating better access for him to tease and suck my clit.

It's fire and ice, my body heating to unbearable temperatures before a chill shudders through me, over and over again.

He knows just how to lick me, suck me, touch me.

And I know before we even get there that he knows just how to fuck me, too.

For a split second, a flash of guilt surges in my stomach. It's so fierce I sit up and grab Jarrett, but then it's gone, replaced by the hunger raging through me as Jarrett takes that as his cue that I've had enough foreplay and am ready for him to be inside me.

He answers the plea by grabbing my ass and pulling me toward him, and then he pushes my feet toward my face, like I'm doing the fucking happy baby yoga pose.

"Hold on," he says, waiting until I grab my feet — *literally* the yoga pose.

Then, he presses up onto his knees, grabs the condom I didn't realize he'd slapped on the bedside table, and rolls it on.

"Spread," he commands, and I pull harder on my feet, opening myself completely. I mean, there is no more vulnerable position for me to be in. I'm spread with my vagina just waiting there, catching a draft, my legs restrained by my own strength like a good little girl.

I shiver as he lowers himself down once more, just long enough to slick his tongue over my asshole, my pussy, sucking my clit long and hard and releasing it with a yelp from my lips.

Then, he's at my entrance, one hand holding my thigh as the other presses the tip of his cock inside me.

And he nails it home.

I gasp at the sensation, at the fullness of him inside me, at the forbidden juiciness of not having him for so long, of him somehow being off-limits and yet never anyone else's but mine.

Jarrett groans when he withdraws and presses inside again, feeling every inch of me taking him in. "I hope you're as ready as I am," he breathes like he's in pain. "Because I'm not going to last long."

He slips out and back in, finding a rhythm — slow at first as he reaches down and strokes my clit with his thumb. He knows just how to circle, just where to apply the pressure so it builds my orgasm without hitting any too-sensitive spots.

It's like fucking magic, how fast I build for him, how fast my heart races and blood pumps right where I need it.

"Come on," is all he says, and as if that invitation was what I was waiting for, I explode, holding onto my feet even tighter and spreading my legs wide enough to know I'll be sore in the morning. My glutes clench as I ride the wave, reaching for more, *begging* for the orgasm not to recede too early.

Jarrett takes my moans as permission to find his own release, and I'm glad Erin is with Bear tonight when he comes, because his screams are as loud as mine, the deep baritone of his voice rumbling off the walls like a fucking lion's roar.

I don't have time to come down, to pant, to wrap my slick body around him and laugh at how fast we both came. As soon as he finishes, Jarrett pulls out, disposes of the condom in the trashcan by my bed, and rolls another one back on in its place.

I gape at the sight, and he just arches a brow, smirking at my dumbfounded expression.

"I know you didn't think one round would be enough," he says, shaking his head before descending on me like a predator. "It's been too long since I've touched you, kissed you," he says, pressing his lips to mine before he whispers, "*fucked* you. I'm nowhere near satiated."

My body heats to life again at his words, at how much this man desires me, how badly he craves my body. And with another bruising kiss and lust-drunk moan, Jarrett flips me, pulling me into his lap.

He grabs my hips and guides me down, my sore, wet pussy opening for him once again.

Round two.

Ding ding.

Skyler

A THOUSAND BEAR HUGS wouldn't be enough.

I never thought I'd say the words, never thought there was *anything* a hug from my best friend couldn't fix. But even lying on his couch, my feet in his lap and a fetus-sized burrito in my belly, even with a half-bottle of wine swimming in my system, even with an entire evening of talking and laughing, and even with the dozens of hugs I've stolen tonight — I'm still on the verge of tears.

I've been feeling it for months, the constant knot in my throat, the pain and aching in my chest. Like at any moment, at any time, I could just burst into tears and then into flames.

Unstable.

Unsettled.

Unknown.

I've been keeping my shit together in front of everyone, working hard in my last semester as president of KKB, acing my classes as I prepare for graduation, being there for Ashlei through her injury, supporting Cassie in her long-distance relationship, and Jess in her difficult decision she knows she has to make soon. I've cheered Erin on in her case against the guys who violated her, and called home to check in on Mom and Dad, to promise them I'd be home for the holidays before going wherever post-graduation would take me.

I'm graduating.

The realization always makes those tears I've been holding at bay build a little stronger.

Because I've dreamed about this for so long, but I never dreamed I'd feel so fucking lost when the time actually came.

"You know," Bear says, rubbing my arches with his eyes still on the TV. "You could call him."

"And say what?"

He shrugs. "Whatever you're feeling."

"I don't know what I'm feeling," I say on a sigh. "That's the problem."

"You know exactly what you're feeling," Bear argues. He finally looks at me then. "You're sad. You miss him. You love him. You're hurt by what he did. You don't know if you can forgive him."

"Exactly," I say, pointing at his chest when he says that last part. "So, if I don't know if I can forgive him and move forward, why would I call him? What would it change?" I look at my chipped nail polish where I balance the half-empty wine glass in my hand. "Besides, he's apologized, yes, but... he doesn't even understand *why* he has to apologize."

"I'm sure that's not true."

"He doesn't see Natalia the way I do. And he feels like I should be understanding with the show, with his career. And I *am* it's just..."

"It's just that you want to know where you stand in his life," Bear finishes for me. "If you're less important than his career, on the same level, or more."

My stomach cramps. "Yes," I whisper.

We're quiet for a while, me sipping my wine while Bear pretends to watch the TV. I know he's just giving me space to process, to think.

"Maybe I am being too hard on him," I confess. "Maybe it wasn't as big of a deal as I'm making it."

"Don't do that," Bear says. "Don't make yourself feel crazy. I would have been upset, if it were me."

"You would have killed her," I said with a smirk at my best friend. "You would have grabbed her wet hair and slammed her head against the tile."

"Jesus, Sky," he says with a frown. "That's so violent." A pause, and then a tilt of his head. "But, not *entirely* far-fetched."

I chuckle. "I'm just saying, maybe his apology was more sincere than I'm giving him credit for. Maybe it's *me* being dramatic."

"You? Never."

I roll my eyes, but then my nails are tapping against the wine glass, and I suddenly shoot up to set it down and reach for Bear's phone.

"What are you doing?"

"I'm pulling up his Instagram."

Bear's eyes widen, and he snatches his phone out of my hand before I can even unlock it. "Um, first of all, why do you need my phone to do that?"

"Because I blocked him," I say with a shrug. "I had to. It made me physically ill every time he liked one of my photos, or any time I saw him post something."

Bear sighs. "Yeah. It would make me sick, too... which leads me to my second point of caution — I don't think this is a good idea."

"I just want to see what he's been up to. You were right," I confess. "I do miss him. And maybe this will help push me over the edge, help me get the lady balls to just call him."

Bear's mouth pulls to the side.

"Please."

He sighs, handing me his phone before kicking back on the couch again. "I still feel like this is a bad idea."

"Noted," I say, but I'm already typing *Kip Jackson* into the search bar on the app. He and Bear are friends, so Kip's profile pops up before I even finish typing the full name, and my heart squeezes at the sight of that familiar smile, those ocean blue eyes framed by thick black glasses.

I tap the little circle.

And then I freeze when I see the most recent post.

For a moment, my thumb just hovers over it. I don't want to see it blown up to full-screen. I can tell just from the small thumbnail what it is.

Kip, dressed to the nines, full suit and bow tie and dress shoes and a watch I bought him in Vegas.

And Natalia, in a short, silver, slinky dress with thin straps.

He has his arm around her waist, and she has hers around his, and when the picture was snapped, he was smiling at the camera.

She was smiling up at *him*.

I nearly vomit when I finally tap it and pull it full size — especially when I see all the likes and comments underneath it. The caption reads *That's a wrap on editing! Can't wait to bring* Black Number Four *to your laptop screens and home TVs, and for you all to see this amazing girl in action.*

The comments range from *congratulations!* and *can't wait!* to *cute couple!* and *wow, you're both glowing!*

The more I scroll, the more those tears I've been holding back threaten to break loose. I feel them blurring my vision, feel them tightening my throat, feel them suffocating me and demanding to be felt.

"Sky..." Bear says, leaning up to look at the screen with me. When he sees it, he mutters, "shit," and takes the phone from me, tossing it on the coffee table.

I look at him.

And then I break.

Covering my face with my hands, I do my best to breathe through the terrible sobs that wash over me like a thunderous, relentless wave. Bear pulls me into his chest and holds me close, whispering that it will be okay.

But I know it won't.

When we had our fight, I was angry. I was pissed off. I was so fucking hurt that I couldn't see him. Over the summer, I needed that space. And even when he left to go back to California, I was still upset, but I think...

I think deep down, through all that, I just always assumed it was a phase.

I always assumed it was just a fight, just a summer apart, just something we would have to work through.

I thought we'd make it through.

The realization that I was wrong strikes me like a fist to the gut, and I double over, surrendering to another massive attack of painful cries.

He's having the time of his life while my life falls apart.

And somehow, I can't help but feel like it's all my fault.

Jess

"SHIT!" I CURSE AS the contents carefully balanced on the top shelf of my closet tumble out and rain down on me, a shower of shoes and yoga equipment and long-forgotten hobbies.

Erin runs over from her room, makeup half-done and hair pinned back. "What was that? Are you okay?"

I grunt, looking at the mess on the floor. But spotting what I was looking for, I swipe it off the ground and plop onto my unmade bed. "Just peachy."

Erin offers a soft smile at that, her shoulders deflating a little. She strolls over to me and sits on the edge of the bed. "Is this your favorite pair of shoes or something?" she asks, tapping the lid of the old shoebox in front of me.

"It's my own personal form of torture that I like to succumb myself to from time to time."

Erin cocks a brow.

I sigh. "It's a memory box," I explain, flipping the lid off to reveal the contents inside. "Mostly of Jarrett. And then..."

"Kade," Erin finishes for me, fishing out a picture of us from that first formal we attended together.

"Yep."

Erin smiles at the picture, setting it aside before holding up a greasy pizza napkin. She wrinkles her nose. "Pictures, I understand. But this?"

"They're memories," I defend, swiping the napkin from her. I smile at the nasty thing. "This was from when Jarrett flew in to visit from New York. We had amazing sex when he first landed, and then knew we weren't leaving the room. So, I ordered pizza, and we stayed in." I bite my lip. "All. Night. Long."

"Okay," Erin says, holding up her hands and standing. "I think this memory box is a personal experience."

I chuckle. "You off to class?"

"Leaving in ten. Are you going to work?"

I shake my head. "We had three weddings this weekend — Friday, Saturday, *and* last night, so we all have today off to recover."

Erin nods. "I'll be back tonight. If you want to talk," she adds, her eyes falling to the box before they land on me again.

"You sure you're up for that crazy ride of me talking through my feelings right now?"

"Always."

She blows me a kiss, and then she's out the door, and I settle back into memory lane.

The last week has been a whirlwind.

After Jarrett left — which wasn't until very, *very* late the morning after Halloween — I nearly had a breakdown. All the memories of us had come rushing back, completely washing over the foundation I'd just rebuilt and fortified with Kade.

I thought after the karaoke event that I knew. I thought I would just call Jarrett up and tell him that while I did care about him, I couldn't see him.

But then stupid me *had* to see him.

And stupid me remembered why I'd loved him so fiercely, why he'd broken me so completely, why even when I tried — I could never forget him.

I pull a thin, lacy, hot pink bra out of the box, smirking when I remember Kade's face the time I wore it for him, the time I punished him for being a jerk to me over the summer, for blowing off the plan *he* had made for us. That was the closest I'd ever been to a Dom, and I loved it.

And God, I love *him*.

I love that he rose to every challenge I gave him, love that he wanted to learn, that he wanted to please me, that he wanted to be my every sexual desire. I love that it quickly became so much more than that, that he snuck into my heart and made me fall for him without so much as trying.

I love how effortless we are, tried and true.

A team.

My eyes catch on a box of matches with *Ralph's* in script on the front, and I pull them from the box, smiling again. I snatched them from the supply closet that night Jarrett railed me on Halloween, reminding me that playing the games of flaunting college boys in front of him wouldn't work.

And I love him, too.

I love how just one look from him can strip me utterly naked, how he knows me better than I know myself sometimes. I love that he's not afraid to push my buttons, that he calls me on my bullshit, and that he fucks me like a goddamn pro.

I love that toxic, completely addicted feeling of losing him and winning him back.

The most beautiful mess.

I close my eyes, sighing before I pull out more items, one by one, each little menu or picture or scrap of clothing or stolen tchotchke another memory pulling me this way or that.

It's a vicious tug of war, one where no one wins.

My phone buzzes in the sheets next to me, and I hitch a breath at the sight of Kade's name.

Can I see you?

I sigh, shaking my head and typing back a response before I can think on it more.

Not today.

Erin calls out a goodbye from down the hall, and then the condo door opens and shuts, and I'm alone.

Another ping of my phone.

Were you with him on Halloween?

Him. He doesn't even have to say who for me to know.

I didn't post anything on the holiday, not a single picture, which is unlike me — since everyone knows I love my costumes. I'm sure he put two and two together that I wasn't with Erin and Bear, nor was I with Ashlei — who posted a sad, albeit cute, picture of her dressed as a mummy on the couch with Brandon — and I certainly wasn't with Skyler and Cassie at Ralph's wooing Cassie's soon-to-be Little.

And still, I can't bring myself to answer him.

Suddenly, my phone rings, and I jolt, thinking it's Kade. But it's Herb at the front desk, and I answer surprised, "Herb?"

"Good morning, Miss Vonnegut. You have a visitor."

I swallow. Maybe Kade isn't taking my non-answer as an answer. "May I ask who?"

"The young man who picked you up for Halloween, Miss."

My heart jolts again, but this time, in a traitorous, excited way.

"Send him up, please."

I jump off the bed as soon as we end the call, fussing with my hair a bit and changing out of my giant sweatpants into a small, cute pair of sleep shorts. I'm wearing a tank top without a bra, and decide I shouldn't bother putting one on.

When I see the box and its contents on my bed, I curse, gathering everything and shoving it back inside before kicking the whole box under my bed. I close my closet door to hide that mess, too, and then scuttle down the hall.

My phone buzzes as I do.

Kade.

You're killing me, Jess.

When I open the door and see Jarrett smirking, holding two coffees in a carrier and a bag of what I assume are donuts from one of the best places downtown, my heart cracks.

"I'm on my way to the office," he explains, a beautiful smirk on that beautiful face of his. "But I had to see you first."

I bite my lip against the smile I feel building, opening the door more for him to come inside.

My phone feels like a bomb in my hand.

I read Kade's text again, and then I type back the most honest thing I can.

I'm killing me, too.

Before he can respond, I toss my phone on the kitchen counter face down, following Jarrett inside. I lead him back to my bedroom, snatching the bag of donuts from his hands.

"Mmmm," I say, inhaling the intoxicating scent as I pull out the first one. "Blueberry cake. How did you remember my favorite?"

"Come on, like I could ever forget. You ate *five* in one sitting the first time we went."

I laugh around the mouthful I've already started chewing on. "Hey, I never said I was a lady."

"I never said I wanted you to be one."

Jarrett takes a bite off the other end of the donut, and I swat away his victorious smile when he takes half the thing with him.

When we're done chewing, Jarrett sits on my bed, patting the seat next to him until I do, too.

"I feel like we didn't get to talk much," he says with a wry smile. "On Halloween, that is."

My cheeks heat. "I don't think either one of us had an issue with that."

"At the time, no," he agrees. "But... I don't want you to think that's all I want. That that's all you are to me."

I frown. "I didn't. But now..."

Jarrett laughs under his breath, opening his arm and pulling me under it. His lips press against my temple, and I melt at the touch, at how soft and sweet it is, at how good and lovely and *right* it feels when his hand rests on my waist.

"I want to take you on a date," he says, but already I can feel it — that magnetic field between us firing to life. His hand tightens where it holds me, eyes falling to my lips. "An actual date where we talk and catch up and maybe get to know something new about each other, too."

"Okay," I say breathlessly, and my fingers trail up the buttons of his shirt, hooking over the collar. "When?"

"As soon as you'll let me," he purrs, his free hand finding my knee. It trails up, slow and steady, leaving chills in its wake.

I unfasten the first button of his shirt, then the second. "This week is kind of busy at work... can I let you know?"

Jarrett's hand splays over my thigh, fingertips so long they brush the hem of my tiny shorts. "As long as you *actually* let me know, yes."

"I will," I promise, mouth parting, eyes flicking to his. "We could talk now, you know," I offer, but even as I say the words, I'm undoing the last of his shirt buttons and shoving the fabric back, over his shoulders, down to his elbows where it catches.

"We could," he muses with a smirk, helping me get his shirt the rest of the way off. As soon as he's topless, my eyes roaming the painted valleys and ridges of his abdomen, he grabs my hips and tosses me like a teddy bear back into my pillows. "*Or* you could take your shorts off, pull those perfect tits out of that thin little thank top they've been teasing me through, and let me make you come a couple times before I have to go to work."

My pussy tightens at the words, and without me having to answer, he's already slipping his fingers under the bands of my shorts and tugging. I lift my hips to allow him access to strip them off, and then he reaches for my tank top, roughly yanking until my tits pop up through the neckline.

He bites his lip on a moan, sucking my left nipple hard between his teeth before moving on to the right. When they're both puckered and I'm writhing beneath him, he kisses his way down, and then flips us so that I'm on top.

Straddling that beautiful face of his.

"You're always so hungry in the morning," I tease, but the words lose their bark at the end when he flicks his tongue against me, his hands grabbing my ass and pulling me into him.

"Insatiable, really," he growls.

My hands fly to the headboard to keep me steady when he licks me long and slow, seam to bud, and then sucks my clit with just enough pressure to make my legs quake around him.

And just like that, any attempt at talking is forgotten.

Jarrett's hands are steadfast on my ass as he helps me ride his face, sucking and licking and biting and kissing like eating pussy for breakfast is his favorite pastime. I lose myself completely with him, succumbing to not one, not two, but *three* orgasms. The first one comes from his tongue, the second from him taking me from behind, and the third time in the shower where we're both trying to be good and get clean.

But we're naked, and *wet*, and steamy... like we could keep our hands off each other.

By the time he forces me to let him go so he can get dressed and go to work, I'm sore and aching in all the best places, my eyes ready to close for a long nap when he kisses my forehead and lets himself out.

I surrender to sleep the second he's gone.

And somewhere in that strange state of not quite sleeping but not quite awake, I swear I can hear my phone buzzing on the kitchen counter down the hall.

Bear

"GO, GO, GO!" ERIN screams beside me, jumping up and down like a wild animal, and now that she's stripped off her beanie, her dark blonde hair is flying everywhere — including right in my face. She nearly steps on my toes before I grab her waist to hold her steady, laughing when she turns to face me with wide eyes. "What?"

"I love that you're excited," I tell her. "Just... watch for other people's feet. And faces."

She smiles — and *God*, the sight knocks my next breath from my chest. It's not a small smile or a soft, reserved one. It's full on, eyes crinkled, teeth dazzling and lips spread smiling.

My happy Erin.

How I've missed her.

She whips around again in time to see my little brother get tackled to the ground about five yards from the end zone, and she throws her hands up in victory, jumping up and down again before crushing me in a hug.

"He's amazing!" she says, stripping her scarf off. "And so *tall* and massive. He's going to kill it when he gets to college. I'm sure he'll have the ladies all over him, too." She pauses, then starts unzipping her jacket. "Do you think he'll go pro?!"

I laugh, stopping her before she can remove the puffy Patagonia. "Hey, don't take off too many layers. You're warm now because you're jumping around, but I don't want you catching a cold."

"I love this," she says breathlessly as the team lines up for the next play. "Football, cold weather, hot chocolate, fire pits, pumpkin everything... *this* is fall."

"I don't know how you do it in Florida," Mom chimes in from next to her, shaking her head. "Still eighty degrees in November? No, thank you."

"*Ninety* when we left for the airport," Erin corrects her.

"Maybe you'll end up here one day," Mom says, and I don't miss the mischievous look in her eyes when she says it. I also don't miss how bright *her* smile is, how full her cheeks are, how healthy and happy she looks compared to the woman who'd run off my freshman year of college.

Whatever happened in Mexico, it seems to have set her right. And I'm thankful, at least, Clayton gets to see this side of her, gets to grow up with a mom who's present and working and *sober*.

"Real subtle there, Mom," I tease.

She shrugs. "Hey, I'm just saying, Erin has only been here two days and she's fallen in love already."

"It's true. I mean, how could I not? Just driving through that tunnel, being in the country one second and then *bam*," Erin says, illustrating with her hands splaying wide like a panorama. "A whole city!" She looks at me and shrugs. "Who knows where life will take us after I graduate."

My heart flips in my stomach at the thought, at the way she's watching me, at the fact that she sees *me* in the picture after graduation, sees a future where we might possibly move to my home city.

The ball is snapped on the field, and we all turn in time to watch the quarterback throw a perfect spiral to Clayton, giving him the touchdown he almost had on the play before.

We go wild, along with the rest of the stadium, and Erin jumps into my arms, pressing a celebration kiss to my lips that makes me wish for my little brother to get at least a dozen more touchdowns just like that one.

After the game — which we win by a landslide — we all go to our favorite family-owned sports bar for a late-night dinner. Clayton might as well be a celebrity for how many people want to shake his hand or take a picture with him or get his autograph when we walk through the door. He gets interrupted the whole time we're there, but I don't mind at all.

I'm so fucking proud of him, my chest is the size of a hot air balloon.

"Stop looking at me like that," he teases, his voice a deep baritone I'm not used to. He's grown up so fast, in the blink of an eye it seems, and that stubborn, cocky teenage attitude I had is settling in on him just the same. He's got longer hair now, dreaded and styled, and when a few girls walk by giggling, I laugh at the lazy-eyed smile he gives them.

If Palm South thought *I* was trouble...

"Like I'm proud of you?" I shrug. "No can do, little brother. Going to have to get used to it."

Clayton throws a French fry at me.

"Did you see the scouts?" Mom asks him, eating a sweet potato tot from her own plate. "This is the third game that one from Alabama has been to."

Clayton shrugs. "He can come to as many as he wants. I'm going to PSU."

"I love that you love my alma mater so much," I tell him, clapping a hand on his shoulder. "But there's nothing wrong with exploring options. Alabama is a D1 school."

"Doesn't matter. I know where I'm going. I've known since I was twelve," he says, meeting my eye.

The admiration there, the respect... it's enough to make my throat squeeze tight like there's a fist around it.

Erin smiles, leaning her head on my shoulder as she says, "Well, I for one think you've got your head on straight. Palm South is the best university there is."

"And they're going to be the best *football* team there is when I'm there," Clayton says.

The two of them high five across me, and Mom and I shrug, knowing that — at least for now — we've been beat.

I'm on a high after dinner, and with Clayton going out to celebrate with his friends and Mom going to sleep, it leaves only Erin and me. Once I confirm she's as far from sleepy as I am, I bundle her up and pack a few blankets, taking her to my favorite rooftop.

"Wait, wait, wait," she says through a mixture of laughter and tears around midnight. The moon is hidden behind thick, navy-gray clouds tonight, but it somehow illuminates her just enough for me to see that beautiful smile. "You're telling me that *you*," she says, pointing at me. "And *Skyler*?"

She laughs again before she can even get the rest of the sentence out.

I nod. "Yep. Right here," I say, patting the rooftop under our blanket. "It was her first time coming to Pittsburgh with me. She was single at the time, and so was I, and we were very, *very* drunk." He shrugs. "Everyone always asked if we had ever had feelings, I think we just got curious."

"And did you?" Erin asks, her voice a little tinged with something akin to jealousy. "Have feelings for her, I mean?"

"God, no," I say instantly, shaking my head. "Not like that, anyway. We made out, got about as far as me taking her shirt off, and then we both burst into laughter."

"Sounds like you two."

"We're best friends," I explain. "We've been through a lot of shit together. I'd kill anyone who hurt her, and I know she'd do the same for me."

"So I should call Kip and warn him?"

I sigh. "Don't get me started on that fiasco."

Erin chuckles, then crawls over from where she was reclining on the blanket to cuddle with me. "Okay. *Now* I'm cold," she says.

"We can go back to the hotel," I say softly in her ear, dragging the tip of my nose up her neck. "I know many ways to warm you right up."

"Mmmm," she says. "Yes, please. But let's stay here a while. This view..."

We both sweep our gazes over the city lights, the way they dance over the river and twinkle like stars all around us.

"You really think we could end up here one day?" I ask her after a while.

"I think it's as possible as staying in Florida. I mean, it's not like you're super in love with your job, right? And I could go anywhere after graduation."

"You know," I say. "I've been thinking about that, actually. My job. You know the account manager I work with, the one who hired me as her personal trainer?"

"Giselle, yeah?"

I nod. "Well, she thinks I might be onto something with my training and nutrition. She thinks I could open my own business."

Erin goes stiff in my arms, then turns to face me, her eyes wide. "Oh, my God. I can't believe I didn't think of that first."

"You really think I could do it?"

"Are you *kidding* me?" she asks, knocking on my abs like a wooden door to illustrate.

I laugh.

"Look at you! You know more about fitness and nutrition than anyone I know. I'm in the best shape of my life since we started dating, and I didn't even have to hire you."

I shrug. "I don't know."

"I do. And you have the graphic design skills, the coding experience to do a website. You might need to hire some help eventually, but you could get started on your own. For sure."

"Giselle said the same thing."

"Well, she's a smart woman." Erin kisses my cheek. "I can help you with a business plan."

"Will you be my sexy little lawyer on call, too?" I tease, biting her neck when she turns back around and leans into me.

"I'll wear your favorite pencil skirt and everything."

That earns her a moan from me, and she chuckles, but then goes silent for a long while.

"They're questioning me this week," she says.

I swallow. I don't have to ask who. The case has been slow going, but the detectives and lawyers have already questioned me, the girls, and the fucking assholes who raped Erin, as well as their disgusting friends. Who would go to bat for them, I can't imagine — but they have to be pure scum.

"You're going to crush it," I whisper.

"It's going to crush *me*," she whispers back.

I hold her tighter, kissing her neck and wrapping her up as much as I can, letting her know I have her, that she's safe, that it will all be okay.

"I just... what if we go through all this, and they win anyway? What if we go to court and the judge rules in their favor?" She pauses. "What if it doesn't even *make* it to court?"

"They won't win," I tell her. I don't say anything further. Those three words are everything she needs to know, everything I firmly believe.

"I love you," she whispers into the night, those words sweeping up on a soft breeze to caress my ears.

"I love you," I tell her. "And I'm proud of you, for stepping forward, for speaking out against them."

"I hope I don't regret it."

"No matter what happens, you shouldn't," I tell her. "Win or lose, court or no court — you're an example for other victims, an inspiration for other women to tell their stories, too."

Erin nods softly, but I don't miss the single tear that wells up and rolls down her right cheek.

I thumb it away, tilting her chin until she's facing me, and seal my admiration for her with a long kiss.

"So," I ask her, knowing she needs a break in the subject. "Will we live in the city, or the outskirts?"

"City, of course," she says. "How about that building there?"

She points at one across the city that I know costs at least a half-a-million dollars for a two-bedroom condo, but I nod anyway.

"Looks perfect."

Erin turns, wrapping her arms around my neck. "Perfect is wherever I am with you."

Cassie

I CAN'T TELL IF Skyler wants to wrap me up in the biggest hug ever...

Or strangle me.

On the one hand, I know her heart is full that I'm taking a Little, that our family is growing, that our legacy in Kappa Kappa Beta will live on after we're gone. Erin never took the news well that I didn't want a Little, but Skyler supported me no matter what. Still, I know deep down she's always wanted me to take a Little, too, and I know she was ecstatic to hear I'd changed my mind.

On the other hand, I made her dress up like Ron from *Harry Potter* for the reveal.

With a gold and garnet scarf around her neck, a long black robe down to her knees, an orange wig, a stuffed toy rat in one hand, and a wand in the other — she looks absolutely adorable.

And also ready to kill me.

"She should be here soon," I promise Skyler, checking the time on my watch. "If she followed all the clues and spells correctly — which I have no doubt she did — we've got maybe ten minutes."

"I'm fine, Little," Skyler says, and her smile tells me maybe she *is* closer to wanting to crush me in a hug rather than cut off my oxygen supply.

"You really do look great."

She chuckles. "Your hair is ridiculous."

I laugh at that, touching the frizzy curls I pulled off to complete my Hermione look — thanks to an overwhelming amount of teasing and hairspray.

"You're excited," she says after a minute, that small smile holding firm.

I nod. "I really am. Tera is awesome. If anyone is going to take on our family number and reputation, I couldn't have asked for anyone better than her."

"She's lucky to have you for her Big."

I frown. "For a couple more months. Then, we both leave her."

A light flashes in Skyler's eyes at something behind me, and her smile grows. "Something tells me she'll be *just* fine."

We're on one side of the reflection pond, the water backlist and spraying up into the night, and when I turn to look where Skyler's gaze has fallen, I can't help but burst into laughter.

I set up a scavenger hunt of sorts for Tera all across campus, giving her clues of where to find hidden mystery items to complete her Harry Potter costume — like his glasses, a gold lightning bolt tattoo for her forehead, her robe, her Gryffindor scarf, and even a stuffed Hedwig. Along with finding the objects, she had to perform "spells" to random people I had in on the event in order to get her next clue.

And the last task? Defeat the cardboard Voldemort I had printed out and staged in the middle of the pond.

It looks like a scene out of a movie, the way her hair is flying back behind her, scarf in the wind, her wand held high as she banshee screams and runs through the water toward the cardboard cutout. In dramatic fashion, she stops right in front of him, the most determined look in her eyes, and then she holds her wand right to his nose and screams, "*Avada Kedavra!*"

When nothing happens, she pauses, breathing heavy and looking around.

So, I take my cue, sprinting from our hiding spot and splashing into the pond, too.

Tera's eyes light up at the sight of me, and to match her energy, I land a kick right to the cardboard cutout Voldemort's chest, bending him in half before he falls into the water.

Then, Tera and I are screaming and laughing and hugging and crying and all the memories of when I found out Skyler was *my* Big rush back to me in the most vicious, most beautiful flood.

"I'm so glad it's you!" Tera says when we pull back, both of our eyes glossy.

I sniff. "Welcome to the family, Little."

Skyler joins us then, and when Tera sees her, she covers her laugh before wrapping Skyler in a hug.

"A fine Ron Weasley you make, President."

"You can call me G-Big now," Skyler says, and when they're done hugging, she holds up her wand and says, "Now, what's the spell to make a very strong cocktail appear?"

We all laugh, already making our way out of the pond and waving to the spectators who had watched the scene. Some of them are snapping pics, so we pose with our soggy Voldemort and take a few of our own.

"Are we changing before we go out?" Tera asks.

"Absolutely not," Skyler answers. "Fully committed to the *Harry Potter* theme tonight. We need to look up a recipe for spiked butter beer and order it at Ralph's."

I wrinkle my nose. "Something tells me we can't trust any bartender at Ralph's to even remotely know how to make a drink that isn't three parts whatever alcohol you want and one part soda."

"Fair," Skyler concedes. "But we should try anyway."

"Oh! Before we change, I told Adam we'd video chat him," I say, pulling out my phone.

Tera is all bright smiles and red cheeks, and she, Skyler, and I cuddle in close to make sure we're all in frame as the phone rings. Skyler touches up her hair while Tera fixes her glasses on her nose, and then the screen connects.

"Merlin's beard!" Adam answers, completely on theme. "Looks like we've got ourselves a new Gryffindor."

"Hi, Adam! Nice to finally meet you," Tera says. "Virtually, anyway. I've heard so much about you."

"Same here, Tera. Welcome to the family."

There's a voice somewhere near Adam — a female voice — that makes my heart stop.

It's then that I notice his surroundings, a candlelit restaurant with plush, deep red booth-like seats and chandeliers hanging above him. Mahogany wood trims everything in sight, and he's not in his normal Alpha Sig polo, or in any of his chill clothes.

He's got on a suit and tie.

"Yes, it is! Here, come say hi," he answers to the girl, patting the seat next to him. A second later, she scoots over next to him and waves at us on the screen.

Which means she couldn't have been that far away to begin with.

"Hi, Cassie! Oh, my gosh. You guys look amazing!"

Skyler and Tera do some silly movements with their wands to get the full effect, but I just stand there, trying to remember to breathe, trying to force a smile.

Because I know without looking at myself in the screen that I look crazy right now — wild, frizzy hair, baggy cloak, puffy scarf around my neck.

But *she* — the girl with Adam — is the one who looks amazing.

Her dark hair is pin straight and hanging over her shoulders, her eyes lined like a cat's, and tinged with smoky eyeliner. Her lips are painted a blood red, spread wide to reveal her perfect, straight white teeth. I can't see everything she's wearing, but I *can* see her quite impressive cleavage and the thin black straps straining to hold said bosom in place.

Skyler gives me a look, and it's enough to make me clear my throat and remember to speak.

"Hi!" I say.

Simply.

Stupidly.

"I'm Chandler," the girl says. "Adam has told me *so* much about you. I can't wait to meet you when you come visit!"

"Same here," I manage, and it's not a complete lie. Adam *has* told me a lot about her, too.

The part about not being able to wait to meet her, though...

"Chandler scored a free dinner at one of the nicest restaurants in town," Adam explains.

"It was a gift since we booked our dinner before our semi-formal here," Chandler adds. "But I didn't want to come to this fancy-schmancy steakhouse by myself, so I dragged your boyfriend here with me and told him we could talk business."

I force the most pathetic laugh of my life.

"Where are you girls off to now?" Adam asks.

"Ralph's, of course," Skyler says. And she must sense that I'm uncomfortable, must know that Tera is about two seconds away from knowing the same, so she grabs the phone from my hands and smiles wide at the screen. "And we better get going. So much to drink, so little time."

Adam chuckles. "Take care of my girl. And hey, Tera," he says, waiting for Skyler to put her on the screen again. "Nice to meet you. You picked the best Big there is."

Tera beams at me. "I know. I'm the luckiest Little."

The smile I wear is a little less forced then, my heart caught between surging with love and happiness, and breaking from jealousy and insecurity.

"I love you, babe," he says to me next, blowing me a kiss. "Call me tomorrow."

Skyler ends the call before I can get out my answer, and then she immediately loops her arms through mine and Tera's, taking up the middle. "Alright, bitches — let's party!"

She and Tera give a little hoot of approval, and then we're making our way across campus. Skyler holds up the conversation as we try to find a cab once we hit Greek Row, and when Tera runs inside the KKB house real quick to meet up with some of the other pledges and take some pictures, Skyler pulls me to the side in the yard.

"Hey, she's just a friend. Adam loves you. She is not a threat."

I nod, but almost start crying.

"He loves *you*," Skyler says again, holding my arms and searching my eyes.

"I know," I say. "But people cheat on the ones they love all the time."

Skyler frowns, pulling me in for a long hug. "He's not cheating on you. Okay? I promise. I know Adam. *You* know Adam. He could never."

I nod, sighing when she releases me from the hug. "I'm just being crazy."

"No, you're being *normal*. Long distance is hard."

Skyler's attempt at being strong dies with that, as if she's just remembered the distance between her and Kip — both literally and metaphorically — at this very moment.

She clears her throat. "Let's go out and have fun with your new *Little* tonight, okay? You can talk to him in the morning. Tell him how you're feeling. Let him clear your worries."

I blow out a breath. "You're right. I want to make sure Tera has the best night."

And then like we've summoned her, Tera is bolting across the yard, waving her wand around and saying random spells as we laugh and watch.

A cab pulls up. We all pile in.

And then we celebrate the new addition to our legacy.

Skyler

I PLOP INTO BED with a sigh heavier than any I've ever released in my life, freshly showered and bleary-eyed after a long, but fun, night out with the girls. My legs are sore from dancing, my throat sore from screaming, and I already know that regardless of not drinking a crazy amount, I'll have a headache in the morning.

But it was worth it.

Seeing Cassie take a Little, getting to know Tera more, celebrating with all our sisters as our sorority gets bigger and stronger... it's the best feeling in the world. Perhaps what touches my heart most is knowing I'm a part of it, knowing these are friendships that will last a lifetime, values that will settle in and help young women grow into professionals, maybe mothers or wives, maybe country leaders.

The possibilities are endless, and I get giddy when I think about how something so seemingly small — a sorority at a tiny private university — can have such huge impacts on so many lives.

On the world, really.

I didn't even bother getting dressed after my shower, and now I'm wishing I would have thought to plug in my phone to charge and shut off the light before collapsing, because it's going to take every ounce of energy I have left just to roll over and do those things before I pass out.

Except when I make my move and reach for my phone to plug it in, it vibrates in my hand.

And Kip's face fills the screen.

I swallow down the knot that immediately builds in my throat, pressing my free hand to my chest to try to ease my racing heart. We haven't talked in so long, and the only time I've seen his face was when I stole Bear's phone to stalk his Instagram and immediately regretted it.

I let it ring for a long time, debating just letting him hit voicemail.

But at the last second, I answer.

"Hello?"

There's a brief pause on the other end, and then a half-shocked, half-relieved sigh. "You answered."

I bite my lip. "Don't make me regret it."

He blows out a breath, and even though I can't see him, I can imagine him — the way he pinches the bridge of his nose, moving his glasses up in the process, and the way he runs his hands back through his hair, the way his eyes look when he's sad or distraught, how they somehow morph into an even deeper blue.

"What are you doing?" he asks after a moment. "It's late there. I thought you'd be asleep."

"It was Big/Little reveal. I just got home from Ralph's."

"Oh." I hear the hesitancy in his voice, the questions he wants to ask but doesn't dare — like if I was there with another guy, if I danced with another guy, if I kissed another guy, if I'm with another guy in any capacity.

It would kill him.

Just like the thought of him and Natalia has been killing me.

"So, Cassie did take a Little, huh? I bet you're excited."

"I am. She's sweet." I pause. "What do you want, Kip? Why did you call?"

He lets out another long, slow breath. "I called to tell you I'm sorry."

My shoulders deflate at the words.

"But not like I did before."

I sit up a little straighter in bed, pulling the sheets to my chest and waiting.

"Skyler, I hope you believed me when I said I never meant to hurt you, and that I was sorry that I did." He sighs. "But... I didn't fully hear you out. I was stubborn and didn't want to believe I'd done anything wrong, because I'd been so far up my own ass that I didn't stop to consider how my actions might be affecting other people around me. It's a good excuse, right? To feel like you don't have to apologize if you didn't do it intentionally? But I was wrong. I was so, so wrong."

I close my eyes against the tears building there.

"Not only was I wrong for not seeing your side, for not agreeing with you because you were right — if it were me in your shoes, I would have felt the same way. Hell, I would have been even angrier, I wouldn't have been nearly as controlled as you." He pauses. "And you were right about Natalia."

My heart squeezes so painfully in my chest that I can't help the choked sob that rips free from me. To see the picture of them together was enough pain to last me a lifetime, but if he's called now to tell me they're together, to tell me I was right about them...

I'll fucking die.

I will *die.*

"The other night, we got together for a mini premiere night. It was for cast and crew to watch the series before it hits the small screen."

I can already feel it, my body breaking down, because I know he's about to tell me that something happened that made him realize his feelings for her.

Bile rises in my throat.

"The show is good, Sky," he whispers. "It's so fucking good."

I want to tell him I'm proud of him, that I'm happy for him, but every word — every *breath* is lodged in my throat.

"We were on such a high afterward, and we decided to go out. We were at this rooftop club. The music was going, we were all dancing and drinking and..."

My stomach turns again, and I double over on myself, squeezing my eyes shut against the burning urge to cry. Images of Natalia dancing with him, her ass grinding against his crotch, his hands on her waist...

I want to beg him to stop. I want to beg him to hang up and cut me out of his life and just leave me to rot without him.

I can't handle it.

I can't take this pain.

"She said she needed air, needed a break, and asked me to go with her. We went to this little corner garden with benches and a fountain, and we were just sitting there, talking, looking out over the skyline." He pauses. "And then... she kissed me."

I can't fight against it this time, the guttural cry that rips free from me, the tears that pour down, the ugly sobs that free themselves.

"Skyler, baby, don't cry," Kip pleads, and I swear he sounds like he's in just as much pain as I am, like hearing me cry is a dagger to his chest.

I can't even catch my breath long enough to tell him not to call me baby, not to coddle me as he breaks my heart.

"I saw it then," he says. "I saw everything you'd been telling me, everything I'd been ignoring, everything I'd said was innocent even when I knew deep down that it was suspicious, that it was maybe a hair too much."

"Kip, please," I finally manage to beg. "Please, stop. I can't breathe. I can't..." My next sentence is robbed by another painful squeeze of my chest.

"I know. I'm so fucking sorry, Sky. I didn't want to tell you, but I knew I had to. I wanted to be upfront and clear about everything. If I stand another chance at having you, at getting back into your heart, there can't be any secrets between us."

Those words make me pause, though my rib cage is still painfully tight around my lungs. "What?"

"I'm sorry," he says again. "I should have listened to you. I should have respected you. I should have sat Natalia down and had a conversation with her about professionalism, about drawing a clear, dark boundary so she understood. More than anything, I should have been there to pick you up." His voice catches. "I should have been there. And I'll live every day of my life regretting that I wasn't."

I sniff. "I don't understand. What happened between you two? After... after she kissed you?" My stomach knots.

Kip blows out a breath. "Well, I grabbed her arms and pushed her back to stop her. She basically said I was fighting it and she knew I wanted her too, which I immediately informed her was a gross misinterpretation."

My chest kicks in my chest, and I can't help but feel a small twinge of petty victory.

"I told her she'd been drinking and needed to sleep it off, then the next day, I sat her down and told her it was out of line. She was pissed," he adds. "But I was disappointed more than anything. Disappointed that I didn't see it, that I'd hurt you, that she was the star of my first show, that she plays the most amazing woman in the world, the woman I love, and I can't go back and change that now."

I swallow. "You can't go back and change it," I finally say. "And maybe it happened for a reason. You said it's good, right?"

"It is," he admits. "But now, it all just feels... tainted."

I nod, even though he can't see me, because I can only imagine how contrary those feelings must be — pride and shame all at once.

"I don't ever want to work with her again," he says after a while. "And I don't plan on it. I just wish I would have seen it sooner. I wish..." He curses. "God, I wish so many things. Most of all that I was with you, right now, holding you in my arms and looking into your eyes when I tell you that I love you, that I'm truly, *truly*, sorry, and that I'm begging you to give me another chance."

His words release another wave of tears, but they're silent, slipping down my tears like assassins in the night.

"Will you ever forgive me?"

I swallow down a sob, and it takes me a long while before I can answer.

"I want to," I admit, my voice raspy and strained. My heart is already breaking before I say the words. "But I don't know how."

My face warps with the admission, with the truth that Kip has hurt me so much — possibly past the point of fixing. But it's the truth.

And if there are no more secrets between us, then I won't keep one, either.

"You know more than anyone how hard it is for me to trust," I say. "How hard it was for me to trust *you* again, specifically, after what happened with your dad and Vegas and... just... *everything*."

"I know. I know," he says, and I wait for more, but he doesn't say anything else.

"I love you," I whisper. "But I've forgiven you once. I... I don't know if I can do it again."

I hear something on the other end, something that sounds like a restrained cry, like a grunt of a grown man trying to hold it together when he's on the verge of breaking down.

For a long while, we sit on the phone together. Sometimes it's just breathing, sometimes one of us is crying, sometimes it's more silent than a desert in the middle of the night.

After what feels like an eternity, Kip speaks.

"Hold onto us, Skyler," he pleads, his voice rough. "You know me. You know my love for you. Hold onto that. Hold on."

I close my eyes, sending one last set of hot tears rolling down my cheeks.

And though my heart surges in my chest with the urge to do what he's asking, and I can already feel every molecule of my being latching onto him, onto our memories, onto everything I know and love and trust in him, I end the call and force myself to make peace with the truth.

It's over.

EPISODE 4

Erin

THERE'S SOMETHING UNIQUELY HORRIFYING about reliving sexual abuse.

For years, I've blocked out that night — the shock of it, the pain, the embarrassment. I've blocked it out so hard, so fiercely, that it almost feels as if it never happened at all.

Did I imagine it, the way I'd felt more drunk than usual, the way the chandelier light spun and spun above me as we danced at semi-formal? Did I imagine the way Landon's warm eyes turned cold, the way he gripped my wrist when he pulled me back to that room, his brothers following us? Was it all a dream that I sensed something was off, that I got uncomfortable when his friends started touching me, kissing me... that I tried to fight... tried to leave?

Sometimes, it feels like it. It feels like it happened to someone else, or never happened at all.

But reliving it with a room full of lawyers and detectives, it was more real than it ever had been.

The questions they asked, the notes they took, the looks they gave me... it was the perfect combination to split open the carefully constructed cast I'd worn all this time, I relived it all — the feeling of being unknowingly drugged, the confusion of being dragged away from the ballroom, the fear when I felt them all moving in on me, their laughter and soft words of assurance that everything was fine like the most vivid nightmare.

Candice, my lawyer, begins to silently cry when I tell the room how Landon slapped me when I tried to run for the door, how he threw me on the pool table hard enough to knock the breath from me, how he wasn't the first to molest me — but rather, he held me down, his hands bruising my arms as one of his friends took the first turn.

No, not one of his friends. Not a nameless brother.

I list out their names in order of how they raped me — Nick Simmons, Daniel Cole, Landon Turner, and last, Aiden Harrison.

There is a young girl with the lawyers of the boys who raped me. From the way she's taking notes and listening intently to every move Landon's lawyers make, I gather that she must be an intern or a new employee.

Her eyes well with tears, too, when I tell the room how I cried through the first one, begging them to stop, but that when Daniel pushed inside me and I knew there was no stopping them, I fell silent. I numbed out. I grasped onto the only survival mechanism I could in that moment, which was to just hold onto that pool table and wait for them to be done, wait for them to finish.

And silently pray that they would leave me alive in the end.

I didn't know if they would, at the time. I wondered if they'd kill me, if those terrible moments of embarrassment and pain would be my last.

And in that moment, telling that room full of people what had happened to me, I knew every detail was true — down to the painting of a mermaid sitting on the edge of a sailboat, which I had stared at while they raped me, holding her gaze, letting the anchor she sat beside anchor me, too.

The room is quiet when I finish, and I hold my head high, looking each of them in the eye. I answer all their questions — clarifying timelines and terms, repeating names, explaining *again* why I didn't go to the police immediately, why I didn't get a rape kit, why none of my friends knew until very recently.

By the time we finish, I'm so tired I could pass out on the spot.

"Thank you, Erin," Candice says, her eyes still red as she leans over to squeeze my wrist.

My mind goes fuzzy after that, a blur of legal jargon as they explain to me that the process of arresting the offenders is complex, and this is only one step. They inform me that should Landon or any of the other offenders try to contact me, I should call the police immediately, and that they'll keep me informed on what happens next.

After a formal goodbye handshake with each of them, I excuse myself, and as soon as I'm out of the door, my legs begin to shake, all the adrenaline that had been coursing through me leaving my body at once.

I stare at the tile floor as my heels click along it, and in its natural fashion, my mind begins to erase the last couple of hours. I feel it almost like a black wall of steel slowly stretching toward the sky and blocking that part of my memory, as if to say *you don't need to see this, let's just leave it in the past where it belongs.*

When I make it to my car, I shut the door and stare at the steering wheel for a long time. I'm supposed to go to therapy, but all I want is to go home.

No, all I want is to go to Clinton.

But I know after such a traumatic event, therapy is the best place I can go. I know I can't just leave it all buried, can't ignore it, can't pretend like nothing is happening or never happened in the past. I have to face it, sit with it —
no matter how uncomfortable it is.

So, I fire up the engine and make my way across town.

I'm about five minutes late to the meeting, thanks to South Florida traffic and a random thunderstorm. So I rush inside with my hair a frizzy mess, not bothering with an umbrella now that it's just a drizzle. I take my usual seat as quietly as I can, trying not to interrupt the person talking — a young boy, newer addition, talking about his addiction. I give him my full attention the moment I'm seated, even as I smooth out my damp clothes and try to fix my hair a bit.

When he finishes speaking, Jackie, our therapy leader, smiles and thanks him for sharing.

There's a brief moment of silence, some of the other attendees offering words of encouragement to the young man, and I take the opportunity to fully settle in, letting my gaze wander the room to see who's here tonight.

And that's when I see him.

How I walked in without sensing him, without feeling those brazen eyes on me, I don't understand. I could blame it on the afternoon I've had, I suppose, but even that shouldn't have kept me from noticing my ex sitting in the same chair he used to, right across the circle from me.

Smiling.

Smiling, as if he never left.

Smiling, as if he didn't leave me with nothing but a note to explain.

Smiling, his eyes heated, ankle crossed over his knee and leather-jacket-clad arms folded across his chest like he owns the place.

Like he still owns *me*.

Gavin's sky blue eyes watch me unabashedly as I gape back at him, and it's only when Jackie says my name that I snap out of what I convince myself *must* be a daydream.

"How are you this evening?" she asks.

"I…" I swallow. "I'm fine."

Jackie gives me a sympathetic smile. "Do you want to talk about what happened today? I believe you told us last week that you were meeting with the lawyers and detectives. How did it go?"

I open my mouth to answer, to do what I came here to do, but then my eyes snap back to Gavin, and I have to zip my lips closed again to keep them from trembling.

He's not smiling anymore.

I want to scream at him. I want to demand answers. I want to punch him in his stupid face and throw him out of *my* safe place and tell him to never come back.

I want to ask him why he left.

I want to tell him his letter wasn't enough.

I want to make him feel the way he broke me.

But more than anything, I want to get far, *far* away from him.

"I'm sorry," I say, shaking my head and immediately reaching down for my purse. I don't offer any other explanation before I'm heading for the door, and I don't take my next breath until I'm through it.

I know Jackie will tell the room that it's okay, that I'll be alright, that she'll check in on me — and she will. I know I'll have a call from her likely as soon as session is over. She'll move on and ask someone else to share because that's what has to be done.

She won't press me to stay.

That's what I love about her.

The rain has mostly stopped when I push out into the evening air, warm and humid, the sky quickly fading from gray to deep navy as night settles in. I fumble in my purse for my keys, the familiar *beep beep* of my car unlocking hitting my ears right before an even more familiar voice calls my name.

"Erin," Gavin repeats when I don't stop, and his footsteps splash through the puddles behind me as he jogs to catch up. "Hey, please, wait."

"You don't get to ask a damn thing of me," I say, whirling on him. I point my finger right in his face — his face that is far too close for my taste. "You don't get to show back up here, in *my* space, in my *life*. I don't know why you're here, why you're back, and I don't want to know. Okay? So just fuck off."

The words shock me more than him when they roll off my tongue with ease, but I hold my chin high as I turn on my heels and set for my car again.

"I'm sorry."

I stop at the sound of those words, but I don't turn. I just stand there with my hand on the smooth metal handle of my car door, waiting.

"I'm sorry I left like that. I'm sorry I did that to you. I'm sorry for..." He sighs. "For everything."

Tears burn my eyes.

"I can explain, if you'll give me the chance."

I shake my head. "No."

"Please," he begs, and I feel his hand warm on my shoulder before I shrug it off.

I turn on him then. "How dare you," I spit.

"Don't be like this. I care about you, Erin. I know you still care about me."

"That's where you're wrong."

Even as I say the words, they burn as only lies do. I *do* care about him. I *do* want him to be okay.

But I also want him to leave me the hell alone.

"I know I hurt you, but if you just give me another chance—"

"No," I say, more firmly than the last time. "I'm sorry, Gavin, but I've moved on and you should, too."

I open my car door, slipping inside and slamming the door shut. Gavin stands there dumbfounded for a moment, the drizzle soaking his shirt and jacket before he taps on my window.

I grit my teeth but roll it down just an inch.

"Moved on, huh?" he asks, hurt evident in his voice. "It's Bear, isn't it?"

I don't answer.

Which is answer enough.

He laughs. "Well, that was fast."

"Goodbye, Gavin."

"Wait," he says, slipping his fingers in the gap my rolled-down window has made.

He must trust me an awful lot more than I trust myself to think I won't smash his fingers.

"It doesn't have to be romantic. It doesn't have to be anything more than..." He pauses, blowing out a breath. "Can I take you for a drink? Please."

I swallow, my chest tight and heavy with all the things left unsaid and unfinished between us.

"Maybe another time," I whisper, but when our eyes meet through the crack, I know he sees what I'm really saying.

Never going to happen.

His jaw is tight when he withdraws his fingers, and I roll up my window and peel out of the parking lot without a glance in my rearview mirror.

I don't even tell Clinton I'm coming, just burst through his front door when I finally make it to his house. He's on the couch watching a basketball game, a full plate of chicken and veggies in his lap.

One look at me, and the plate is tossed aside.

He runs to me, swooping me into his arms as the first sob chokes through me.

"It's okay," he promises. "I'm here."

And with that permission, I fully let go.

Adam

"THIS IS FUCKING HORSE shit!" I bang my fists on the wooden table for emphasis, rattling the entire thing and causing half-a-dozen students to startle at the sound.

"Shhh!" the librarian immediately scolds, her brows folded hard as she shakes her head. She points her bony finger at me as one last warning — likely because this isn't my first outburst in the last four hours, but she's saying it'll be my last, or else.

I murmur an apology before letting my head fall into my hands again, digging my palms into my eyes enough that I see colors behind the lids. I suppress the urge to groan, to growl, to flip the fucking table and try to force a calming breath.

This is supposed to be the easy part.

It's November. I'm supposed to be coasting after fighting with the alums and the exec board, supposed to be watching all the fruits of our labor come together, supposed to be taking my hands off and letting these brothers ride their metaphorical bikes on their own, supposed to be more focused on planning what Cassie and I will do when she visits for Thanksgiving than anything Alpha Sigma related.

Instead, I'm nose deep in books far too thick with words far too big explaining policies far too complicated — all because the alumni brothers decided to be twats.

"Wow," a voice purrs over me. I look up to find Chandler smirking, her fingers toying with a few pages of one of the books spread out around me. "I haven't seen this much fun since senior year Spring Break."

I try to smile, but know it falls flat as I slump back in my chair.

Chandler chuckles, shrugging off her small backpack and tossing it on the table before taking the chair next to me. She peers over at the book currently splayed at the center. "Aspen University Student Organized Event Policies," she reads, arching a brow at me.

"Don't even ask."

"Too late."

I sigh, sitting up a little straighter as the back of my hand slaps against the open pages. "I've been working with the brothers on an event that will hopefully help put them back on the map — an Anything But Clothes Bubble Bonfire." I pause when Chandler has to fight back a smile. "Hey, they came up with it, alright? And honestly, as cheesy as it sounds, they've been working their asses off and it's going to be a kickass event. They got a popular band on campus to come play, have an epic set up for the bonfire, all these different seating areas and photo ops, plus a foam pit."

"Girls *do* love a foam pit."

"And the theme being Anything But Clothes? Can you even imagine?"

She laughs. "I know me and my sisters would have been *all* over that."

"Everyone on Greek Row is talking about it, and the guys are so stoked." I sigh. "They're going to be crushed when I tell them it can't happen."

Chandler frowns. "Why not?"

"Apparently, there's some policy that states that student-run events can't have any kind of open fire. I mean, I get it," I added. "It's Colorado. And even though we're out of fire season, I'm sure they don't want some fraternity event causing the next wildfire that runs rampant across the Rockies."

"Is it an open fire?"

"I guess," I say, waving my hand at the books. "That's what the asshole alumni guys I've been working with explained to me this morning. I've been digging through these books all afternoon trying to find the exact law, but so far, nothing. I figure there's got to be a loophole, or some way we can still have the event but be in line with the policy."

Chandler frowns even deeper, and then she scoots her chair in closer to the table and digs her laptop out of her bag. I watch as she types in the university website, fingers clicking away a lot faster than I can type.

"What are you doing?"

"Helping," she says easily.

"You don't have to do that. It's Friday, I'm sure—"

"I've got nothing to do," she says with a look that tells me she's not too happy about that fact. "Besides, you helped me once. Remember?"

Her eyes find mine, and the smile we share is one I imagine only kids caught between being in college and being an adult could really understand.

"You can leave at any time," I say as I turn back to the books.

"Shut up and keep digging."

Silence envelops the library again, other than the soft sounds of students whispering, typing, and flipping pages. Every now and then, Chandler will pause me to show me something, or I'll show her something, but we never quite find what we're looking for.

Until...

"Aha!" she says — loud enough that the new librarian on shift gives her a look. She apologizes before moving her laptop over closer to me and whispering, "Look at this."

I follow her cursor, reading to myself. When I finish, I sigh, pushing back in my chair again.

"So it *is* a real rule." I shake my head. "I mean, not that I doubted it, but I hoped there would be a way. Stones around the fire or... or... a number of fire extinguishers on hand, buckets of water, something."

"Adam, you didn't read it all."

I frown, looking at a smiling Chandler before I lean forward again. She lets me take the laptop from her, and I scroll down until I see the starred amendment at the bottom.

The amendment that says bonfire events may be approved by the Student Union so long as the following requirements are met and sufficient paperwork is provided.

The article goes on to list out the requirements — and just like I thought, it's all things we can manage.

"I fucking knew it!"

"Shhh!"

Chandler and I bite back our laughs as we apologize, yet again, to the librarian. Then, we huddle closer as we look through the website.

"Okay, so we just need to make sure the fire is contained within a permanently structured area — easy enough, we could have it be a new addition to the house — and have a hose hooked up to the house for emergency." I shake my head, and when I turn to Chandler, we're nearly nose to nose. "Holy shit, you figured it out."

"*We* figured it out," she says, and as if she realizes how close we are, she clears her throat and sits back in her chair. Her hand sweeps out over the screen. "So, once you get those things taken care of and provide the paperwork and proof? You'll be good to go."

"Thank God," I say, pushing her laptop back toward her. "Can you email that to me? I'll get started in the morning." I pause. "*After* a round of very stiff drinks tonight."

She chuckles. "You got it."

"Thank you," I say earnestly.

"No problem," she insists, her cheeks turning a soft shade of pink.

"Is there any way I can repay you?"

"Well, I kind of owed you, anyway," she reminds me. "But... if you insist, how about not letting me hang out alone on a Friday night?" Her eyes meet mine then. "I'm so sick and tired of being the old girl on campus with no real friends."

I bark out a laugh at that. "You are *far* from old."

"Tell that to these eighteen-year-old bitches."

Another laugh from me before I look at my phone, frowning at the time. "I'm supposed to have a video chat date night with Cassie in about an hour."

When I look up at Chandler again, it's just in time to see her playful smile slip, her eyes going back to her laptop as she sends off the email before closing the lid. "Oh," she says, forcing a smile again and waving me off. "Well, consider us even, then. I've got some shows to catch up on, anyway."

She's already packing her things away, but I sigh, because I know exactly how she's feeling. It *does* feel weird, to be too old to party and be a student, but too young to be an adult. It's the strangest in-between, and being in a new place with no friends...

Well, it's lonely.

"Wait," I tell her, stopping her before she can stand. "Let me just step out and call Cassie. We can reschedule."

Chandler shakes her head. "No, no, don't do that, I'm sure she's looking forward to it."

"We talk all the time," I assure her. "And I'm going to see her in just a couple weeks. She'll understand."

Chandler bites her lip. "You're sure?"

"Positive. Give me a sec."

We walk out of the library together after putting away all the books I'd strewn out, and then I excuse myself to the corner of the building, cursing against the biting cold as I find Cassie's contact and let my thumb drop on the screen.

"Hey, babe," she answers. "I thought we had another forty-five minutes."

"We did. Uh, *do*. Um..." I grab the back of my neck, casting a look at Chandler. "Hey, would you mind if we rescheduled?"

A pause on the other end was my only answer.

"I can explain later, but a friend just helped me out of a bind, and... well, again, I can explain later. But if you're cool with it, could we have our date tomorrow night instead?"

The silence is long before Cassie finally says, "Sure. I mean... Yeah, I don't see why not." She pauses again. "Who's the friend?"

"It's Chandler, the one you met when we video chatted after Big/Little reveal." I let out a breath of a laugh that fogs in the cold night air. "She literally just saved my ass. I owe her a drink."

"Oh."

I smirk, narrowing my eyes as I turn even more so Chandler can't read my lips or overhear. "Is someone *jealous*?"

"No!" A pause. "I just... you promise she's just a friend?"

I don't mean to laugh, and by the way Cassie screams my name when I do, I know it's an asshole mistake. "I'm sorry," I say, still laughing. "It's just, the fact that you think I've got eyes for literally any other woman but you is hysterical."

"You're a prick," she says, but I can tell by the way she says it that she's smiling, too. "I'm sorry. Of course, you should go have fun. I know you don't know anyone there, and I'm glad y'all have become friends. I just..."

"You miss me," I finish for her. "And I miss you, too. And if it'll ease your mind, I'll tell you a million times. She's just a friend. You are the love of my life. You have nothing to worry about."

She sighs. "That does help."

"I love you," I say softly. "Call you in the morning?"

"Text me later tonight," she says. "When you're home."

I chuckle. "Yes, ma'am."

"And Adam?"

"Yeah?"

"Have fun."

I blow her a kiss through the phone before we both hang up.

Ashlei

BALLING UP ANOTHER DOVE chocolate wrapper with my left hand, I close one eye and stick my tongue out, aiming for the ceramic decorative bowl on the coffee table.

"She lines up the shot," I say softly. "And... she shoots!"

With a flick of my wrist, the blue and silver foil wrapper goes flying.

And completely misses the coffee table altogether.

I blow out a breath through flat lips, looking at the empty bowl and the tiny foil balls littered all around it. Then, I look at the TV, at the rerun of *America's Top Model*, and then out the window at the palm trees swaying in the breeze along the beach.

Sighing, I grab another piece of chocolate.

I know without a mirror that I look as pathetic as I feel, and I wish with everything in me that I could snap out of my pity party and get back to the bad bitch I was before the accident. So far, I've only been able to pull myself together long enough to go to work, give it all the energy I had, and then come home and cry about the fact that I can't go to the pole studio.

Not that I haven't been invited.

Karen has called me almost every day, has even popped by unannounced a few times, saying the girls miss me and they'd love to have me back — even if just to coach from the sidelines until I'm well enough to get back on the pole.

But she doesn't understand how much even the thought of that scenario breaks me.

To be watching and unable to *do*, to coach without being able to *show*, to have this vital part of me ripped away... possibly forever...

It's been akin to losing a lung, each breath reminding me that I'm closer to death.

I'm close to being able to start PT — or so my doctor says. But I'm healing slower than he first anticipated, and every time I hear him tack another week on the end of my sentence, despair creeps in and grabs ahold of me tighter and tighter.

I thought I knew heartbreak, thought I knew depression.

I've never known any kind of pain quite like this.

A whistle shakes me from my thoughts, my unfocused eyes drifting from the TV screen to where Brandon is standing at the edge of the hallway. He's freshly showered after his long run this morning, his short hair damp and glistening, gray sweatpants hanging deliciously off his hips. Without a shirt on, I have a front row show to the phenomena that is his abdomen, with his pecs and biceps a solid opening act.

"I didn't know I was dating a basketball star," he muses with a grin, eyeing the wrappers all over the ground.

"Watch out, Lebron James."

He chuckles, arching a brow at the TV as he makes his way across the room to the couch. He plops down next to me, carefully pulling me into him while being mindful of my shoulder. "So, what was wrong with her?" he asks, nodding to the model now wrapped in a blanket and looking pale as hell at the judging ceremony.

"Food poisoning," I explained. "But look, she still showed up."

"Think it'll gain points with Tyra?"

"It should. She nearly died and still got her ass to work." My heart sinks, and then against every ounce of willpower I have, tears burn my eyes.

Brandon notices immediately, and he looses a breath, tucking me closer as he balances his chin on the crown of my head. "It's going to be okay."

"When?" I manage on a shaky whisper.

The question breaks me — even more so when Brandon just holds me tighter in answer.

He doesn't know.

No one does.

"Will you take a walk with me?" he asks after a while.

I groan, but before I can reject, he pulls back and meets my eyes with his.

"Please?"

I sigh. "That's not fair. I can't say no to you when you look like that."

"Then say yes."

I do a little temper tantrum flail, whine, and then concede, letting him help me up off the couch.

Once I'm dressed in shorts and a tank top, Brandon and I take the elevator down to the lobby and push out into the pleasantly warm morning. Fall in Florida may not be cold, but there's a break from the humidity, and the temperature hanging in the mid-seventies with little puffy white clouds and an otherwise blue sky make me smile in gratitude.

Brandon takes my hand as we cross the street to the park, a lush, green patch of land with running trails along the water and right to the beach. This was where we ran into each other in the spring, when he was trying to pretend like he didn't still want me.

The prick.

He smooths his thumb over my wrist as our hands swing gently between us. "I know it seems like your world has crashed down around you," he says, eyes on the water, then his shoes, then me before doing the circle all over again. "It's hard not to lose hope when something so important has been taken away from you."

"It is," I agree, but already just being outside has my soul feeling lighter, my heart a little less tight. "But thank you for being here for me. For *always* being here for me. I..." I swallow at the truth of what I'm about to say. "I honestly don't think I could do this without you. I think if I had lost pole in the spring when I'd just lost you, I... I..."

I couldn't finish the sentence.

Brandon squeezes my hand tighter, and then leads us to a little bench in the shade under a wide oak. Spanish moss hangs from the limbs, and I stare at the sun rays peeking through it as we listen to the waves, to the people, to the soft sounds of a Sunday morning.

"You'll never have to do anything without me," he promises after a moment. "I'll be by your side through PT, and when you go back to the studio and no doubt come home frustrated every night until you're doing the tricks you were before the accident."

I chuckle. "God, I will try my best *not* to be a nightmare, but..."

Brandon smiles, and it's then that I see it — the worry etched in his features, the way his hands are trembling slightly.

"What's wrong?" I ask him.

"Nothing," he lies.

"Brandon..."

"Nothing is wrong, Ashlei," he says, his eyes meeting mine. "And that's just the thing, isn't it? When I'm with you, when we're together, it doesn't matter what we're facing. Everything feels right. Everything feels... whole."

I smile, looping my arm through his and laying my head on his shoulder. "I love you."

He's silent for a long time, and again we sit and enjoy the sun's warmth, the ocean's breeze, the feeling of being together — even when things suck.

And then, out of nowhere, he says the absolute last thing I expected.

"Let's elope."

I balk, sitting up ramrod straight so I can look at him and make sure it isn't some sick joke. But when I meet his gaze, it's as serious and level as if he'd just made a business proposal.

"What?"

"Let's elope," he repeats, turning to fully face me and folding his hands in mine. "Ashlei, I know without a fragment of doubt that you're it for me. You're the one. You're *my* one. I want you and me, forever, and I want it right now. I want to put the biggest fucking diamond rock on your finger so everyone knows it, and I want to marry you somewhere far away where it's just the two of us, and I want to make love to you on a tropical shore, and I..." He swallows. "I want you to say yes. I want you to pack up what you need right now, today, and I want to be on a jet or my yacht by dinnertime."

"Why by dinnertime?"

"So I can marry you in the morning."

My heart is beating so furiously in my chest that I have to steal one of my hands from Brandon to press it against the bones, trying to soothe, trying to calm.

"Tell me what you're thinking," he begs.

I sniff against the tears welling in my eyes. "I'm thinking I can't say no to you when you look like that."

"So say yes."

I laugh, nodding as tears slip free. "Yes."

"Yes?"

Another laugh as I climb into his lap and kiss him all over, not even caring when he points out that I'm not supposed to lift my arm that high to rest around his neck. "Yes. Yes, right now. Yes, forever. What do I pack? When do we leave?"

He slams a kiss hard to my mouth, holding the back of my head in his palm as we breathe each other in.

The kiss grows deeper and more urgent the longer we sit there, until Brandon finally helps me up off the bench and we half walk, half run back to the condo. It doesn't take long to pick the place, and though I know we're forgetting things we'll need, we decide we don't care as we haphazardly pack our bags in twenty minutes' time.

And then we're boarding the yacht and sailing off into the horizon.

Jess

"SHIT," I MURMUR TO myself as I scurry along the side of the dance floor being built. Or should I say, the dance floor that *was* being built... before the entire crew we hired for the event decided to go on strike.

Literally.

"Everything okay?" Brittany asks when I pass her. She's looking over something on the iPad with our intern — likely the bride's instructions for centerpieces or the seating chart.

The smile I force comes too naturally, and it scares me a little how easy the lie spills. "Yep! Right on schedule. You good here? Need me?"

She waves me off. "No, just going to wrap this up and then we're both leaving. You should go, too. You'll need rest for tomorrow."

"I just have to check on a few more things and then I'm out."

She nods to excuse me, and when she's back in the works with the intern, I resume my cursing as I run back to the kitchen where the owner of the event company we hired is desperately trying to get her crew to stop packing up their things.

"We told you," one of the guys says when I push through the swinging doors. "Meet our demands, or we're out. You thought we were bluffing. Well, now you know we're not."

"Jeremiah, we can discuss this at the office on Monday," the owner tries to say — calmly, especially now that I've made myself present. "But right now, we have half a dance floor to assemble, chairs and tables to set up, lighting, and—"

"And you can do it yourself," one of the other guys says, which earns him some enthusiastic agreement from his comrades.

I watch in horror as this fight continues on, something about Christmas bonuses being canceled this year, as well as them having to work all through the holidays, plus some murmurings about what they're being paid. Whatever is going on, the crew isn't happy.

And no matter how hard the owner, Sammi, begs them, they don't go back into the ballroom I need turned into a glamorous wedding venue by the morning.

They all just leave.

Sammi sighs when it's just the two of us alone, pinching the bridge of her nose and muttering something that sounds like a prayer in a language I don't recognize under her breath before she turns to me with a dazzling smile.

"Well," she says, and I wait for the solution.

But instead, she just throws her hands up, let's them clap down on her thighs, and starts crying.

Another curse word finds my tongue.

"It's okay," I soothe her, running a hand along her back.

She blubbers something about being a failure and how her father is going to gut her like a fish, and as much as I feel for her, as much as I would comfort her even more if I was her friend, the fact of the matter is that I'm the woman who hired her.

And now I'm in a bind.

"Why don't you go home, talk to your dad, figure out what can be done to get your crew happy again, okay?"

She sniffs. "What about you? What about the wedding in the morning?"

I tongue my cheek, but force a smile against my urge to scream. "I'll handle it."

"Are you sure? I... I can stay to help, I can—"

"Go," I insist again, already shoving her toward the back hallway that her entire crew left through. "Just leave all your supplies and I'll... figure it out." *God help me.* "Can I call if I have questions?"

"Of course, but—"

"You're not going to be any help to me or anyone like this," I interrupt before she can argue again. "Go work through whatever needs to be worked through. It won't ruin our relationship with you, okay? We'll give you another chance, but you've *got* to get your crew happy."

She nods, nearly bursting into tears again when I tell her she'll have another chance. In this industry, a mishap like this can be the difference between a booming business booked every weekend, and a sad sap going door to door at event agencies begging for work.

I don't want to be the one to hang her up to dry.

But I also have to do *my* job.

As soon as Sammi leaves, Brittany pops her head into the kitchen. "Alright, we're heading out." She frowns, looking around the empty space. "I thought I saw the crew come back here. I was going to tell them they need to move the dance floor about seven inches to the left. It's not going to be center with the stage."

"They just took a quick break to eat," I explain. "Ran down to their favorite restaurant. Don't worry, I'll stick around until they get back."

She arches a brow. "You sure?"

"I got this," I assure her. "I want to take a second look at the cake, anyway, and you know how picky I am when it comes to table runners. I just want to make sure it's all in order, then I'm out the door. Promise," I added when she went to argue with me.

"Okay, but don't stay too late." She sighs, shaking her head. "A *morning* wedding. Who does that? I'm already crying thinking about setting my alarm for three AM."

My smile is tight. "You and me both."

With a salute, my boss leaves, and then I'm alone.

"Motherfucking shit balls!" I scream, grinding my teeth as I lean back against the countertop. I tap my fingers on the edge of the granite, thinking.

The wedding is huge — two-hundred-and-sixty guests, plus all the vendors. There's no way I can set up the tables, chairs, linens, centerpieces, and dance floor by myself. I'd be lucky to get even half done before Brittany showed back up in the morning.

I sigh, pulling out my phone and dialing the first person I can think of who might be able to help.

Which, coincidentally, happens to be the last person who was inside me.

The phone rings and rings, but Jarrett doesn't pick up. I debate just hanging up but decide I don't have time for pride right now.

"Hey, I need your help. I'm texting you an address now. Can you grab some of your coworkers or a couple buddies and help me with some event set up? I can pay. Long story but... I'm in a bind."

I don't know what else to say, so I hang up and text the address.

As soon as I do, Jarrett texts back with a line of question marks. Then, he texts *Is this where I should go when I'm ready to ravage you after the rally?*

The rally.

Shit.

I close my eyes and force a breath as I text back *Going to be honest, completely forgot about the rally. Disregard my voicemail and have a good time. Text me after.*

Jarrett asks if everything is okay next, to which I lie and say of course. His agency is running a rally downtown for the guy they want to support in the next election for mayor. I know how important it is for him, and how hard he's been working on it. I can't steal him away just because my vendor left me in hot water.

My stomach twists as I pull up my next option — who would have been the first person I called, if I'm being honest with myself, had I not been avoiding him for weeks.

I just don't know how to face him, now that I've spent time with Jarrett.

I don't know how to tell him that I still have really intense feelings for his brother.

I don't know how to tell him that I might...

No, I think to myself, shaking my head. *These thoughts can wait for another night.*

Before I can talk myself out of it by reminding myself just how shitty a person I am, I find Kade's contact in my phone — heart squeezing at the photo of me on his back, arms wrapped around his neck, both of us smiling.

"Jess?" he answers on the second ring.

"I need you."

And that's all I have to say.

It's an absolute masterpiece to watch, Kade and his brothers whipping a ballroom into immaculate event shape in under three hours. They're all so brawny and attentive that I just point and instruct and like little worker bees, they do exactly what I ask of them.

Of course, it's a *little* rowdy, too. After all, it's a Friday night and I've suckered them into working. But when Kade said he could come and he'd have a crew, I immediately ran to the store and grabbed provisions — meaning lots and lots of booze.

And pizza, of course.

Someone hooked their phone up to one of the giant speakers and has been blasting dubstep all night, and I've seen just as many shots being taken as I've seen tables being set up.

But I don't care.

Whatever gets the job done.

And as much as I'm running around and supervising everything, helping where I can, ensuring all the details are exactly as the bride described, I can't keep my eyes from wandering to Kade.

He was emotionless when he got here — no hug or kiss for a greeting, just a thin smile and a *What should we do first?*

I can't blame him. He knows I've been with Jarrett. He knows I *haven't* been with him.

I know it's killing him.

It's killing me, too.

He must be working his frustrations out in the gym, because his already-impressive physique is even more cut than I remember, and I watch every muscle ebb and flow as he unstacks chairs and places them around the room, helps his brothers rebuild the dance floor, and sets up the band's equipment on the stage.

It's almost midnight by the time we get everything where we need it, and Kade dismisses his brothers after I hug them all and pay them cash out of my own pocket.

What Brittany doesn't know won't hurt her, and they saved my ass tonight.

When they're gone, taking what's left of the bottles and the music with them, the ballroom door swings shut and an eerie silence falls over me and Kade.

My soul wants to jump out of my body, the way he's looking at me. His hands are in his pockets, eyes under folded brows, jaw tight. He still doesn't have a shirt on, and I can see the band of his briefs peeking out above his basketball shorts — a sight that makes me ache for him right between my thighs.

"Thank you," I finally manage. I open my mouth again to say that I would have been fucked without him, that he saved me, that I love him, that I've missed him.

But I close it just as quickly, because the menacing look in his eyes tells me he doesn't want to hear it.

He watches me for so long I can't bear to meet his gaze anymore, and I don't know why, but my eyes sting with tears when I look away.

Kade sighs, and then he slowly crosses the space between us, until he's just inches from me.

"Jess."

I close my eyes at the sound of my name on his lips, at the tender way he says it.

I don't deserve that tenderness.

"Look at me," he commands, and when I don't, his finger and thumb gently touch my chin, tilting it until I'm forced to meet his gaze.

And the way he's watching me now, it's like *he's* the one who's been a class A prick.

"I'm sorry," I whisper.

He nods, the gesture cutting me off before I can tell him all that I'm sorry for.

His eyes search mine, his tongue snaking out to wet his lips. "I never had to leave, you know."

I frown, tilting my head, but Kade just steps into me, his palm sliding along my cheek as I lean into it and close my eyes to soak in the touch.

I *have* missed him — it wasn't a lie.

And feeling that connection with him again, seeing him again, everything inside me swirls like a nasty storm. I want to vomit. I want to pitch myself off the nearest roof. I want to whip myself and lock myself up.

Because I still love him, with every cell in my body I love him.

And I've been fucking another man.

"I never had to lose you to know," he continues, his voice soft, just a rumble over my skin as I let my eyes flutter open to meet his gaze once more. "I've known since the moment I saw you, since you thought I was just some douchebag frat boy," he adds with a smirk that makes me smile, too — though the smile releases two hot tears down my cheeks. "And I was already so far gone, Jess. I was so far gone. There was no saving me, and there was no way I could ever live without having you."

"Kade..."

"I know you've been with him," he says, his jaw hardening, chest heaving with a deep breath. "And I meant it when I said it's fucking killing me to know that."

I roll my lips together as more silent tears slip free, but Kade wipes them away as quick as they come.

"As angry as it makes me, and as much as it fucking *wrecks* my heart," he says, beating his fist on his chest with a break in his voice that I feel in my own soul. "I understand. I understand why you have to give him another chance, why you have to see if there... if there's something still..."

He can't finish the sentence.

I wrap my arms around his waist, and he pulls me in closer, letting out a long, slow breath as he drops his forehead to mine.

"Please," he begs. "Give me my chance, too. Don't write me out of the story yet."

I shake my head because I haven't — I *can't* write him out.

But before I can answer, the ballroom door swings open.

And Jarrett flies into the room.

"Jess?" he calls, and then his head snaps in our direction, his eyes dilating when he sees us — Kade's hands still framing my face, my hands on his hips.

His hands curl into fists at his sides, and Kade releases me with his jaw so tight I think he might chip a tooth.

Fuck.

"I got your voicemail," Jarrett says, his eyes on his brother even though he's talking to me. He doesn't move an inch.

Kade blinks at that, a brief look of confusion washing over his face before he turns to me.

And the pain in his eyes makes my knees wobble.

"You called him first?" he asks me, but I can't answer. I just swallow, reaching for him, wishing I had the words to make everything right, to make this all go away.

For both of them.

For *all* of us.

But he rips his arm away before I can touch him, sniffing as he grabs his shirt off the back of one of the chairs and storms toward Jarrett.

"Kade, wait," I try, but he doesn't so much as give me another glance.

Jarrett tries to catch his arm as he storms past, but Kade rips away from him, too, turning on him with a menacing glare. "Don't you fucking *touch* me, you backstabbing bastard."

He doesn't react — not physically — but I see the way those words shred Jarrett, the way he knows he's hurting his little brother, but can't help himself.

Kade shakes his head, stepping right up to Jarrett's face, the two brothers chest to chest as he says, "You left."

Jarrett closes his eyes, a long blink before he opens them to face his brother again.

"You fucking *left* her. You *broke* her. And you know who loved her when she was in pieces, who helped her find herself again, who watched her build an even stronger version of herself with you out of the picture?" He jabbed a thumb into his chest. "*Me*. And now you have the fucking *nerve* to show up again, rip open her wounds, play with her like you always played with every fucking girl growing up? They didn't deserve that shit, and neither does she."

I frown, but don't have time to wonder what he's referring to before Kade shoves Jarrett — hard.

"Wake the fuck up and let her go, let her be happy," Kade says as Jarrett steps right back up into his space. "Because we all know you don't have any intentions past fucking her until you're bored again."

"You don't know shit," Jarrett seethes.

Kade just laughs, shaking his head and looking his brother up and down as he puts space between them. "I know everything about you. And I know even more about her. I *love* her, you piece of shit," he says.

My heart squeezes so violently I feel my ribs creak with the pressure.

"So do I," Jarret responds. "And I loved her first."

Kade's jaw clamps shut at that, but after a moment, he shakes his head and shoves through the ballroom door, letting it slam shut behind him.

I flinch at the sound, closing my eyes as my throat burns.

When I open them again, Jarrett is already on his way over to me, but I hold up my hands. "Stop."

He does.

I shake my head. "You should go, Jarrett."

"I'm sorry I didn't come sooner. I'm sorry I—"

"Jarrett, please," I beg, and my eyes shine with fresh tears that make his shoulders slump, make him nearly cry out that I won't let him come closer. "Please, I need to be alone. Please. *Please.*"

I can't stop pleading, can't stop crying, and though I can tell it kills him, Jarrett scrubs a hand over his jaw and nods, backing up, giving me space.

"Okay," he says, holding up his hands. "Okay. Just... call me. Tomorrow. Please."

I nod, but it's a dismissive one, one that says I can't make any promises.

To anyone.

Not even myself.

He watches me for a long moment before he finally rips his gaze from mine and leaves through the same door Kade did.

And I collapse onto the floor and succumb to every heartbreaking sob my body lashes me with.

Erin

THE HOLIDAY SEASON ALWAYS feels a little off in Florida.

While the rest of the country is bundled up, drinking hot spiced pumpkin drinks and reading by the fire, it's business as usual in South Florida — which is to say it's very, very hot.

My hair is already damp at my neck after talking outside with a few people from therapy, and a single bead of sweat slides down my back as I trek toward my car, a heavy sigh leaving my lips after a long day.

A long *week*, really.

Candice has been keeping me in the loop with the trial, but unfortunately, there won't be any news one way or another until after Thanksgiving. So for now, there's nothing more for me to do but try to forget about it all and enjoy myself.

Those were her words.

As if I could forget.

As if I could focus on school or on calling my mom to see if she wants me and Bear to come home for the holiday or *literally anything else* other than the fact that Landon and his brothers have been questioned, as have I, as have all other witnesses in question.

And a decision will be made.

A decision I have absolutely zero control over.

I'm so lost in thought — something that seems to be happening to me more and more lately — that I don't notice Gavin leaning against my car door until I'm about ten steps away. He straightens at the soft *beep* of me unlocking the vehicle, and while he offers a sheepish smile, I only give him a glare in return.

"What?" I clip, moving around him to toss my purse in the car before I stand — door still open — waiting for whatever he wants before I climb in and peel out of here.

"You shared a lot in therapy today," he said, tucking his hands in his pockets. "I... I didn't realize you were going to court for... for what happened."

"I might not be."

He frowns. "But you said—"

"We were all questioned, yes. I'm trying to press charges, yes. But nothing is certain. The detectives and lawyers have done their jobs for now, and it's up to the prosecutor what happens next."

"They're going to pay," he says, his jaw tense. "They will, Erin."

I shrug, mostly because I don't want to cry — nor do I want to get caught up in this conversation with the boy who broke my heart and left me behind because he couldn't handle me.

"I'm proud of you," he says after a quiet pause from me. "I know it couldn't have been easy, to come forward after all this time. But you're setting an example. You're doing the right thing. And I believe the justice system will do its job and make them pay for what they did."

I fight the urge to roll my eyes.

"Is that all?" I ask.

His shoulders deflate, and it's then that I see how though his eyes are red from what I assume is lack of sleep, he *does* look better than when I last saw him. He's filled out, his skin a bronze instead of that translucent gray, his cheekbones no longer hollow. Maybe he did get help. Maybe he meant what he said in his letter to me.

Regardless, I don't owe him anything — least of all this conversation.

"Erin, I truly am so sorry," he says, his voice just above a whisper. "For hurting you, for leaving the way I did. For... everything. I know it doesn't matter now, I know you're happy with Bear and I'm happy *for* you. But..." He shakes his head, running a hand back through his hair as he looks away from me. Sweat beads along his neck. "Goddamnit, Erin, you are so fucking important to me. To my life. You were instrumental in my recovery. And I don't know if I helped you the way you helped me," he says, his eyes meeting mine then. "But I meant what I said. I would really like to be friends. *Just* friends. Not the creepy kind of friend who says that's all they want and then tries to make a move."

I can't help how my nose stings, eyes pricking with tears that dry as soon as they appear. Because as he said those words, that I helped him, I know he helped me, too.

"I just don't want to lose you in my life," he pleads. "And with everything going on in yours... I want to be there."

I sigh, biting my lip as I mull over his words. To his credit, he *does* seem genuine.

And in so many ways, I feel the same as he does.

I never wanted him to leave the way he did. In fact, him breaking up with me because I'm not pretty enough would have been easier to handle than that letter he left me with.

But if he really did check himself into a treatment center, if he really was in that low of a place... and now he's back... and we can be friends?

I know how much it would mean to him.

Even more — I know how much it would mean to *me*.

He was there for me when no one else was — not because they wouldn't have been if I'd have told them, but because I didn't have the strength to own what had happened to me. He was the first to touch me, the first to make me desire after having something so viciously taken from me.

He was — *is* — part of my recovery.

And it seems I'm part of his.

After a long moment debating, I sigh again, extending my hand. "Friends," I say, pulling back a little when he goes for the shake. "*Just* friends. The second you try to cross a line, it's over."

Gavin throws his hands up. "Just friends. I swear. It's all I want."

I nod. "I'd like that, too."

His smile is one of relief, his shoulders sagging with the breath, and then we shake hands.

And on that touch, the first time touching him since he broke my heart, I feel an all-too-familiar aching pain radiate right to my heart.

"What are you doing now? Want to go grab a drink, catch up?" he asks. Then, he laughs, grabbing the back of his neck. "Or, well, maybe grab *you* a drink. I don't drink anymore."

"At all?"

"Nope."

I smile. "I think that's a good thing."

"I do, too."

"I have plans tonight," I lie. The only plans I have are with my bed, but this *friendship* is new, and I'm too tired to dive in deeper than just agreeing that it's okay. "Maybe next time."

Gavin's smile is a bit flat, but he nods. "Sure, next time."

He grabs my door to open it farther for me, waiting for me to climb in before he carefully shuts it and taps the top of my car.

Adam

"I JUST HOPE YOU'RE ready to barely leave the hotel room," I tell Cassie under my breath, looking around the bar to make sure no one's heard me. Of course, not that I really care — but I am *trying* to be polite to any innocent bystanders.

Cassie giggles into the phone. "I wish I could just talk to you all night."

"Me too," I tell her, my chest squeezing with the admission. "But we'll see each other in just over a week. That's not too long."

"I might die waiting."

"Better not. You've got your first cosplay convention to go to."

She squeals a little at that. "You really think I look okay? I'm excited to dive into Tera's world a little bit, but I don't want to embarrass her."

"Are you kidding? You make the absolute sexiest Daphne Blake I've ever seen..." I whistle. "I just wish I was there to be your Fred Jones."

"You'd need a very good wig to pull that off."

"And I'd wear it," I say. "For you."

A pause passes between us, and then Cassie sighs. "I really should get going. I'm picking Tera up from her dorm room across campus."

"Take lots of pictures and videos and tell me all the crazy things you see."

"I will," she promises. "Eight days."

"Eight days," I repeat on a sigh. "I love you."

"I love you."

When she hangs up, I hold the phone to my ear a while longer, heart heavy and aching with the need to hold her, see her, *be* with her. I finally set my phone down on the bar, signaling to the bartender to pour me another IPA as I polish off the last of the one in front of me.

It's been a long time since I've gone to a bar by myself — let alone on a Monday night. But with the Alpha Sigma bonfire behind me and the semester winding down as the brothers focus on holidays and finals, I'm in a pensive move.

And I'm lonely.

I miss my own brothers, miss how busy it always was this time of year back at Palm South. I miss having a purpose as president, and though I thought this position would fill that need, the simple fact is that it just doesn't.

I'm not in a fraternity anymore.

I'm not in *college* anymore.

Lost is the sad term that keeps coming to mind, and as the bartender slides a fresh beer in front of me, I sigh, drinking down the feelings that come with that admission.

My eyes find one of the big screens hanging above the bottles on the back wall, watching as the Cowboys and Steelers take the field. At least I have football to distract me.

"This seat taken?"

I blink, frowning at first when I turn to find Chandler beside me. But then a surprised smile curls on my lips. "Looks like it is now. What are you doing here?"

"Same as you, I'd imagine," she says with a sigh, propping her hands on the bar to help her up until she plops down onto the barstool next to me. "Drinking away Monday."

I laugh. "What are you having? I've got a tab open."

"What's that?" she asks, nodding to my glass.

"IPA."

"Perfect."

I get the bartender's attention, and once Chandler has a cold beer in front of her and has shrugged off her jacket and scarf, we clink our glasses together and take a long chug.

"Ah," she says, smacking her lips. "That's *exactly* what I needed." Her eyes find the television, and she wrinkles her nose. "Ugh. Football."

"Not a fan, I take it?"

"Not after growing up with a dad and three brothers who were obsessed with it, no." She shakes her head. "Constant screaming on Sundays, I tell you. No peace."

I laugh. "*Three* brothers? Your poor boyfriends."

"Very few made it past the *meet the family* stage," she says. "And as you can tell by my glorious single state of being now, no one lasts long after."

I smirk, not allowing myself the opportunity to take in her appearance any lower than her eyes. She knows as well as I do that she's a very attractive woman — unique, edgy, with a rack that you can see from outer space. "I doubt you stay single long. Unless you want to, that is."

She shrugs. "I don't know what I want."

"What a loaded statement," I say with a sigh of my own. "I've been feeling the same, actually."

Chandler takes a long drink. "Trouble in paradise?"

I frown, not understanding until I meet her gaze and then piece together that she thinks I mean Cassie.

"Oh, *God* no," I say quickly. "Cassie is the only thing *right* in my life." I pause. "Honestly, it's been that way for a while, I think."

"I don't know, it looks like you've done a lot of good here. My girls can't stop talking about Alpha Sigma's *transformation.*" She does a little move with her hands to illustrate the word, her voice going up a pitch.

I chuckle. "And I'm happy for them. It's been fun, it's just..."

"Not what you thought it would be."

"Not at all," I admit.

"You thought it would be like college 2.0, that you would get the same satisfaction as a Field Executive that you did as president."

"You're too good at this."

She smiles. "I know the feeling is all. It's not the same when you're not an active member. It makes you feel old, like an outsider. And fuck, it's lonely."

I nod in agreement. "I think I'm done after this year."

"They'll be sad to lose you."

"Maybe. But the bigger issue is that I have no idea what I want to do next, only that it has to be in Baltimore."

Chandler nearly chokes on her next sip of beer at that. "Jesus Christ, *why* Baltimore of all places?"

"That's where Cassie will be going to med school." I meet her gaze. "Johns Hopkins."

Chandler's brows shoot into her hairline. "Wow. Gorgeous *and* smart as hell... it's just not fair. Some girls get all the fun."

I smile. "She's had to work her ass off for it."

"I don't doubt it." Chandler taps the bar for a moment, watching me like she wants to say something. But she keeps biting her lip, her cheek, looking away just to look back again.

"What?" I ask.

"Nothing, it's just..." She shakes her head. "This is crazy, and I doubt you'd be interested but..." She stops. "Never mind."

"Chandler," I say, arching a brow to let her know I don't like playing these games.

"Okay, okay," she says, turning to face me more. "It's just... what a small fucking world. *I'm* from Baltimore."

I blanch. "You are?"

"I am. My whole family is. That whole football hate I was talking about earlier? Try being in a house full of Ravens fans."

I chuckle.

"Anyway, my dad's parents own a pretty big company based in Baltimore... Simmons Snacks."

It was my turn to choke on my beer. "Simmons Snacks? As in the potato chip company?"

"Potato chips, popcorn, salsa and queso, cookies, crackers..." She nods. "Yep."

I gape at her. "What the fuck, Chandler. You never told me you were the granddaughter of some of the wealthiest people in the world."

"It's not my wealth," she says quickly. "Anyway, they've been hounding me for about a month now to come work for them. They're in desperate need of someone to head their Public Relations and Events team." She pauses. "In Baltimore."

My ears heat.

"I have no interest," she adds quickly. "And they know that. They've wanted me to work for the family business since I was born, but I just... I don't want anything to do with it. Not because it isn't a great company," she clarifies. "Because it is. I just want to make a name for myself outside of it." She pauses. "Also, I don't want to live in Baltimore."

I laugh at that. "So, why are you telling me this?"

"Isn't it obvious?" She shrugs. "What if *you* lead their team?"

I blink.

"Don't look so surprised," she says with a smile. "You'd be great at it. I mean, that's essentially what you're doing here, what you did all through college — public relations and events. You'd get to do what you love professionally, outside of a fraternity organization. For a company you know and love. In the city where your girlfriend is." She cocks a brow. "Did I lose you?"

"I'm just trying to decide if you're a figment of my imagination," I say, playfully swinging at the air around her like she's a ghost.

She chuckles and swats my hand down. "Look. Come home to Baltimore with me for Thanksgiving. They're stubborn, but I know once my PopPop meets you, he'll jump at the opportunity to hire you. He probably won't wait for you to finish out your job as Field Executive," she adds with a cringe. "But as long as you're not opposed to leaving before Spring semester..."

"I'm not. I mean, that's when Cassie is going, so... it'd be perfect."

"Well, there you have it."

My smile is so big it nearly breaks my face. "I don't know what to say, Chandler."

"Well, it's not done yet. But you can start with a thank you."

"Thank you," I say hurriedly, but then my stomach sinks to my shoes. "Wait... *fuck*. Cassie is coming here for Thanksgiving."

Chandler frowns. "Can she come out a different time?"

"It's her last semester at PSU, and she's in a sorority. You know how that goes."

"I do." Chandler's mouth tugs to the side as she thinks. "I mean, I could try to talk my grandparents into coming out here to visit, but their schedule is so crazy... we're lucky to pull them away even for a single day for things like Thanksgiving and Christmas."

"Do you think they'd meet with me over the phone?"

"Possibly, but I'll be honest... PopPop doesn't sway lightly. I think charming him in person would be your best bet."

I curse again.

"Look, I know it would suck to call off the trip for Cassie to come, but on the heels of that disappointment would come the best news ever — that you both get to be in the same city again. You could *live* together." Chandler reaches over to squeeze my wrist. "A little sacrifice now could pay off in a big way later."

I nod. "Or Cassie could castrate me and break up with me for good measure."

"You really think she'd do that?"

I sigh. "No. But I don't want to tell her about this, just in case it doesn't happen. She'll get her hopes up and then... if I don't get the job..."

"You'll get the job," Chandler says quickly. "But whether you want to tell her about the meeting or not is up to you. For now, I'm going to tell my mom to have another setting at the table for dinner. And you need to figure out what to tell Cassie."

I frown, nodding. Then, I turn to face her. "What's in this for you?"

"Well, one, they'll get off *my* back about the damn job," she says. "Two, I'll have a friend to hang out with over the holidays instead of my insufferable brothers. And three?" She shrugs. "I think we've got a pretty good track record of helping each other out. I don't want to break it."

I smile. "Friends, huh? I didn't think I'd find one of those out here."

"That makes two of us. Now," she says, downing the last of her beer and holding the empty glass up to the bartender. "Let's get another round and you start taking notes. I'm going to tell you every single way to woo my grandfather."

I grin, chugging the last of mine to match her, and once we have new beers, we get to work.

The fire burning in my belly is unmatched, fueled by the thought that this might be it, this might be how I can do what I love but not be away from Cassie any longer.

No more long distance.

No more video chat dates or texts or calls.

Just me and her, in the same city, the same *house*, potentially.

My pulse races at the thought, at the surprised look on Cassie's face should I be able to land the job. It'd be the best Christmas gift I could ever give her — the news that we'd both be in Baltimore come spring.

So, with that as my motivation, I took detailed notes, and by the time we asked for the check, we were booking me a flight to Baltimore.

Ashlei

"YOU LOOK ABSOLUTELY RADIANT, Miss Daniels," Riel says, tucking a beautiful fuchsia flower into the crown she's been weaving into my hair. The electric blue water of St. John can be seen out of every window of Brandon's yacht, and it reflects off Riel's dark eyes as she puts the final touches on my updo.

She pulls back with a smile, clapping her hands together. "All done."

With her hands on my arms, Riel gently turns me to look in the full-length mirror in my cabin.

And I gasp.

I did my own makeup, wanting to be sure I still looked like *me* for such a special day, but I chose not to look in the mirror after I slipped my dress on, nor did I sneak a glance as Riel did my hair.

And now here it is, all at once.

Me, in a delicate, flowy, A-line wedding dress — the straps delicate around my collarbone, waist cinched, elaborate beading covering the bust and a weightless, silky, long skirt with four deep slits all the way to my upper thigh. I know with just a little turn that those slits will allow the fabric to flow all around me in the Caribbean wind.

My hair is woven into a thick braid, the most colorful flower crown playing with the warm pinks and oranges of my eyeshadow and bringing out the gold in my hazel eyes. Brilliant Swarovski crystals cover the straps of my high heels, highlighting my immaculate pedicure.

I touch my neck, the simple diamond hanging on the end of a slim gold chain.

And that makes me look at my ring finger — the one about to be covered with the perfect engagement ring Brandon picked out for me.

And a wedding band, too.

My eyes well, and I turn back around to wrap Riel in a hug. "Thank you," I whisper.

We met Riel when we first arrived in St. John, and she's been our wedding planner of sorts, helping us find everything we desired for our ceremony — which wasn't much, but what we *did* want, Brandon wanted top of the line.

She's been a saving grace to me, helping me with flowers, choosing a photographer, decorating the bow of the yacht, and ensuring we have the best local chef onboard for our wedding night dinner.

"One last thing," I tell her, turning around to face the mirror again. "Help me get this off."

I'm already fidgeting with the straps of my arm sling when Riel stops me. "I don't think that's a good idea."

"Riel, I am not wearing this monstrosity while I get married. I refuse."

I sigh when I see the worried look on her face.

"I'll put it on as soon as the vows are exchanged and that man gives me the kiss of my life, okay? Just... please. Don't make me wear this out there."

Riel smiles softly, and with a nod, she does as I ask.

When the arm brace is off, I chuckle a little at how that arm is slightly paler than my other, but nevertheless, I feel one-hundred times lighter.

I let myself take in the whole image one last time before my eyes wander to the bits of Cruz Bay I can see off in the distance through the magnificent windows in my cabin. The lush green mountains stretch up over the cerulean blue water, sailboats and yachts peppering the shoreline, and my heart leaps into my throat as I realize where I am.

Realize what I'm doing.

I close my eyes on a smile, thinking of how many times I've played through what this day would be like. From the time I was a little girl, I've dreamed of what I'd wear, the kind of cake I'd have, the party...

And now, it's just me and the man I love on an island far, far away.

It couldn't be more perfect.

"Okay," I breathe, opening my eyes and taking a long, slow breath. "I'm ready."

Riel nods, leading the way for me out of my cabin and carefully down the stairs to the main deck. She hides me in the back of the parlor, curtains pulled over the usually open airway that leads out to the bow. I haven't seen the decorations come all together yet, haven't seen the lilies and roses and baby's breath wreaths or arch that match my bouquet. I haven't seen the freshly polished teak deck, or the fairy lights hung in a zig zag fashion over the bow.

And I haven't seen my groom — not since dinner last night.

It was torture for both of us to sleep in separate cabins, but it was the one thing I wanted to keep old-fashioned.

And when Riel comes back in through the parlor bar entry, nodding to let me know that everything is ready, I step up to stand right at the edge of the curtain as two of Riel's friends pull open opposite ends of it back in sync.

And I see him.

And he sees me.

And all the wait, all the time apart was worth it.

I wish I can say I hear the music playing — the sweet, soft sounds of a violin from the musician we hired our first day on the island. I wish I could hear her playing our song, "Unchained Melody," as I slowly drift across the teak toward where Brandon waits for me at the bow. I wish I could take in the golden rays of sun on the island, the shockingly blue water, the waves softly lapping at the sides of the boat, the flowers and the lights and everything we'd set up for this very occasion.

But I can't see, can't hear, can't feel anything or anyone else but Brandon Church.

He stands tall and regal as ever at the bow, his cream suit casual yet sophisticated, highlighted by the Carolina blue dress shirt underneath. Diamond studs glisten in each earlobe, his hair in a neat, styled fade, facial hair trimmed to perfection. Every inch of the outfit is tapered to fit him, hugging and hanging off all the right places.

I take my time letting my eyes wander the length of him, feeling the pulse of his heartbeat even with the distance still between us. It's an energy, I realize — one I've been in tune with since the moment he stepped onto the same elevator with me at *Okay, Cool*.

When my eyes finally crawl up to meet his, he lets out a slow, steady breath. His jaw tightens, nose flares, and he shakes his head once, twice, before he tears his eyes away from me and bows his head down.

He pinches the bridge of his nose, one shake of his shoulders telling me he was moved to tears before he finds the strength to stand tall again.

And those warm brown eyes glistening in the sun, those slender wet streaks staining his cheeks, those lips rolling together as he tries to fight back his emotion — they're what undo me.

My own eyes water, and a single tear slips free before I can even think to stop it.

I don't make it all the way to him before he's meeting me halfway, pulling me into him for a soul-shattering, life-altering, *you're mine forever* kiss.

His lips are warm and commanding, his hands wrapping around the beaded bodice of my dress, and he still shakes with emotion as he holds me tighter and tighter.

When we finally pull away, our foreheads pressed together, I chuckle. "I think you were supposed to wait until the end to do that."

"I couldn't."

I smile, pulling back to look him in the eyes, and he shakes his head, his gaze one of absolute reverence.

"You are a masterpiece," he whispers.

My eyes gloss again, and I press up on my toes to kiss him again before Riel clears her throat and ushers us the rest of the way down the make-shift aisle.

The sea breeze is cool and lovely, the sun still warm on our skins as it slowly makes its descent over the island. Brandon holds my hands in his, our tear-filled eyes flicking back and forth between each other's as Riel's officiant reads the sweet but short ceremony we selected. He has us laughing and smiling all the way up until he says it's time for us to exchange our personal vows.

The entire time, all I can focus on is where Brandon's thumb smooths the top of my knuckles, a sensual promise of what's to come *after* the vows.

"Brandon Church," I say first, and his dazzling smile makes me smile, too. "I wish I could say I've known since the moment I met you that you'd be my husband one day, but the truth is, I was doing everything I could back then *not* to think of you as anything other than my boss."

That earns me a chuckle from Riel and the officiant, both.

"But I knew... something. From the moment you stepped into the elevator, from the first time our eyes met and I heard your voice, a part of my heart that had been dormant all my life came alive. I stirred beneath your gaze, and though I tried to deny it, tried to fight it, I think I knew even then that there was no way I'd be able to stay away from you."

"That makes two of us," Brandon chimes in.

I chuckle. "I don't think either of us can deny our chemistry, but it's our love that makes me happiest. I know at the end of the day, no matter what we go through — you have my back, and I have yours. There's no better feeling than that." I squeeze his hand. "There was a time when I didn't know if I'd walk life alone or with someone by my side, a time when I wondered if life was worth living at all. But then I found you. And you saved me."

"We saved each other," he amends.

I smile, nodding with tears glossing my eyes once more. "I love you. And I am yours, for today, tomorrow, and evermore."

Riel sniffs and wipes a tear from the corner of her eye before it can fall. I offer her a soft smile before Brandon clears his throat, pulling my attention back to him.

"Contrary to the many public events in which I have delivered speeches deserving of a standing ovation, I have to admit... I failed every time I tried to write down in words what you mean to me, Ashlei Daniels."

My heart throbs in my throat, and I swallow it down as my eyes blur.

"I never knew what it was to be truly hungry until I laid eyes on you and knew I couldn't have you. That desire, that wanting is something I will never forget. But as you said before, what started as something so carnal swiftly turned into something I couldn't place, couldn't name, because I'd never experienced it before in my life." He takes a breath. "*Love*. Love so pure and powerful and sweeping that I had no choice but to get caught up in the wave of it."

I bit my bottom lip.

"You are, without a doubt, the strongest, smartest, most incredible woman I have ever had the pleasure of knowing. You own every room you walk into. You command the attention of every man, woman, and child. You, my sweet wife—"

"*Almost* wife," I correct.

"Are going to take this whole damn world by storm," he finishes. "And I am just honored beyond measure to be the man who gets to stand by your side while you do it."

I smile, squeezing his hands, desperate to get to the kissing part now.

"Our love has been tested," Brandon says. "But if nothing else, we have proven that even when we hurt each other, we know at the end of the day that there is no one else. Your love was meant for me, and mine was meant for you. We are souls destined to find each other in this lifetime and every one after. I vow to treasure each moment with you as if it were my last, and to spend every moment away from you praying for your return to my arms. I will make you happy, Ashlei. I will care for you, protect you, and most of all, respect you." Brandon's eyes are sincere, heavy as they hold mine. "That is my promise."

My bottom lip trembles as I nod, accepting his vows, knowing their truth. And once again, everything fades into the background — the water, the breeze, the sunlight, the music, and even the officiant's voice as he declares us husband and wife and allows Brandon to kiss his bride.

In the next moment, I'm swept back in a dramatic dip, and all around us, sailboats and yachts and tourist ferries alike roar with applause.

But for me, it's just Brandon's arms around my waist, his lips on mine, his heart forever joined with the one beating in my chest.

And just like that.

I'm Mrs. Ashlei Church.

"Please don't make me."

I cross my arms and bat my lashes, hoping the wedding hair and makeup is still intact enough after our breezy sunset dinner for Brandon to show mercy on me.

He chuckles, crossing the space in the master bedroom to hold my elbows in his massive hands. "I'm not doing it to be mean, my love. You've gone all day without it. The doctor said—"

"I know what the doctor said," I growl, wrinkling my nose. "But it's so ugly, and bulky, and *not* sexy."

"You are sexy no matter what you wear."

"You say that now, but when that strap is smushing down my boob..."

Brandon plants a soft kiss to my lips. "First, let me help you out of this," he says, fingertips walking down my hips and slipping under the high slits of my dress. He tugs at the fabric as my breath catches. "And then, we put the brace on, and I fuck you as my *wife* should be properly fucked."

I pout. "But—"

Brandon catches my bottom lip with his teeth, biting hard enough for me to yelp before he releases me. "Stick that lip out one more time and I'll bend you over my knee."

This time it's *me* who bites my lip, my thighs clenching with the thought of being punished, of being spanked.

Yes, please.

Brandon's lips are on mine in the next breath, his kiss soft and slow and purposeful as he backs me up more and more until my spine hits the window. With the added support, he presses me into it, careful of my shoulder as he hikes one of my legs up and slides my dress skirt up over my hips.

"Every time the wind blew, I'd see your thigh, this little spot where your hip meets the muscle," he teases, running his fingertip along my hip flexor. "And it drove me mad, knowing I'd have to wait to kiss that spot, to have this pussy," he husks, his hand dipping between my legs without warning. His fingers skate under my panties and slide through my desire, a groan of approval on his lips when he adds, "*My* pussy."

"All this talk, but no action..." I tease, wrapping my arms around his shoulders. I want desperately for him to pin me against the window and let me hold on for dear life as he eats the pussy he was just raving about.

But the bastard is too worried about my safety.

He laughs against my lips, giving me a brief kiss before he pulls away. "Too much pressure on your shoulder to hold on like that," he says, reading my mind. "Tonight, you'll have to be content with me ravaging you the way I want to."

I'm tempted to pout again, but then Brandon holds my hand in his — the one connected to my good shoulder

— and gives me a little spin, the skirt of my dress flaring as I turn to face the window.

His lips are warm, little kisses pressing against my neck and the top of my spine as he carefully undoes each button at the back of my dress. When it's loose enough, he slips one strap off my shoulder, and then the other, letting the fabric pool at my feet.

He moans when he sees what he no doubt suspected with the open back of the dress — that I'm not wearing a bra — and before I can prepare for it, his hands palm each breast, weighing them, massaging as he presses his hard-on against my ass.

"I can't believe I get to touch these for the rest of my life."

"Even when they're old and saggy."

He almost laughs, but the slight pressure change on my nipple has me gasping, moaning, arching back into him and begging for more contact.

"No more jokes," he whispers in my ear, and then his fingers slip under the bands of my lace panties, and he strips them down my thighs, too.

I want to protest again when he pulls out the brace, but I'm so desperate to have him inside me that I just let him help me into it. I catch a glimpse of how stupid I look in the mirror and make to tell him so, but he kisses me silent.

I'm swept into his arms in the next breath, his mouth still on mine as he carries me over to the master bed. It's lush on an average day, but with brand new sheets with a higher thread count than anything I've ever slept in, it feels like being laid down in a cloud of cool silk when he deposits me.

He stands then, his eyes drinking in every inch of me as he shrugs off his suit jacket, unbuttons his dress shirt, makes quick work of his belt and his dress slacks. Hunger grows in his gaze as much as I feel it burning in my soul at the sight of this powerful, sexy man stripping for me.

My man.

My *husband.*

Desire pools between my legs at the thought, at the ownership, and as soon as he's out of his dress shoes, I pull him onto the bed and down on top of me.

His mouth eagerly devours mine, swallowing my next breath as the hard length of him slips between my thighs. His shaft glides through my wetness and over my sensitive clit, making me shudder, making my nails dig into his flesh to beg for more.

"Easy," he teases, kissing my brace as I fight the urge to roll my eyes.

"I'm fine."

"I want to keep it that way."

Brandon balances on his elbows then, his eyes searching mine as he sweeps a bit of my fallen braid out of my face. His thumb drags down my nose, over my lips, tracing my jaw before he wraps my neck in a gentle but possessive embrace. "I meant every word I said," he whispers. "I am yours, Ashlei."

My brows tug together, and I nod, pulling him down to kiss me. I don't have to say it. I know he feels it without my words.

I'm yours, too.

I want him to fuck me against the window. I want to be bent over the railing so all of St. John can watch. I want him fast and hard and furious, desperate and needy — the way he was the first time he had me on his private jet.

But I know we'll have a lifetime for that.

Tonight, I'm limited, and perhaps more than that, it feels... *more*. It's not just his skin on mine, our mouths fused, our breaths labored between us as our bodies ache to be connected.

It's a union, a promise, a tender turn of the page that starts a new chapter in our story.

"I love you," Brandon whispers against my lips.

And then he hikes one leg up, kisses me with enough pressure to bruise, and fills me.

I cry out at the first thrust, the way it leaves me breathless as always. His long, hard, thick length stretches me, but the burn fades quickly, pleasure taking its place.

The waves rock the boat in time with him flexing inside of me, in and out, and I hold on with my good arm while letting my other rest.

Fire licks at my core quickly, with the way he brushes my sensitive clit with every thrust. Or maybe it's the wedding, the vows, the fact that this man is mine in every way there is to be.

Forever.

"Ashlei," he groans, kissing me hard as his pace intensifies. "Come with me, baby. Find it."

I reach down between us, and he presses up onto his palms to give me the space I need to rub my clit and find my release. It doesn't take long, not with him towering over me like that, not with the wicked grin he gives me as he watches me play with myself, watches himself sink inside me deeper and deeper with each thrust.

My legs spread wider, toes curling as I quicken my circles and find my release, panting and screaming out his name. And he comes undone with me, a grunt loud and feral ricocheting off the cabin walls as he spills inside me.

Yes.

Yes, yes, yes.

Even after he's done, he continues to move, in and out, feeling his slick release leaking out of me. And before we have the chance to come down, to breathe and prepare, he's already hardening again.

"Round two already, Mr. Church?" I ask, arching a brow.

"Followed very quickly by round three, *Mrs.* Church."

I bite my lip at that, and Brandon smirks, rolling until I'm on top.

And this time, I ride my husband until we both come again, and realize my wedding night might be the most sleepless of my life.

Jess

A WEEK BEFORE THANKSGIVING, I text the girls and call an emergency video chat call.

It takes more back and forth than I'd like for us to nail down a time for the call, given everyone's schedules, but somehow — miraculously — I get them all to agree on six p.m.

Erin comes over to my room for the call, her hair wet from her shower and a bottle of wine in hand — along with two glasses.

"I don't know what this is about," she says, shuffling in in her fuzzy slippers. "But something tells me we'll need this."

I motion for her to hand me the bottle as I connect my laptop to the video chat, and then I pour us two full glasses as the other girls click into frame one by one.

Cassie and Skyler are together, too, cuddled on Skyler's bed. Ashlei looks happier than I've seen her since the accident where she sits on her and Brandon's couch — and a little too tan for all the moping she's been doing.

I don't even let the small talk happen. I just take a long swig of wine and say, "I'm calling an emergency Friendsgiving."

Skyler frowns. "What's going on, J-Love?"

I shake my head, tears already forming in my eyes — and provided I cry about as much as Cassie skips class, all the girls instantly sit up straighter, Erin's hand smoothing over my back.

"I need you. All of you. I have no idea what to do. I feel lost and guilty and fucked up and *sad*. I'm so, so sad,"

I admit. "I don't care where we go, but I need us all to get away. Out of town, out of the vicinity of everything here. I just... please. I need you."

"I'm there," Erin says instantly. "I can't bail on my family for Thanksgiving. I'm bringing Bear home for the first time. But I don't have to be back at the office until Tuesday, so... long weekend?"

"That works for me," Skyler says.

"Same," Ashlei chimes in. "I can't take more time off work, but we have Black Friday and the following Monday off already."

I arch a brow. "What do you mean *more* time? Are they seriously punishing you for the whole two days you were out of the office for your surgery?"

"Um... not exactly."

She bites her lip, and the girls and I exchange glances, waiting.

"Instead of a Friendsgiving... how would y'all feel about a belated bachelorette?"

I blink.

Cassie tilts her head.

Skyler and Erin both frown so intensely I'm worried they might get wrinkles on the spot.

And then Ashlei bites back a smile and holds up her left hand.

Showcasing a very large, very shiny, very *new* diamond ring.

Chaos erupts. Skyler and Cassie are bouncing up and down on the bed, their video frame shaking wildly as they squeal and demand details. Erin claps and grabs my laptop from me to see the ring closer, to which I smack her hand and grab it back, pushing a shortcut on the keyboard to make the window go full-screen.

"Jesus Christ, Lei! It's gorgeous!" I scream.

"It's *huge*," Erin adds.

"What the hell happened?" Skyler asks.

Ashlei holds up her hands to calm us with a giggle. "He proposed," she says simply with a shrug. "And then… we eloped. We just packed a bag and got on the yacht and sailed away. We shopped for everything we needed when we got there."

"Got *where*?" Cassie probes.

"St. John."

A collective sigh from the group makes Ashlei chuckle.

"You better have pictures, bitch," I warn, pointing my finger at the camera. And though I'm joking and smiling and joining in the celebration, I can't deny the way my chest aches, the way I feel both happy for my best friend and still wholly gutted for me.

"I do. Video, too," she promises.

"Alright, that settles it," I say, clapping my hands together. "Bachelorette party, next weekend, Black Friday through Cyber Monday. I'll take care of everything. All you bitches need to do is pack and show up at the airport. And also help me figure out my life once we get there."

"Where are we going?" Skyler asks.

I wave her off, letting her know she can find out once I do.

"Um, small problem…" Cassie says, holding up her finger. She sighs. "I'm sorry, but I'm flying to see Adam. And I don't want to miss this. *God*, I don't want to miss this, Lei," she says more pointedly at Ashlei. "But I haven't seen him since July, and things have been so hard lately, so…"

Her voice fades, and Skyler gives her a sympathetic look before squeezing her arm. We all know how hard it's been for her and Adam doing long distance.

Long distance is what killed me and Jarrett.

It's what killed Skyler and Kip.

We don't need another casualty.

"I'll allow your absence," I say. "Just this once. Only because I love Adam, and you, and the two of you together. But you're sponsoring a round of shots."

"Of course," she says, but her smile isn't one of relief. I know that look of FOMO, and I'd have it, too, if I were in her shoes.

"We'll party when you're back, too," Ashlei promises. "Don't worry."

Cassie nods, and then I rub my hands together again.

"Don't stuff yourselves too full of turkey and mashed potatoes, ladies," I say with a wicked smile as I pull up my phone, already searching for resorts. "I'm thinking... *Mexico*."

That earns me a group of squeals, and Skyler starts talking about which swimsuits to pack as Ashlei says she's almost positive Brandon has a timeshare at a resort in Cabo.

Already, my heart feels lighter, my soul warmer knowing I'll have my girls to help me sort through this mess I'm in — and that we can celebrate our girl finding the man of her dreams, too.

There's a short round of catching up and happy holiday wishes before we end the call.

And when we hang up, I get to work planning the most epic bachelorette party ever.

EPISODE 5

Cassie

"PLEASE SAY SOMETHING."

Adam's voice pierces through the ringing in my ears, the fog clouding my vision as I grip my phone tighter than necessary. I blink, over and over, processing what he's said.

"Cassie…"

"I don't know what you want me to say, Adam," I finally whisper, sniffing back the urge to cry. I'm not sure if they would be sad or angry tears at this point.

"It's not ideal, I know."

"Not ideal?" I scoff, and Lindsey — my roommate — widens her eyes before closing her textbook and popping off her bed. She gives me a little wave to let me know she's giving me space, and closes the door on her way out.

I grit my teeth.

"Not only are you saying that the trip to Colorado to see you that I've been looking forward to since the day we said goodbye is now not happening, but you're also saying you're going to have Thanksgiving with *some other girl's family.*"

"In Baltimore," he adds for me. "In order to secure a job that would put me there permanently." There's a long pause before he says, "With you."

I shake my head. "Is there something going on with her? Are you…" Bile rises in my throat. "Are you cheating on me?"

My bottom lip wobbles with the question, and Adam curses. "Of course not. Baby, how could you even ask that?"

I don't answer.

"Hey, look down. You see that silver chain and those two letters hanging around your neck?" he asks.

And I do. I wrap my fingers around the charm, closing my eyes and freeing a silent tear.

"That was a promise to you. A promise that I love you, more than anyone, and that I will be true to you. Always. You're my person, Cassie."

"But things change. You've been away for a whole semester almost, and you've spent so much time with this girl." I sniff again. "I wouldn't blame you if you... if you found other interests. If you outgrew me. If you..."

"Stop. Stop right there," he says. "First of all, you would kill me if that were true, and you know it."

I almost smile at that.

"Secondly, I love you. I *miss* you — and that's exactly why this is important to me. I know it sucks in the short term. It breaks my fucking heart to have to make this call," he admits with a strained voice. "But what if this is the key to us being together come spring? What if we could not only be in the same city, but in the same house?" He pauses. "Or apartment, or whatever."

My heart squeezes at that. "You want to move in together?"

"If I get this job? Hell fucking yes, I do. I want to be able to kiss you every night before I go to sleep and kiss you as soon as my eyes open in the morning."

I clutch my necklace, slumping back against the headboard. "I hate this."

"I know. I do, too. I tried to do it through just a phone call, but... I mean, this is Simmons Snacks, Cassie. They're a big deal. They're not going to be won over by a resume and some guy they don't know on a phone call — if they would even take it. But to Chandler, they aren't Fortune

100 business owners — they're Nana and PopPop. It wouldn't be an interview, it'd be a family meal, maybe a cigar and a glass with her grandfather. And *maybe,* a job offer."

"This is a lot to give up for *maybe.*"

"It's a sacrifice, yes," he agrees. "And I hate asking you to make it. But I'm willing to, if it means I might have a chance to have a great job with a great company in the city where my amazing girlfriend is moving."

My heart wars with my brain, logic and emotions clawing and hissing over who's right and who's wrong. In the end, it's confusion who wins, and I slump even more.

"I'll see you at Christmas," he adds when I don't respond. "That's just one more month."

My mouth tugs to the side. That *is* true, but it doesn't change the fact that my Thanksgiving plans have been blown to smithereens.

And that he's going to some other girl's house for a holiday.

"Trust me," he begs after another long silence, as if he can hear my thoughts shredding me apart. "I would never do anything to hurt you."

And I know he's right.

I know he'd never hurt me.

I nod even though he can't see me, and then let out a long, slow sigh. "I trust you."

We talk for a little while longer, and eventually, the tears dry up and I'm laughing and aching with how much I miss him. We end the call with a million *I love you*'s and I feel half-assured that everything really will be okay in the end.

The other half of me feels like a woman unhinged, like I'm teetering on the edge of a dangerous cliff.

I flop back on the bed, eyes losing focus as I stare up at the ceiling.

And then, I grab my phone and group text the girls.

Change of plans. Got room for one more?

Bear

MY NAILS ARE DUG so deep into my palms, I'm about to draw blood.

These balled-up fists are all that's saving me from trashing Erin's room and this whole damn condo as she calmly, casually packs her bag for her girls' trip.

I'm not mad about the girls' trip. No, I'm happy for her. I'm happy she's getting away. I'm happy she can take a break from the trial and school and therapy. I'm happy for Ashlei, too — for her and Brandon and the whole celebration.

What I'm *not* happy about is the text that came through Erin's phone on our way home from her parents this morning, having had a very pleasant Thanksgiving dinner last night.

Hey, any word from lawyer?

From Gavin.

My jaw clenches so tight it gives me a headache as I remember those words flittering on her phone screen in the console between us as she drove, his name in bold letters above it.

It'd been all I could do to wait until we got home to discuss it.

"I'm not hanging out with him outside of therapy," Erin repeats as she folds another swimsuit and tucks it into her bag. "He's asked, but I've said no every time."

"But he's back," I say as calmly as I can. "He's back and you didn't tell me. He's back and you're friendly with each other. He's back and he's *texting you.*"

Erin sighs, pausing with her hands in her bag as her eyes meet mine. "Are we really doing this?"

"Hell fucking yes, we're doing this. Why did you keep it from me?"

"I didn't keep it from you. I planned on telling you by inviting Gavin over for dinner. With *both* of us. So you could see that while he's back, he's nothing to me."

"If he's nothing to you, then why are you talking to him at all?"

She frowns. "Okay, maybe not *nothing*."

My blood boils, but before I can scream, Erin holds up her hands.

"He's nothing like *that* — romantic or anything past a friend. Okay? I just..." She bites her lip, eyes focusing on something across the room. "I don't expect you to understand this, but Gavin is important to me. He's important to my recovery." Her eyes meet mine then. "He's part of the closure I'm seeking, as well as a very important part of my entire healing process. He was there for me, Bear. He was there when no one else was."

That makes me growl, and Erin shakes her head.

"You can be upset if you want to, but you weren't talking to me. You were pissed off and dating someone else and," she adds, pointing at me. "I'm not mad at you for that. I don't blame you. You had every right to be upset with me, and to be in love with another woman. But similarly, I had the right to be with another man, and to lean on him when I had no one else."

I'm breathing like a bull now, nostrils flaring as I try to see her side, try to calm myself.

But I simply can't.

"This is all bullshit," I spit. "Gavin, therapy, all of it. He wasn't part of your healing, Erin. He was part of the problem."

I expect those words to hit her hard, but instead, her shoulders slump, brows folding together. "Therapy is bullshit?" she repeats, shaking her head. "We're back to this?"

"You know what I mean," I say flippantly.

"No, I don't think I do. And I don't think *you* understand how therapy didn't just help me — it *saved* me. And in a lot of ways, so did Gavin. I'm sorry you hate to hear that, but it's true."

I force a long inhale, folding my arms over my chest and shaking my head over and over as I stare out her floor-to-ceiling window at the Miami skyline.

"Look, I'm glad you're perfect and you've got everything figured out in your life," she says, tossing a pair of sandals into her bag with more force than necessary. "No trauma in your life. No feelings to sort through. Absolutely no family drama at all for you, right?"

I grit my teeth. "Don't bring my family into this."

"Oh, of course not. Why would I? We never talk about them, do we?"

Her words slam into me.

"That's how it always goes," she continues. "I'm the crazy one for going to therapy, but you're completely sane not talking about your mother's abandonment, her addiction, the way that addiction spread to your older brother, how she's back now, how Clayton's relationship with her is different – will forever *be* different from yours."

I swallow the knot in my throat, still too angry to admit she might be right.

"I have to get to the airport," she says, forcefully zipping up her bag.

Her declaration snaps me back to the present moment, to the whole reason I was angry in the first place.

"I don't want you seeing him."

"Well, that's just too damn bad."

I hook her elbow when she tries to swing past me. "What would you do if this were me? What if Shawna showed up and wanted to be my *friend*?"

Erin's brows pinch together, and she shakes her head. "Are you kidding?" She rests her hand on my forearm, giving it a gentle squeeze. "I would be *happy* for you. After what happened between you two, the way things went down? I would be ecstatic for that closure for you, for that opportunity to mend a relationship that meant so much to you — even if was just platonic now."

"I don't need a relationship with her. I don't ever want to talk to her again."

"And that's *your* choice. I respect it." She shakes her head, her doe eyes searching mine. "Why can't you do the same for me?"

My jaw muscles pop, and I look away from her, trying again to see through my fury and understand what she's saying.

But I just fucking *can't*.

Erin sighs, dropping her hold on me and moving for her door again. "You can let yourself out. Just lock up before you go."

"Erin," I say, catching her elbow again.

She pauses at the door, turning to look at me with eyes that tell me more than her words that she's not just sad we're fighting.

She's disappointed.

In me.

And I wish I could be level-headed, that I could see it from her point of view, but regardless of how pissed off I am, I don't want her to leave like this.

I gently tug until she lets me pull her into my arms, and I wrap her in a fierce hug, letting out a slow breath at the way she feels in my arms, her head against my chest, the scent of her hair in my nose.

"I love you," I remind her.

"I love you, too."

I swallow as she pulls away, waiting for me to say something else. But I don't have anything to say that wouldn't upset her more — or me.

So I say nothing at all.

She leaves.

And I punch a hole through her wall.

Skyler

"SHOT SKI! SHOT SKI! *Shot ski! Shot ski!"*

You would think it's Spring Break instead of a family holiday weekend by the amount of twenty-something year olds gathered around the pool at *La Rose Roja Resort*. The girls and I were all pleasantly surprised to find it so packed and happening when we arrived yesterday, the resort employees handing us our first fruity cocktails.

And the party has raged on ever since.

As to be expected, we nearly blacked out on our first night, not even bothering to get all dolled up to go out. We just got to our penthouse, freaked the fuck out over what Brandon had set up for us, and then promptly changed into our swimsuits and went down to the pool party.

After that, things got a little fuzzy.

A few things I remember...

One, Jess dancing on the bar during a wet t-shirt contest and winning easily when she decided the wet t-shirt was just getting in the way, so she stripped it up over her head.

Two, Cassie and Ashlei making a giant, teetering pyramid out of beer cans, stealing empties from every guy and girl alike to add to their masterpiece. They let out a victorious cheer when it finally got so big that it crashed to the ground and half of it ended up in the pool.

Three, Erin letting loose more than I'd seen her since *maybe* my freshman year of college. She took shots and danced in the pool, and even played along with some guy who's here for a bachelor party and needed to get a girl to ride around on his shoulders to knock an item off their scavenger hunt list.

And four — yet another text from Kip lighting up my phone, haunting me even through my buzzed haze.

Where are you?

Maybe it's self-preservation, how I've ignored every message from him since that night he called me to apologize. He told me to hold onto him, but inside, I know I have to do the opposite.

I have to let him go.

So I've been focusing on school, on Kappa Kappa Beta, on my new Grand Little, on my meetings with the guidance counselor to figure out where I'm going after graduation.

I've ignored every call, every *how are you, I miss you, are you okay, where are you, please call me* that he's sent.

Being out of the country with my best friends has made it easier to do so — well, as easy as letting Kip Jackson go can be, at least.

Which is to say, it's slightly less torturous.

Now, it's day two of our trip, and after a successful morning brunch, afternoon of relaxing by the pool, and evening of massages — we're back for round two, the sun setting over the resort, bass thumping from the DJ's booth perched over the pool.

Erin, Cassie, and Jess have a shot ski in their hands — an old wooden ski painted with the resort's colors and fitted with shot-glass-sized holes that now host a full mouthful of tequila. It takes precision to get the shots lined up with each of their mouths and to pour them down without spilling all over someone, but they pull it off — to the roaring approval of the crowd.

When they finish, Erin holds the ski over her head in victory, and then someone at the resort is taking it from her and carrying it to the back to wash it and no doubt line it up for the next victims.

"I'm drunk," Cassie slurs, slinging her arm around my neck.

"Easy, Little — it's only nine."

"Come dance with me," she says instead of acknowledging how young the night is, but I oblige her, letting her take my hand and drag me to the shallow end of the pool right in front of the DJ.

Everything is warped and blurry, not because I'm drunk, but because that's just the state of being I've existed in since Kip and I fought last semester. It's like being half-frozen, half-numb, like a dream where you're underwater and try to punch something but can't.

My hands are up in the air, hips swaying to the rhythm, eyes closed and lights coloring my eyelids green and blue and pink and purple as we dance.

But inside, I'm sitting alone in a dark room, staring at the ceiling.

Existing.

Cassie finally decides she needs water, and we make our way through the crowd and over to the VIP booth that comes with our penthouse rental. It's got three massive day beds and two dedicated servers to bring us alcohol or food — or water, which is very much needed in this moment.

Jess and Ashlei are kicked back on one of the day beds, lost in conversation, and Erin is somewhere still dancing in the pool when Cassie and I slip through the roped-off entryway.

I can't help but smile at the sight of Ashlei in her all-white bikini, the gold sash across her chest reading BRIDE-TO-BE — except *to be* is scratched out and ALREADY is written in Sharpie above it. Even with her arm in a sling, she's radiant, glowing only the way a new bride can.

Bride.

She's *married*.

As if the thought has just finally sunk in, I wrap her in a fierce hug as soon as I'm inside our little area, and she giggles, squeezing me in return.

"You're married," I whisper in her ear.

"I know. How crazy is this?"

"Insanely crazy. Also, insanely amazing."

She nods when I pull back, her eyes glossy. "I love that rich bastard."

I bark out a laugh. "I know."

"Oh, here," Jess says when I'm standing again. She tosses my phone to me before I'm prepared to catch it. It bobbles a little in my hand before I grip it tight. "That thing has been blowing up."

I frown, looking at the dozen missed call requests on the screen. They're from a number I don't recognize, an area code I've never seen before.

I chew my cheek, wondering if it's Kip trying any means necessary to get ahold of me. I can't think of anyone else it would be.

"Just call him back," Erin says from over my shoulder. I jump, not realizing she had joined us, and she gives me a knowing smile as she squeezes my arm. "Hear him out. Even if your choice is still the same and you think it's over, you at least owe it to him to put him out of his misery and make sure *he* knows that's your decision, too."

My mouth tugs to the side, stomach roiling at the thought of ever saying those words, at ever officially admitting that we're done. But I nod, letting her know I hear her.

And then I grab my bag and tell the girls I'll be back in a bit, disappearing through the hotel lobby doors.

It's a quiet ride up the elevator, though I can still hear the music thumping on when I make it to our suite. It's absolutely massive, three bedrooms and a huge sitting area finessed with the finest furniture and interior design. There's a fireplace and an infinity plunge pool that has the illusion of hanging off the deck and over the ocean below, as well as an expansive balcony, and a stacked minibar that we've more than taken advantage of.

I slip my bag off my shoulder, laying a towel out on one of the daybeds on the balcony before I pull up the missed call notifications on my phone. I almost regret setting up international calls and texts with my service provider for this trip, but I wanted to make sure I was available in case my parents needed me.

Or maybe, deep down, I *wanted* Kip to call.

I sigh at the absolute mess I am before tapping the number on the screen to call it back. I tap the button to put it on speakerphone next, leaning back against the plush pillows and waiting as it rings, my eyes on the last rays of sun touching the beach.

"Where the hell *are* you?"

The voice that answers is not what I expected. Female, angry, and... and... *familiar*.

"Who is this?"

"Natalia."

I snap upright, eyes narrowing. "You have a lot of fucking nerve to call me."

"Yeah, well, you can tell me how much you hate me later. Right now, I need you to tell me where you fucking are. Actually, I need you to answer Kip and tell *him* where you are."

"How about I hang up and you go fuck yourself?"

I'm about to do just that when she screams, "Wait!"

I pause with my finger over the red button that will end the call.

"Just... look. I know you hate me."

"I don't hate you. Hating you would require that I give a shit about you in some way, and I don't," I clarify.

"Fine. But just... please. *Please* call Kip and talk to him. He's worried sick about you."

I swallow. "And you would know this how?"

"Oh, don't worry — he's not talking to me anymore than he has to to wrap up the show," she says with a scoff. "So, you won. If that's what you're wondering."

"I never knew I was in a fight."

"That's a lie and you know it."

"And you're a *bitch* and you know it."

There's a pause, then a sigh. "Maybe. Or maybe I just know what I want and have learned in my short life that sometimes you've got to do some fucked-up things to get what you deserve."

I shake my head.

"Look, I didn't call to fight you. I called to... to... I don't know, try to talk some sense into you, or at least plead to whatever part of you still cares about Kip."

"Don't you dare question my feelings for him."

"Well, he's fucking sick over you. He's not eating, barely sleeping, and tonight is the premier and he's nowhere to be found."

I blink, my heart stopping dead before kicking back with a violent thump in my chest. "It's premier night?"

"Yes. And not just for the cast — for *everyone*. There's going to be a packed theater. Professors, students, even some well-known indie film producers. It's a big deal,

Skyler, and this series is good enough that Kip should be entering it into film festivals. But he hates it. He hates *himself* for how he hurt you when he was making it. It's tainted."

"Not just by me," I seethe. "And you know damn well if it's anyone's fault, her name starts with an N."

"I'm just asking you to call him."

"And I'm telling you that I don't owe you a single damn thing. You say you did what you thought you needed to do to get what you want? Well, let me tell you this. I saw talent that day you auditioned. I saw a sweet, kind, humble girl who deserved success. But the more I got to know you, the more games you played, the more I realized you're nothing but a snot-nosed brat too big for her britches, an entitled little girl who thinks she's owed the world before having to work for it. You will burn more bridges than you can build if you keep this up. So, from one woman to another, drop the games and the manipulation and *work* for what's important to you." I pause. "You already had the gig. You didn't need to have the man."

"But the man was a tie to my dreams."

"Get your dreams on your own."

I hang up before she can answer, and nearly throw my phone but refrain. I do grip it so hard the screen protector cracks, though, and then I force a breath, dropping it to the side and flopping back on the daybed.

The sun has set now, the moon sliding in to take its place, and I stare up at the navy and purple sky with my heart racing.

Racing, and aching, and bleeding out.

I close my eyes, holding back the tears I feel burning behind my lids.

Slowly, I peel myself up again, reach for my phone, and pull up Kip's contact.

I'm okay. I'm in Mexico for Ashlei's bachelorette. Long story.

I pause, not yet sending it as I debate what to say next.

Go enjoy the premier — you've earned it.

Another pause, and then I add.

I'm so proud of you.

I send it before I can overthink it.

The little bubbles letting me know he's typing appear in an instant, then disappear, then appear again, then disappear.

His heart is just as much at war as mine.

Finally, one simple text comes through.

Thank you.

For texting him back, for telling him where I am, for saying that I'm proud of him? I don't know which.

I love you, I type out, the blinking cursor at the end of the sentence my only point of focus.

But I delete the words instead of sending them, and then I head back downstairs to the party, leaving my phone in the room for the rest of the night.

Bear

A LOW GROWL RIPS out of me as I thrust the barbell up again, chest puffing, lips flat as I force myself to keep breathing through the reps.

Seven.

Eight.

My muscles quake in protest, but I grit through the pain, willing my mental capability to be stronger than my physical as I thrust the bar up again.

Nine.

"Come on, one more," Giselle says, standing over me with her fingertips under the bar like she could actually help me if I needed it.

She's a buck thirty soaking wet, and I'm benching two-hundred-and-fifty pounds.

With all the effort I have left, I grunt and shove the bar away from my chest, hooking it on the rack as soon as I've extended my elbows to get the full lift.

A few guys around the gym murmur various encouragements to me as I sit up, mopping my forehead with my towel. They say *damn, bro* and *nice* and *yes, sir* as Giselle walks around the bench to face me, holding up her hand for a high five with a proud grin on her face.

I slap her hand. "Why are you looking at me like *you're* the trainer?"

"For that little show, I was."

I try to smile, but it comes up short. I haven't had a full smile since Thanksgiving, since before I found out Gavin was back in town and Erin was talking to him.

And that she didn't tell me.

The fact that she left town right after to go on Ashlei's bachelorette didn't help. She's texted me a few times checking in, but I know she's hanging with her sisters and I don't *want* her to be glued to her phone.

I just wish she hadn't left after a fight like that.

Planting weight onto my feet, I push off from where I'm seated on the bench and over to the barbell in front of the mirror. I start loading it up, preparing for a heavy deadlift when Giselle touches my shoulder.

"Hey, don't you think we've pushed it hard enough for today?"

I shake my head without looking at her. "I need the release."

"Well, what you *don't* need is an injury."

"I'm fine."

"Maybe so," she says, stepping in front of me to block me from putting more weight on the bar. "But as your boss, I'm calling it."

"You're not my boss," I say, arching a brow.

"Your superior, whatever." She waves her hand, and then when her arms fold over her chest again, she frowns. "Come on. Let's hit the sauna. You can sweat it out."

I hang my hands on my hips, body aching and so tired I know the possibility of injuring myself is actually higher than I want to admit.

"Sauna," Giselle says, snapping her fingers in front of my face. "Now."

I sigh, but relent, tossing my towel over my shoulder and cleaning up our space before I let her lead the way.

The gym is quiet for a Saturday evening, likely because most people are still spending time with their families. I'm thankful Giselle was down for a training session. I needed to get out of my house, out of my head.

We both sigh in relief when we take a seat on the warm wood in the sauna, the dark room already soothing us — body and soul. Hot rocks cook in the middle of the room, steam rising all around us, and we nod to the only other two people in with us — two girls who look fresh off a swim in the lap pool.

"God, I'm going to be so sore tomorrow," Giselle groans, leaning back to balance her elbows on the wood behind her. She rolls her shoulders, hissing. "I know leg day is the worst, but upper body day sucks, too."

The corner of my mouth lifts. "I loved it."

"Yeah, well, you're a masochist," she says, eyeing me for a second before her attention is back on the rocks. "Besides, sounds like you were blowing off some steam. There's always more energy when you're pissed off."

I clench my jaw, but don't reply.

"What's going on?" Giselle asks.

The swimmers must think we want privacy, because they give us a little nod and smile before they see themselves out, and then it's just the two of us.

I sigh. "I don't really want to talk about it."

"Come on. Maybe I can help. Besides, I'm nosy and the workplace drama has been unfortunately dry lately. Give me something."

I shake my head on another fake smile. "It's nothing, really. Just... Erin and I got into a little disagreement before she left for her trip."

"Uh-oh. What'd you do?"

I actually chuckle at that. "Overreact, most likely. I don't know. Her ex is back in town, and he goes to therapy with her, and they've been talking. I saw a text come through from him and I just... I lost it."

"She didn't tell you he was back?"

I shake my head, and Giselle whistles, massaging the side of her neck for a moment.

"Well, I'd be upset, too."

"They're just friends," I say with confidence — which is funny, considering I didn't want to hear it when Erin told me that same thing.

"Friends, with an ex?" She shakes her head. "I don't know if that's possible."

"With them, I think it is. They have a complicated relationship, one that's tied up in a lot more than just romance." I frown. "I think he's been an important part of her recovery."

"Recovery?"

That makes my throat go dry, and I shake my head. "It's not my story to tell. Just... I guess what I'm saying is that talking to you about it now, I realize I trust her, and I'm not threatened by him. But I certainly didn't act that way originally. And she said some things, some *true* things, but still... they stung."

"Like?"

"Like calling me out on the fact that I have a lot of family shit in my life that I've never properly dealt with, that I laugh at her going to therapy when in reality I probably need it, too."

"This is your therapy," Giselle says simply, and when I turn to look at her, it's with a gaze of wonder.

Because she just nailed what I have been trying to tell Erin forever, I just never knew how.

"I mean, you come here to be silent, to sit with your thoughts, to work through frustrations. And from what you've told me, it's always been this way, yeah?"

I nod. "Yes."

She shrugs. "Not everyone has to talk about what's happened to them. Sometimes, we handle trauma by working through it physically, overcoming it the same way we overcome a challenge in the gym."

I watch her for longer than appropriate.

"What?" she asks on a smile.

"I just... yes. That's exactly it."

She looks at her nails before polishing them on her sports bra. "I know. I'm good."

I smirk, relaxing a little bit and digesting her words as silence falls between us. After a long while, Giselle clears her throat, wiping at a bead of sweat rolling down her neck.

"You know," she says softly, tentatively. "There are other ways to find that release you need."

My heart halts in my chest.

"I could help," she continues, and to my absolute horror, she scoots a little closer, angles her body toward mine, and touches my knee with one hand. Her eyes find mine, and where I hope she can read the warning in my gaze, I find only heat and lust in hers as she slides her hand up my thigh, higher and higher. "No one would have to know."

"Giselle..."

Her smile turns wicked when I say her name, and unabashedly, she runs her hand up even more, wrapping around my cock before I can stop her.

I jerk away quickly, grabbing her wrist with more force than necessary and keeping hold of it as she giggles and bites her lip.

"You want to take control?" she asks. "I like that."

"Giselle," I say again, this time more firm. "This is inappropriate."

Her smile wanes, and she blinks a few times before ripping her arm out of my grasp. "Oh, *calm down*. It's not that serious." She rolls her eyes. "It's just a little fun. And trust me — you're in need of it."

"I have a girlfriend."

"And I went to bat for you so you could have an extra-long weekend to take said girlfriend home to Pittsburgh, remember?" she challenges, arching a brow at me. "Erin is out of town. She also doesn't know me and never has to find out." Her gaze falls to my lap. "And I don't know if you've noticed, but you're hard as fucking tungsten right now."

"I would never cheat on her," I clip. "I would never hurt her like that. And if you're implying that I somehow owe you for what you did for me, then you should have explained those terms before you assumed I'd agree to them."

Giselle scoffs, her little mouth falling open as she shakes her head and watches me with narrowing eyes. She closes her lips together, rolls them, and then, like she was under some sort of spell, all the anger disappears. She smiles, genuine and calm, and stands up.

"No worries, it was just a miscommunication." She throws her towel over her shoulder before grabbing her gym bag from the floor. "I'm going to shower and head out. See you Monday?"

She doesn't wait for me to answer before she leaves me alone in the sauna, and as soon as she does, I bark out a curse, elbows coming to my knees as I dig the heels of my hands into my eyeballs.

The heat soaks into my skin.

And along with it — the most severe doubt I've ever felt in my life.

Every ounce of trust I had for Giselle has been vanquished. What if she didn't mean what she said about me starting my own business, about me having the chops to have my own company? Was she just spitting that nonsense to try to get close to me?

To try to fuck me?

I grimace, cursing again as I kick back in my seat.

And Erin...

What if she meant what she said to me in the spring, that she didn't have anything to give me? Did I push her? Did I ask too much?

What if she rushed into this because she felt like she had to?

What if she's not ready?

I swallow, thinking of how I acted when I saw that text, the jealous rage that consumed me.

What if *I'm* not ready?

Thought after thought pummels me like fists to a speed bag, and I take every blow harder than the last until I can't take it any longer. My fists ball, legs quake, lungs seize up as they try to calm me with fresh air.

But it's no use.

I might be able to work out my physical frustrations, but there's no escaping this hell that lives inside my head.

I grab my duffle bag and sling it over my shoulder, shoving through the sauna doors and barreling out of the gym.

And I drive straight to the office.

Skyler

"JESUS SAID SUNDAY IS the day of rest, y'all," Erin tries, popping a grape into her mouth while we lounge by our plunge pool.

"And we *are* resting. Until..." Jess looks at her watch. "About two hours from now, in which case we will be transitioning into pre-gaming and then full-on party mode."

Erin shakes her head. "My liver will never recover from this trip."

"How often is it that your best friend gets married?" Cassie remarks.

"It better only be once for this bestie," Ashlei says, holding up her finger. "Because if I lose a man this fine, just hang me up to dry, y'all, I'm done."

We all laugh and raise our water bottles in a cheers before chugging — which may very well be our most important chug of the day. If we're going to hit up the pool party again tonight, we'll need all the hydration we can get.

Electronic dance music softly thumps up to our room from the pool deck below, and we tap our feet along to the beat as we soak in the sun's rays. Ashlei has taken off her sling to avoid tan lines, and she and Cassie are reminiscing on the night before as Erin flips through a textbook — one we tried to get her to leave behind, but to no avail.

That girl is nothing if not serious about law school.

Jess and I are quiet for a while, just enjoying the breeze and the nice weather and the music, and then I notice her looking at her phone. She sighs, flipping between two photos. I lean in a little closer and chuckle when I see one is of her and Kade, and the other is her and Jarrett.

"Sadist," I tease.

She groans, closing her screen and throwing her phone onto the table face down. "I know, I know. I can't stop."

"I don't think swiping between pictures is going to make the answer come to you."

"No, probably not. But they *are* nice to look at."

I offer a sympathetic smile. "How are you feeling? After getting away and clearing your head a bit."

Jess is silent for a long pause. "Sick. Absolutely sick."

"Because you still don't know?"

"Because I think I *do* know, and somehow that makes it even worse."

I frown. "How so?"

Jess's maple eyes meet mine. "I have to hurt one of them, Skyler. I've already hurt them *both*." She shakes her head. "I don't deserve either of them after the way I've played them back and forth under the guise of needing time, needing space, needing... whatever. The truth is I fucked Kade and then fucked his brother two weeks later." Her eyes water. "I'm the most awful human to ever walk the face of the Earth."

"You love them," I say, sitting up. "And they both knew what they were getting into. If either of them was against it, *really* against it, they would have told you to kick rocks already."

"*That's* what I deserve."

"Well, love makes us do some crazy shit," I say with a laugh. "I mean, come on — this group is nothing if not proof of that."

Jess nods. "They really love me. And I really do love *them*." She swallows. "But like Cassie said — I can't have them both."

"No, you can't."

There's a knock at our suite door, and Cassie pops up, already jogging inside. "Room service is here!"

Jess closes her eyes and sinks down into her lounge even more, ignoring the call for food. "It's going to hurt him so bad. It's going to *kill* me."

"It's going to hurt *who* so bad?" I ask.

Jess sighs, opening her mouth to answer me, but then her eyes go wide as basketballs at something behind me.

I whip around, scared there's a bug or a monster or a fucking tsunami.

Instead, I find Kip.

My jaw drops as he walks onto the balcony with Cassie trailing behind him, her face just as shocked as mine. He looks like absolute shit — wearing what I can only assume is the tux he wore to the premier the night before, a five o'clock shadow on his jaw, his eyes red and puffy.

In his hand is a bouquet of flowers.

"What are you doing here?" I breathe.

Kip's eyes search mine, a thick swallow bobbing his Adam's apple before he shrugs. "I came to fight and win my girl back."

Jess rolls her lips together and smacks my arm as Cassie, Ashlei, and Erin all do a miserable job of hiding their collective sighs at his declaration.

"Actually," he clarifies. "I came to grovel, and plead, and put all my chips on the table, to pray like hell my measly pair of deuces is enough." He takes a confident step toward me. "Pray that *I* am enough."

My heart squeezes in my chest, tears pricking my eyes.

"I am sick without you, Skyler. I could say my entire world has been flipped upside down, but the truth is that *you* are my world. The show, school, whatever future career I might have — none of it matters without you." He swallows. "You are my dream. And without you, life is just... sleep deprivation. Punishment. Unrelenting torture."

"Kip..."

"I am so sorry for hurting you, for not listening to you, for having my head so far up my ass I couldn't see my mistakes. Please," he begs, his own eyes watering, nose flaring. "Please forgive me. Please tell me you'll give me another chance. I swear I won't waste it. I swear, if you let me, I'll spend the rest of my life making sure you know you are my everything."

"If you don't kiss him, I will!" Jess says, shoving me until I have no choice but to either tumble out of the daybed onto my face or stand. I choose the latter, and Kip smirks at Jess before his eyes are on mine again.

Sincere and more apologetic than I've ever seen.

And I hate myself for putting him through this, for making him so sick he thought he could ever truly lose me.

As if I haven't been his since the moment I laid eyes on his stupid glasses and his stupid perfect smile.

I inhale, exhale, and slowly make my way over to where he stands.

But I don't say a word.

I just nod.

In the next breath, I'm swept into his arms, and then I'm spinning, my hair flying behind me as the girls laugh and cheer. I don't have the chance to laugh, though — because Kip captures my mouth with his, holding me to him in a beautiful, long-overdue kiss.

"I will never hurt you again," he swears against my lips. "I'm so sorry, Skyler. I'm so fucking sorry."

"I'm sorry, too," I breathe into him.

"You have nothing to be sorry for."

"Sure, I do. I put you through more torture than you deserve. I didn't accept your apology."

"Well, I didn't apologize correctly. I was blinded... I couldn't see your point of view, and I'm sorry for that."

"Okay, okay," Jess says, making a gagging notion with her finger, tongue sticking out. "He's sorry, you're sorry, we all get it. Now, can you two get out of here and go fuck already?"

I cover my laugh by burying my face in Kip's chest, peeking up at him. "I... I love you, and I'm so happy you came all this way but... I'm here with the girls. It's Ashlei's bachelorette."

"I know, I know, and I don't want to take you from them. I just had to see you." He sweeps my hair from my face, and I lean into his palm as he says, "I had to know you were okay. That *we* were okay."

"We are," I promise.

"Skyler, I swear to God, if you don't have that man naked in the next ten minutes," Jess warns.

I spin in Kip's arms, throwing my hands up. "But we're going out!"

"*We* are going out," Ashlei corrects, pointing to the four of them and purposefully leaving me out. "*You* are getting railed." She pauses. "Sorry, Kip."

He throws his hands up with a smile.

"If you still have energy after, come join us," Erin says.

I bite my lip, looking at all of them. "Are you sure? I don't—"

"GO!" they all yell in unison.

And then I'm swept up again and carried out of the suite.

My feet don't hit the ground again until I'm halfway across the resort in Kip's room. It's much smaller than the penthouse suite Brandon booked us, but I couldn't care less as I immediately slip my hands under Kip's suit jacket and shove the fabric back over his wide shoulders.

"Help," I pant against his lips, trying unsuccessfully again to strip him.

Kip chuckles, shrugging out of his jacket and unfastening his tie. "Are you sure you don't want to talk for a while? We haven't—"

"Later."

I don't wait for him to unbutton his dress shirt. Instead, I grab at the collar with both hands and then rip them in opposite directions, sending the first two buttons skittering to the floor. Kip roars a laugh at that, and then helps me rip it the rest of the way because two buttons was all I got with all my might.

I laugh then, too, before Kip steals my breath with a passionate, demanding kiss — one that has me pressing up on my toes for more as he tugs at the string of my bikini top. It falls loose, dangling from the string wrapped around my neck, and Kip palms my breasts with a groan that makes me ache and clench and tingle.

"*Fuck*, it's been so long..." he husks, pressing his forehead to mine and looking down to appreciate the view of what his hands are doing to me.

I capture his mouth again just as my fingers start fumbling with the button and zipper of his pants, and in-between bruising kisses and lip biting, I manage to undo them, yanking as hard as I can to get them down over his ass.

Kip shoves them the rest of the way down, hopping a little as he frees one leg and then the other. I'm in his arms in the next instant, and then I'm falling into the lush comforter, pillows making a soft *whoosh* when I collapse into them.

It's a glorious sight to behold, Kip watching me from the foot of the bed as he slowly strips his boxer briefs down. His length springs free of them, making me bite my lip, and when he palms that impressive cock with his heated gaze on me, I spread my knees, leaning up on one elbow as I slowly slide my other hand down my exposed breast, my navel, and dive beneath the small triangle fabric of my bikini bottoms.

"Have you touched yourself thinking about me?" Kip asks, his eyes on where my fingers move under the swimsuit.

"Only every night."

He closes his eyes on a hot breath, stroking himself as his cock twitches at my words. "Me too. I've come so many nights thinking about you, about how fucking tight you are, how perfectly you fit around me."

"Why don't you remind me what that feels like?"

"Soon," he promises, and then he's prowling onto the bed, climbing between my legs.

His shoulder hits the bottom of one of my legs and then the other, until my knees are spread even farther, and he nips my fingers through the fabric of my bottoms.

"My turn," he says, and I remove my fingers just in time for him to pull at the string over my left hip, then the one over my right, the fabric falling away like silk and leaving my bare pussy right in his face.

Kip growls, carefully trailing his middle finger from my clit down through my slick lips as I tremble and quake.

"Perfect," he mutters, shaking his head and sliding his finger up again. He circles my clit in a swift motion that makes my legs convulse, and then that finger slides down again, entering me with a shock between pleasure and the pain that comes with having been empty for so long. I arch into the touch, and Kip smirks, kissing my inner thigh. "So goddamn perfect."

That featherlight kiss on my thigh turns into a tongue gliding along the seam where my leg meets my pelvis, and then he's sucking and biting and teasing his way to where I want him most, his finger slowly moving inside me and making me writhe.

It's like a dream and the most alert awakening of my life all at once. My head is fuzzy, focus distant, as if I'm both experiencing and watching it happen from above. At the same time, every nerve in my body is sensitive and buzzing, coming alive at the faintest touch from this man.

This man whom I've missed.

This man who traveled halfway across the world to get me back.

This man whom I love.

This man I can't live without.

Kip's mouth finally descends on my clit as he slips another finger inside me, and I cry out at the warmth, the pressure, the all-encompassing feeling of being connected again. When he groans and sweeps his tongue long, hot, and flat over my sensitive nerves, I buck into the touch, twisting my fists in the sheets and grinding my hips.

He knows just how to lick me, how to tease me, how to move his fingers inside me along with the rhythm of his tongue. He knows to move slow at first, exaggerating the movements, and then to pick up speed as my breath hitches, my hips moving of their own accord as I reach for my climax.

And he knows just where to press a third finger at the sensitive opening below where his other two are now, giving me a shock of forbidden pleasure. He glances up at me, his tongue still sweeping, eyes asking me for permission.

"Yes," I breathe, pleading, and he slicks his finger through my desire before gently, slowly, inching it inside my ass.

I cry out, seeing stars, and then he's sucking on my clit and moving his fingers inside me in a slow, hypnotizing rhythm that pushes me closer and closer to my release with every pump. The finger inside my ass is just barely in there, barely moving, but it's pushing all the sensitive, bundled-up nerves in just the right way.

And with his name barreling off my lips, I fly apart.

I know if anyone is in the rooms around us, they hear every moan as I find my release, tearing at the sheets with my nails and arching my back and riding out every blissful wave. Kip smirks against my clit before blowing a gentle *shhhh* on it that only makes me convulse harder.

I come for longer than possible — at least that's how it feels — and when I'm done, everything falls lax, my legs opening wide, arms flopping out, sweat-sheened skin sticking to the cool sheets.

Kip kisses my clit gently, but it still makes all my limbs shutter, and he slowly makes his way up to capture my mouth with his.

"That was fucking hot," he says, smirking.

"Your turn," is my only response before I'm flipping us over, pinning him to the sheets as I make my way down his body, kiss by kiss, on shaky, sated limbs.

"Wait," he says, halting me before I can reach the promise land.

I look up at him with a pout that makes him chuckle, but he pulls me back up until I'm straddling him, and he kisses me long and hard.

"I want these lips around my cock," he says, biting my bottom one to emphasize. "But not before I fill that beautiful pussy I just had the pleasure of tasting."

I moan when he kisses me hard again, our teeth clashing, but I don't have time to tell him how much I love his dirty talk before my hips are lifted, and he's situated at my entrance, and then he grabs my ass and guides me down over him, flexing his hips as I swallow him whole.

We both cry out at the sensation, at him stretching me and filling me so fast it steals both our breaths. I sit there for a long moment, him completely inside me, our breaths heavy and hot between us as we soak in the way it feels.

And then he spanks my ass, lifts me, and slams into me again.

A long curse leaves his lips, and he arches back, eyes squeezing closed as I press my hands into his chest and take control. I ride him slow at first, letting him hit deep and feel every inch of me opening for him. But after every thrust, I pick up the pace just a little, just enough to have him biting his lip and groaning and peeling his heavy eyelids open to watch my breasts swell above him or to look down at where his cock disappears inside me.

I know without him telling me that he's not going to last long — not after months of being apart, after just spending so much time going down on me, after being inside me again with my tits bouncing in his face.

I ride him a little faster, moving my hips just like I know he loves, tucking my pelvis anytime I sit fully down so I can take him as much inside me as possible. And when he groans loud and heavy, his hands gripping my hips hard enough to leave a mark, I know he's close enough.

I hop off him without warning, which makes his eyes shoot open wide, a desperate *no* almost flowing off his lips.

But before he can say it, I flip around, putting my pussy in his face again as I take his cock deep in my throat.

"Oh *fuck*, Sky," he curses, and I bob my head up and down, taking advantage of the angle that lets his cock curve into my throat just right.

I hold myself steady with one hand and slide the other down over his balls, rubbing them in time with my mouth. Then, I press my index finger just between his ball and his ass, finding that sensitive spot and massaging it as I deep throat him again.

And that does it.

With a curse, Kip holds my head down and spills into my throat, his body pulsing and trembling under me as he releases. I swallow every last drop, soaking in the way it feels to make this man fall apart from my touch alone.

Kip shutters when he's fully spent, and then just like I did, he falls lax, his breaths tickling my pussy as he comes down. I swirl my tongue around him one last time before I release, and then I carefully crawl off of him, sitting on one hip and looking back at him with a grin before wiping the corners of my mouth with my thumb.

He shakes his head. "You wicked little girl," he growls.

And then he pulls me back up the bed, his mouth finding mine, and we slip easily into round two.

We finally hit a point where we need water, and food, and rest.

Kip orders us far too much from room service, and when it arrives, we have a buffet in bed.

And I beg him to play the web series for me.

It's surreal, seeing our story brought to life on the screen, and past the gut reaction the first time Natalia's face shows, I don't even feel animosity toward her. It's like I slip in so easily that I feel like it's me, not her, and it's Kip, not the actor playing him. It's *our* story.

She'll never be able to taint that.

We're on episode three, me sucking on a chocolate milkshake while Kip draws lazy circles on my hip between pressing gentle kisses there, when my phone buzzes loud on the bedside table.

My breath hitches in my chest at the simple text on the screen.

S.O.S. Get down here. Now!

Jess.

Cassie

I SLAM BACK ANOTHER shot of tequila.

I've lost count which one I'm on.

All I know is that I don't even need the salt or the lime anymore. It doesn't burn, it doesn't sting, it just makes me let out a victorious cheer and slam my hand on the bar, ready for another.

"Ooohkay," Ashlei says, peeling me away before I have the chance to get the bartender's attention. The girls I just took the shot with are high-fiving me as Ashlei steals me from them — they're a bachelorette party, too, from New York. "Maybe we hold off on another shot for a while."

"But I want another one," I pout.

"I know you do, but let's give that one time to set in first, mmkay?"

I wave her off, shrugging free of her grasp before I blow a breath through flat lips. "*Fine*. But then I'm going to dance."

"Dancing we can do," Ashlei says, and she leads me down into the pool, the water warm and pleasant as we join the other dancing bodies right in front of the DJ booth.

The music is loud and energetic, bass thumping through me as the lights sway above us and reflect off the water, too. I throw my hands up and move my hips, enjoying the buzz.

Or, at least, trying to.

Under that joy and fun is a thick layer of slimy anger holding on for dear life and refusing to let go.

Kip showing up to surprise Skyler was the sweetest thing I've ever seen. It reminded me of something out of a movie, and the way he looked at her, the way he flew hundreds of miles without sleeping because he was so sick at the thought of losing her...

It makes my stomach hurt.

Because it's beautiful.

And because I want it to be Adam who showed up like that.

I want it to be him who surprised me, who said he couldn't wait to leave Baltimore after the Thanksgiving meeting, couldn't stand to be away from me any longer. I want it to be the two of us holed up in a room somewhere in the resort, making love for hours. I want it to be me wrapped up in my guy's arms, smitten from the fact that he flew all the way here just to find me, just to have me and remind me that it's us against the world.

Instead, I've had a string of measly text messages that make my blood boil.

We barely talked on Thanksgiving, save for the early call he made to wish me a happy holiday. We watched part of the Macy's Day Parade together before he said he had to go, and my gut soured at the sound of Chandler's voice in the background of that call.

It shouldn't have upset me. He said all the right things, assured me everything was okay, and I *knew* he was doing it for us. He wanted a job in the same city where I would go to school so we wouldn't have to be apart any longer.

But he was willing to sacrifice being with me to do it.

And I hate that fact.

I hate that he didn't say no to Chandler, that he didn't say he could find a different job. As selfish as it sounds, because I *know* Simmons is an amazing company he'd be lucky to work for, I just don't want to have to share him.

Not even like this.

Perhaps what's driven me past sad to angry is how he hasn't called since then, nor has he been attentive over texts. Sure, I'm with my girls and want to be present to celebrate Ashlei, but when my texts go unanswered for hours only to get a *sorry, it's really busy over here, but I miss you so much and I think I've got this job in the bag!*

Well...

It just hurts.

And maybe it's the alcohol swimming in my body, the music thumping through my soul, and the hopeless romantic still swooning after what Kip did — but I'm sad and lonely and pissed off.

The more the night goes on, the more I fear that may be the most dangerous combination of emotions.

"I want another shot," I tell Ashlei, and I don't wait for her before I'm making a beeline through the crowd, back to the stairs that exit the pool.

She chases after me, catching my elbow just as I hit the bar.

"I don't think that's a good idea."

I shrug her off. "I'm fine. You want one?"

Ashlei frowns. "No. And I don't want *you* to take one, either."

"Come *on*, Lei. Loosen up! This is your bachelorette party and I feel like you've been the most tame of all of us."

Lei frowns, and then her eyes are scanning the crowd.

I have no doubt she's looking for Erin, or Jess, or both of them for backup, so I make my move before she can stop me.

"Two tequila shots," I tell the same bartender who has been helping me all night, and he smiles, shaking his head before he pours them up.

"Be careful, señorita," he warns.

I wink at him, taking the shots and fully preparing to take both, but then a warm hand wraps around me from behind.

"Looks like you could use some help with one of those."

The voice is deep and seductive, the words whispered into the shell of my ear as I'm pulled against a rock-hard body. For a moment, I let myself imagine it's Adam, that he's come to apologize, to tell me he hated being away from me so badly he couldn't stand another minute apart, to dance with his girl and take her back to his room and...

I sway my hips against the stranger in time with the music, letting my head drop back against his chest. I feel his lips smirk against my neck as his hands find my waist, and he moves with me, taking the weight of me as the alcohol sets in even more.

I'm dizzy, the world spinning, my legs barely holding me up anymore. But it feels so *good* to be touched, to be held, to have warm arms wrapped around me and warm breath touching my skin.

The stranger trails his hand down my arm, grabbing one of the shots from me before he carefully, slowly spins me around to face him. Or maybe he spun me quickly and I was just moving in slow motion, because some of my shot sloshes out of the glass, and he laughs, steadying me with a, "Whoa, there."

I smile, peering through the drunken haze to study his face.

He's absolutely gorgeous.

His dark blond hair is wet from the pool, sticking up this way and that, his skin a little red from being in the sun. He's got a goofy, charming sort of smile, a broad jaw, a little dent in his nose like he maybe got into a fight once and took a blow he never recovered from.

He's still holding my hip with one hand, his other wrapped around the shot glass, and he clinks it to mine before throwing his back.

I know I shouldn't do it.

I know I'm well past my limit.

But I throw mine back, anyway, this time grimacing and fighting down the roil of my stomach that immediately comes once I've swallowed.

The guy smirks at me, taking both our empty glasses and setting them on the counter.

Then his hands are on my hips again.

And his eyes are searching mine.

And I press up on my toes, launch myself into his arms, wrap my hands around his neck...

And kiss him.

He groans, sliding his hands around my hips to palm my ass and pull me more into him as I thread my hands through his hair. He smells like sunscreen and chlorine and tequila, his lips foreign, not moving the way they should with mine, his hands too aggressive, his hair not the right texture.

And when he slides one of his hands beneath my swimsuit to grab my bare ass and squeeze, my eyes shoot open and I realize what I've done.

I press my hands into his chest and shove him back, making him stumble into a group of girls who curse at him and shove him back toward me. His eyes are wild, hands up as he stares at me like I'm crazy.

"Oh, my God," I whisper, covering my mouth, shaking my head as my eyes blur with tears.

I whip around and find Jess staring at me as she makes her way through the crowd, and Erin is behind her, screaming into her phone, her face bent in anger.

When Jess finally reaches me, she wraps a hand around my wrist and tugs. "Let's go."

"I kissed him," I breathe, letting her pull me.

"I know."

"I kissed him."

She sighs, stopping her rampage through the crowd and turning to face me. She braces her hands on my arms, leveling her gaze with mine. "I know. It's okay. You're drunk. It didn't mean anything."

But I just shake my head, over and over, the fiercest chill of my life breaking across my skin as my stomach twists and turns, my throat burning.

And before Jess can pull me any farther through the crowd, I rip away from her hold and rush to the nearest bush, surrendering what little dinner I ate and every ounce of tequila I consumed.

Then, I drop to my knees and sob.

Jess

IF ANYONE WERE TO look down upon this scene from an aerial view, they would likely remark that it's a lovely and serene sight to behold.

A stunning penthouse suite at a gorgeous Mexican resort, the sheer white curtains floating in the breeze, the expanded balcony with a private hot tub and plunge pool all so alluring and beautiful. The magical backdrop of a pristine white beach and turquoise water, currently reflecting the full moonlight overhead, and the distant sound of the waves washing ashore.

From the outside, it appears to be an absolutely extraordinary slice of paradise on Earth.

But inside?

It's a goddamn disaster.

"I... I... I'm a monster," Cassie cries to herself, snot and tears dripping down her face as she rocks herself back and forth on one of the daybeds. She sniffs, not even bothering to wipe away the mascara staining her cheeks. "How could I do that to Adam? How can I ever live with myself again?" She balked. "How do I tell him? Oh, God."

She covers her face and sobs even harder, and Skyler winces, rubbing her back and doing her best to comfort her Little as she falls apart. She got down to the pool just in time to see Cassie vomit in the bushes after I sent her the S.O.S. text — and that was before I even knew about Cassie.

I sent it because of Erin.

Erin, who is now pacing back and forth, arms folded hard over her chest as she shakes her head over and over, tossing between murmuring to herself and screaming curse words loud enough for the entire resort to hear. Something happened to her around the same time Cassie had her meltdown, about an hour ago amidst the thumping music of the beach club, but she has yet to tell us what, exactly.

All we know is she looked at her phone, screamed bloody murder, cried, and has been pacing ever since we all dragged Cassie back here to console her.

Ashlei disappeared into the bathroom as soon as we got back, and for how long she's been in there, I can only imagine she's ralphing up the fruity shots we've been knocking back all night.

And then there's me, swiping back and forth between two pictures on my phone, each depicting a different man I love.

Swipe.

Me on Kade's back, my arms wrapped around his shoulders, lips pressed to his cheek as my hair falls over us like a curtain. His warm brown eyes are bright with love and adoration, his smile megawatt in size as he snaps the selfie.

Swipe.

Me and Jarrett in bed, his beast of a body encompassing all of mine as I curl my back into his chest like a cat. The morning sunlight reflects on our soft, sated smiles, and his dark eyes smolder at the camera, promising he's nowhere near finished with the girl in his arms.

Swipe.

Kade.

Swipe.

Jarrett.

Swipe. Swipe. Swipe. Swipe.

Back and forth, over and over, I stare at those men

— the men who own my heart — and feel it break at the realization that I will hurt one of them.

That I've *already* hurt them both.

I don't deserve the patience they've given me — the space, the time. And I definitely don't deserve their love.

But I have it, and though I love them both in return, I know there's no putting off the decision I have to make.

The decision I made long before I was ready to admit it to myself, if I were being honest.

Talking to Skyler earlier was the first time I was ready to admit it out loud, and Erin took her place tonight, asking me all the hard questions and not letting me change the subject until I answered them.

I know what I have to do.

But I also know it will kill me to do it.

In my daze, I don't realize Erin is screaming and Cassie is having a full-on panic attack until I snap out of the trance my phone has me in. I close the screen and drop it to the cushion beside me, popping up and running over to Erin first.

"It's not fucking fair! This whole system... this whole *world* is fucked!" she screams.

"Will you bitches shut up?!" Ashlei yells from inside the bathroom. "It's impossible for a girl to poop with all this racket going on!"

Skyler gives me a look that says she's got Cassie, so I grab Erin's hand and lead her to the edge of the balcony, letting the fresh sea breeze calm us both. I don't say anything, just hold her there and smooth my hand over her arm, letting her take a moment for whatever it is that's going on.

She opens her mouth to say something when my ringtone sounds from the chair I was sitting on, and Erin and I both look at the screen, stilling at the sight of Jarrett's name in bold above the new message.

My chest caves in on itself, and I close my eyes for a long moment before I open them to find Erin staring back at me.

"What are you going to do?" she asks, her voice just a whisper.

Before I can answer, Ashlei clears her throat from where she's now standing in the middle of the balcony between us all. Her hair is a mess tied loosely on top of her head, her arm still slung up from the accident, and her face is ghostly pale.

She doesn't say a word.

But when I spot what she's holding in her hand, she doesn't have to.

Her eyes lock on mine, and I exhale, stomach roiling for a whole new reason. Skyler is the first to say what I know we're all thinking.

"Oh, shit."

And Ashlei smiles, *smiles* so wide her eyes water in the process. She shakes her head, staring at the stick before finding my eyes first. Everything is silent somehow, the music from below muted, the ocean waves quiet, the universe balancing in the wake and waiting along with the rest of us.

"I'm pregnant," she whispers.

And then she covers her mouth and cries.

EPISODE 6

season and series finale

Adam

"PLEASE SAY SOMETHING."

Cassie's voice is weak, hoarse, pained as if she's being tortured and I'm the one holding the whip.

All I can do is stare at the string of Christmas lights hanging above me in the Alpha Sigma courtyard, somehow immune to how freezing it is, and unable to hear the party raging inside. With finals next week, the brothers are letting loose and trying to have a little fun before they're chained to their textbooks.

I imagined this call so differently.

I've been anxious to talk to Cassie since Thanksgiving, since I hit it out of the park meeting Chandler's grandparents. Mr. Simmons was in a fraternity, too, when he was younger, and we bonded over our love of brotherhood. He had also been raised by his grandfather, so sharing stories about the lessons we learned and how we grew up only strengthened our easy friendship. Pair that with the fact that his wife, Mrs. Simmons, thought I was absolutely adorable and nearly fainted when I helped her clean up the kitchen and washed every dish instead of joining the other guys in the living room watching football?

It was a smash hit, a home run, an all-around win.

I had a job offer by the time we got on the plane to head home Sunday night.

I'd tried to call Cassie then, eager to share the news, but her service had been shoddy at the resort and I wasn't surprised when the call didn't go through. She was exhausted after her flight home yesterday, so our call had been short and sweet, and I told her I got the job with all the intention of filling her in on every single detail today.

This call was supposed to be excitement and celebration. It was supposed to be *let's shop for an apartment* and *oh, my God, we're going to live together*. It was supposed to be our Thanksgiving sacrifice paying off, and a new date marked on the calendar for when we'd be together again, and a moving truck rental and...

It was just supposed to be so *happy*.

Instead, it's a heavy, hard fist to the gut.

"Adam, please," she begs again when I don't answer.

My heart is in my throat, chest so tight there's little room for the breaths I'm trying to force. "I don't know what to say."

She whimpers, and we don't have to be on video chat for me to know how she looks right now, to know that beautiful face is blotchy and red and tear-stained.

It's sick that I want to hold her, to comfort her, when she's the one breaking *me*.

"I'm so sorry," she says again, a broken record at this point. "I... I was drunk, and upset, and *stupid* and I—"

"Didn't listen to me," I finish for her.

"What?"

"You didn't listen to me. Or, at least, if you did, you clearly didn't hear me when I said I was doing this *for us*. I gave up seeing you for the holiday so that I could find a way for us to be in the same city. *Together*. For us to *move in* together. For us to..."

I can't finish the sentence, tears stinging my eyes, nose flaring as I shake them off.

"But you didn't call me," she says through her tears. "We barely texted. This whole semester has felt like... like... like we aren't even a couple."

"We've had dates almost every weekend," I argue. "We talk *all* the time."

"It's not the same. It's not enough."

"I know!" I scream. "Which is exactly why I flew to fucking Baltimore to get a job near *your* future school. So we could be together. So we wouldn't have to do this anymore. And you…"

Again, my words are cut short, throat constricting with the effort to say them. I'm so sick I have to stand and pace for fear of actually vomiting.

Cassie is silent.

The longer she is, the more my mind races, the more I think about how many times I had the opportunity to do the same to her, but never would have even considered it.

I couldn't stomach the thought of kissing another woman.

And the thought of *her* kissing another man…

I close my eyes, jaw popping, chest tight with a mixture of rage and the fiercest despair I've ever known.

"How could you do this, Cassie?" I ask, voice just above a whisper. "How could you so much as *look* at another man that way, let alone act on it?"

"It meant nothing. I was drunk, I don't even remember what he looks like, I—"

"Well, that makes it better, doesn't it? That just makes it all forgivable. I guess if I get rip-roaring drunk tonight, I can kiss whoever I want and it's fine, right?"

Her silence is answer enough for me.

"Tell me what you would do, if it were you," I say. "If you were on this end of the call, and I told you I got drunk and kissed another woman. What would you feel?"

She sniffs. "You can't possibly hate me as much as I hate myself right now."

I let out a long exhale.

"Adam, I love you," Cassie whispers. "I'm so sorry I hurt you. I can't even look at myself in the mirror. I swear, it will never happen again. It was a mistake. A stupid mistake. Please," she begs. "Please forgive me."

My chest is on fire as I pinch the bridge of my nose and fight back the emotion threatening to strangle me.

"I have to go."

"No," she cries. "Please, Adam. Please."

"I can't talk to you right now, Cassie. You have to respect that. Just... I need some time."

"Adam—"

But I hang up before she can say another word.

My fist curls around my phone, desire to crush it surging through me. I shove through the back door and inside, instantly feeling suffocated by the heat coming from the fireplace. I jog upstairs before any of the guys can ask me what's wrong, but I don't miss the way they watch me, the concern in their eyes.

When I make it to my room, I slam the door shut, finally letting myself heave my phone across the room. It hits the wall and bounces off, the screen cracking when it hits the hardwood floor. And with the music loud enough to drown it out, I let out an animalistic scream, one loud and long enough to make my throat hurt when I finish.

I stand in the middle of the room, panting, and then the anger starts to fade, and my imagination turns even more cruel in its absence.

I can see it, another man's hand sliding in to caress her face, her neck, tilting her chin up, finding those big, innocent green eyes staring up at him, those light pink lips parted and waiting, those soft hands twisting in his shirt...

I barely make it to the trash can by my desk before I vomit, mostly stomach acid burning my throat and my nose as I release.

I stay there for a while, waiting, expecting more before I finally kick back and lean against my bed. I can't stop shaking my head, can't stop closing my eyes tight and opening them again only to discover I'm not stuck in a nightmare the way I wish I was.

I just want to wake up and this all be gone.

I want to wake up and laugh at the audacity, at the outrageousness of even thinking Cassie could hurt me like this.

Barbed wire shreds my guts as I crawl over to my desk, pulling the top drawer open and reaching my hand inside. I feel around until I find what I'm looking for, and then I sit back on my heels, staring at the box in my hand as the hardwood digs into my knees.

I pop it open, and the diamond ring glistens in the Christmas lights, sending another pang of torture through my chest.

I fall back against the bed again so hard it moves, banging into the wall a bit and scraping against the floor.

Then I clutch the ring to my chest.

And I break.

Jess

I CAN REMEMBER A time when walking this very same walk would fill me with power.

I remember the sound of my heels clacking on Greek Row, the Boss Bitch energy flowing through me with the knowledge that I wore nothing but lacy lingerie under my long coat. I remember storming inside the Alpha Sigma house like I owned it, like I owned Kade.

And I did.

I had him wrapped around my little finger, and he had me.

It doesn't seem possible that that moment was in this same lifetime, let alone just a little over a year ago. We were so new then, exploring each other, having fun — all under the premise that I was training him to be good in bed, to be good with girls, and he was just helping me medicate my broken heart.

How quickly that turned to love.

How easily he became one of my best friends.

How comfortably he fit into my life, and made me fit into his.

The thought makes me sick as I walk Greek Row now, feeling about as out of place as a bride wearing black. This wasn't my home anymore, these weren't my streets to rule, and this wasn't my man to own.

I don't even know what I'll find when I get to the Alpha Sigma house now, if the boy who first caught my attention on that cruise ship will shine through, or if the man I fell in love with will still be there, or if they've both been replaced by the shell of who he's become in the time it's taken me to damn near kill him.

It's an effort to hold my dinner down when I walk through the door — open, as per usual, the living room filled with brothers. Half of them are at the long dinner table in the back, textbooks and laptops spread out around them, and the other half are trying and failing to be quiet as they play video games on the big screen. I don't get more than a few glances when I walk in — and since I look like absolute shit, no one stares long enough to care who I am.

I walk slowly back to Kade's room, stomach in knots, but find it empty.

"He's outside hanging Christmas lights," one of the brothers says to me, and then he's texting away on his phone and walking back down the hall.

I blow out a breath, following him until I'm rounding the dining room and making my way to the courtyard.

I stop at the sliding glass door when I spy him, standing at the bottom of a tall ladder and pointing at something on the roof as he instructs the brother at the top of the ladder where to hang the next strand. His face is aglow, the light and shadow of the night playing against his muscles. It's pleasantly cool tonight, and he's wearing a long sleeve A Sig shirt and black sweatpants that make me want to curl up with him on the couch.

My eyes water, heart stinging in my chest.

And as if he senses the spirit of our past, too, he stops what he's doing, frowns, and turns to find me staring at him.

There's no confusion in this face when he finds me, no surprise or shock. It's a lifeless sort of stare, one laced with pain and accusation and something a lot like hope. He swallows after a moment, muttering something to the brother on the ladder before he makes his way to me.

I open the sliding glass door, meeting him halfway, and the brothers who were working outside with him give me a polite nod and hello as they squeeze past me and inside, shutting the door behind them.

An eerie quiet falls over us, brothers laughing and talking inside, but the sound muted by the soft hum of the night. The Christmas lights that have been successfully hung glow above us, the other strands curled at our feet, waiting for their turn.

Kade's eyes search mine for a long moment before his body ebbs toward me, like he wants to wrap me in a hug, but he stops himself, shoving his hands in the pockets of his sweats, instead.

"Can we go for a walk?" I ask, my voice cracking.

Kade closes his eyes, opens them again, his gaze on his shoes. He nods.

We don't say a word as we walk around the side of the house and back onto Greek Row, and I start the trek that leads into the heart of campus, listening to the sound of our sneakers on the sidewalk.

"How are you?" I ask when we're far enough from the house.

Kade glances at me like he's not sure he actually believes I asked him that before shaking his head a little.

You already know — that's what he says without words.

I tuck my hands in the back pockets of my jeans on a nod, my eyes watering. I don't know where to start other than the obvious place.

"I'm sorry, Kade," I whisper.

He blows out a breath — long, slow, and shaky.

"I don't have an excuse for how I've behaved. I don't have any words that will make any of it right, make it go away, or make it feel better. I just don't. All I have for you is honesty," I say, glancing at him before my eyes are on my shoes again. "I vow to give you that."

Kade doesn't say a word, but I know he's listening.

"When Jarrett came back," I start. "It blew up my entire world. Everything I thought I knew about him, about you, about *us*... it just became clouded behind this big, heavy fog. But when we finally talked, I got some clarity, some... closure, I guess, that I didn't realize I needed. I thought everything was going to be fine. And I meant it," I say, looking at him then. "I meant what I said to you last semester. That I love you."

"I know," Kade whispers. His voice is laced with such pain it feels like it's splitting my ribs in half.

"I never expected to ever see him again. I damn sure never expected for him to tell me he still had feelings for me." I bite my lip as tears blur my vision. "I have been the most atrocious person, all because I was confused, trying to hold onto what I have with you, while also reaching for what I had with him."

We make it to the reflection pond, the palm trees around it decked out in red and white lights, and I tug Kade's sleeve, guiding him over to one of the benches. When we take a seat, he scoots away from me, his back rigid, eyes on the pond.

"I am so sorry, for everything I have done, for everything I can't take back," I whisper.

I reach out for him, covering one of his hands with mine and heaving a sigh of relief when he doesn't jerk away.

"Please, look at me," I beg.

Kade closes his eyes on a burning exhale before he does as I asked, and the moment our eyes meet — *really meet* — both our lips tremble with emotion.

"Kade, I love you," I whisper, tears pooling in my eyes and falling over my cheeks, silently carving rivers down to my jaw. "I love you. And I want to be with you."

Kade cracks then, a brief moment of shock washing over his face before he crumples, pinching the bridge of his nose in one hand as his shoulders begin to shake. He can't fight back the emotion, and seeing him succumb to it makes my tears come even faster.

"I want to be with you," I repeat. "But..."

His eyes snap to mine.

"But I don't know if it's right to be."

"Jesus Christ, Jess," he says. "What are you saying?"

"I'm saying that I want you. I want *us*. But what I've done to you... I don't think I could ever forgive you, if it were me in the reverse. I don't deserve you, Kade. Or your love. I..."

My words choke off on a sob, and I cover my mouth with my hand, shaking my head as tears sting my cheeks.

Kade lets out a breath, something of a smile on his lips before his arms are around me, pulling me across the space between us on the bench and crushing me to him. He inhales my scent once I'm in his arms, and I do the same, crying harder at the way it feels to have him hold me, at the warmth of his body, at the familiar smell of his cologne.

"You deserve so much more than me," I sob into his chest. "So much better than what I have done to you."

"Shhh..."

"No," I say, shaking my head as I pull away from him. I look right into his eyes when I continue. "I can't ever forgive myself. I don't know how you could. I want to be with you, but how could I honestly ask that of you, after everything?"

Kade sighs, rubbing my arm with his hand as his eyes flick between mine. He doesn't say anything for a long while, and I know he's realizing it, too — I've hurt him too badly to ever repair it.

"I won't deny that I have been sick for the last four months," he says. "And I won't say you didn't hurt me, because you did. But, *fuck*, Jess, if I didn't think you were worth the pain, if I didn't think you were worth the wait, and if I didn't believe in us the way I do, do you honestly think I would have stuck around?"

I sniff. "But—"

"You say you wouldn't have been able to do the same, but I know that's a lie, too. Because if I would have asked you for time, for space, you would have given it to me. And if I would have asked you to wait for me to figure out what I needed, you would have done it. Tell me you wouldn't have."

I bite my bottom lip hard against the emotion building in my throat. Kade just lifts a brow, waiting.

"I would have," I whisper.

"And why?"

I close my eyes, then, releasing more tears. "Because I love you."

"Because you love me. And I love *you*, Jess. In case you haven't realized it yet, love isn't some beautiful painting hanging in a museum. It's scarred with pencil marks and eraser stains and layers of paint trying to hide the one underneath it and failing miserably. It's messy — perfectly so. Maybe you don't deserve me. Maybe I don't deserve *you*. But we love each other enough that none of that matters."

"I just don't know if I'm good for you..."

He smiles then, swiping away a fresh tear with his thumb before I lean into his touch.

"Why don't you let me be the one to decide that."

I don't get the chance to answer because he frames my face in his hands and pulls me into him, his lips warm and salty when they meet mine, and I taste our tears when I open my mouth and he slides his tongue inside.

Our hearts breathe a sigh of relief at the kiss, hands trembling where we hold each other, and suddenly it's far too cold to be comfortable. I climb into his lap, holding on tight as I soak in every kiss I've missed in the last four months, and he holds me just as tight, wrapping himself up in my warmth.

"Come on," he whispers, reluctantly breaking our kiss and pulling me to stand. "I don't want to fuck you in a public place this time. I want you all to myself."

I blush at the memory of the karaoke event, laughing a little as he tucks me under his arm and steers us back toward Greek Row.

Time seems to pass unnaturally on that walk, our hands intertwined, words no longer needed, our hearts beating soundly for the first time in months. When we make it back to the A Sig house, he quietly leads me inside and back to his room, locking the door behind him once we're inside.

It's pitch black, not a single light on, and his blackout curtains shielding the Christmas lights from the courtyard. I feel his hands on me before my eyes adjust, and even then, I can barely make him out, barely see more than an inch in front of my face.

But I feel him.

I feel his breath on my skin, his lips against my neck as he tugs me into him and presses his body flush against mine. He kisses blindly until he finds my mouth, his hands exploring in the dark, gliding the length of my ass before cupping and slipping between my legs.

I loose a breath at the feeling, at being touched, at knowing he'll be the *only* one touching me forever—

Or, at least, until he's sick of me.

Anxiety tries to fight its way through, but Kade's next kiss silences all attempts, and then I'm led backward, the back of my knees hitting the bed before we tumble into it.

"Everything that I am," he whispers against my stomach as he peels my sweatshirt off, my hair tumbling through the neck hole and over my breasts as he discards it. "Everything that I have," he says as he wrangles me out of my sports bra. "It all belongs to you."

I run my hands through his short hair, pulling him to me until I can find his mouth, and I kiss him with the promise that I feel the same.

Slowly, piece by piece, I strip him down as he does the same to me. We climb under the comforter and pull it up over our heads, our hot, needy breaths warming us as we explore every inch of each other in the dark.

I flip him onto his back, tasting his abs on my way down to his shaft, and he hisses a breath when I take him inside my mouth, swallowing him whole.

I don't even get to adequately tease him before it's me being flipped, my legs spread wide, Kade's fingers parting me at the seam before his tongue lashes the part of me aching for him most.

Gone is the urgency, the rush, the need to claim that we both felt surging through us that night at the concert. In its place is reverence and understanding, wonder and awe, disbelief and gratitude. I touch him like it's both the first and the last time, and he makes love to me like these hours here in this bed are the last we have on Earth.

Neither of us chase our orgasm. Neither of us speed up our pace or do the things we know will make the other unravel. We soak in every second, moaning and tasting and biting and licking. He fucks me from behind, and then I roll him over to ride. He straddles my face to fuck my mouth while he sucks on my clit, and then I'm spread underneath him, hooking one leg on his shoulder.

All night long, we exist in that dark room of a universe.

My soul is at peace. My heart is finally home.

But in the back of my mind, I know the worst part is still to come.

Because I've finally made my choice.

And there's still one person left to tell.

Bear

THE RAIN PELTS MY jacket as I exit the parking garage and make a left, hands in my pockets and head down. I wish I had my umbrella, wish I would have been smart enough to check the weather before I left my house, but I'm a bundle of nerves, and it was all I could do to choke down breakfast with my stomach like this.

I thought I'd already tackled the hardest part earlier this morning, that walking into the agency and handing in my two weeks' notice would be the biggest challenge of the day. It wasn't easy — especially when my boss offered me a raise to try to keep me. Giselle glaring at me from her office didn't add to the comfort, either, but I ignored her altogether.

I made up my mind over the weekend.

And there was no amount of money that could change it.

I spent the morning making a list of the projects I'll need to finish before I leave, and listing out who I think will be the best to delegate my work to once I'm gone.

And now, on my lunch break, I'm checking the next thing off my list.

I thought this would be the easy part.

The way my ribs are closing in on my lungs suggests otherwise.

The last two weeks of my life have been spent preparing me for this exact moment. I've dedicated every waking hour not at work to researching, analyzing, planning out strategy, compiling the documents I need, and filing the necessary paperwork to get this lunch meeting in the first place.

I've been so focused that I haven't even seen Erin since she got back from her trip.

In all fairness, she told me she needed some space, too. I don't know what happened in Mexico, but I do know the way we left things couldn't have had her in that great of a mood. I wanted to see her the moment her plane landed, wanted to hold her and talk through everything that had happened.

But she said she needed to get sleep for school, that she had finals coming up, that she needed to focus. I think I've known in my gut that it's a lie, an excuse, but the truth is I've been busy, too.

Maybe this is what we both needed.

Space. Time. Distance.

The rain lets up a little as I make it to the high brass doors that lead into the Palm South University Credit Union, and I pause under the overhang to remove my jacket and shake off the water as best I can. Wiping my feet on the mat, I take a deep breath, pull my shoulders back, and push through the door.

The downtown branch is much nicer than the one on campus, mahogany wood desks lining the left side of the main space, while private offices span out to my right. There's a hall in the back that a group of women walk down as soon as I enter, and directly in front of me are seven teller windows, the brass and wood making up their stations playing well with the warm burgundy carpet.

"Good afternoon, sir," a young man greets me from his place by the door. "How can we help you today?"

Holding my soaked rain jacket away from me as much as I can, I pull the binder full of paperwork from inside my suit jacket, relieved to see it's still dry. "I have a meeting with Mrs. Jarwolowski."

"Inquiring about a small business loan?" he asks.

My stomach somersaults when I answer, "Yes, sir."

With a beaming smile, the young man leads me to the small waiting area stretched out in front of the glass-window offices, letting me know Mrs. Jarwolowski will be with me soon. He takes my jacket and hangs it on the rack near the door, and I take a seat, smoothing my clammy hands over my slacks.

I've never been more prepared for anything in my life, and yet I'm so nervous I think I might actually shit myself.

I barely studied for tests at Palm South, depending on my skill set and good luck to get me by most of the time. I never cared much about getting A's. I just wanted to pass and get my degree — which I did by the hair of my chin.

But this...

This loan is the difference between a pipe dream and a reality. It's the difference between being jobless and being an entrepreneur. It's the difference of being a struggling graphic designer with a major lack of experience and being the CEO and Owner of my own business.

This loan isn't just money.

It's everything.

When I left the gym after what happened with Giselle, I couldn't shake myself from the thoughts assaulting me — not just about Erin, but about what would come next for me. I wondered if what Giselle had said, what Erin had agreed with, could ever be true.

So, I started crunching numbers.

The more research I did, the more ideas started flowing. Before I knew it, I had Word doc after Word doc of a business plan — rough in nature, but fleshing out slowly and surely. I stayed up every night until well into the early morning, passion flowing out of me like sunlight. It was just after midnight about a week after the gym incident when the realization dawned on me.

I wanted it.

I wanted my own business.

I wanted it so bad I could taste it, see it, *feel* it.

What started as a *let's just see what this could be like* quickly turned into me making an exit plan from my job and a business plan for Pennington Personal Fitness, LLC.

And now, I couldn't stop until I had it.

The binder in my hand is heavy and weighted with dreams and numbers that I hope will add up to whatever this bank needs to trust me with their money, to trust I can pay them back and succeed. I tap my thumb against it, knee bouncing as I wait.

My phone vibrates in my pocket, and I fish it out, swallowing hard when I see Erin's name.

Erin: *Hi.*

I blow out a breath.

Hi I type back.

Erin: *I miss you.*

I close my eyes on another long sigh.

Me: *I miss you so much it hurts.*

Erin: *Come over tonight.*

My stomach ties up in knots, because as much as I want to see her — *need* to see her — I have no idea what shape I'll be in tonight. I might be high on life and celebrating, or I might be a depressed mess who realizes he quit his job before having a steady plan in place. I have savings to get me through for a while, but it's not much, and if I don't get this loan...

"Bear?"

I look up from the blinking cursor on my phone, still having not answered Erin, and find a young woman staring at me.

She's petite, slim, dressed in a creamy pink blouse and beige dress slacks that hug her long legs all the way down to her nude high heels. She looks familiar, and I tilt my head, trying to place her.

It isn't until she pushes the rose-gold framed glasses up her nose and smiles that I realize.

"Oh, my God, it *is* you, isn't it?" she asks, adjusting her purse on her shoulder. She takes a tentative step toward me as I stare at her in disbelief.

It can't be her...

It can't be the same bright green eyes I stared into so many nights, the same plump, rosy pink lips I kissed more times than I can count. That jet black hair, it can't be the same that was once shaded a shocking violet, that I once bunched in my fists between the sheets.

But when she takes another step, I know without a doubt that it is.

"It's me..." she says shyly, tucking a strand of hair behind her ear. "Shawna."

I nearly drop the binder of papers from my lap as I shuffle to stand, fumbling with the folder until I have it secured under my arm. Then I just stand there, looking at the girl I used to have such deep feelings for it nearly killed me.

Almost as much as the way we broke up.

Her brows fold together, bottom lip disappearing between her teeth as her eyes flick between mine. The last time we talked, she told me she couldn't stand up to her parents, that she couldn't claim me as her boyfriend because I was black and her parents were *old-fashioned*.

The memory makes my jaw clench.

"I... I'm sorry," she says, shaking her head and already turning to leave. "I shouldn't have said anything. I'm going."

"Wait."

She stops, turning over her shoulder.

I sigh, swallowing. "How are you?"

I see the relief swell through her, her shoulders releasing a bit of tension as she turns to face me again. "I'm well. I was just dropping off a deposit for my boss," she says, tapping her purse. "And I'm certainly happy I ran into you."

A tight smile is about all I have to give.

"Are you waiting to see someone?"

"I'm inquiring about a small business loan," I answer.

Her eyes light up at that, smile wide and glowing. "Really? What kind of business?"

"Personal training and nutrition."

"Wow," she breathes. "That's... that's actually quite perfect for you, isn't it?"

My heart surges with the assessment, because it does feel perfect. It feels right.

But I still can't move, can't do much other than answer her questions as I stare at the ghost I never thought I'd see again.

Shawna's mouth pulls to the side as she motions to the chair next to the one I was seated in. "Mind if I join you for just a few minutes? I'm not exactly in a rush to get back to the office."

I blink out of my daze, nodding and gesturing to the chair for her to sit. I wait until she does before I take the seat next to her, rigid and uncomfortable and yet I'm glad she stayed.

"So," she says, balancing her purse in her lap with a wide smile angled at me. "Starting your own business, huh?"

"Hopefully." I tap the binder. "We'll see if I make the cut."

"They'd be crazy not to offer you a loan. I've got to say, though, after hearing Skyler won second place in that tournament in Vegas, I'm kind of surprised you're not asking *her* for the loan."

I sigh. "Well, to be honest, she's my backup plan. But that's *her* money, you know? She's about to graduate, and I know she's got her own dreams to go after." I pause, sniffing. "I want to do this on my own."

"You will," Shawna assures me.

A silence falls between us, her looking at me and me looking at the binder in my hands.

"Clinton, I am so sorry for what I did to you."

I close my eyes on a breath. "It's—"

"Not okay," she finishes for me. "I could sit here and give you every excuse in the world, repeat all the ones I did when everything happened... tell you my family is old-fashioned, that they were my money source, that I was scared, that I needed time, but the truth is that what I did to you, the way I behaved, the way my *parents* behaved... it was racist. Plain and simple. And I'm sorry. I'm sorry I treated you that way, that I hurt you like that, that I was too blinded by what I thought was okay to see what was really right and what was so blatantly wrong."

I finally meet her gaze, and finding such sincerity there makes my chest ache. "Thank you."

She nods. "I know I can never go back and undo what happened, but running into you today... well, maybe it was the universe giving me one last chance to make amends. The right way."

"What if I would have cursed at you and spit on your shoes?"

"I would have gladly taken the lashing," she says with a smirk. "Although, I would have been pissed about the shoes. These are Michael Kors."

I smile, relaxing a little more in my seat.

"So, other than opening a business, how are you?" Shawna asks.

"Good," I lie. She must see right through it, because she arches a brow that makes me chuckle in surrender. "Or well, I *was* good... until about two weeks ago when everything blew to smithereens."

"What did you do?"

"How do you know it was me who did something?"

She just gives me a pointed look, which makes me laugh again.

I run a hand over my fade, but don't reply to her question. The truth is, I don't know Shawna Ballentine anymore. I don't trust her the way I once did. And while it was nice to hear her apologize, what's going on between me and Erin, between me and myself... it's not for her to be a part of.

My phone lights up where I dropped it on top of my folder, and Erin's name fills the screen. I curse, thumbing open the text I had yet to respond to. She sent through a question mark after the text asking me to come over, and I shake my head, knowing I probably gave her a heart attack by not responding right away.

See you at seven. I'll bring dinner.

She replies with a little heart emoji, and then I tuck my phone away again.

And find Shawna grinning at me.

"What?" I ask.

"You and Erin Xanders, huh?"

Though my skin is dark enough not to show it, I blush. "Yes."

She shakes her head, sitting back and folding her arms. "It's about damn time."

I arch a brow.

"I always knew it would be you two in the end," she says. "I'm so happy you finally figured it out."

I want to laugh, but the gesture gets cut short when her words hit me square in the chest with the force of a tow truck.

I always knew it would be you two in the end.

She's not the first to say it to me, not the first to see it, to know it.

And I knew it, too.

I knew it all along — from the first time I really talked to her on that bench on campus, when she saw what no one else saw and offered to help me when no one else even knew I needed a hand.

From the first time I danced with her, silly and uncoordinated.

From the first time I tasted her lips, even as drunk as I was.

From the first time I woke up next to her, even though she kicked me out in a panic.

I knew.

"Bear?" Shawna asks when I sit there for far too long, but I can't help it.

It's all hitting me.

It doesn't matter that she's friends with Gavin, that he's back, that he may have other intentions than the innocent ones he's painted for her. Who cares if he texts her, or if he even tries to make a move?

Because just like I did with Giselle, Erin would turn him down.

She loves me.

As unyieldingly as I love her.

I want to kick myself for being so stupid, for fighting with her, for letting my stubborn pride and jealousy threaten the one thing in this world that I truly love.

"Mr. Pennington?" a soft voice calls from one of the glass offices, and I blink, standing abruptly.

An older woman with long silver hair and a youthful smile strides over to me, shaking my hand as Shawna stands to join us.

"I'm Mrs. Jarwolowski," she says. "Sorry about the wait."

"It's no problem at all," I assure her, and then I turn back to Shawna, who watches me with a warm, genuine smile so different from the one she used to hold for me, but familiar all the same. "It was really nice running into you," I say. And I mean it.

"You, too. Take care of yourself, Bear."

I smile and nod, and then Shawna makes her way to the front door, and I follow Mrs. Jarwoloski back to her office where I plead my case for Pennington Personal Training, LLC.

All the while, I make an even more important plan for this evening.

Erin

YOU KNOW WHEN YOU say a word so many times, it stops making sense?

The first time you say fork, you think of the shiny metal instrument you eat with. You say it again, and the same happens. But say it out loud, over and over, twenty times in a row, and suddenly you're wondering if it's a real word, wondering what words even *are* and who decided what sounds and syllables equate to a definition. And what of a definition? Isn't it just more strange sounds forming strange words that we have somehow come to agree *mean* a certain something?

It's enough to make my head spin, and it has been — for two long weeks, I've done nothing but stew and steam and boil over thinking about one stupid word.

Dropped.

Dropped, like a football meant for a receiver, a touchdown opportunity lost. Dropped, like a slippery wine glass, crashing to the floor and shattering. Dropped, like a façade, someone finally admitting what they've truly desired all along.

Or dropped, like the charges against Landon Turner and the three other men who raped me.

I've been through enough trauma in my life to know how the grieving process goes. I fully expected the anger, the denial, the painful sadness and despair. I knew I'd cycle through it all, and I have been, every waking moment since Candice called to tell me the news.

I heard her voice replaying in my nightmares, little snippets of jargon and disappointing phrases nestled between sincere apologies.

321

Due to lack of evidence...
If we'd have had a rape kit...
Their word against yours...
They had multiple witness testimonials...
There were videos and pictures taken that night that dispute our claimed timeline...
Clinton was your only witness...
Without evidence we can't...

It's all blurry. All of it. Even after formally meeting with Candice upon my return and going over it more thoroughly in person, all the details are lost behind the one bold statement I can't fully process.

The charges against Landon and his brothers have been dropped.

They won't go to trial. They won't have to answer for what they did to me. They won't have so much as a pencil smudge on their permanent record.

They're free to go.

They're free to live their lives.

They're free to keep working at their jobs and dating their girlfriends — who likely don't even know what they've been accused of.

They're *free.*

It is the most jagged pill I have ever had to swallow.

I know I don't look much better than I feel when Herb calls from downstairs to let me know Clinton has arrived. I light a few candles and pull a fresh bottle of wine from the fridge, lining up two glasses on the counter and uncorking the bottle to let it breathe.

Jess is spending the evening with Ashlei — likely trying to convince her that it's time to tell Brandon what she discovered during our trip. The poor girl is so scared of his reaction that she's taken four more tests since we returned home, all with the same result.

With Jess out of the condo, I have it all to myself, and I'm finally ready to see Clinton and tell him what happened.

Three firm knocks signal that he's at the door, and when I open it, my tongue turns to sandpaper at what I see. He looks just as devastated as me, bags under his bloodshot eyes and shoulders sagging. Suddenly, all the fighting, all the silence after and the space I thought I needed from him to process feel like the most pointless, stupid waste of time.

My bottom lip wobbles, and that's all it takes for Bear to rush through the threshold and crush me into his arms.

"I'm here," he whispers into my hair, and I nod vigorously, clutching him tight as I reluctantly give in to emotion.

I don't want to cry over them, over what they did to me — not anymore.

But I can't deny that this hurts.

Clinton holds me until I give him the cue that I'm ready to go inside, and when I do, he takes my hand and guides me. Soft jazz plays from the small speaker in our kitchen, and that along with the candles set a soothing scene.

He drops the bag of food he brought on the kitchen counter, ignoring it as he pulls me over to the couch. He sinks down first, then guides me into his lap, holding me once more.

"I'm sorry," I breathe.

"Stop," he says, kissing my forehead. "It's me who should be sorry."

"I don't have to see him anymore if it's going to hurt you. Gavin," I clarify. "I care about him, but I care about you more."

"I'm not threatened by him."

I lean back at that, arching a brow.

"Contrary to how I acted," Bear adds with a sheepish smirk. "I was wrong. I trust you, and while I hate that Gavin ever got the pleasure of being with you, I know you're mine now, and I also know he's an important friend to you. I'm sorry I put you in that position and acted like a child."

My brows fold together, and I shake my head in wonder. "You've really grown a lot in the time I've known you, Clinton Pennington."

"Yeah, well, I've had a few badass women in my life to slap me into shape along the way."

I chuckle at that, and then with those apologies still dancing in our eyes, Clinton slides his palm along my cheek to frame my neck, and I lean into the touch on a content sigh.

Home.

The word flitters through me like a warm wind, and I blink my eyes open, smiling as I realize it's not being here in this condo that makes me feel this way.

It's being with him.

"I've missed you," Clinton croaks.

I nod, leaning in to kiss him, and he wraps his arms around me even tighter.

"I have some news," he says.

"I do, too."

"You first."

I shake my head. "I'd rather hear yours. Especially if it's good, because mine is not."

That makes him frown, but I smooth my thumb over the line between his brows.

"I'm okay. But you first," I say again.

He sighs, and I know he wants to argue, but he refrains. Sitting up a little straighter, he covers my hand with his, fingers trailing the skin of my palm. "I don't think there's any slow and easy way to say this, so I'll just get to the point." His eyes meet mine. "I quit my job."

My eyebrows shoot into my hairline.

"Well," I say. "That wasn't what I was expecting."

"Trust me — I didn't expect it either. But I had a sort of... I don't know. *Awakening*, maybe? While you were gone, and over the last couple of weeks that we've been apart. I've had a lot of time to think, and when I wasn't mulling over how stupid I was to pick a fight with you over Gavin—"

"You're not stupid."

"—I was thinking over what comes next. For me. For *us*," he adds, bringing my knuckles to his lips. A gentle kiss, and then he holds them there, his eyes on mine. "I went to the bank today and applied for a small business loan."

My jaw drops. "Oh, my God, Bear."

"And I got approved."

That makes me jump off the couch. "Oh, my God!" The smile that splits my face is so big, so wide that it hurts a little as I yank Clinton off the couch and make him jump around with me. He laughs and picks me up with a spin, and when my feet are on the ground again, I slug him in the arm.

"Ouch!" He pretends it actually hurt, rubbing his arm.

"Why didn't you tell me?! I would have gone with you!"

He chuckles, holding my arms in his hands. "I wanted to do it on my own. Besides... things have been strained between us. I thought maybe if I showed up with some good news, you'd forgive me easier."

"I forgave you before you even thought to apologize."

"And that's just one of the many reasons why I love you."

I blush, plopping back down on the couch and tugging Clinton to follow. "So, what does this mean?"

"It means..." He laughs, shaking his head. "It means I have my own business. Or, well, I have the *start* of it, anyway. I found a few small retail spaces that I could potentially rent out for the studio. Now that I have my loan, and my business plan, I just need to get my website up and running, plan out a marketing strategy, get the studio set up with everything it needs and then..."

"And then make a million fucking dollars in the first year," I finish for him.

He barks out a laugh at that. "I'm pretty sure that's impossible as a personal trainer, but I appreciate your enthusiasm."

"I'm going to help you. We'll make videos for social media, and everyone will fall in love with you and be clamoring to get your time. It doesn't have to be confined to *just* the studio, you know. You could have virtual clients."

He frowns. "Virtual clients... I hadn't even considered that."

"You're welcome."

"Want to be my VP?"

I scoff. "More like *you're* the VP. I've always been El Presidente, babe."

Bear smiles, his warm eyes searching mine as he leans in and presses a slow, soft kiss to my lips. "I can't tell you how much it means to have you in my corner. I have no idea what I'm doing, so I'm going to need you. As per usual."

"I'm here," I promise.

"There's one more thing I need to tell you," Bear says with a sigh. "Giselle hit on me."

I blanch. "*What?*"

"It was while you were gone. We were at the gym, went to the sauna after, and she started by asking why I was off.

I thought she was just being there for me as a colleague, but then she had her hand on my thigh and was—"

"I'll kill her."

Clinton chuckles, squeezing my hand in his. "No need. I put her in her place. And then promptly quit."

"Is that *why* you quit?"

"Partly," he admits. "But not completely. I believe in this dream. Almost as much as I believe in us."

I smile, shoulders deflating. "Well... I still want to kill her, but I also feel all warm and fuzzy knowing you handled it."

Clinton leans in for a long kiss before he sits back, tapping my knee. "Your turn."

My stomach sours, then, smile instantly slipping.

I can't sit still while I talk about it, so I stand, pacing the living room for a moment before I finally say the words.

"The charges got dropped."

A pause.

A breath.

And then a roar.

"*What?!*"

Bear jumps to his feet, his chest puffed, fists clenched.

"What the fuck do you *mean,* the charges got dropped?"

"Exactly what I said. They got dropped." I wave my hand in the air. "Lack of evidence."

"Lack of—" Clinton's jaw drops, and then he smiles — a sadistic, twisted sort of smile as he shakes his head. He hangs his hands on his hips, tongue in cheek. "I'll kill them."

As if he's going to do it right in this very moment, he stomps toward the door, and because I don't trust that he's kidding, I hook him around the elbow and pull him to a stop.

"It's over, Bear."

"Like hell it is. It's not over until they're all behind bars or dead. And since the first apparently isn't happening…"

"Bear, please," I plead, and he looks at me then, seeing the hurt in my eyes. "I've been agonizing over this for two weeks now. I don't want to get angry again. I've finally come to accept it."

"Two *weeks*? Erin, why didn't you tell me sooner? Why wasn't I the first one you called?"

"Because just like you needed to get your loan on your own, I needed to process this first — *before* letting anyone else in. I needed to be alone."

He frowns. "I hate that."

"I know. But thank you for respecting it, anyway."

A ginormous sigh leaves his chest, and his eyes find the windows, the lights of the city reflected in his hazel irises. "So… that's just it? There's no fighting it, nothing else we can do?"

"That's it," I whisper.

He shakes his head. "I'm so sorry, Erin."

"Me, too."

Bear pulls me in for a hug, resting his chin on the crown of my head.

"I'm proud of you," he whispers. "It took a lot of guts to do what you did. I'm sorry the justice system failed you, but I hope you don't regret coming forward."

"I don't," I assure him, pulling back to look into his eyes. "In fact… I don't want to stop here."

He frowns. "I thought you said there was nothing else we could do."

"About Landon? No. There's not." I swallow. "But I want to help other victims. I want to be there when a woman is brave enough to come forward, and I want to fight for her, fight against the system set up to continue making this something to be ashamed of, something to be afraid to do."

Bear just rubs my arms, waiting.

"I'm shifting my focus into criminal law. I want to be a prosecutor."

He whistles. "Damn, girl. That's a tough career to get into."

"It'll take a lot of hard work, a lot of persistence, and likely a lot of luck. Everyone wants an internship at the prosecutor's office this summer. I just have to somehow find a way to make sure they pick me."

"How can I help?"

"I'll let you know when I figure it out. For now, I need to focus on finals and getting through the rest of this semester. I'm heartbroken over the prosecutor's decision in my case," I admit. "But if anything, it's lit a fire in me. I feel stronger now that I've faced those monsters head on — even if they never have to pay for what they did to me."

Bear's fists curl again at that.

"I may not be able to win every time, but I promise this," I say, pulling back to gaze up at Bear. "I will never stop fighting."

His chest swells again. "And I thought I was proud of you before."

I smirk, and then his lips are on mine, warm and comforting and safe.

"I have something for you," he says almost sheepishly when he pulls away.

"Okay..."

"I have to run down and get it from the lobby. Why don't you pour us a glass of wine and I'll heat up our food when I get back?"

I nod, and then he's gone, leaving my door cracked behind him as he jets into the hallway.

I take my time pouring us the wine, taking the first sip and sighing at the release it brings. I'm staring out the window with my thoughts running wild when the door creaks open again.

And when I turn, I nearly drop my wine glass.

There he is — my Bear, my man, my *everything* — smirking in that sexy way he does.

And cradled in his beastly arms is the tiniest, fluffiest puppy I've ever seen.

"Oh, my God! Bear! You got me a puppy?!" I set my wine glass down without caring that I spill a little in the process, and then I rush over, swooping the golden fluff ball out of Clinton's arms and holding it to my chest.

"I got *us* a puppy."

I giggle as the little thing licks my face. It has floppy auburn ears and fluffy golden fur, but its paws tell me that it won't be this little for long.

"Boy or girl?"

"Girl. I didn't name her yet. Wanted to let you have the honor."

"She's so cute," I whine — and it really is a whine, my voice three octaves higher than I realized it could even reach as I move us over to the couch and sit down.

I plop the puppy beside me, laughing when her little leg slips between the cushions and she sinks before rolling over and offering me her belly. I pet it as her tongue lolls out to the side.

When I look up at Clinton, he smiles down at the puppy before sitting on the other side of her, petting behind her ears as I rub her tummy. Then, his eyes find mine, a bit of fear mixed with adoration in those irises.

"Move in with me."

My hand stalls.

"Erin, I realized a lot of things in this time we've been apart — like that I drive myself absolutely insane thinking about the possibility of ever losing you."

I roll my lips together, eyes glossing.

"You were right. I do have a lot of things in my past that I haven't faced, haven't handled. And we *both* have a lot of hurdles ahead of us. But I want you there for all of it. I want you to know everything about me, to be there through the good and the bad, and I want to be there for yours, too."

"Bear..."

"I want forever with you, Erin Xanders."

My heart swells like a balloon, and I choke on something between a laugh and a sob as Clinton grabs my hands in his.

"And I don't care if it's in Pennsylvania or Florida or middle of nowhere Kansas," he says as I laugh, squeezing his hands. "I'm never going to be perfect. I'm *always* going to find new ways to frustrate you and piss you off."

"Ditto."

"None of that matters, though. As long as we have each other, I want it all." He slides a little closer as the puppy climbs on top of our laps, nipping at our shirts for attention. "Move in with me, Erin. Start a life with me. Because I can't live without you, and I never want to try."

Tears blur my vision as I nod, but I can't speak the word.

"Is that a yes?"

I laugh, setting the first rush of tears free. "Yes," I whisper.

I'm swept into his arms in the next instant, and the puppy takes it as a cue to play, nipping at us and letting out the cutest bark I've ever heard. We both pull back on a smile, and Clinton pulls a little toy from his pocket, offering it to the pup who eagerly chews on it.

"You had that the whole time?"

"Oh, you should see the supplies in my truck right now."

I laugh. "So... when do we do this?"

"Is now too soon?"

"Maybe," I say on a chuckle. "I need to pack. And Jess..."

"Will be just fine," he promises me. "How about you focus on getting through the rest of the semester, and I'll handle packing and moving. Deal?"

I nod. "Deal." Then, I shake my head, covering my mouth with both hands. "We're moving in together."

"We are."

"We need a Christmas tree."

"That can be arranged."

"And we have a *puppy!*"

He laughs. "We do. What do you want to name the little girl?"

He grabs one end of the toy, playing tug of war as the puppy presses weight into her haunches and fights against him. She loses her grip, plopping down on her butt and looking up at me with the cutest face before she's up and going again.

Knocked down, but never defeated.

"Zelda," I whisper, eyes flicking to Clinton.

"A little warrior, huh?" he muses, ruffling the fur behind Zelda's neck. "Just like her mama."

"Does that make you *daddy?*" I purr, arching a brow when Bear freezes, his eyes flashing to mine.

"Say that again, and I'll show you just how *daddy* I can be."

"Swear it?"

And with a wicked smile, he pulls me into him for a hot, promising kiss.

Ashlei

EVERYTHING IS QUIET UNDER here.

Eyes closed, breath locked in my chest, hair floating all around me.

The bath water is warm, pleasant against my sore muscles after physical therapy. And while nothing has been able to calm my racing thoughts over the last couple of weeks, this is pretty close to peace.

Here, submerged, I can hear my heartbeat.

And I swear I can almost hear hers.

Or maybe it's *his*. I won't know for a while. But she feels like a girl. She feels like she's got my sass, my competitiveness, my will to never back down. I find myself wondering about her far too often already. Will she be athletic? Intelligent? Funny? Charming? Will she have her dad's eyes or mine? Whose smile? Whose temper — because either way, she's likely in trouble, and so are we.

My lungs start searing in my chest, and I come up for a breath, warm water dripping down my face as I blink my eyes open.

The bathroom is dark, save for the little bit of sunlight streaming in from the door I left open. It gets too hot in here when I take a bath, but the open door lets in a draft, and I relax as a gentle breeze wafts over my face.

Everything is loud up here.

Out of the water, anxiety attacks me, pressing me to tell Brandon while also warning me that when I do, I might not get the reaction I want. What reaction *do* I want? I don't even know. But fear has me gripped, has the microphone on the stage of my mind as it swears to me that he won't want our baby — or me once he finds out I slipped on my birth control and made this possible at all.

That anxiety leads straight into wondering if I could do it alone, if I could be strong enough to raise a child without him. How badly would I damage her if I did it on my own? How many times would I fail her in the process of trying to raise her right?

I suppose, partner or not, we all mess our kids up somehow.

Rich, poor, doting parents, or alcoholics — we can trace so much of our trauma back to the mother and father who bore us.

That sends another pang through my chest, and I sigh, sinking down under water once more to block out all the noise.

I think I knew even before I took the test. I think I knew the moment it happened, the very second I felt him spill inside me. It's like I sensed his little swimmers on their mission, felt my eggs drop and open up. I woke in the middle of the night that night, my back to Brandon's chest, his arms around my stomach, and I swore I felt it — that little connection inside me that would spark life.

It's why I didn't drink at my own bachelorette party.

I faked shots, putting the liquid in my mouth only to spit them into the drink I pretended to chase the shot with. When the girls ordered me a drink, I'd sip on it so lightly I barely tasted it at all until they weren't looking and I could ditch it. When I ordered my own, it was soda water and lime.

I knew.

I just *knew*, and the anxiety was too much to not see proof on a little stick.

I took my first pregnancy test before we left for the trip, but of course, it was too soon then. It hadn't even been a full week since Brandon and I had returned from St. John. But that last night of the bachelorette, when Cassie was wailing over kissing a stranger, and Erin was fuming over something she wouldn't tell us about, and Skyler was getting railed by Kip somewhere across the resort, and Jess was swiping between two photos of the men she loves... I felt it again.

That kick in my chest.

That stirring in my gut.

I just knew it was time to take the test again.

And when I did, the word *pregnant* showed up on the little screen just like I knew it would.

Since then, I've taken multiple tests, just to be sure — and it's been the same result every time. There's no denying it.

I have a little human growing inside me.

A smile spreads on my lips, warmth washing over my soul at the thought, and then I'm jerked out of the water and back to reality.

"Ashlei! Jesus Christ, are you okay? What are you doing?"

I wipe the water out of my eyes to find a worried Brandon holding me by the arms — careful of my still-healing shoulder — and searching my eyes like he's sure he just saved me from a suicide attempt.

"I'm taking a bath. Wanna join?"

"You were under water."

I shrug. "It's just quiet."

He sighs, releasing me and taking a seat on the edge of the tub. He pinches the bridge of his nose, laughing a little as he shakes his head. "God. Sorry. I just... I thought..."

"I hate physical therapy, but I don't hate it that bad," I tease.

He gives me a grim smile. "It's just... you've been different lately. You've been... distant."

I grimace. "I know."

"Did I do something? Did I... did we rush into getting married and now you're regretting it?"

I balk, sitting up so fast some of the water splashes onto the edge of the tub. "Oh, my God, no. Of course not." I squeeze his forearm. "Baby, I'm the happiest I've ever been now that I'm Mrs. Church."

His shoulders release again, and he covers my hand with his. "Is it your shoulder?"

I chew my lip, knowing I can't keep it from him any longer.

All I can do is pray this won't be the end of our fairy tale.

"My shoulder is sore," I confess. "PT is kicking my ass. But... there's something else. Something I need to tell you."

"Okay..." Brandon swallows. "Tell me. Anything."

I take a long breath, releasing it fully before I grab his hand in mine. Slowly, I sink it into the water, pulling him forward a little until he's touching my stomach.

He frowns at first, and then heat glosses his eyes, those dark irises flashing with want when he looks at me again. He smirks, just a little, and slides his hand down farther.

"Is this what you want, Mrs. Church?" he asks, his fingers brushing against my clit as he leans in for a kiss.

My pussy flutters at the touch, legs clenching, but I laugh in his face before pulling his hand back up. "No, pervert." I pause. "Well, at least, not right now. Hold that thought. First..." I hold his hand to my stomach again, pressing my palm over his and holding it there.

He looks down at the water, at where he's holding me, frowning when he finds my gaze again. "I don't understand."

I swallow, applying a little more pressure so that his palm is splayed flat against my belly. My eyes search his under lifted brows, waiting, not able to say the words.

And just like it did for me, I see the exact moment it hits him.

His frown disappears, the line between his eyebrows wiped clean as his eyes double in size. His lips part, gaze falling to my stomach before slowly crawling back up to my eyes.

"You're..."

"Pregnant," I finish for him, and my eyes water with the admission, with the weight of releasing the truth. I nod. "Yes."

He lets out a short breath through his gaping mouth, but it's slack, no emotion one way or another evident in his eyes or lips. He looks as if he's seen a ghost, or has just been told the meaning of life and finds it impossible to fathom.

His eyes slowly trail down again, sticking to the spot where his hand is pressed against my stomach. His fingers curl, just a centimeter, the tips of them indenting my skin softly.

Then his eyes snap to mine, brimming with tears, and he makes that same sound again — the short puff of air through his open mouth.

Only this time, it's a laugh.

"You're pregnant," he whispers, the first tear slipping free. It falls so quickly off the apple of his cheek that I don't even have time to reach for it.

"I'm pregnant," I repeat, and I blame the damn hormones for the way my eyes instantly water, too.

"We're having a baby."

My heart pinches to the size of a penny before exploding into a hot air balloon. "We are. I mean... if... if you want to."

All emotion leaves his face then, frown back in place. "Are you fucking kidding me?"

"I just... I understand if you don't want to be a part of this. We didn't plan it. I know you've been avid about me taking my birth control and being careful. We haven't even *talked* about kids and..." I rub my belly next to where his hand still rests. "I can do it on my own, if you—"

I'm swooped out of the tub in the next instant, the words stuck in my throat as water sloshes out of the tub and off of me, soaking the rug and the bathroom floor and all of Brandon's suit.

"You are fucking *mad* if you think you'll ever have to do it alone," he breathes against my lips before kissing me, punishing and promising all at once. "You're *mine*, Ashlei Church. And that little boy is *ours*."

"*Boy?*" I say on a laugh, the release of which seems to deflate my anxiety in one fell swoop. "How do you know if it's a boy?"

"I just know."

"Well, I think it's a girl," I say as he carries me out of the bathroom and plops me into our sheets, not a care in the world that we're both soaking wet.

Brandon takes a moment to appreciate my body splayed out on the bed before he lowers down over me, gently, carefully, and starts peppering my stomach with soft, slow kisses.

"Should we make a bet?" he asks between them.

"Only if you want to lose."

"I think I win either way," he argues, those kisses trailing up over my breasts, my neck, my jaw, until he's at my lips. "Because boy or girl, they have you as a mom. And I have you as my wife."

I can't help the visible swoon that rolls off me at his words, and he chuckles into my mouth as he kisses me, rolling over to the side a bit so his hand can splay on my stomach once more.

"Can I ask you something?"

"Anything," I whisper, arching a little into his touch as his hand inches down.

"Why does knowing you're carrying my baby make me want to fuck you so goddamn bad I can hardly breathe?"

My legs squeeze together of their own accord, but Brandon reaches down to grab my thigh and pulls it toward him, spreading me once again.

"Because you love to own me," I say, biting his lower lip. "In every. Single. Way."

A growl is affirmation that I'm right, and then Brandon squeezes my thigh before jumping off the bed. His eyes bore into mine as he unfastens his belt, shoves the button of his pants through the slip, and rips the zipper down. He tugs at his tie next, undoing the knot with expert hands as I spread my knees wider for him, one hand palming my breast as the other slips between my legs.

His breathing turns wild, erratic as he watches me, but he doesn't fumble with his clothes. He takes each layer off with precision and power radiating off him, just like always, until he's nude and hard and pulsing with need.

He descends on me like a wolf, his mouth crashing into mine before he sits back on his heels, admiring the view of me spread before him. He trails a finger down one of my legs, pulling my ankle to his lips before setting it on his shoulder. He does the same with the other leg, hiking it up high, until my back is flat in the sheets and both ankles are balanced on his shoulders.

I've seen Brandon lust for me — ever since that first day in the elevator at *Okay, Cool,* I've seen how badly he desires me. But this... the carnal way his hands grip me, the somehow careful yet relentless way he fills me as I stretch and arch and cry out his name?

This isn't just want, or need, or dominance.

It's love.

It's the kind of love that drives a man mad, that sends soldiers to war, that breaks up continents and rains down hellfire on earth.

It's the damning, redeeming, torturous and ecstasy-inducing rush he'll never get enough of, an always-present yearning that will never leave him sated.

But I'm the lucky woman who gets to watch him try.

Brandon makes love to me for the rest of the evening, and well into the night and early morning, until we're both so sore and weak we can barely move to give ourselves sustenance.

Turns out my fears were unfounded.

Turns out this man of mine is everything I knew he was and more.

Turns out I'm going to be a *mom.*

And boy or girl, my baby is going to have the best dad *ever.*

Jess

IT'S AN UNBEARABLY HOT night for December, sweat beading at the base of my neck and dripping down my spine as I walk through downtown. It doesn't help that work was chaotic today, holiday weddings being of a special kind of demanding nature all their own. I thought we would have a lull in the season until spring, but since Florida is about the only state not covered in snow right now, we're a hot spot for winter weddings.

In a way, I appreciate the workload. Because while my heart and soul feel at peace for the first time in months, keeping busy has helped me avoid one unfortunate fact.

I have to tell Jarrett my decision.

Kade assured me there was no rush when he saw how anxious I was after our night reunited. He even offered to do it for me, to take the brunt of his brother's pain so I wouldn't have to. But it's not his battle to fight.

I got myself into this mess.

I have to be the one to crawl out of the mud.

My heart beats loud and off rhythm in my ears as I approach the building where Jarrett's office is. The building itself is owned by a bank, the floors above it occupying small and large businesses alike, everything from tech companies and law firms to advertising agencies and nonprofits.

I take a seat in the lobby at five after five, crossing my legs and balancing my hands in my lap as I wait. I didn't have the lady balls to ask him to meet me. Hell, I didn't even know today was going to be the day I'd break the news. I just felt it. About halfway through the afternoon, my stomach flipped violently, chills breaking on my skin, and I knew it was time.

At five-thirty, I start to wonder if he's already gone for the day. The holiday season seems to be a weird one for anyone working in a nine-to-five. It's like the month of December allows permission to leave early, come in late, and take longer weekends without explanation.

But just as I'm thinking maybe I should text him, the elevator dings, and he walks off with a group of four other individuals.

Two of them are laughing at something on a phone screen while Jarrett and a middle-aged woman converse quietly, Jarrett speaking animatedly with his hands as she listens.

The first sight of him makes my stomach drop.

Dressed in relaxed navy slacks and a crisp cream button down, he looks every bit relaxed as he does business-ready. His head is freshly shaved, beard trimmed neat, and though he's smiling as he talks with the woman, I see the same evidence in him that I saw in Kade, that I've seen in myself, proof that sleep hasn't come easy.

Dark bags under his eyes.

Slumped shoulders.

Strained concentration as he tries to listen to the woman's response to whatever he's said.

Emotion tries to strangle me as I stand, tries to tear me from where I stand on that marble floor and steer me outside before he can see me.

But I'm tired of running.

I'm ready to face him — even if I know it will hurt like hell.

He almost blows past me, and I'm fully prepared to chase him out into the streets. But just as his colleagues sweep through the revolving door, he stops dead in his tracks, stilling like a deer spotted by a hunter before he slowly, carefully, cranks his neck to look at me.

A myriad of emotions wash over him in a split second, everything from shock and delight to pain and fear. I watch each of them show themselves in his eyes, his lips, his stature before he takes a tentative step toward me.

The woman he was speaking to pops her head back to check on him, and he tells her to go on, that he'll catch up. Her eyes skirt to me suspiciously before she leaves, and then it's just the two of us in the vast, echoing lobby.

His eyes warm the closer he gets, one hand holding a messenger bag, while the other slips into the pocket of his slacks. He takes his time trailing the length of me, no doubt noticing that while I wear the same pained expression as he does, I look better than I have since the day he showed back up at Palm South.

I think he knows already, before I can say a word.

"Hello," he says after a long pause.

I offer a small, apologetic smile in return. "Hi."

Jarrett sniffs, looking away from me and out the large windows before his gaze reluctantly travels back. "I think I need a drink for this."

He doesn't say another word before turning for the door, and I follow him outside, the two of us walking silently next to each other until we duck inside a small bar a block over.

It's already filling up with patrons in business-casual dress, each of them eager for happy hour after a hellish day. Jarrett orders himself a rye whiskey neat, and I opt for a glass of red wine, knowing I won't be drinking much of it so I can say what I need to with a clear head.

I wait until Jarrett takes the first sip of his drink, hissing through his teeth a bit when he does. And when he finally looks at me again, his dark eyes shielded under bent brows, he sighs.

"Well," he says. "You've been ignoring me. I guess I should have known this was coming."

"I'm sorry," I breathe. "I... I've been a coward."

He shakes his head once, frowning even more, but doesn't say anything else.

"I don't know where to start," I admit.

"How about by telling me you've made your choice," Jarrett says, and then his eyes hit mine again. "And that it's not me."

My nose stings. "I'm sorry," I whisper.

He nods, looking away again, his eyes on the bottles lining the back of the bar.

"I loved you," I start, not knowing where the right place is, just knowing I have to say *something*. "And... I love you still."

His eyes shoot to mine.

"Maybe that will never change," I confess. "I think... I think there's a part of me that will always belong to you."

He swallows, Adam's apple bobbing hard in this throat.

"But what we have," I continue, circling the rim of my glass with my fingertip. "At least, what we have *now*... it's purely physical. It's chemistry and carnal need," I say, meeting his gaze once more. "But it's not real love. I think we both know that."

"It could be."

"Maybe," I say. "But... I'm not sure what we have anymore, Jarrett — past that desire to fuck."

The words slap him across the face, the sting visible to anyone around us.

"I don't trust you," I admit on a cracked voice. "And I don't think you trust me, either. Do we want each other? Yes. But you broke me. And I broke you, too."

Jarrett nods, taking a long pull of his whiskey.

He doesn't say a word.

"I've done a lot of thinking in the past few months, a lot of self-reflection, a lot of thinking about why I feel the way I do, why this has been so hard for all of us." I tilt my head a bit. "It's the strangest thing, thinking back to that time when we were together. Because... *so much* of the time, we weren't *actually* together."

Jarrett opens his mouth to argue, but I continue.

"Think about it. The first time we met, we fucked in a parking lot. Then, we found out you were the graduate assistant for one of my professors." I wet my lips. "I became your mouse. You wanted me because you couldn't have me, because I was off-limits, and I loved to play that game, to make you want me, to parade other guys in front of you to drive you mad until you snapped. And it worked. You *did* snap, and then..."

"We dated."

"Kind of," I admit. "But think about it. For a long while, we played games. Mostly me, I admit that, but even when I showed up at your door and confessed that I had deeper feelings, I remember being so scared I nearly vomited on my way up to your place."

His brows fold in at that.

"You scared the shit out of me," I whisper. "Because I knew, even then, that you aren't the kind of man who is kept by any woman."

I know the look washing over him in this moment, that realization, that uncomfortable feeling of being viewed under a microscope and having someone peg you down in a way you didn't even know yourself.

"When we were *finally* official, you left. And I don't blame you for that," I say quickly when I see him growing on the defense. "You were going after your dream job, what you want in life, and you should. But that's what I'm saying. How much time did we *really* spend together, where it was truly us?" I pause. "How much do you really know about me, other than the way I moan your name?"

"Jess..."

"You wanted me so badly when you couldn't have me," I whisper, tears blurring my vision of him. "And then found me an annoyance as soon as you did. When you were in New York, I felt like a stain on your shirt that you couldn't get rid of, like a rash you so desperately wanted to hide."

"I came to visit you," he argues. "I took you and your friends out, I—"

"Once, Jarrett," I interrupt. "One time. And we fought even then."

Silence.

"The only reason you want me now is because you came back and I was taken. You get a rush over me being off-limits to you — especially when you can break those walls and prove that I still want you, despite the consequences."

He swallows hard.

"It's toxic — to *both* of us. And I won't do it. I refuse to participate any longer."

Jarrett's shoulders slump, and he shakes his head, an argument building on his lips.

"If you wouldn't have had to come back to Florida for work," I say, reaching over to squeeze his forearm and make him look at me. "You never would have thought of me again."

"I thought of you every day."

His words kick me in the chest.

"Maybe so," I say softly. "But you don't love me. You love the chase."

His jaw tics, and he shakes his head, but tears his gaze away from me, unable to stare the truth in the eyes.

"I want happiness for you," I say after a long while. "I do. You are such a—"

"If you say *great guy*, I swear to God, I'm pitching myself off the first rooftop I can find."

I swallow, picking at my nail polish with my eyes on my hands. "I'm sorry."

Jarrett sighs, deep and heavy, like all the hope he was holding onto left him with that breath. He holds his tumbler in his hand lightly, giving it a toss with his wrist, and then downs what whiskey is left before turning to face me.

"I hope my brother knows how lucky he is."

I try to smile, but it falls flat. Instead, the tears I've been holding at bay slip free, the realization that Jarrett and I will never be sinking in and tearing my soul to shreds.

"And if he ever fucks up," Jarrett warns.

"I know," I say before he can finish, reaching for his hand. He turns his palm up, letting me hold him, and I squeeze his hand tightly. "I know."

He nods, his eyes searching mine, and tears well in his eyes before he sniffs and jumps up without warning. His hand pulls from mine, digging into his pocket for his wallet. He slaps down a twenty to cover our drinks, and I slowly stand to mirror him.

"So, I guess this is it," he says.

"I guess so."

He bites the inside of his cheek, and then opens his arms, and without hesitation, I slip into them, both of us sighing when he wraps me in a tight embrace.

"You're wrong about one thing," he says against the shell of my ear. "I *do* love you."

I nod against his neck, squeezing him tight, and we hold that hug for just a second, or was it a lifetime, before finally letting go.

And we do.

We let go.

In that moment, with that final embrace, I feel the last bit of Jarrett that has always stuck to my heart washing away, the waves taking him out to the Sea of the Past. And when I look into his eyes, I know he feels it, too.

The cleanse.

"Goodbye, Jarrett," I whisper.

And then I leave him behind.

Later that night, Kade draws lines on my skin with his fingertips, my back to his chest, his chin on my shoulder as he holds me.

"So," I say after a while, rolling in his arms to face him. Every limb is sore from how much we've made up lately, but it's the delicious kind that I don't mind at all. "What now?"

"What now?" he repeats, kissing my nose before he looks up at the ceiling, thinking. "Hmm... well, I'm thinking we might need a little food, maybe a shower, and then I have this position I want to try where—"

I flick his forehead, laughing when he pins me down into the sheets and kisses me breathless. I finally push him away and hold my hands to his chest where he balances over me.

"I'm serious," I say. "With all this behind us... now what?"

Kade smiles, smoothing my hair out of my face. "Well, I've got a semester left of school," he says. "*You've* got a busy wedding season coming up in the spring. And then..." He shrugs. "The world is our oyster."

"What does that mean?"

He laughs, leaning down to press a brief kiss to the frown line between my brows. "It means we don't have to have it all figured out right now. We're young, Jess. Young and *madly* in love. I'm finishing up school, you're starting a new career, and we're building a future... together."

The corner of my mouth lifts. "We are, aren't we?"

"I don't know that I'm ready to dive in as head-first as your bestie has but..."

I snort laugh. "Oh no, I'm not ready for babies either. Although, I *do* plan to spoil the shit out of hers."

"Oh! Can we be the cool aunt and uncle who gives the kid ungodly amounts of sugar and loud toys and then send them home again at the end of the day?"

"Obviously. I also plan to buy them any and everything they want so that they know when they're old enough to need beer for a high school party, Aunt Jess has their back."

"That's illegal."

I snort. "Like that ever stops anyone."

Kade chuckles, settling more in-between my thighs, and when he nestles into my warmth, I feel him start growing hard again.

"Insatiable," I whisper against his lips as he kisses me.

"Only when it comes to you." He nibbles my lip before pushing up to balance on his elbows again. His eyes search mine, his smile warm and just... *happy.* So, so happy. "I don't have a ten-year plan for you, Jess. Or a five-year one or hell, even one for the next three-hundred-and-sixty-five days. But I can tell you this. One day, I will get on my knee, and I will ask you to spend your life with me — officially, because to be clear, you've already agreed to that whether you know it or not."

I laugh, but it's against the tears building at his words.

"And one day, I'll cry like a fucking baby when you walk down the aisle to me. And one day, I'll hold your hand when you give birth to the first of our twelve babies."

"*Twelve*?!" I laugh. "And what if I don't want any of those things? What if I said I never want to get married or have kids?"

Kade shrugs. "Then I would say whatever you want in this life, wherever it may take you — count me in. Traveling the world, joining the circus, partying until we're too old to take drugs," he says as I laugh. "Whatever you choose — I'm your co-pilot." He swallows. "For as long as you'll have me."

I curl my fingers in the hair at the nape of his neck, reaching up to press a kiss to his lips. "What if I want you longer than you want me?"

"Impossible."

"What if I drive you insane?"

"Oh, you *absolutely* will," he says, and I pinch his side. "But I wouldn't have it any other way."

I bite my lip when he rolls his hips against me, doing his best to distract me from this conversation — and it's working.

"So, no matter what comes next, it's me and you."

"Me and you," he echoes, kissing me deeply.

"I love the sound of that," I whisper, wrapping my ankles around his hips.

"And I love *you*."

With that promise, he captures my mouth with his, effectively silencing the conversation as he rolls against me once more.

And finally — *finally* — every jagged little piece of me falls into place.

Cassie

I SHOULD BE GETTING ready for my last semi-formal.

I should be laughing with Skyler as she does my hair and I help her pick out the perfect accessories to go with the dynamite black dress she bought a few weeks ago for the occasion.

I should be taking Tera under my wing, showing her the ropes, passing the torch to her as Skyler and I leave and she starts the new line of our family.

Instead, I'm on a flight to Denver, my tail tucked firmly between my legs and what's left of my bleeding heart on my sleeve.

It's all I have to offer Adam. No apology will be enough. No amount of admitted regret can take back what I've done. Nothing I ever say or do will be able to atone for how I betrayed him in the most fundamental and hurtful way there is to betray someone you love.

In my heart, in the very pit of my gut, I know I'm walking into a losing battle. Like a soldier on the front line against an impossible force, I know I won't walk out a survivor. But I can't let him go without a fight. I can't let go of him without knowing I did everything I could to hold on.

A soft, quiet voice whispers in my ear that Adam loves me, that we can make it through anything, that it will all be okay — but I don't see how it ever could. Adam hasn't spoken to me even once in the three long weeks since I confessed what happened in Mexico.

I wouldn't speak to me, either.

For all I know, he's written me out of his life forever. For all I know, he's shacking up with any girl who looks his way and trying to fuck me out of his system. For all I know, he's moved past the grieving stage and right on to the *fuck her* stage where he firmly believes everything between us was a lie.

I cover my mouth against the bile burning my throat at the thought, closing my eyes and willing myself to calm down as the captain announces we're descending into Denver.

I was supposed to be on this flight three weeks ago, flying in to spend a long holiday weekend with the man I love.

Instead, he went to try to secure our future.

And I put my mouth on another man.

If I hadn't already cried out every bit of moisture left in my body, I know I'd be sobbing once again. None of the girls have been successful at pulling me out of my depression — no matter how they tried. It's taken all my energy just to drag myself to class and pass my last finals. I barely passed them, my long run with all A's slipping from my fingers. I'll still graduate just fine, and I'm already set for Johns Hopkins, but it doesn't change the fact that not only did I fail Adam, but I've failed myself, too.

Regret and longing sour in my gut as I grab my carry-on out of the top compartment once we land, wheeling it behind me. My mind races, trying to grasp words out of thin air, to string together the right declarations that will somehow prove to Adam that I'm still worthy of his love.

How can I convince him when I don't even know that I believe it myself?

My phone pings to life when I turn it off airplane mode, texts from both Tera and Skyler filling the screen. They send pictures of their outfits, of them doing our sorority hand sign in front of the house, and the latest is them piled into the back of the limo, loading up to go to dinner and then to the venue.

Fire burns my chest as I type back that I miss them and hope they have the best time. Skyler just types in all caps GO GET YOUR MAN while Tera sends a string of emojis.

I'm still staring at the pictures when I hear my name called.

"Cassie?"

My feet stop moving.

My heart stops beating.

My lungs cease to provide air as the familiarity of that voice sinks in.

Everything comes back to life in slow motion, and I turn just the same, finding Adam sitting in a chair by gate C45. His phone balances in his hand, brows furrowed together as he blinks over and over like it can't actually be me he's seeing.

When he realizes it is, he's off his feet in the next instant, his phone dropped on top of his duffle bag and left behind.

I immediately start to cry.

And then I'm swept into his arms.

I clutch him so tight my knuckles whiten, and he crushes me in return, soothing me as I sob and struggle to catch my breath.

"Cassie? What are you doing here?" he asks, but still, he holds me, kissing my hair before pulling back to search my eyes. "Why didn't you tell me you were coming?"

"I didn't want you to tell me not to."

My bottom lip quivers with the admission, and Adam sighs, shaking his head and pulling me into his chest again. "Oh, baby. I would never say that."

"Not even after the monster I've become?"

His laugh is soft, blowing up the tendrils of my messy hair. "You're not a monster."

"Sir," a stern voice interrupts behind us. "Please don't leave your bags unattended."

It's one of the flight attendants working the gate desk, and Adam nods, grabbing my hand and my bag before pulling us both over to where he was sitting. When we get there, he drops his hold on my bag, but keeps his hold on me.

"I'm supposed to be boarding a flight in twenty minutes," he says with a laugh. "To come see *you*."

I sniff, looking at the monitor behind him. Sure enough, Miami is written in big letters at the top.

"You were coming to see me?"

"I was going to crash semi-formal," he says on another laugh. "I mean, come on — you know it's my favorite thing to do when it comes to you."

"I seem to remember it being *me* who crashed through your bedroom window last year."

"True," he admits. "And then we went to semi in our pajamas."

The memory makes him smile, but it makes tears well in my eyes again, and I cover my mouth, shaking my head as they relentlessly fall free.

"Hey," Adam says softly, pulling me into his chest. "Shhh, it's okay, it's okay."

"No, it's not," I sob, wiping my nose with the back of my wrist as I press space between us. "Adam, why were *you* coming to *me*? I'm the one who messed up. I'm the one who... who..."

I can't even finish the words, and Adam frowns, rubbing my arms. "Have you been torturing yourself this whole time?"

"How could I not?"

I sob harder, and Adam sighs, looking pointedly at an older man staring at us before saying, "A little privacy, please?" The man looks away, and Adam grabs our stuff and leads us to the corner of the waiting area, tucked between a wall and a window.

I finally find the strength to look into his eyes, my hands clinging to his shirt. "I'm so sorry, Adam."

"I know," he says. "I already know. Okay? Trust me — I've been on that side plenty of times to know you didn't mean to hurt me, and even more that it meant nothing to you."

"It didn't," I swear. "I was so drunk I don't even remember it, which I hate admitting, but it's true."

Adam just smooths his hand up and down my arm for a long moment, letting me breathe, willing me to steady my racing heart. His touch alone is enough to do it, and slowly, my tears start to dry.

And then I hiccup.

Adam smiles. "There's my girl."

"I hate myself," I whisper on another hiccup.

"Don't. Look at me," he says, lowering his gaze to mine. "*I'm* sorry, too. I should have made you more of a priority this semester, should have listened to you when you told me you missed me and we weren't spending enough time together. I was so focused on the fraternity, on the drama with the exec board, and then my focus shifted completely to getting a job in Baltimore. When the opportunity came up with Chandler, I just... I couldn't see all the ways it might threaten you or upset you because I was too zeroed in on what it would mean if I landed the job. I promised you last year that I wouldn't mess things up over this, and I meant it. But I failed you. I just hope you see that it's always been us in my mind — even if I didn't do things the right way."

"You were doing it for us," I say. "I know that now. I see it. But in the moment, I was just..."

"I know. And you had every right to be. I'm sorry I didn't follow up on my word to you. I'm sorry I ever made you doubt that there's anything or anyone more important to me than you."

That makes my nose sting again, and I stifle the tears threatening to spill. "How can you say that after what I did?"

"You fucked up," he says — simply, casually, as if I left my purse in a restaurant rather than kissed another man. "And you know what, so did I. I have. Multiple times. I mean, have you forgotten the absolute ass I made of myself in the first two years I knew you?"

I laugh a little at that.

"I don't care about some loser in Mexico," he says, waving his hand. "He might have got one kiss. But I want the rest of them. I want them all, every kiss from here on out, from now until the end of time."

"So dramatic," I tease.

"Have I ever been any other way?"

I shake my head, tentatively leaning into him. "So, you forgive me?"

"I do. And I'm sorry it took me so long. I hate that I made you sick all this time. I know you've been sick, because I have been, too."

"It's been the worst three weeks of my life," I admit. "I thought I lost you. For *real*, this time."

"Silly girl," he says, lining my jaw with his thumb. "Were you not listening to me at Spring Break last year?"

I try to smile, but my chest is still so tight, it's impossible to hold in place.

"Cassie McBee," he says softly, tilting my chin until I look into his eyes. "What did I say?"

I swallow. "That I'm your now. And your forever."

"Yes," he says. "And that means you're my pain in the ass and no one else's."

A little laugh breaks free from me at that, and before it can turn to tears, Adam pulls me in for a sweet, slow kiss.

"You know, I had a whole plan for tonight," he confesses, and it's then that I notice his hands trembling, his breath a little shaky. "Semi-formal has always held such significance for us. I almost fought Clay at your first one, nearly killed Grayson after he broke your heart at the second one, and came pretty close to losing you forever last year, thanks to my pride. We don't have the best track record when it comes to them, so I was really hoping to set that straight tonight."

"Well, I beat you to the punch," I tease. "I just... I couldn't go. I couldn't get dressed up and dance and pretend I'm okay."

"I was flying in for your graduation, too," he adds. "Which is in three days. So we need to get you back home."

I nod.

Adam sighs, still thumbing my jaw.

I frown, covering his shaking knuckle with my hand. "Are you okay?"

"About to shit myself, actually, thanks for asking."

I laugh, searching his eyes, confused. "What? Why are you—*ohmygod*."

My hands fly over my mouth, eyes bulging out of my head as Adam carefully lowers down onto one knee.

Distantly, I hear the collective gasp around us, traveling strangers as shocked as I am as they pull out their cell phones and watch Adam dig into his jacket pocket.

"Like I said," he starts, freeing the box. "I had a whole plan for this. But I guess if we've learned anything by now, it's that plans don't ever work out the way we think they will. Not for us. The world loves to throw us curveballs, to test us, to throw every hurdle at us it can just to see if we'll break." He smiles then. "But we don't. We *won't*. We never could. Because you and me, Cassie? We're indestructible." A pause. "Just like diamond."

He pops the lid open, a chorus of squeals and swoons echoing all around us. Nestled inside the cream cushion is a delicate gold band with a solitaire round diamond glimmering in the light.

"Adam," I whisper, shaking my head, eyes flicking from the ring to him and back again.

"No more games, Cassie McBee. No more letting other people get in the way, or cursing bad timing, or letting miles stretch between us. I want you — *all* of you — from this very moment until my last full breath. I want to follow you to Baltimore and then to wherever you may go next. I want to be the only man who has the pleasure of cuddling you in your sweatpants and feeding you mint chocolate chip ice cream," he says, and another round of laughters and *awww's* reverberate around us. "I want to wipe away your tears, even if I cause them. I want to be the first one to call you doctor when you get that white coat — and I know you will. But more than anything else," he breathes, taking the ring from the box and holding it in his shaking fingertips. "I want you to know with every beat of your heart that I am yours, that you are everything to me, and that we can face anything this crazy universe throws at us. Together."

He reaches for my hand then — my left hand — and I tremble as he takes me in his grasp.

"Marry me, Cassie," he says, his green eyes shining where they look up at me. "Marry me, and I promise, I will spend all my life infuriating you."

A laugh rips from my chest, but tears invade my vision all the same as I nod, vigorously and relentlessly. "Yes," I whisper for good measure.

And he slips the ring on my finger.

The crowd at the gate cheers, whistles and claps and hoots and hollers ringing in our ears as Adam rushes to his feet and pulls me into his arms. I kiss him in a way that is *far* from airport appropriate, but I don't care. No one else exists to me in this moment. It's just me and Adam floating on a cloud, his promise weighing down my finger, his love forever in my heart.

"Thank God you said yes," he breathes into my ear for just me to hear. "It would have been *really* embarrassing if you'd said no."

I laugh. "You knew my answer before you even thought to ask."

"You've been known to surprise me."

"That's true," I concede. When we pull back, I hold my hand up between us, moving my finger at the shiny, unfamiliar ring now occupying it. "Wow," I breathe.

"Do you like it?"

"I would have said yes to an onion ring."

He laughs, but I can't take my eyes off the rock.

"Damn, that would have been a lot more affordable. Why don't we return this one and just hit Burger King on the—"

I press my finger to his lips to shush him, and then kiss him to silence him even more, allowing him nothing but a satisfied chuckle against my mouth.

"Alright, before I lose myself completely and check us into the nearest airport hotel, we need to go beg that flight attendant to give us another ticket for this flight."

I frown. "Wait, we're still going?"

"Are you kidding? It's your last semi-formal. Besides," he says, kissing my hand. "We've got to get you graduated."

Graduated.

I've been so lost in my heartache that I haven't had time to let it sink in, that this is it, this is the end.

My time at Palm South University is almost up.

Adam collects my bag and then his, shrugging the duffle over his shoulder as he wheels mine behind him. Then, his blazing eyes find mine, and he crooks a smile.

"Ready?"

There he is. My fiancé. My future husband. The man who owns me, body and soul.

I slip my arm around his, the diamond on my finger catching the light. And I know that no matter what happens next, life will be the biggest adventure with him by my side.

"Ready."

Skyler

"OKAY, BITCH," JESS SAYS as soon as we're in my room. To call it *my room* at this point is kind of a stretch, seeing as how I have until tomorrow morning to have all my stuff moved out of the house. My sheets and comforter are the only thing still in place, everything else packed in boxes lining the walls. "Time to show me the money."

"You *really* don't believe me?" I ask.

"You *really* want her to prove it?" Cassie mirrors with a wrinkled nose.

Jess waves her off, popping one of the bottles of champagne we snuck into the house and covering the opening with her mouth to save any drops from spilling over. She snaps her fingers and points at me, then at the floor, telling me without words what she wants.

I laugh. "Alright, but remember you asked for it."

"Oh, God. *She* did but *we—*"

Erin doesn't have time to plead her case before I dramatically unzip my graduation gown, letting it fall to my feet in a puddle of polyester.

"Ow ow!" Ashlei screams as Cassie covers her eyes and Erin laughs uncontrollably.

Poor Tera, the newest edition to our room squad, is blushing so hard I could probably fry an egg on her cheek.

Jess just smirks, shaking her head and filling red Solo cups with champagne before divvying them out to everyone except Ashlei — who has a water bottle, instead. "I knew you weren't lying. I just wanted to see your tits."

"Well, take a long, hard look, baby," I say with a wink, jiggling them a little bit to further prove that I did, in fact, go commando under my gown.

"Does Kip know you did that?" Cassie asks, hands still over her eyes.

I pull a pair of sleep shorts and a tank top from one of my duffle bags and slip them on. "Please. He was the first to find out. Why do you think I was almost late?"

"I'm surprised you got him to let you come back here instead of straight to a hotel with him after that little fact," Ashlei muses.

"He's with the rest of the guys at Ralph's until we join them," Cassie answers for me. "Good thing we all picked smart men. They know sisters come first."

"Damn straight," Jess says, but eyes the glistening rock on Cassie's finger. "Although, is that still the case?"

"Always," Cassie promises, holding out her hand to admire the ring. "He's my future husband, yes. But you bitches are my soulmates." She wraps Tera in a hug next. "Yes, that includes you."

Tera squeezes her back. "I think I picked the best sorority on campus."

"Duh," Jess answers easily. "And you've got a legacy to uphold, so, allow me to bestow upon you three golden rules."

I roll my eyes as the rest of the girls groan in unison.

"Number one: sisters before misters, always. You've just been reminded of how long that one lasts. Rule two: always be the funnest bitch at Spring Break."

"Funnest, J-Love? Really? I think I need to see that degree you supposedly got..." Erin teases.

Jess waves her off. "And rule three: avoid dating brothers *at all costs*." She pauses. "But if you become an Eskimo sister? Well... whatever. It happens."

"A... what?" Tera asks.

"Listen, the only rule out of all of that is number one.

And trust me," Cassie says, pulling her Little in closer. "It's not hard to follow."

"I'm going to miss you. It sucks I only had one semester with y'all here," Tera says to Cassie, her eyes finding me next.

"Don't worry. We won't be far," I promise her.

Erin gives Tera a sweet smile before wrapping her in a hug, too, and even Jess looks a little emotional before she covers it with declaring we all drink.

We clink our plastic cups together in the center, take a big gulp of champagne, and then climb into my bed.

Cassie is still in her gown, the other girls in beautiful dresses for the occasion, but we all flop onto the bed and cuddle up, not caring.

"This poor old bed," Erin says, patting the mattress. "She's seen more than she probably would have liked."

"She's definitely had her share of drama," I agree. "God, I can still remember us in here when you told us your master plan for Kip."

"Stop," Erin says, holding up her hand with a cringey smile. "That's a time in my life I would very much like to forget."

"I'm sure there are *many* things we'd classify in the *Happy to Leave That Shit Here* category," Ashlei says.

"Not me," Jess chimes in. "I don't have a single regret."

"Not once?" Cassie asks.

Jess frowns, thinking. "Nope. Not one. Well... except maybe when I was a dick to you and Bo, Lei," she amends. "I haven't quite forgiven myself for that."

Ashlei reaches over to squeeze Jess's ankle.

"I don't think I have any regrets, either," I say. "In fact, I don't think any of us should. We lived a lot of life in this house, on this campus."

"A lot of mistakes," Ashlei says.

"A lot of fun," Cassie adds.

"A lot of booze," Jess says with a tilt of her cup.

"A lot of sisterhood," Erin whispers, and when we turn to see her eyes welled with tears, we all smack her.

"Not yet!" Cassie warns. "Please, I've cried so much in the last month. Don't make me bawl again."

Erin laughs, wiping her face. "I can't help it. I mean, I've already graduated, you'd think it wouldn't be that emotional for me but... this is it. This is the last time we'll all be here, in this room, in this bed."

We all fall silent then, looking around the room, at each other, the words we can't say written all over our faces.

"Hey, maybe not the last time," Tera finally says. "Who knows? Maybe... Maybe I'll be president one day."

I swear, Erin beams so bright at her Great-Grand-Little that I'm surprised she doesn't steal all the wattage from every lightbulb in the house.

"You'd be an excellent president," Cassie says.

"Think the girls would be down with a cosplay themed social?" Tera asks with a smirk.

We all laugh, knowing that's answer enough.

"Well, you're all welcome into my bed in L.A. anytime," I say. "It's going to be a hell of a lot nicer than this one."

"I still can't believe you're moving across the country," Ashlei muses, absentmindedly rubbing her belly. "I mean, I *can*, because... well, because you're a badass. But, moving to Hollywood, starting a casino-event business..."

"Starting a *life* with Kip," Cassie adds.

"It's surreal," I say, smiling. "But... I'm ready. And with Kip entering his show into the film festival this upcoming summer? Who knows what life will bring us next."

"Riches," Jess says over a sip of champagne. "And I'm sure glad you bitches are taking care of our money, because the wedding planner life isn't one of fame and fortune, I'll tell you that."

"Yet," Ashlei says. "You just wait. You're already making a name for yourself, and you're only a year removed from college."

"Says the one who's likely to make partner at her agency before next year is up."

"I don't know," she says, looking down at her stomach with a serene smile. "I might take a little time off. Not a lot," she adds quickly, eyes wide when she looks at us again. "But... maybe a little."

"I don't blame you. I'd want to do the same thing," Cassie says.

"I can't wait to spoil the brat," Jess says. "Kade and I have already decided we're taking on the role of aunt and uncle for all of your little ones. So just be prepared for them to love us more than you."

"I feel like I should keep them far, *far* away from you once they're sixteen," Ashlei says with an arched brow.

Jess just gives her a mischievous smile in return.

"What about you, Little?" I ask Cassie, tapping her foot. "You ready to plan a wedding?"

"Not yet," she says with a laugh. "I need to get through medical school first."

Erin frowns. "Long engagement?"

"At least a few years."

"Okay, I'll allow that," Jess says, pointing her finger at Cassie. "But I will *not* allow you to elope like this bitch did." She points at Ashlei next. "I expect God-awful bridesmaid dresses and a proper bachelorette party and an open bar with a dance floor I can occupy all night long. Got it?"

"Yes, ma'am," Cassie says with a chuckle.

"I'm so envious of y'all who are *done* done with school," Erin says with a longing sigh. "Poor Cassie and I won't be free for years."

"But then she'll be a badass doctor and you'll be a badass prosecutor and Ashlei will be running the world from her and Brandon's yacht and Skyler will be throwing an illegal poker tournament *on* said yacht."

"And you'll be…" I prompt her.

She scoffs. "Probably banging Kade on the balcony."

"It *is* a rather fun place to canoodle," Ashlei says with a reminiscent sigh.

"Jess, seriously. What about you?" I ask. "Stop downplaying like you're not just as badass as all of us — if not all of us *combined*."

"Seriously — I don't know," she confesses. "And I think that's okay. I'm only twenty-three. I don't *need* to have everything figured out. All I know is, right now, I love my job, I love my boyfriend, I love my messy, no-direction life, and I *love* being here," she adds, grabbing us in a group hug. "Celebrating you bitches."

We're quiet for a moment, all of us lost in thought as we look around the room again, snuggling into each other's arms.

"We can't ever lose this," Cassie whispers. "No matter what happens, where life takes us… we always have to have each other."

"Come on, Grand Little," Erin says. "Didn't you know that when you rushed? Kappa Kappa Beta isn't just for four years." She shrugs. "It's for life."

Another silence falls over us, and my heart swells in my chest, tears pricking my eyes.

"Okay," I say, leaning up to face them all head on. "I don't want to get super mushy, but I have to say this, so you all just sit there and let me say it." I point at Jess. "Shut up," I tease before she can get the words out.

She smiles. "Fine. Two minutes only. Go."

I take a deep breath, looking at each of them. "I couldn't have survived the last four years without you. I mean it. I came into this university not knowing who I was or who I wanted to be, and while I still might be figuring that second part out, you girls loved me every step of the way. In the in-between," I whisper. "And I know if you loved me then, you'll love me always."

Ashlei squeezes my hand.

"Thank you for being my friends," I say, and then I can't help it — I start blubbering, which makes them all peg me with pillows before we're wrapped in a tight group hug, our heads resting on each other as we sigh and soak it all in.

"We shouldn't make the guys wait all night," Ashlei says. "Especially since I'm not sure I trust Brandon with a bunch of ex-frat boys."

"Technically, Kade still *is* one for another semester," Jess reminds her.

Ashlei taps her nose. "Even more reason to get to Ralph's."

"You're just being driven mad by your hormones and want to sneak off with Mr. Church," Erin teases.

Ashlei shrugs, not denying as we all start making moves.

"Wait!" Cassie cries out before we can get off the bed. She jumps off long enough to grab her phone before piling back in, and we all huddle in close so she can snap a selfie.

She flips to the camera roll to show it to us, and for a long time, we just stare at the picture, at our smiles, our red, puffy eyes.

"I love you," Jess whispers, wiping her tears before they can fall. "All of you. So much."

We wrap her up in another fierce hug and stay there, fighting back emotion for as long as we can before Jess claps her hands and hops up first.

"Alright! That's enough. Come on," she says with a wicked smile, yanking us up off the bed one by one. "Skyler, put on a dress. Cassie, ditch the gown. The rest of you, in the bathroom so we can fix our hair. And in ten minutes exactly, I'm calling a cab and we're going to Ralph's one last time."

"One last time," I echo.

"Guys," Cassie whines, about to cry again, but Ashlei smacks her arm.

"No," she warns with a laugh. She points at Tera next. "Get your Big in line, Tera."

"Aye-aye, captain," she salutes.

Once we're dressed and ready, we link our arms together as we walk across the yard to where the cab waits. But Erin pulls us to a stop at the street, making us all turn back toward the Kappa Kappa Beta house.

Memories flash like rave lights in my mind — socials and formals, sisterhood events and boys snuck into our rooms, Spring Breaks planned and Halloween costumes assembled, happy tears... and plenty of sad ones, too.

We stand there for a long while before Erin sighs, turning us toward the cab.

"Come on, girls," she says. "Let's make it a night we'll never forget."

And as we join our guys at the bar, I start to feel it — this unnamable spark.

It flickers to life when Bear wraps me in a hug, telling me for the hundredth time tonight how proud he is of me.

It grows a little stronger when he then turns and takes my Big into his arms, his eyes on her like she's everything his world revolves around.

That spark burns brighter at the sight of Brandon's hand on Ashlei's stomach, her eyes wide and bright as she stares up at him before he leads her to the dance floor. It nearly blinds me when Adam takes Cassie's hand in his, kissing her ring, and then her lips.

Tera joins up with a group of our active sisters at the bar, taking pictures and laughing with young women I *know* will play a huge role in her life now and forever.

Jess and Kade order a round of shots, doing some awkward kind of hand dance at the bar that makes us all laugh and sets the spark into a full-blown fire.

But I can't name it — not until the exact moment Kip slides up behind me, wrapping his arms around my waist and setting his chin on my shoulder. He kisses the sensitive skin under my ear, and I sigh, warmth and light flooding through me.

And then I feel it in my bones, deep in my soul, the truth that anchors us all.

This isn't the end.

No, this is only just the beginning.

The End

A Note from the Author

THANK YOU FOR READING *Greek.* Palm South University has been my passion project for seven years now, and I'm thrilled you have joined me for the journey. To say I'm emotional after this final installment would be a gross understatement. I'm just simply not ready to leave the world of PSU.

Now, YOU star as the main character, and while you'll be able to play some of the main story lines from the books you love, you'll also get to make different choices and unlock bonus scenes and other paths!

Download and play today. https://bit.ly/DorianPSU

If you liked this book, check out my new box set – The Pain in Loving You (https://geni.us/PILY) – where you can read THREE of my angsty all-time bestsellers. You'll get *Weightless, A Love Letter to Whiskey,* and *Make Me Hate You* all in one epic collection.

You might also enjoy my Becker Brothers (https://geni.us/OnTheRocksKS) series, following four rowdy brothers in a small town in Tennessee as they solve the mystery of their father's death – and find love along the way. Keep reading for a sneak peek inside!

For my angst fans, check out Close Quarters (https://amzn.to/3oNNA3Y), a sexy, angsty billionaire romance set on a yacht in the Mediterranean. If you're a fan of Brandon Church, this one is right up your alley.

I also love to hang out with my readers online. My favorite place to hang out is Instagram (http://www.instagram.com/kandisteiner), but I'm also on TikTok (https://www.tiktok.com/@authorkandisteiner?lang=en)

if that's your jam. And, my group on Facebook (http://
www.facebook.com/groups/kandilandks) gets exclusive
giveaways, sneak peeks, and more – so come hang out.

You can also sign up for my newsletter (http://www.
kandisteiner.com/newsletter) if you don't want to do all
the social media, but also don't want to miss any new
releases from me.

And again, thank you for picking my book out of the
millions you could have selected to read. I truly appreciate
it.

More from Kandi Steiner

The Red Zone Rivals Series
Fair Catch
As if being the only girl on the college football team wasn't hard enough, Coach had to go and assign my brother's best friend — and *my* number one enemy — as my roommate.
Blind Side
The hottest college football safety in the nation just asked me to be his fake girlfriend.
And I just asked him to take my virginity.
Quarterback Sneak
Quarterback Holden Moore can have any girl he wants.
Except me: the coach's daughter.
Hail Mary
(AN AMAZON #1 BESTSELLER)
I used to love Leo Hernandez, but that was before I hated him. And now, I have no choice but to move in with him.

The Becker Brothers Series
On the Rocks (book 1)
Neat (book 2)
Manhattan (book 3)
Old Fashioned (book 4)
Four brothers finding love in a small Tennessee town that revolves around a whiskey distillery with a dark past — including the mysterious death of their father.

The Best Kept Secrets Series
(AN AMAZON TOP 10 BESTSELLER)
What He Doesn't Know (book 1)
What He Always Knew (book 2)
What He Never Knew (book 3)
Charlie's marriage is dying. She's perfectly content to go down in the flames, until her first love shows back up and reminds her the other way love can burn.

Close Quarters
A summer yachting the Mediterranean sounded like heaven to Jasmine after finishing her undergrad degree. But her boyfriend's billionaire boss always gets what he wants. And this time, he wants her.

Make Me Hate You
Jasmine has been avoiding her best friend's brother for years, but when they're both in the same house for a wedding, she can't resist him — no matter how she tries.

The Wrong Game
(AN AMAZON TOP 5 BESTSELLER)
Gemma's plan is simple: invite a new guy to each home game using her season tickets for the Chicago Bears. It's the perfect way to avoid getting emotionally attached and also get some action. But after Zach gets his chance to be her practice round, he decides one game just isn't enough. A sexy, fun sports romance.

The Right Player
She's avoiding love at all costs. He wants nothing more than to lock her down. Sexy, hilarious and swoon-worthy, The Right Player is the perfect read for sports romance lovers.

On the Way to You
It was only supposed to be a road trip, but when Cooper discovers the journal of the boy driving the getaway car, everything changes. An emotional, angsty road trip romance.

A Love Letter to Whiskey
(AN AMAZON TOP 10 BESTSELLER)
An angsty, emotional romance between two lovers fighting the curse of bad timing.
Read Love, Whiskey – Jamie's side of the story and an extended epilogue – in the new Fifth Anniversary Edition! (https://amzn.to/3FB1B7E)

Weightless
Young Natalie finds self-love and romance with her personal trainer, along with a slew of secrets that tie them together in ways she never thought possible.

Revelry
Recently divorced, Wren searches for clarity in a summer cabin outside of Seattle, where she makes an unforgettable connection with the broody, small town recluse next door.

Say Yes
Harley is studying art abroad in Florence, Italy. Trying to break free of her perfectionism, she steps outside one night determined to Say Yes to anything that comes her way. Of course, she didn't expect to run into Liam Benson...

Washed Up
Gregory Weston, the boy I once knew as my son's best friend, now a man I don't know at all. No, not just a man. A doctor. And he wants me...

The Christmas Blanket

Stuck in a cabin with my ex-husband waiting out a blizzard? Not exactly what I had pictured when I planned a surprise visit home for the holidays...

Black Number Four

A college, Greek-life romance of a hot young poker star and the boy sent to take her down.

The Palm South University Series

Rush (book 1) FREE if you sign up for my newsletter!
Anchor, PSU #2
Pledge, PSU #3
Legacy, PSU #4
Ritual, PSU #5
Hazed, PSU #6
Greek, PSU #7
#1 NYT Bestselling Author Rachel Van Dyken says, "If Gossip Girl and Riverdale had a love child, it would be PSU." This angsty college series will be your next guilty addiction.

Tag Chaser

She made a bet that she could stop chasing military men, which seemed easy — until her knight in shining armor and latest client at work showed up in Army ACUs.

Song Chaser

Tanner and Kellee are perfect for each other. They frequent the same bars, love the same music, and have the same desire to rip each other's clothes off. Only problem? Tanner is still in love with his best friend.

About the Author

KANDI STEINER is #1 Amazon Bestseller and whiskey connoisseur living in Tampa, FL. Best known for writing "emotional rollercoaster" stories, she loves bringing flawed characters to life and writing about real, raw romance — in all its forms. No two Kandi Steiner books are the same, and if you're a lover of angsty, emotional, and inspirational reads, she's your gal.

An alumna of the University of Central Florida, Kandi graduated with a double major in Creative Writing and Advertising/PR with a minor in Women's Studies. She started writing back in the 4th grade after reading the first Harry Potter installment. In 6th grade, she wrote and edited her own newspaper and distributed to her classmates. Eventually, the principal caught on and the newspaper was quickly halted, though Kandi tried fighting for her "freedom of press."

She took particular interest in writing romance after college, as she has always been a die hard hopeless romantic, and likes to highlight all the challenges of love as well as the triumphs.

When Kandi isn't writing, you can find her reading books of all kinds, planning her next adventure, or pole dancing (yes, you read that right). She enjoys live music, traveling, playing with her fur babies and soaking up the sweetness of life.

CONNECT WITH KANDI:
NEWSLETTER: kandisteiner.com/newsletter
FACEBOOK: facebook.com/kandisteiner
FACEBOOK READER GROUP (Kandiland):
facebook.com/groups/kandilandks
INSTAGRAM: Instagram.com/kandisteiner
TIKTOK: tiktok.com/@authorkandisteiner
TWITTER: twitter.com/kandisteiner
PINTEREST: pinterest.com/authorkandisteiner
WEBSITE: www.kandisteiner.com

Kandi Steiner may be coming to a city near you!
Check out her "events" tab to see all the
signings she's attending in the near future:
www.kandisteiner.com/events

Acknowledgments

I'LL BE QUITE HONEST — I'm not sure how to properly thank every soul who has helped make Palm South University what it is. So many friends, strangers, lovers, shows, and books have inspired this series, and it has been fueled by avid readers for many, many years.

I want to start by thanking you, the reader. I always refer to PSU as my "passion project" — which is just a fancy way of saying it doesn't make me money, but I love to write it so much that I don't really care. For whatever reason, PSU has been a hard sell, but those who do read it understand why I love it so much.

That's you.

So, thank you for reading, reviewing, spreading the word and being as excited as me every time school was back in session. These past several years are filled with joyous memories around this series, and it's all thanks to you.

Elaine York of Allusion Publishing has been by my side throughout this whole series — and bless her, she's even stayed with me through three format and cover changes. Thank you, Elaine, for loving my college babies as much as I do and for always polishing them up to a beautiful shine.

A special shout out goes to Staci Hart, who read the first book in the PSU series and believed in me. She believed in me so much that she threw all her energy into helping me be better, critiquing me like no one ever had — which is a large reason why there is so much growth in my writing from book one in this series compared to the last few. Thank you for always being my ride or die. I love you.

To my mom, who taught me to do what I love no matter what, thank you for constantly reminding me that these books were worth it.

To my incredible team of alpha and beta readers for this installment: Lindsey Barnett, Jan Cassi, Trish QUEEN MINTNESS, Jayce Medina, Kellee Fabre, Carly Wilson, Sarah Green, and Michelle Myers — when I say this book (and this series) would be flat out awful without you, I mean it. You were there every step of the way, reading as I wrote, providing crucial feedback that helped make these books better and better. Thank you, from the bottom of my heart, for all your hard work and dedication to making my books shine.

Tina Stokes is my rock, my friend, my keeper — and without her, my life would be a complete mess. If you ever see her at a book signing, give her a big half and thank her, because she's the reason I'm still here. I love you, Tina. Thank you!

To the groups who have supported this series from its inception — the Palm South University Discussion Group and Kandiland — thank you for making the internet a cool place to hang out. Whenever I need good vibes, I know I can find them with y'all.

A big shout out to my friends at Valentine PR for spreading the word about this series and helping others fall in love with it. And to our blogger community (that includes you, Bookstagrammers and Booktokers). No one would even know I WRITE books if it weren't for you. You're the backbone of what we do, and I thank you.

A final, heartwarming thank you to my fiancé, Jack, who believes in me and my dream just as much as I do. Your love and support make romance easy to write, my love, and I can't wait for all our adventures to come.

www.ingramcontent.com/pod-product-compliance
Lightning Source LLC
Chambersburg PA
CBHW020901060726
47591CB00004B/1036